JADE

"How kind of you to invite me to dinner, Griggs. And how presumptuous of you to assume that I would accept." Jade tried to make her smile a little brighter to take some of the sting out of her words and cautioned herself against letting bitterness get in the way of her plans.

Griggs only chuckled as he helped her on with her coat. "My, you haven't changed a bit in years," he remarked. "Still able to strike with a rapier tongue." His black stretch limo was waiting for them at the curb and the chauffeur expertly helped Jade into the car. A short time later they were entering one of Manhattan's most elegant restaurants. Jade adored the place on sight, even though she had been prepared to scoff at anything Griggs might like. After they had been seated, he turned to Jade and examined her candle-lit face for long minutes.

"What ever happened to us, Jade?"

"Was there ever any 'us'?" she returned.

He wrinkled his handsome brow. "There can be this time around, I promise," he replied, then leaned across the table to kiss her gently on the mouth. With that one kiss he wiped away her resolve, and Jade found herself unable to resist him . . .

CONTEMPORARY ROMANCE
FROM ZEBRA

ASK FOR NOTHING MORE   (1643, $3.95)

Mary Conroy lived her life as daughter and wife in the safest way possible—always playing by the rules. But this didn't guard her from cruelty and pain. Mary found a new way of experiencing the world as mistress to a very attractive, but married, man. A world where desires and betrayal were separated only by a plain band of gold.

WINTER JASMINE   (1658, $3.50)

The beautiful Beth wanted Danny and longed to be a part of his exciting life style, but Danny was tired of the fast lane and yearned for stability. Together they shared a searing passion and searched for a world in between.

SOMEBODY PLEASE LOVE ME   (1604, $3.95)

Cat Willingham was every woman's ideal of success. She was smart, wealthy, and strong. But it took Wall Street millionaire Clay Whitfield to bring out the sensuous woman trapped deep inside her, and to teach her the passions that love can bring.

JADE

NANCIE
MacCULLOUGH
WEIR

ZEBRA BOOKS

KENSINGTON PUBLISHING CORP.

ZEBRA BOOKS

are published by

Kensington Publishing Corp.
475 Park Avenue South
New York, NY 10016

First printing: January 1986

Printed in the United States of America

*This book is dedicated to
Tom MacCullough . . . my
very first hero*

PROLOGUE

Only in Manhattan would it seem perfectly normal to have a gymnasium in a penthouse. Of course, Ivan & Igor's was not a run-of-the-mill gymnasium. The hideous odor of sweat socks would never permeate the dressing rooms here. From the moment one stepped off the super-high-speed elevator that whisked patrons to the tower suite, one was acutely aware of having entered a rarefied atmosphere.

The first sight that greeted each patron was a huge, antique-silver samovar, gleaming like a lustful eye and ever full of fragrant hot coffee to be sipped while awaiting a class to begin. Classes at Ivan & Igor's were never larger than six people—more often just two or three—and were generally composed of socialites, celebrities, or career women who wanted to keep their already slim and graceful bodies "in shape." It was a far cry from the health spas where middle-class, middle-aged matrons went in the hope that the machines that whirred and pummeled would whir and pummel their gone-to-flab bodies back into some semblance of acceptability.

At Ivan & Igor's, the decor was plush but the class

procedures were Spartan—twenty minutes of strenuous floor exercises before going on to individual gymnastic routines consisting of handstands, headstands, back-bends, forward flips, backward flips, workouts on the rings and the uneven parallel bars, with a final stretch on the trapeze by an ever-watchful instructor. Ivan & Igor's was one of a handful of select "beautiful people" gyms in Manhattan, which also included such places as Kounovsky's, Alex and Walter's, and Pilates—places where it was "in" to work out.

Of course it was rumored that Jackie used to come there.

No one had ever seen her there for sure, but then everyone was afforded the luxury of egalitarian treatment at Ivan & Igor's. First names of both the instructors and the clients were used almost exclusively, and once a woman was reduced to the standard uniform of leotards and leg-warmers, she became simply another member of the class; that is, unless a famous face or well-known accent gave her away. Even then, in this clubby atmosphere, it was considered bad taste to in any way acknowledge anyone's uniqueness.

Each morning at eight, Darlene, the lip-glossed and Kenneth-coiffed receptionist went rapidly from curtained dressing-room to curtained dressing-room, checking to see that the miniature floral arrangements in each were still fresh, that the powders and colognes kept on small, filigreed shelves were in order, and that the delicately lighted makeup mirrors were on. Then she would flip on the overhead lights in each of the white-leather-matted gym rooms so that bulbs would blaze and reflect back off the mirrored walls and ceilings. After starting coffee in the samovar, she meticulously watered the numerous potted palms and other jungle greenery that lined the elegant reception area.

Lastly, she would fumble in her desk drawer for the secret compartment that held the key to Ivan & Igor's private office. After unlocking the office door, she would fold back the silk-covered Chinese screen that concealed Ivan's most cherished possession, a four-track tape machine with enough complicated switches and dials to resemble the control panel of a 747. Each night before he left the gym, Ivan would personally select a tape for the next day, place it in position on the machine, and then carefully lock up his office. Darlene was permitted to touch only one switch on the machine, the one that would activate the monster and flood the establishment with the syrupy, muted tones of piped-in music. Then she would leave the day's mail on his desk, carefully relock the office, and replace the key in its hiding spot.

Earlier this morning Darlene had checked the shower, sauna, and steambath rooms to make sure that the ever-present stock of thick, thirsty white terry towels, each embroidered with the golden crossed dumbbells and a discreet "Ivan & Igor's" at the hem, were in plentiful supply. At nine the masseuse arrived and made herself available to those who wished to have the self-inflicted aches of their workouts soothingly rubbed away.

Darlene settled back behind the long slab of white marble that served as a reception desk and prepared to enjoy a cup of coffee along with a quick perusal of the morning's *New York Times*. The large, avocado-colored, hand-tooled leather appointment book that lay open on the desk beside her showed only cancellations today for the eight o'clock slot, and she knew that neither Ivan nor Igor, ever arrived before ten.

This morning proved to be the exception, however. At exactly five after eight the elevator doors parted ominously and the glowering, towering, silver-haired Ivan appeared.

With barely a curt "Morning" in Darlene's direction, he unlocked and stalked into his small private office to the right of the reception room, only to appear again almost at once and mumbled a request for coffee as he impatiently riffled through the morning's mail that he held in his hand.

Money problems, Darlene could only surmise. Though the clientele was rich and the classes well attended at Ivan & Igor's, Ivan had a definite knack for turning a fortune into a shoestring overnight. In contrast to the more conservative Igor, Ivan loved beautiful clothes, fine wines, and being seen at all the right places. With his continental manners and carefully preserved Russian accent, Ivan was considered a charmer by the women who frequented the gym, and he was often included in their social gatherings—this despite his sometimes insufferable egotism and the fact that he was called "Ivan the Terrible" behind his back by instructors who often endured his volatile displays of temper.

At sixty-eight, he was still a striking figure of a man, with a lean, hard body on which he lavished all the loving care one might give a fine antique. Aside from his daily schedule at the gym, he was regularly invited by the husband of one of his gym class patrons to play squash and tennis at one of the more exclusive clubs.

His favorite indoor pastime, however, was social climbing, and nothing delighted him more than casually being able to drop a well-placed name into a conversation.

He did so now, while absently ripping open the envelopes in the stack he held.

"Ah, there it is, as usual," he enthused, letting a check flutter out of his hand to land on the desk in front of Darlene, where she could scarcely miss noting its famous signature.

"Her daddy sends the check from Grosse Pointe *every* month. She is one of the few who is *never* in arrears," he revealed smugly.

Darlene brushed the check off the front page of her *New York Times* with a careless gesture and remarked in a bored voice, "If you ask me, I think it's a bit peculiar that a woman *that* age still has Daddy paying the bills. God knows, she's married enough money in her time—not counting the chauffeur, of course," she added offhandedly.

It was a point of pride with Darlene to beat Ivan at his own game of knowing the insider's personal life, and seeming to do so effortlessly.

"Everyone has some minor peccadilloes in his past," Ivan snapped as he stalked back into his office.

No one would know better than you, thought Darlene, smiling to herself at his churlishness. She had worked at the gym as a receptionist for over two years now and had heard the story of Ivan's past life—both his inflated version and the more commonly accepted truth.

Born after the turmoil of the 1917 Revolution, Ivan Petrovich eventually fled his native Russia and made his way to this country in the early 1930's. Equipped with an obscure title and striking good looks, he possessed very little else when he first arrived, but he quickly fell in with other Russian exiles better endowed with earthly goods. With these connections and his magnetic charm, it was only a matter of time before Ivan was being kept by one wealthy woman after another. He was well into his thirties before it occurred to him that the career he was pursuing was one that age would eventually force him to abandon. So he wisely pressed one of his lady friends to put up a considerable sum of money so that he and Igor, a boyhood friend of his from Russia, could open a gymnasium. The dowager did it on a whim, but to everyone's surprise, the place caught on with the society crowd. Soon Ivan found that he was capable of supporting himself without the aid of his patroness, and it was with great relief that he left the rather overripe lady's bed and board and found himself a luxurious co-op apartment on Central Park South where he had been residing ever since.

As he sat in his private office, his mind was even now considering his long-time abode. The maintenance on the apartment was steep, he reflected, as was the upkeep on his Mercedes. And the weekly backgammon games that he had begun attending at the Park Avenue apartment of the Marquis du Rochelle were slowly, though exquisitely, breaking him. He leaned his aristocratic head upon one well-manicured hand as he thought of the money he had lost last night. It was all very gentlemanly, of course, and IOUs were never written, but the total was clearly etched in the minds of all those involved. And the money he had lost last night, added to the debts he had accumulated in other weeks, was astronomical. He simply had to put his hands on some extra cash, and he had to do it fast.

There was one conceivable avenue open to him that he had been loathe to pursue until now, but seeing the checks that had arrived in the mail today, and quickly glancing over the books, convinced him that the time was right for drastic measures. There were several large outstanding debts that the gym had to collect within the next week in order to avoid serious trouble. It was not something Ivan could discuss with Igor because his personal financial situation had forced him to borrow heavily from the business and he had not wanted to burden Igor's mind with such knowledge. The innocent Igor assumed that all the gym's commitments were being scrupulously met on schedule. It would distress him, to say the least, to learn otherwise.

The gym's monetary problems, combined with the extent of his backgammon losses, were forcing Ivan into a course of action he had no taste for. Emitting his Slavic sigh, he reached for the white phone on his desk and began to dial.

Chapter 1

The window in India's tiny kitchen looked out onto a courtyard. Across the court was the window of another kitchen in an apartment that was a duplicate of hers. Every day she saw a woman there doing the same things she did at the same times. Breakfast in the morning, dishes at mid-morning, feeding a toddler in a high chair his lunch at noon. India began to wonder if the window were a mirror.

She recalled a poem she had written during the summer after her senior year in high school, when she had taken her first job and had been dismayed to find her days filled with the detritus of minor office chores:

Four walls do not a prison make—
But they help.
Four walls in which to do the same things
In the same way
Each day.
My mind cries out for help from behind bars of
    boredom
But no answer will come.
My cage
Is myself.

She shook her short brown hair back from her face, as though to dislodge such discouraging thoughts, and flicked the kitchen light switch to "off."

Passing through the small dinette, she paused briefly at the gilt-framed mirror on the wall and checked her hair. Noting a few more gray strands, she tried to tuck them out of sight. There were too many to pluck anymore.

Hate that gray? Wash it away!

She stopped for a moment as she passed the door of two-year-old Toohey's bedroom and peeked in to make sure he was indeed taking his morning nap. With Heather going a full day to third grade at Chapin now and Drew off to the fun-fraught problems of ad agency commercial producing, the time had begun to hang heavily on her hands. She had been too used to being a working wife and mother to adjust to the placidity of domesticity in only two brief years.

Noting that Toohey had dropped his sneakers on the floor in the hallway, she swooped down and scooped them up without breaking her stride.

The quicker-picker-upper.

In the large bedroom that she and Drew shared, she found herself irresistibly drawn to the large oval mirror that hung over their bureau. Leaning close, she examined the crinkles around her hazel eyes for signs of any new inroads of time.

Stop it, she silently chastised herself. You've simply got a bad case of thirty-nine-itus. One's fortieth birthday next month doesn't automatically mean instant old age. But why is it that nobody ever expects forty to actually happen? Jane Fonda, yes. You, not in a million years! Besides, what's so bad about being forty when you have everything a

16

woman could want? You found a devoted husband, albeit your second one—but sometimes finding the right person takes time! And there are your two, if not always lovable, always interesting, children, and your great apartment on Manhattan's fashionable Upper East Side. Were you any happier years ago, living in the Village, with personal problems almost as staggering in number as the roach population?

Suddenly she began to wonder if she was becoming one of those New York neurotics who was never happy unless she was gloriously unhappy.

She had made the bed upon rising, an old habit from the days when she had to be up, dressed, and fully made up by the time the nursemaid arrived to take care of little Heather while she took off for her job as a sportswear buyer at Macy's. God knows, there had been days when she hadn't looked forward to going to work and fighting the same old battles over again. And yet there was something comforting about the routine of one's own office, one's own secretary, one's own problems. Her first big mistake, she supposed, had been deciding to stay home after Toohey's birth, just to give him that all-important mother love for the first few months. With Heather, she had needed the money too desperately to indulge such uncharacteristic maternal instincts, and she had turned over the child to a nursemaid at six weeks, with the result that Heather had survived—and *flourished*. Toohey clung to her skirts like lint now that he was toddling, whereas Heather had waved her a cheery bye-bye every morning from the time she was able to sit up.

India threw herself down on the neatly made bed, clasped her hands behind her head, and studied the slight crack in the high ceiling as intently as if it contained the secrets of the universe.

Would you believe it? I'm cleaning my bathroom bowl?

The trouble was, though thousands of housewives would probably slaughter her in cold blood for saying it, there wasn't enough in a three-bedroom apartment to keep a grown woman's mind from succumbing to dry rot. The place was tidy, though not immaculate, for India had no inclination to exclaim over the smell of clean laundry or compare floor waxes with the zeal of a religious fanatic. Little Toohey was a delight, but he took two naps daily, and by 4:00 P.M. his inane baby conversation started to pale on her. She had begun to look forward to Drew's homecoming each evening with an intensity that frightened her. She felt like a leech that eagerly awaited his return to fasten upon the details of his day and suck them dry. She had nothing to report about her day, God knew, and she wondered if Drew were finding her as dull as she found herself.

He was such a wonderful, kind, understanding man that she could hardly believe it—even now—that he had fallen as deeply in love with her as she had with him when they had first met six years earlier. It was the production of a TV commercial that had brought Drew over to Macy's to check out several outfits for his client's approval. India had been acutely aware of the gold band on his finger and was therefore slightly surprised when he had called her for lunch the next day. But his first marriage had been a disaster too, as she learned over lunches and walks in the park, and finally dinners together in restaurants where no one would see them. She had been divorced for two years, but she had had to relive the same ugliness while Drew set about getting his. It had been worth every minute of the agony, though,

18

for the joy they had together now.

Was there still joy?

Stop it, thought India for the second time that day. The problem is *you*. You're fifteen pounds overweight, going gray, approaching forty, and never talk to anyone over four feet tall until evening.

For God's sake, if you don't *like* yourself, *change* yourself! Nobody else is going to do it for you.

She jumped up from the bed, stripped off the ratty green slacks and faded old shirt of Drew's that she had been wearing, and stepped onto the sleek, modern scale in the master bedroom. Fifteen pounds over is right, she told herself, but let's lose twenty to be on the safe side.

Staring into the bathroom mirror for her third close inspection of the day, she decided to shower then right after Toohey got up from his nap, she would go down to the drugstore, get some Clairol, and rid herself of the offensive gray hair. The sandbox in the park would have to live without her scintillating presence today.

Adjusting the hot and cold to somewhat bearable, she stepped into the shower and began considering which of the newly popular diets she would begin this very day.

And what *was* the name of that midtown gym where all the beautiful people went faithfully, to keep their beautiful bodies beautiful?

Chapter 2

"And *that's* the way the world shapes up today! Have a *great* Tuesday!"

"Thank you, Jade!"

"Thank *you*, Jack. 'Bye, everyone. See you tomorrow."

The familiar, sophisticated theme music came up as the camera held on Jade Greene's handsome features and copper-colored hair for a few seconds longer before cutting to the closing montage shots of early morning New York.

In the cavernous gloom of Studio Eight, the two principals of MBB's *The Morning Hour* seemed to be sitting on a small island of light in the center of a sea of darkness. As the set lights were killed and the regular lights came up, Jade reached down to detach the tiny lavaliere microphone from the front of her dress and rose to stretch wearily.

Jack Jackson, her co-host on the show, allowed himself the luxury of running his hands up his temples, thereby ruffling the precisely sculptured, blow-dried hairdo that his hairdresser took such pains to perfect each morning.

"They were late with that damn clip about the

pickets in Newark at the beginning of the second half," remarked Jade irritably as she smoothed her skirt and gathered her papers together. "I'm gonna kill those guys in the booth if they do that to me again. I had visions of telling my life story for filler, but at this hour of the morning, I couldn't remember it!"

Jack Jackson rose also.

"I think that's *their* problem, too. Everybody's half-asleep around here."

"Everybody's asleep but the brass up on the twenty-second floor. They *never* sleep, and I'll get some half-assed memo about that later this morning. See you tomorrow."

Jade gave Jackson a friendly wave and a grin as she left the set for her own office, floors above in the television complex.

What the hell, she could afford to be friendly toward Jackson, she mused silently. After seven years of being on the program with billing that read *"The Morning Hour,* hosted by 'Handsome Anchorman . . .' *with* Jade Greene," she had finally won out and achieved the coveted title "co-host" at the contract negotiations at the beginning of the year. "Handsome Anchorman" had always said that it would be over his dead body and—son of a gun—it was. And Jade hadn't even had to be the one to do it. It was a macabre and senseless accident that finally took his life; he had choked to death on a piece of steak in his favorite local restaurant in Greenwich last year, and after observing a proper period of mourning—about five minutes, Eastern Standard Time—the network officials had auditioned everyone in town but Captain Kangaroo for the choice spot of host on *The Morning Hour.* After a lot of desk pounding and foot stomping, Jade had finally managed to communicate to the brass that they *had* a perfectly competent host right in their midst. But still they had insisted that a compromise would have to be reached with the "co-host" title. She would be given equal billing and allowed to vote on the choice of her fellow newscaster, but they would not let her handle the show alone. Jade had never expected to win out as sole host, so she took this for the victory it was and after seeing Jackson's audition tape, she agreed with the powers-that-be that he was the one. Jack Jackson was an amiable, good-looking young guy from the Middle West who could do the early morning news without making people want to throw their shoes at the TV set. He gave Jade a lot of leeway and proper respect for the fact that she was the only major woman broadcaster, aside from Barbara Walters and Jane Pauley, who had made it this far up the ladder. The choicest interviews went to her, and she willingly settled for her half of the screen after years of battling to get a fair shake. She'd come a long way for a "nice Jewish girl from Augusta."

Her forthright style was such that viewers either adored her or loathed her. No one was ever neutral about Jade Greene. When seven o'clock came each weekday morning, her devoted fans roused themselves wearily and tuned in their television sets to be greeted by those piercing emerald-colored eyes, those features a trifle too sharp to be pretty that were framed by her impeccably groomed mop of copper hair, and heard her familiar, slightly grating voice announce briskly, "Good morning, world! This is *The Morning Hour* and I'm Jade Greene . . ."

This way of life suited Jade perfectly—for now.

Stepping off the elevator at her floor, Jade made a sharp right turn and headed for her office to check her calendar and the day's mail. She hoped she would have some time to work with an editor on the moviola to edit and synchronize the interview she had done yesterday with the Ambassador from Sweden. She knew that her schedule included a luncheon and a late afternoon interview with an author, but her secretary would fill her in on what ever else had come up. Her watch said 9:10. She would have to hurry.

Today was Tuesday, and on Tuesdays and Thursdays at 10:00 she went to Ivan & Igor's, the fashionable midtown gymnasium. There she donned leotards and bent and stretched for an hour in order to better prepare herself to do battle with the world out there that she greeted so impudently each morning.

Chapter 3

The pert young stewardess in the familiar blue and white uniform of Nordic Airways was almost past her seat before Cricket could manage to attract her attention.

"Yes, ma'am? May I help you?"

"What time do we land at Kennedy?"

"We should be landing at 8:16, New York time," she answered with her most treacly smile. Moving on quickly down the aisle of the 747 before Cricket could even thank her, she disappeared into the economy section of the plane.

Cricket checked the gold Gucci watch on her wrist and noted that she had at least an hour to kill before landing. She squirmed restlessly in her seat and wondered what she could do to avoid seeing the rest of the dreadful movie that was relentlessly unfolding on the large screen in front of her. Deciding that since her internal clock was all screwed up anyway she might as well go up to the bar and have a drink, she stood up and climbed over her sleeping seatmate.

Anyone watching the slim, long-legged, loose-limbed young woman making her way up the circular staircase to the upper deck would scarcely have guessed her to be what she was—a syndicated travel writer. In a field dominated by the middle-aged, she had made it spectacularly. She was spectacularly young and spectacularly successful.

Beginning as secretary to one of the most important writers in the field—the travel editor of the national leisure time magazine, *Festival*—Cricket had taken on whatever small writing assignments he had allowed her. This had only served to whet her basic urge for travel, and soon she was writing a small column of her own for another magazine. With this, she was on her way. Her column had proved enormously successful and before long was in syndication—a coup for any columnist.

Reaching the top of the steps, she surveyed the empty lounge area with a slight lift of spirits. At least she wouldn't have to make pointless conversation with anyone. She was bone-weary from this last trip. Lately, the invitations for trips came in so frequently that she had been forced to sort out those that would make the most interesting columns and regretfully turn down the rest.

With the retirement of her former boss at *Festival* last year, she had been asked to return to the magazine's staff as a full editor, and she had accepted instantly. The prestige of the magazine greatly enhanced her own, and Cricket enjoyed every minute of it. Mostly she enjoyed the picking up and going anywhere in the world on very short notice.

In her elegant apartment on Fifth Avenue, she kept her clothes separated into four different closets, one for each season of the year. She could pack in minutes for any place on the globe simply by going to the closet that corresponded to the climate of the country that was her destination.

She had thrown in her choicest Bogner skiwear for

this last trip to the Arctic Circle. But the trip from Lapland to Helsinki had been arduous, and now she longed only to see her plush, king-size bed in New York once again, a bed she shared only when the spirit moved her.

She sat in a swivel chair at one of the tiny round tables in the bar area and glanced around impatiently for someone to take her drink order. Noting that the entire lounge was empty, she hesitated only a moment before getting up and going over to the small service bar to mix her own.

"The Lord helps them that help themselves!" her widowed mother had always told her.

Selecting a glass from the shining array against the wall, she reached into the ice-maker to scoop up some cubes.

"How 'bout mixing one for me, too, while you're at it, sweetheart?" a self-confident male voice boomed.

Cricket whirled around in annoyance and looked for the source of the request. She found it in an unlikely place.

Standing in the frame of the door to the flight deck was a ruggedly handsome blond man, his airline cap tipped back on his head and a big grin on his face.

"Mix it yourself," she snapped, lightening the irritation in her voice with a trace of a smile that tugged at the corners of her mouth.

"Um, couldn't do that," he answered seriously. "I've got to get back up front and fly this thing."

Cricket's shoulders drooped in astonishment as she put down her glass and started to giggle in spite of herself.

"I *don't* believe it! Now I *have* heard everything! You are the pilot and *you* are asking *me* to mix you a drink! Isn't that against regulations?" she queried, her amazement elevating her beautifully shaped eyebrows.

Again the irresistible grin from the pilot.

"I won't tell if you won't," he countered.

"You're incorrigible," she answered, smiling and reaching for another glass. "Is a Bloody Mary all right with you? It *is* morning, New York time, you know."

"Sounds great!" answered the blond man. "Why don't you just bring it up here and join me when you've got them both ready." After this casual invitation, he vanished back into the flight deck.

Cricket shook her head in disbelief as she opened two cans of the Bloody Marys and mused that airline people were all kooks, and this particular pilot was the kookiest of all.

Still, she decided, it might be fun. In all her travels, she had never had a drink on a flight deck with the flight personnel. And Cricket Wells could never resist a new experience.

With a glass carefully balanced in each hand and her flight bag slung over her shoulder, she eased her way through the small door that led to the front of the plane.

She saw that the cabin was also occupied by two other airline personnel. She wondered briefly why her outrageous pilot friend hadn't ordered drinks for them all.

"Hi, honey," the pilot greeted her casually, never taking his eyes off the control board in front of him. "This is Al Swanson, first officer,"—he gestured to the man in the seat to the right of him—"and this buzzard here,"—he jerked a thumb over his shoulder to the man sitting in the movable seat at the right rear—"this is Per Stabos, flight engineer. Make yourself comfortable," he added, indicating that she take the seat directly behind his.

28

Cricket settled herself and looked around with interest. Though she had often toured the flight decks of other planes with fellow travel writers, she had always been fascinated by the complexities of the systems control station. The multitude of dials and switches boggled her mind.

The pilot's mind, however, appeared to be anything but boggled as he reached a hand over his shoulder to receive his Bloody Mary. She thought she detected the faintest hint of disapproval in the first officer's expression, for he seemed to square his already square-jawed face a trifle more firmly, but he made no comment.

Cricket handed the pilot his drink and said cheerily, "I'm afraid I didn't get your name."

"Sorry 'bout that, ma'am. Shows you haven't been listening to the flight announcements. This is your captain speaking," he intoned in a solemn voice. "My name is Tex Harrington and I will be your pilot on our trip to New York."

Cricket sipped her Bloody Mary and giggled again.

"You're right. I never listen to those things. After the millionth trip, they begin to grate on you."

"Oh?" The pilot turned slightly and she could see that he had raised a bushy eyebrow. "You travel all that much?"

"Almost constantly," Cricket answered primly, not volunteering any more information. Let him wonder, she decided.

"What were you doing in Helsinki?" he asked curiously.

"Coming down from Lapland."

"Okay, I give up. What were you doing in Lapland?" he asked in amused exasperation. Her game intrigued him.

"Oh, I was just up there for the reindeer roundup,"

Cricket tossed off as casually as she could.

"Reindeer roundup?" Tex couldn't conceal his amazement anymore and swung around to look at her full face, to see if she was pulling his leg.

Cricket finally broke up.

"Yes, the reindeer roundup. They hold it every year in September."

Tex turned back to his controls and took another sip of the Bloody Mary.

"Next thing, you'll be tellin' me that you're a reindeer cowboy!" he commented.

"Nope. But I've got a driver's license. A reindeer driver's license, that is," she added, putting down her drink and rummaging through her flight bag.

Triumphantly she handed him a small card.

Tex squinted to read it.

On the front was the picture of a reindeer's head and the legend "Reindeer Driving License." Flipping it over, he saw her picture in one corner, her name, Cricket Wells, written in as the owner of the license, who "has today passed the reindeer driving test and on this ground has earned the right to drive a reindeer sled in the wilds to be present among the untamed reindeer without escort, and will, in an emergency, use the lasso. Sunglasses are to be used while driving. Remember, acceleration and high speed increase the consumption of 'fuel' and 'cutting in' may cause irreparable damage to reindeer hide. This license is valid for three years. Suomi— Finland." This was followed by the signature of the teacher of the reindeer driving school—an unintelligible scrawl to Tex—and an official-looking seal.

Tex grinned broadly and handed it back to her.

"Now I've seen everything! And I thought you were kidding me!"

"No, *I've* seen everything," said Cricket mischievously. "Do you always entertain ladies on the flight deck with cocktails while you're flying?"

"Only when they're as pretty as you are," Tex threw back gallantly.

"Are you going to let me take a turn at the controls?" she asked impishly. She had an impulse to know how it would feel to handle a plane this big.

"Now *that's* against the regulations," he answered, suddenly serious.

Cricket was miffed.

"This is a hell of a time to go official on me," she pouted.

"Sorry, honey, but flying this thing is *my* job." His tone was firm.

Cricket sighed. She sensed that she could inveigle him no further. In that instant, the fun of the situation began to wane for her.

Gathering her flight bag and her drink, she rose to leave. She saw by her watch that she would have only half an hour until landing, and she wanted to freshen up.

"Hey, you don't have to run off like that, just 'cause I won't let you drive," Tex called after her in disappointment.

"Sorry," Cricket replied pertly. "I just remembered a previous engagement. Thanks for the ride."

With that she whisked herself out the rear door and, stopping only long enough to deposit her half-empty glass on the bar, she skipped down the spiral steps and back to her seat.

It had been fun, but what she really would have liked would have been to try her hand at the controls.

Anyway, she *had* just remembered an engagement, and suddenly the incident on the flight deck was forgotten.

It was Thursday, and if she got a cab right away and dropped her luggage with the doorman at her building, she could make it to Ivan & Igor's in time for her ten o'clock gym class.

Her muscles, stiff from the long flight, could certainly use the workout.

Chapter 4

Anastacia rolled over and slipped out of bed before Ferrago could wrap his strong, well-muscled arms around her.

"Where ya goin'?" he mumbled drowsily.

After stretching languorously, she settled her long, brown, naked body into the huge, plump, leather-covered chair beside the bed and reached over to the nightstand for a cigarette. Her flesh broke out in goose bumps at the contact with the cool, smooth surface.

Ferrago swiftly clamped a restraining hand on her wrist.

"Don't! Why the hell do ya want to start puffing on those things so early in the morning! You're going to ruin that gorgeous body of yours if I don't watch you every minute."

Anastacia shook loose her hand from his grip and pursued her original objective—the red-and-white package of Carltons that was never far from her reach.

Lighting up the cigarette and inhaling it sensuously, she gazed at the rumpled figure on the bed through a cloud of smoke and gave a low chuckle.

"Would you believe, love blossom, that this ole body managed to survive for eighteen years before I met you? If I hadn't ruined it by then, I don't think I'll be able to do it too much harm in the next eighteen, do you?"

Ferrago Anselmo sat up in the king-size brass bed, and the scarlet satin sheets fell back from his pale body to reveal the thick, curly black hair on his chest that Anastacia loved to explore with her fingers. He refused to acknowledge that Anastacia did not share his passionate pursuit of health.

The shelves of Ferrago's bathroom were lined with bottles of megavitamins, and the shelves of his refrigerator with bottles and jars of health food. He was a fervent believer in wheat germ and yogurt. Anastacia favored Big Macs and thick chocolate shakes—junk food.

Ever since she had moved in with him two years before, he had restructured her diet, her habits, her life-style. And he had made it pay off handsomely. In those short years, she had become New York's top black model. This was probably due more to his skill as an accomplished fashion photographer than to his diligence in tending her health. But he was right in his contention that the camera had a merciless eye and would coldly reflect too little sleep and too much carousing.

Anastacia occasionally chomped at the bit, but not often.

Teasingly she let the cigarette dangle from the corner of her wide, expressive mouth and crawled back into bed across the expanse of the silver-fox coverlet to snuggle into the crook of his arm.

Ferrago nestled her there affectionately while gruffly complaining that someday she'd burn down the whole damn loft with those things.

"What have you got on today?" he asked companionably.

"At this moment, absolutely nothing," she answered with a giggle, spilling ashes on the bedclothes.

"You know what I mean," he reproved in his best parental tone.

"I haven't the vaguest idea. I'm going to call the agency at eight and check."

She was a truly magnificent original, Ferrago thought as he looked down at the long, lean, brown body beside him. His eyes, continually confronted by beauty during a long workday of endless shootings of beautiful women, never grew jaded or tired of looking at perfection. Perhaps it was his ability to continually appreciate loveliness and grace that made his pictures so eagerly sought by every fashion magazine and ad agency in town.

Anastacia's sculpted face had the requisite high cheekbones and large, lustrous eyes and perfect, white, even teeth that modeling demanded, but it also had something more. Was it the way her dark eyes could change mood so swiftly, moving from feeling to feeling the way ripples moved over a pond, he wondered, or the fact that her slim, pointed nose seemed to have a certain hauteur about it? Her mobile mouth could look petulant, inviting, teasing, or mischievous on command. Her sensitive face seemed capable of mirroring all the emotions any woman had ever felt since the beginning of time, and he never ceased to enjoy staring at the loveliness of it.

Almost unconsciously, he reached out his hand and smoothed back a strand of her long, thick, black hair that had fallen across one eye. Some unknown ancestor in her background had slipped in a gene that had blessed her with hair that never even needed the ministrations of a hairdresser, let alone that obnoxious concoction known as hair straightener. It sprang up from her forehead and rippled back from her face in luxuriant splendor, as natural and untamed as her zest for living.

She was a truly beautiful woman, and Ferrago had spotted that beauty the instant he had laid eyes on her, two years ago, at that far-out fashion show in a deserted factory in New Jersey. With a connoisseur's unerring instinct, he knew he had to encourage that beauty and nurture it until it could flower into the striking woman that nature had intended her to be.

It had not been difficult to convince Annie Clemmons, born and raised in Harlem, to change her name, her occupation, and her habits. All he had had to dangle in front of her eyes was . . . the world. Everything she could ever desire would be hers, he had told her, with the kind of money he knew she would be capable of making. All she needed was a mentor—someone wise in the ways of the fashion world—who would be willing to handle her. And no one was wiser, or more willing, than Ferrago Anselmo.

Of course, he had fallen in love with her. This had not surprised him, for he had always fallen in love with beautiful things. He cherished them and enjoyed them to the fullest, for as long as he chose to savor them. The odd thing about Annie was that her novelty never seemed to pale on him. Her face, with its half-hinted secrets, never seemed to grow stale to him.

It was only her undisciplined, childlike nature that sometimes threatened to do him in. And having a cigarette before she was even out of bed was a prime example.

He reached down to take the offending object out

of her mouth, but she was too fast for him and slipped like quicksilver out of his arms.

With a leap and a laugh she was out of the bed.

"Wench! Put that thing out and come back to bed!" he growled.

Anastacia flipped back the large double doors of her long closet against the wall and began pawing through the acres of clothing that hung there. She, who had grown up in tattered clothes that had been handed down about five times too many, delighted in buying any beautiful garment that caught her fancy.

Silks, chiffons, cashmeres rippled through her fingers as she idly searched. Impulsively, she pulled out a flame-colored, pure-silk peasant shirt and began threading her long, graceful arms into it. Her small, compact breasts had no need of a bra, yet they were full enough to press ever so tantalizingly against the delicate fabric.

Ferrago followed her every movement with his eyes.

After a few more seconds of riffling through the packed hangers, she selected taupe Ultrasuede pants to go with it.

Before donning them, however, she stooped down and rummaged through the bottom of the closet for a pair of tall, soft-as-butter kidskin boots to complete the outfit.

Ferrago wondered if she were as unself-conscious as she seemed about how attractive she looked with her tiny, coffee-colored buttocks peeping out from under the orange shirt.

Perching on the arm of the bedside chair, she studiously concentrated on pulling on first one brown boot, then the other, over slim, brown legs. The boots came to just above her knees, and when she stood, preparing to put on her trousers, Ferrago laughed aloud at the picture she made.

"Ah, my dear, it's a shame you've got so much class and prestige right now or I'd make a fortune selling some shots of you, just like that, to *Playboy!*"

For an answer, she stuck out a tiny pink tongue at him and then methodically proceeded to pull on her pants.

Ferrago stumbled out of bed and headed for the shower. He patted her on her tiny rump as he passed.

"Aren't you afraid you'll catch cold someday, running around this city with no underwear and no socks?" he chided playfully.

"I've got a fire down inside that never goes out," she called to his retreating figure and broke into an impromptu moonwalk as she headed for the phone.

Even when she wasn't dancing, she had a fluid, rhythmic quality about her that made her a sensation at a fashion showing, though she rarely did any but the most prestigious shows now that she was such a popular photographer's model.

She could hear Ferrago turn on the water as she dialed the rococo French phone, her hips moving sensuously and continually to a silent beat, audible only in her head.

"Hi, Helen. It's Anastacia. Read me my bookings for the day, would ya please. Sure, I'll hold."

She strummed the air gracefully with the long, spidery fingers of one hand.

"Oh?" Her voice rose half a note in slight surprise. "Okay then, I'll be at Jon's at eleven and check back after that to see if they're ready for me at Studio 38."

She jotted a few quick notes on a piece of paper as she hung up the phone, then walked thoughtfully to the center of the room and stood, waiting.

In seconds, the large, dripping hulk of Ferrago, casually toweling himself dry, appeared in the bedroom doorway.

Feet wide apart and hands planted on her hips, Anastacia confronted him.

"*You* are too much! Are you serious about this thing again?" she demanded.

Ferrago's face was full of studied innocence as he brushed the towel over his dark, damply curling hair.

"Serious about what, my love?"

"You know very well what! I am booked out today until eleven. *You* booked me out. Because—I was just informed—I am to be at Ivan & Igor's to resume my regular exercise classes there at ten this morning."

"Oh, that."

"Yes, *that!*"

Ferrago grinned a wide, guilty grin.

"A sound mind in a sound body, m'dear!"

"Ferrago," she whined like a petulant child, "I went last spring because you made me and then you said I could stop—"

"For the *summer*. But summer's over and it's time to get back to work. It'll help keep you in good shape."

Anastacia threw her head back slightly and combed her fingers through her long hair. Ferrago had never known a model who spent so little time in front of a mirror or fussing with her looks—and Ferrago had known most of the great ones. Mirrors held no special fascination for Annie. Her mirrors were other people's eyes.

She sighed in defeat. "You win, as always. God, blackstrap molasses, wheat germ, and now . . . push-ups!"

Her voice was so full of despair that Ferrago laughed as he tossed his wet towel on a chair and walked over to embrace her.

"Everybody who's anybody goes to Ivan & Igor's.

You used to pick up more gossip there in a couple of hours a week than you ever did in those stuffy dressing rooms at production houses." He nuzzled her ear consolingly as he buried his face in her thick, dark hair.

"Besides," he whispered, "it's my last line of defense against McDonald's."

Anastacia pulled back from him abruptly and he could see her pale color flush deeper at his last revelation. She looked appealingly guilty.

"Aha!" he said, holding her at arm's length. "You didn't think I knew that you nip in for a quick one a couple of times a week. My spies are everywhere."

Recovering her poise, she answered sassily, "Woman does not live by soybean alone, you know."

"I'm having Baskin-Robbins staked out too, so don't try any tricks on me, beauty."

He gathered her close to him again, enjoying the warmth that spread through his body as her proximity began to arouse him.

"Now, since it's only"—Ferrago paused and squinted at the clock across the room—"ten past eight, why don't you take off all those gorgeous clothes and come back to bed?"

Annie stayed in his arms for only seconds longer before slipping away from him with a light laugh and heading for the nightstand.

She withdrew four scarlet silken cords, then turned to face him as she twisted them slowly and suggestively through her fingers.

"I'd *love* to go back to bed with you, honey chile, only today, we'll play *my* game. You are gonna suffer exquisitely for what you're puttin' this po' black girl through at that gym."

Annie's tantalizing smile and the anticipation of what she had in mind caused Ferrago's sexual readiness to be obviously displayed.

The sight of his large erection brought a sparkle to her dark eyes, and she began unloosening her skintight pants in the most provocative manner she could muster.

Ferrago moved to the bed, a willing victim, anxious to begin. He stretched himself out, spread-eagle fashion, and watched as she finished shedding her clothes.

With delicious slowness and deliberation, she began to fasten first one wrist, then the other to the brass headboard. Methodically, she moved down to the foot of the bed and secured each leg at the ankle with a length of cord. It was a game they had played many times, taking turns with each other, but one that never failed to drive Ferrago wild with excitement. There was something so immensely erotic in having his masculine perogative taken from him as he lay helpless while Annie performed her ministrations on his body.

At last satisfied that she had rendered him totally defenseless she sat back and surveyed him with dancing eyes.

"You know what I'm going to do with you, don't you?" she asked wickedly. It was all part of the game.

Ferrago could only nod. The throbbing in his groin had become unbearable.

"And I'm going to do it so slowly that I am going to . . . drive . . . you . . . out . . . of . . . your . . . skull."

With a last, teasing smile, she knelt at the end of the bed and began exploring between each of his toes with her small, pink tongue, softly and lingeringly.

Ferrago felt as though he would leap out of his skin.

Gently and unhurriedly, she moved up along the

length of his legs, lovingly invading his most private places.

Her tiny tongue was an instrument of exquisite torture, and his entire body writhed in erotic agony.

When at long last she gave him glorious release, it seemed to Ferrago that the whole room splintered into slivers of brilliance, and then he lay panting and exhausted yet deliciously aware of her slight, dark form draped limply across his pale chest.

Chapter 5

Tuesday, at promptly ten minutes to ten, India stepped off the elevator and into the luxurious surroundings of Ivan & Igor's for her second exercise class.

The polished receptionist whom India secretly suspected was a giant-sized, battery-powered Barbie doll, looked up from the *New York Times* and greeted her with "Good morning, India." Though last Thursday had been her first visit here, the greeting made her feel like an old-timer. The woman at the desk must have a fabulous memory, she decided.

Last week she had filled out an application card and had been issued a gym bag. The class had been fun, even though the next day she had ached in places she had not known existed in her body. But the exercises had made her feel curiously alive, in touch with her physical self.

She had found the gym peopled by exotic butterfly types whose lives were quite foreign to her own. The parade of match-stick-thin models, reedlike young matrons, and leanly-muscled lady executives passing before her had made India confront the perplexing realization that if she had looked like any one of them, she wouldn't have been here in the first place.

One thing she hadn't seen were fat people. India wondered if this was because Ivan & Igor's patrons had already attained divine bodies through exercise, or perhaps because fat people naturally gravitated toward the kinds of places that ran commercials on television advertising that machines did all the work—tacky places that were plushly over-outfitted and patronized by working class people. Ivan & Igor's, on the other hand, was elegantly sleek and so was it clientele.

There was a clubby atmosphere about the place that opened easily to include anyone who had the stamina and money to get beyond the first few lessons. Group classes—never more than six to a class—were $25.00 a session, and one made standing appointments that needed twenty-four-hour notice for cancellation without charge.

India returned the receptionist's greeting with a wave.

Gaily printed cotton draw-string bags hung along one wall in the hallway beyond the reception area and held their owners' leotards. India lifted hers off a hook from under the letter T and passed through to the curtained dressing rooms.

Cultured voices floated outward from each, launching strange balloons of conversation into the air.

"Her mother died in Instanbul last week."

"I wondered why I hadn't seen her at the hairdresser's on Monday."

Then from another came: "She's the only person I know with a sign over her bed that says, 'Come again'!"

And from yet another India heard, "I didn't know

that Esme and Larry had split."

"Oh, yes, my dear. And so elegantly. They each took their lovers along and all four of them flew to Haiti for two weeks for the legalities."

"It was positively a *storybook* divorce!"

India quickly stripped off her camel-hair pants suit and efficiently wriggled into her leotard. She wondered if the voices chattering away were those of people dressing after the nine o'clock class or suiting up for her ten o'clock. She hoped the former, because a large class meant less time for individual work.

As she quickly glanced in the mirror to check her hair, she couldn't help noticing the label in the blouse hanging next to the mirror. "Norell," it read. Obviously, its owner was still in the nine o'clock class. She'd noticed a Halston label on a dress hanging in here last Thursday. Now, her own Lord & Taylor label seemed shoddy by comparison.

After a last quick glance in the mirror to make sure no straps were peeking out from under the scoop-necked jersey top, she grabbed her purse and went out to the reception area to enjoy a few puffs from a cigarette and a sip of coffee before class began.

The lacquered receptionist was deep in a serious phone conversation that involved rescheduling someone's lesson that day.

"All right Ivan, but remember you've got two this afternoon, that Addy somebody or other and Mrs. Vanderbilt wants a half-hour at four."

It seemed a life or death matter from the solemnity of her tone.

Above the long, low, rust-colored tweed sofa where India relaxed, framed articles clipped from *Vogue*, *Glamour,* and other slicks proclaimed the virtues and joys of exercising as practiced at Ivan & Igor's. India noted that they had been written up in almost every publication at one time or another.

Gregor, one of the newer instructors, strolled down the curved staircase from the upper gym and perched on the edge of the desk while craning his neck to scan the day's listings in the large appointment book. He had shaggy dark hair, the inverted-deltoid upper torso of most gym instructors, and reminded India of a Cuban revolutionary because of his large, drooping, brown mustache. She estimated he was probably in his late twenties.

What prompted a person, thought India for the hundredth time, to become a gym instructor in a ladies' gym? For Ivan and Igor themselves, the answer seemed simple—money. People had been known to do sillier things for less. But an instructor here could scarcely be getting rich, India mused.

Last Thursday, India's class had been conducted by a shaggy-haired young man known as Misha, who had such a thick Russian accent that India could hardly understand him. She had mostly watched the others in her class and had tried to follow what they were doing. She had almost gone into a state of shock when she'd recognized one of her classmates as Jade Greene, the TV news personality. But she had struggled to look just as blasé and unimpressed as everyone else there who had seemed to regard Jade as just another body.

Jade Greene had to be about India's age, she was sure, but the woman was in *gorgeous* physical condition—not a bulge anywhere in sight and her workout was fluid and professional. She had spun through the walkovers and handstands as though they were second nature to her and had sailed through her ring exercises with the same ease with which she handled her show.

Give me a couple of months, thought India, then

smiled to herself as she silently added, "Okay, well, how about a couple of *years?*"

Just then the elevator doors parted to emit a fabulously attractive young black woman with a flowing mane of black hair floating above a long, earth-colored woolen cape. The smile she flashed the receptionist was blinding, and India strained to catch the name with which she was greeted. "Annie." Hardly distinguished, India reflected, but she had the nagging feeling that she'd seen the woman somewhere before. Maybe it would come to her. She was to be a classmate, it seemed.

The clock hands were almost straight up to ten o'clock now. A handsome young man with broad, Slavic features came bounding down the stairs. His light brown hair was cut in a Prince Valiant fashion and there was a serious expression on his face. He wore the usual close-fitting olive green gym pants and snowy white tee-shirt adorned with crossed golden dumbbells that all the instructors wore here. He cast a swift look at the open appointment book and then turned to address India.

"You are . . .?"

"India," she answered quickly, astonished at his accent, which was pure American with a tinge of Brooklyn.

The Barbie-doll receptionist said, "Jade's already in there and Annie just buzzed in now."

A slight frown crossed the instructor's face as he addressed both Gregor and Darlene.

"Did Cricket call to cancel?"

Gregor merely shrugged, but Darlene smiled slightly and said, "You know Cricket. Half the time she's out of the country and forgets to cancel, Lanny."

Lanny. That was certainly American enough,

thought India.

"Well, it's ten now and I'm not going to waste class time waiting for her."

Turning his attention back to India, he favored her with his first smile of the day, a truly nice, boyish one, India noted.

"Come on, India. Let's go. I'm Lanny. Is this your first time here?" Lanny questioned, guiding her into the larger of the two gyms where Jade Greene was already working out on the parallel bars. Lanny cast a faintly disapproving look in Jade's direction and admonished, "You're going to pull a muscle, flipping around those things without warming up first."

Jade merely laughed in reply as she swung off the bars in a graceful dismount.

"I've been up since quarter to five, and if I'm not warmed up by now, I never will be!"

"Okay," Lanny announced, turning to face them. "Let's line up and get to work."

Jade dutifully took her place next to India as they both faced Lanny and, behind him, the endless wall of mirrors. India decided that coming to the gym was doing more for her than loosening her muscles. The fact that she had to face her own figure twice a week, clad only in a black, skintight leotard, and watch her body with all its bulges in those merciless mirrors was enough to make even the most weak-willed dieter stick to her Rye-Krisps. She noted the slight thickness around her waist that was nonexistent in the figure of the woman next to her, and India's resolve strengthened as they began their preliminary jumps.

Just then the tall, black woman that India had seen get off the elevator slipped quietly into the room, dropped her purse on the chair where the others had left theirs, and joined the line.

It was all India could do not to stare openly. She had never seen such an astonishing body. The woman was lithe and slim—a streak of slithery black in her leotard—but the most electric thing about her was the suppleness of her body.

She seemed to flow, like water, rather than move. When she joined them in their insane jumping, she bounded up and down so effortlessly that India felt like an elephant in comparison.

Jade smiled at her and said, "Hi, Annie," but Lanny only acknowledged her with a nod of the head, never once breaking his monotonous "three-four-five-six-seven-eight . . . okay, that's enough. Let's run in place. One-two . . ."

Everything here was done to the count of eight. With the foreign instructor that India had had last week, she had seriously wondered whether or not he could count beyond eight in English.

"Okay, now legs apart, stretch it right up to the ceiling. That's right, stretch yourself out. Now, flop down as limp as you can and exhale. Now, up, inhale, down, exhale, up, inhale, down, exhale."

Everyone else seemed to know the routine by heart, but at least this week India could understand the instructions.

"Now, hands out straight to the sides. We're going to cross-over kick, opposite foot to opposite hand. Let's go. One and two and three and . . ."

He droned on and India began to puff a little. They looked like a line of funeral Rockettes, except that both Annie's and Jade's legs were precision-straight as they rose and fell, while India's tended to bend a bit at the knee as her foot came up to make contact with her hand.

"Try to keep your knees straight, India," suggested Lanny, not unkindly, breaking his count only momentarily and picking it up again on the next beat.

"Enough," he announced after the inevitable count of eight. "Now, right hand on hip, left hand up, lean to the right side and bounce once, then reverse and do it on the other side. Begin. One and . . ."

At just this moment, a vibrant-looking young woman with short blond curls, wearing a bright-red leotard and black legwarmers literally bounced into the gym, threw her purse on the others, and jumped into the last place in line next to Annie.

"Hi, Lanny, hi guys," she greeted them all, oblivious to the fact that she was interrupting Lanny's count and everyone else's exercises.

Lanny broke off with a rueful grin and said, "Hi, Cricket! Thought you might be on the other side of the world today. You're late." The last was a rather pointed hint that he wanted to get on with things.

"Sorry 'bout that," answered Cricket, giving little jumps in place. "I just got back about an hour ago."

"Oh, where'd you go this time?" asked Jade with a spark of interest. She lounged against the parallel bars, relaxing.

"You'd never believe it," Cricket said, continuing her jumping. Annie and India also perked up their ears.

"A reindeer roundup in Lapland. How about that!"

Comments of "no kidding" and "how wild" were dutifully murmured, and the women started to chatter.

Finally Lanny broke in, concealing his impatience as well as he could with, "Ladies, ladies, would you mind if we got on with the class? Cricket?" He scowled in her direction, but it was a good-natured scowl, India noted.

She had the feeling that the vivacious Cricket was a

50

great favorite here.

"Where were we?" Lanny shook his head slightly, trying to recall the point at which they had stopped.

"Toe-touching next!" sang out Jade.

"I hope I missed all the ones I hate," giggled the irrepressible Cricket.

Lanny shot her one mock-serious warning look and said, "That's what I was about to say. Let's touch our toes. Bend now, opposite hand to opposite foot. Begin! One and two and three and . . ."

India began to smile slightly as she realized that Cricket was a groaner. She could hear little sounds of pain with each movement from Cricket, and she was glad this pulled the muscles of someone else, too. She had been prepared to suffer in silence since all the rest of the women had seemed to do the exercises so effortlessly.

At the count of eight, before Lanny could signal the end, Cricket called out cheerfully, "Eeeee-nough!"

"Cricket," he said good-humoredly, "why does everything start to go to pieces when *you* get here?"

"Let's walk our hands out on the floor now," said Cricket in a fairly good imitation of Lanny's best instructor-type voice.

Lanny grinned.

"Would *you* like to run this class?"

But everyone had dutifully walked their hands out on the floor at Cricket's command and were now on hands and feet with backs arched and heads stretched up.

"I've a good mind to leave you all in that silly position!" said Lanny. Then, resuming his proper demeanor, he continued, "Stretch, breathe! Now walk 'em back up keeping those knees straight."

Cricket's groan at this maneuver was loud and sincere, and India too felt the muscles at the back of

51

her knees ache with the strain.

"Okay. Everybody over to the mats on your backs."

All four women trooped over to the white leather gym mats lining the wall in front of the mirrors and flopped down on their backs.

"All right now, make yourselves as long as you can. Stretch your hands over your heads and *pull*. Point your toes and *stretch* those legs. Reach, reach, reach. Now, sit-ups, let's go! One and two and three and . . ."

India stretched and pulled with the best of them and wondered if one ever got over the feeling of being a trained seal or an obedient dog, faithfully performing each act on command.

"And six and seven and eight. Enough. Relax for a minute, breathe . . ."

With the continual admonitions to breathe, India was tempted to comment that it really came naturally to her, that she'd been doing it all her life.

"Now, roll back and touch the floor behind your head with your toes . . ."

This command brought such a loud groan from Cricket that the whole class began to giggle.

Lanny continued without deigning to notice Cricket's agony. "Support your hips for the bicycle. One and two and . . ."

Just at this point, Darlene stuck her sculptured hairdo through the gym doorway and said, "Jade, sorry to interrupt, but there's a long distance phone call for you. They said it was urgent."

Jade Greene hopped to her feet and rushed out of the room while Lanny continued in a monotone voice ". . . six and seven and eight. Enough. Now, slowly, touch the floor over your head and then unroll your spine along the floor until your legs are flat."

Chapter 6

Darlene punched the proper button on the beige phone at the desk and passed the receiver across to Jade.

Jade took it, noticing a slight tremor in her hand as she reached out for it and conscious of the fact that her heart was pounding unreasonably. Why did long distance phone calls and unopened telegrams always hold the threat of bad news for her?

Controlling her momentary panic, she answered in a firm, clear voice, "Hello, this is Jade Greene. Go ahead please."

Her relief was instantaneous at hearing the nasal voice of her sister, Rose, in Augusta, Maine, shouting "Hello, hello, hello? Jade, is that you?"

"Of course it's me. Stop shouting, Rose. I could hear you *without* a phone. What's up?"

"I called your home, then your office, and now they gave me this number. What kind of place is Ivan & Igor's? It sounds subversive."

Jade fought back a smile.

"Rose, that's not important. Tell me why you're calling me.

"Well, it's Shelley. . . ."

"Shelley?" A note of alarm crept into Jade's voice. Shelley was Rose and Herb's only child, a lovely sixteen-year-old girl, an *A* student who had never given her parents a moment's worry in her life. On her infrequent trips to Augusta, Jade always looked forward to a visit with Shelley and hearing the latest in the pretty teenager's life. Much as Jade adored her own eight-year-old son, Mark, a product of her brief, unhappy attempt at marriage with Ross Fleming, she would have loved to have had a daughter of her own. And in a small way, Shelley fulfilled that desire. The young girl thought her glamorous aunt in New York was the most wonderful woman in the world, and she enjoyed knowing that she was a special favorite of Aunt Jade's.

"Nothing's happened to her, has it?"

Jade didn't want to upset her prone-to-hysteria sister, but the thought of something happening to Shelley filled her with dread.

"Everything's happened! She's gone, that's what's happened!"

Rose's voice broke and she began to sob into the phone.

"Rose, Rose, please stop crying long enough to tell me what's the matter! What do you mean 'gone'? When did she go? *Where* did she go?"

Rose fought back her crying long enough to flesh out the story for Jade.

"I don't know exactly when, or even where. I just know she's gone—"

"Start from the beginning," interrupted Jade crisply. "When did you see her last?"

"After school yesterday, she came home and asked if she could spend the night at a girlfriend's. Janet Moore's. You remember the Moores. He owns the furniture shop in town—"

"Yes, yes, I know the Moores," broke in Jade impatiently. "Please stick to the point, Rose."

"Anyway, I said, 'Why not?' Janet's a nice girl and Shelley has stayed there on many occasions. So she packed an overnight bag and took her books and off she went."

"And?" prodded Jade.

"And this morning Janet called after first period to talk to Shelley about something and I say, 'What do you mean Shelley? She stayed the night with you. She's in school, isn't she?' And Janet says, 'No, Shelley didn't spend the night at my house and she's not in school.'"

Rose broke down and began sobbing again.

"Listen, Rose, you've got to calm down and pull yourself together so we can get this straightened out. Have you called the police?" Worry gave Jade's voice a sharp edge. "Someone could have picked her up . . . she wouldn't accept a ride from a stranger, would she?"

More sobbing came from Rose before she could continue.

"I haven't called the police, because something else happened . . ."

A fresh torrent of crying began.

"Rose, *what* happened? What else?"

"The man at the bus depot called. They found some school books in the trash basket down there. They had Shelley's name and address and phone number in them and he wanted to know if we wanted them back."

"The bus depot? Where in the world would she go?" Jade pondered this new information.

"I asked the clerk if he had seen her. He remembered seeing a young girl in there yesterday afternoon. He says she bought a one-way ticket for New York."

Lights began to flash in Jade's head and she began to realize why Rose had gotten in touch with her so rapidly.

"Rose, did you have a fight with her or something? Was she in any kind of trouble?"

"Trouble? What kind of trouble could a beautiful young girl like Shelley be in? And fight? I've never had a fight with Shelley. She's a wonderful daughter . . ." Rose began to cry again.

Jade sized up the matter very quickly. "Listen Rose, sit tight, at least for a few hours. I can't believe that Shelley won't try to contact me once she reaches the city. Give me a couple of hours to see what I can turn up, and then if we have no lead, I think you'd better contact the police and have them put out a bulletin on her."

"A bulletin? Like she's one of those crazy runaways or something? Oh, Jade!"

"Rose, listen to me. She *is* a runaway, crazy or not. Now, first we've got to find her. Then we've got to find out why she took off like she did. A sensible girl like Shelley wouldn't run off without a reason. Something is wrong, and we'll find out what it is and she'll be back home before you know it."

Jade spoke with more confidence than she felt at the moment. Eight million people in the city and she had to try to find one blond teenage girl! Jade prayed that it wasn't pregnancy that had made Shelley flee. But she simply couldn't believe that a girl like Shelley would have a problem like that, nor would she consider suggesting such a thing to her already-hysterical sister at this point.

Assuring Rose that she would call her back by early afternoon, Jade rang off and thoughtfully replaced the phone in its cradle. A worried frown creased her brow.

She made three quick phone calls, the first to her home where she spoke with her housekeeper. No word there. The second was to her office, where she alerted her secretary and told her to cancel lunch and the interview. The third she made to her answering service. Nothing. Shelley had not tried to reach her through any of those sources.

The worry she felt gave her a leaden feeling in her chest. She had no heart to go back to her gym class; but there seemed nothing possible she could do at this moment anyway, and she recalled the many times she had managed to rid herself of emotional tensions in the mindlessness of physical exercise.

Asking Darlene to be sure to get her out of class if any more calls came, she reluctantly turned back to the gymnasium.

The individual floor work had begun and Annie was leading off the class in Jade's place. The rest of the class sat cross-legged against one wall, watching as Lanny put Annie through her paces. Jade sat down, folded her legs, and took her position at the head of the line as the next to work out.

The individual work consisted of a handstand, rotations, a headstand, a back bend and variations of rotations.

Lanny stood to one side and slightly forward of Annie to spot for her handstand. The more advanced in the group rarely needed his help.

India watched in fascination as Annie casually stretched her long arms over her head and stepped forward into a perfect handstand, holding that unbelievable position, suspended, upended, and poised. After what seemed to India interminable seconds, she sprang lightly back to her feet.

"Very good, Annie," said Lanny quietly. "Now move to the mat and begin your rotations."

Rotations were a formalized, stylized variation of what had been called a somersault when India was a child.

Standing with her long legs spread wide, Annie carefully placed her forearms on the mat in front of her, tucked her chin down so the very back of her head was the next thing to make contact with the mat and effortlessly rolled forward, keeping her legs apart, knees rigidly straight, and landing upright again in a legs-apart position, just as she had begun.

"Another forward please, and then two backward," said Lanny.

Annie repeated this incredible maneuver and then, placing her hands between her legs, fingers pointed backward, she dropped down to her behind, went over backward, and did the whole thing in reverse—twice, and each time with the fluidity of water.

"Very good, Annie. You haven't gotten out of shape," Lanny commented.

The understatement of the year, thought India.

"Now, back bend, please."

Annie lifted her hands over her head and dropped with incredible slowness into a perfect arch.

"Please walk your hands and feet closer together."

India stared as Annie slowly inched her hands and feet closer, accentuating the arch of her body until India began to fear the slim figure might suddenly snap in two at the waist.

"Not bad for an old lady," commented Cricket facetiously, knowing she was easily ten to twelve years the young black woman's senior.

Annie's beautiful arch collapsed in a heap on the floor as she began to giggle.

"Okay, okay," said Lanny. "Now next, you have to learn to get out of one gracefully. Headstand, please."

Annie placed her head flat on the floor, cupping her two hands around her forehead, and kicked up one long, lean, jersey-clad leg. Lanny had to reach up and catch it as the other leg followed, flailing wildly. He steadied them both and held them straight up, tight together.

"Straight knees, point your toes, arch your back slightly and balance."

At this last command, he very gingerly let go of Annie's legs and everyone in the room held her breath anxiously to see if the position would hold.

Annie crashed to the floor ignominiously and hooted louder than anyone else at her downfall.

India decided this class was a lot more fun than last week's and enjoyed the way everyone joined in the good-natured kidding. She could see that the women took great pride in the things they *could* do while not being averse to laughing at themselves for the things they couldn't.

Jade went through her paces next, and while she did them very competently and smoothly, India sensed that she was not in the jovial mood she had been in earlier, when the class had begun.

India was next and she shuddered inwardly.

She was nowhere near being in the same league as the rest of them, and she hoped she wouldn't make too big an idiot of herself. Trying to kick up into a handstand, she felt like she weighed two hundred pounds at least. Lanny caught her legs expertly and, after admonishing her to arch her back slightly, let go of her legs. To India's complete astonishment, she balanced for a split second before descending downward again.

"Not bad for starters," murmured Lanny approvingly.

She managed to haul her bulk through a reasonable facsimile of the rotations, bending her knees ungracefully now and again.

"Headstand" was the next order, and here India felt a little more secure. As a kid, she had been headstand champion of her neighborhood. She fervently prayed that it was like riding a bicycle—something one never forgot.

Placing her head down on the mat and supporting herself by a triangular pattern of her hands, she nervously lifted her folded legs up slowly. At the last moment, she straightened them, arched slightly, and held.

To her utter surprise, the rest of the class burst into applause. She grinned idiotically from her upside down position, as pleased as any child showing off.

"*Very* good," said Lanny sincerely. "You'd be amazed at how many of these athletic wonders we have here simply can't get their balance in a headstand."

Annie giggled loudly. Jade insisted with deadpan seriousness that it was the weight of her smallish bustline that kept her from perfect form. And Cricket simply protested that her head wasn't flat enough. Lanny disagreed with the latter, saying her head was altogether flat enough.

India, flushed with success and the blood running to her head, inquired timidly if she could come down now, which brought forth fresh laughter from the group.

"Certainly," agreed Lanny, then helped her through a fairly respectable back bend.

Cricket whizzed through her floor work, groaning

occasionally, and then the class completed the trapeze work, rings, and parallel bars.

The class ended with each person getting a "stretch" on the trapeze. This consisted of grasping the trapeze with one's hands and having Lanny push in the small of one's back from behind until one's feet were off the floor and the body stretched out in a perfect arch. India was surprised at how good it made her feel.

Finally, they began leaving the class, gathering their purses and exiting with calls of "Thank you, Lanny," "Good class, Lanny," and "See you Thursday."

Just as India was about to grab her handbag and go, she heard Lanny's voice call to her.

"India?"

She turned in reply and he walked over and stood beside her. He had enormous, kind blue eyes, India noticed.

"Listen, if you want to stay a few minutes after your next class, I'd be glad to help you with your floor work so you can catch up with the others. I have another class right now, or I'd offer to do it today. But it wouldn't take much. Your headstand's terrific already."

India found herself blushing like a schoolgirl at his solicitous offer.

"Thank you very much. I'd like that," she managed to stammer. His candid gaze made her self-conscious, though not unpleasantly so. He was really a very sweet person, she thought. And he had such nice eyes.

Chapter 7

Annie changed quickly after class and was busy checking in with her agency on the public phone as Cricket and Jade waited for the elevator. An easy relationship had sprung up between the two women as a result of the class, and Cricket always enjoyed exchanging tidbits of gossip with Jade when she was in town. Occasionally they met for lunch, but such get-togethers were difficult to arrange because both women had such busy schedules.

"How was the reindeer roundup?" asked Jade conversationally, trying to keep her inner uneasiness over Shelley from showing. "Anything fantastic enough to do a piece on for the show?"

Cricket lounged against the wall, her hands stuffed into the pockets of her London Fog trenchcoat. "Really pretty interesting, but I think it's too far away and too unexciting for your kind of thing. Can you imagine that to get to this one village— Suvanto—we had to cross a river on a *raft?*"

"Come on," teased Jade, "you on a raft? Why do I think of you as the yacht type?" she speculated, her green eyes dancing.

"I kid you not. There's a narrow point in the River

Kitinen where they have this oversize wooden raft that stands—and I mean *stands*—twenty people comfortably and everyone just piles on. It has four wooden paddles attached to a cable and four people at a time push and pull the thing along. Everybody takes a turn at the paddle. I almost burst into the 'Song of the Volga Boatmen.'"

The thought of Cricket standing on a raft paddling was enough to make Jade smile, in spite of herself. Cricket seemed to reek of expensive hotels and cushioned Mercedes interiors.

"You're right. It doesn't sound like a piece for 'the Morning Hour,' 'cause this chickadee ain't gettin' on no raft!" she answered with a laugh.

Cricket's expression grew serious for a moment and her eyes assumed a faraway look. "There's something about that country up there, though—something that is so . . . desolate . . . yet so beautiful . . . really awesome in its stark . . . grandeur, I guess you'd say. Heavens"—she shook her head and her voice lost its musing tone—"I'm starting to talk like one of my own columns."

At that moment, the door to Ivan's private office opened and the tall, impeccably tailored Russian strode through it and carefully locked it behind him.

He merely nodded absently at the receptionist as he passed her desk and headed toward the elevator.

His expression was closed and preoccupied, but as he saw Jade and Cricket standing there, his mask of congeniality quickly slipped into place and he beamed his most engaging smile at them.

"Ah, good morning, good morning ladies! How nice to see such beautiful faces to brighten up my day!"

Both Jade and Cricket fought back amusement, for both were used to Ivan's instant charm when he encountered paying customers.

The elevator chose this moment to arrive and Ivan stretched out a palm and bowed slightly, allowing them to enter before him.

As the car descended, Ivan stood beaming fatuously at them.

"Ever eaten reindeer meat, Ivan?" asked Cricket cheerfully.

"No, I have never had the pleasure," answered Ivan in his most unctuous tone. You ladies are always on some new diet or other, aren't you?" he proceeded to comment very seriously.

Cricket broke up and Jade grinned at the expression of bewilderment that appeared on Ivan's face.

"Never mind, Ivan. You wouldn't understand," said Cricket as the elevator reached the main floor and the doors parted.

Shrugging, Ivan uncharacteristically left the car first, forgetting his usual "after-you-my-dear" routine and both women noticed that his features had assumed their preoccupied look again as he hurried away.

"Wonder where he's off to in such a rush at this hour of the day? He looked upset about something," mused Cricket as the two women strolled leisurely from the building.

"I've always wondered if he made 'house calls' to some of his more mature clients," quipped Jade. "And just *what* would his services consist of, do you suppose?"

"Hell," said Cricket, lighting up a cigarette, "from what I've heard, he did his gigolo routine when he was much younger. Personally," she commented, narrowing her brown eyes speculatively, "I've got him figured for a closet queen at this stage of his life. Have you ever seen anyone so enamored of his own body?"

"Didn't someone once say that you should never make a judgment about someone's sexuality unless you've been to bed with him?" Jade remarked. "And in his case, I, at least, cannot claim that singular . . . ah, shall we say distinction?"

Cricket laughed. "Nor *I*. And you're right, of course. Got time for a cup of coffee?" she asked.

Jade started guiltily as she remembered again the pressing problem of finding her missing niece.

"God, no, not today. Thanks anyway. I've got to get home and check on something. Maybe Thursday. See you then!"

With a quick wave, she darted to the curb to hail a passing taxi.

Both women would have been even more puzzled had they followed the rapidly striding figure of Ivan Petrovich as he threaded his way through the shoppers strolling along 57th Street.

Barely glancing at the traffic light on the corner of Fifth Avenue, he crossed, dodging traffic, and headed north along the east side of the street. Passing the several small, elegant jewelry stores, he did not break his stride until he turned abruptly into the entrance of F.A.O. Schwartz at the corner of 58th Street.

F.A.O. Schwartz, the ultimate toy store of the world, was almost deserted at this hour of the day, this time of year. Life-size plush-covered stuffed figures of animals stared impassively out of unseeing glass eyes in the large windows facing Fifth Avenue. In several more months, this same store would be teaming—from early morning until closing time—with hoards of elegantly dressed, well-heeled adults. Most would be attempting to soothe their conscience by purchasing astronomically priced toys and games for their private-schooled or English-nannied children whom they ignored the other eleven months of the year.

Ivan Petrovich, who had lost all interest in children as soon as he had ceased to be one, was not a familiar figure here. Still, his instructions had been explicit.

Brushing by a counter filled with expensive, exquisitely dressed dolls that could duplicate most human functions short of reproduction, he spied the elevator doors off to his right, toward the rear of the store.

Punching the button impatiently, he glanced at his watch and saw that it was already ten minutes past the hour, ten minutes later than it should have been.

The doors opened to his touch and he strode into the small, empty car and pushed "two" on the board.

The short trip seemed endless. He was beginning to perspire under his custom-tailored, tapered Cardin shirt, and Ivan hated to perspire unless, of course, he was performing some complicated maneuvers on the bars at the gym for the delight and admiration of his patrons. Nervous perspiration irritated him, and he looked again at his watch, then cursed himself for it, knowing full well exactly what time it was.

He stepped off the elevator and peered both ways. To his left he saw endless layouts of trains on tables and complicated aerial toys strung from the ceiling. A few idle clerks lounged against the counters in boredom. To his right was a green sign with white lettering that read "Sporting Goods," and he swiftly headed in that direction, past an enormous, elaborately furnished doll's house.

The sporting goods department was apparently deserted and Ivan worried afresh that he might have missed his appointment as he made his way through intricate setups of tree houses and almost life-size log cabins, which would serve rich children as play houses and could serve in Appalachia to house an entire family.

His eyes darkened and then flickered with interest as he noted one lone figure casually inspecting a child-size model of a Stutz-Bearcat, complete with gasoline-powered engine. The middle-aged man wore a charcoal gray chesterfield coat, a pearl gray fedora, and carried a large, brown, paper-wrapped parcel under one arm.

Hope leapt in Ivan's breast as he slowed his pace and attempted to control his uneven breathing.

The man turned, as though by chance, when Ivan approached him, and he surveyed Ivan carefully with a long, unhurried look.

Satisfied by what he saw, he touched the brim of his hat lightly and inquired in a soft voice, "Mr. Petrovich, I presume?"

Ivan nodded and swallowed, uncertain of what to say or do next.

The stranger solved his dilemma by holding out the brown parcel to him. "You'll find it all in order, I trust. And you are aware of the conditions?"

Ivan nodded as he accepted the proffered package.

Again, the man lightly touched his hat, nodded, and without another word, departed, leaving Ivan standing all alone in a child's dream of outdoor opulence.

Chapter 8

After Jade's departure in a taxi, Cricket turned east on 57th Street and strolled casually toward Fifth Avenue. She felt invigorated by the workout at the gym and the first nip of fall in the late September air. Cricket hated it when summer temperatures lingered on after Labor Day. Ever anxious to rush into things headlong, she eagerly dismissed each season at its end and savored the onset of the next. And, corny as it seemed, she reflected there *was* something about "autumn in New York."

The whole city seemed to come alive again with the return of people from their summer trips and hideaways. The theater season was always bright with promise, the social calendar bristled with invitations, and store windows were aglitter with dramatic new clothes for dramatic new beginnings.

Thinking about it, Cricket wondered why New York didn't have its own separate calendar, with a New Year's celebration sometime in September when everything really began anew in the city.

Pausing for a moment at Henri Bendel's window, she stopped to inspect the clothes displayed there as well as to check her own reflection. It was the time of year to take steps to touch up one's tan with a sunlamp, lest the summer's bronze turn sallow and muddy looking. Making a mental note to spend some time under her own lamp when she got back to her apartment, she smiled in amusement at Bendel's latest display.

Always underdone rather than overstated, the current presentation consisted of three mannequins backed into one corner of the window. Though their bodies were draped with a lovely collection of chiffon printed gowns, their limbs stuck out in strange angles of fright or flight—one couldn't be sure which. The oddest thing of all, however, was that the head of each was covered by a brown paper grocery bag tied around the neck with long, gold velvet ribbons.

Cricket continually wondered whether the windows were meant to be a psychological test of one's own neuroses or simply an overt airing of the window designer's personal mental disorders.

The gowns, however, were pretty, and as soon as she got a fix on her own social engagements this month, Cricket vowed she would treat herself to a shopping spree. She always overspent on clothes, but it was her one indulgence since her travel was always covered by the office and her dates took care of her meals. Her co-op apartment had been a gift from her maternal grandmother, given when she had been informed of Cricket's decision to live in New York rather than in the family's hometown of Paisleyville, Virginia. When Cricket had come north to college at Smith, she had found herself much more comfortable with the manners and mores of the Northerners. The helplessness expected of Southern belles had always hung on her like ill-fitting clothing. So after graduation, she had simply announced to the family that she planned to join the Yankees and pursue success in the colder climes. It was typical of Grandma Todd that she believed Cricket would be safer in a Fifth Avenue co-op apartment than staying at one of the private hotels for women that had now all but vanished from the New York scene. Grandma Todd felt that money protected one from almost anything, as indeed it had protected the dear old lady from the day she had married Colonel Todd and his family fortune.

The apartment was really the only thing that Cricket had accepted from her family since graduation. It was part of the New York experience to see if she could make it on her own, and she had—exceptionally well. There was also the added bonus that travel writers had of being able to purchase many, many luxuries as they traveled through free ports. Cricket didn't know of a writer who didn't have an expensive Swiss watch, an elaborate Japanese camera, shelves and shelves of costly liquers, and bottles of French perfume in which some literally bathed themselves.

It was, for her at least, the best of all possible worlds. It allowed her to avoid the only two things she dreaded—containment in one place and commitment to one person.

She permitted herself only a quick peek into I. Miller's windows at the corner before hailing a cab and heading for her office, where a week's worth of unanswered mail awaited her.

Her secretary, Sheila, was nowhere in sight when Cricket sailed into her own small, windowed office at the *Festival* headquarters. But there by her desk were the usual three brown cardboard cartons that contained the week's accumulation of correspondence.

Sheila, always efficient, had run everything, through the mechanical letter-opening machine and then sorted Cricket's things by a strict set of rules. Carton number one held all personal mail, reader mail, and personally addressed trip invitations; carton number two held press releases, notices, and announcements that had been hand-addressed. Poor carton number three held the stepchildren of the lot, things that had been sent to Cricket but addressed through an Addressograph machine. An Addressograph label signaled to Sheila that the mail contained therein belonged on the lowest rung of the correspondence ladder. All of this saved Cricket a great deal of time and trouble because the mail received had a tendency to pile up during her absences. But never knock the volume of it, Cricket reminded herself. It's when it begins to fall off that you have to worry.

Noting that the contents of carton number one would fit into a large brown envelope, Cricket went out to Sheila's desk and rummaged to find one. Scrawling a quick note to her secretary that she could be reached at her apartment, Cricket dumped all the various-sized envelopes into a large one and departed. Sudden thoughts of a long, hot bath appealed to her more than hanging around the office for the day.

Once home, she kicked aside the luggage that the doorman had placed just inside her apartment door, threw her flight bag and unanswered mail on the large coffee table, and headed for her tiny efficiency kitchen to scrounge up something to eat.

At last fortified with a plate of crackers and slightly aging cheese—the only thing her neglected refrigerator contained—she returned to the living room to riffle through her mail.

Kicking off her Gucci pumps, she spread out all the assorted invitations and letters on the coffee table and settled down to go to work.

Fan mail could wait. The first order of business was to read and sort out the trip announcements according to date and plan her calendar for the next few months.

Festival Magazine left it strictly up to her to decide which trips she would accept and which she would bypass. But she was expected to notify the office of her travel plans for at least a month ahead, preferably two.

The first invitation she withdrew from an envelope read: "You are invited to spend two weeks in the Austrian Alps, courtesy of Austrian Air Lines."

Skimming it quickly to see what the trip entailed, she realized it would be hiking, mountain climbing, staying at small inns along the way, sampling "the wonderfully varied cuisine of Austria." And a lot of beer drinking, Cricket bet. Wonder if the damned hills really are alive with the sound of music, she thought wryly.

The date said the second and third week of October. Nuts, she reflected and tossed the letter into a pile for October. She had just gotten back to the city. Two weeks away; that soon really didn't appeal to her.

The second was an announcement of The Travel Writers of America's annual meeting, to be held the first weekend in October at Greenbriar, a posh golf and country club in Virginia. That one was a must because she was an officer. It also went into the October pile.

The next three read respectively: "See Our Beautiful Country from the luxurious comfort of an Amtrak Train. Travel across the USA by train for *three* days"—Cricket hated trains; then "Five Days in Bali in early November;" and finally "A Glamorous Three-Day Weekend in Rio—End of October."

The next mentioned a four-day trip to Paris, compliments of the Louvre Museum. Cricket checked the calendar. That was the first week in November. Sudden visions of the charming pace of the Left Bank came to mind—visions of dining in the tiny, intimate bistros that dotted the St. Germain des Pres area, which contrasted nicely with the desolate, cold country from which she had just returned. Thoughtfully, she placed the invitation to one side.

A week at Costa Brava in the first part of November, fourteen days in Russia—Cricket had just been, last year, and didn't feel it merited another story yet. Everyone was interested in traveling to China now. Besides, accommodations in the Soviet Union were Spartan, to say the least. Six days in Manila. Why anyone would *want* six days in Manila was beyond her. A five-day junket in Canada, compliments of Air Canada, in mid-October, and four days of castle touring in Ireland, the first week in November. And tomorrow's mail would probably bring more.

Nothing from China, thought Cricket reflectively. Even *Nixon* had been invited to China.

With a sigh, she again began to spread them out on the table before her, the October pile first. She took her calendar from her lap and began making notes with pencil in the proper spaces.

Yes to the Travel Writers meeting in Greenbriar, first weekend in October. No to skipping through the Austrian Alps. No to that dreadful train trip. No to the nice people of Canada. Her fingers lingered over the Paris invitation. It *would* be pleasant. She put it aside for the moment. Yes to the weekend in Rio.

74

That would make a very glamorous piece. No to Russia and no to Manila.

That took care of October. Maybe she's tackle November after a bath. Then she'd phone the office and have Sheila do her regrets and acceptances.

She fingered the Paris invitation again wistfully. She had just done a piece on French fashion three months before and she knew it really wasn't necessary to follow it so soon with this. Still, a Parisian trip would be *so* pleasant. It would be continental and stimulating. Paris was her absolute favorite city in the world and she couldn't imagine passing up a chance to see it again.

And something about Paris just promised romance, a commodity she was short on just at the moment.

Then again, she thought, picking up another already opened invitation, Costa Brava might be nice in November . . . She decided to consider these delightful alternatives while she soaked. Tossing the two envelopes on the table, she got up to run her bath.

Chapter 9

Jade had the taxi driver drop her at Sutton Place and 58th Street, rather than turn into the short street running between Sutton and the East River known as Sutton Square. There were only thirteen houses nestled in this small, exclusive mews, and few New Yorkers were even aware that it existed.

Shortly after her divorce from Ross Fleming, Jade had searched out the tiny jewel box of a house, number thirteen and had bought it, both as a hedge against the skyrocketing rents in Manhattan and as an investment. Located off one of the most exclusive streets in the city, it offered privacy and protection. Sutton Place was lined with expensive apartment buildings and each had its own white-gloved doorman. Many had two. There was scarcely an hour of the day when the air on Sutton Place was not alive with the whistling for cabs.

She turned the corner at a half run and continued down Sutton Square until she reached number thirteen, overlooking the river, and ran up the short flight of steps to the house.

Fitting her key into the ornate brass lock, she let herself in and closed the door behind her.

"Mrs. Swann," she called out, not wanting to

alarm her housekeeper, who might be surprised at her unexpected midday return.

The house was perfect for Jade's needs, precisely because it was so small. The main or parlor floor, into which she had just entered, held both a small front parlor and a larger living room at the back. The basement floor below held the kitchen and a large dining room. One flight up was Jade's bedroom, a small study, a bath and dressing room. The top floor provided two baths and two bedrooms, one for Mrs. Swann and one for Jade's eight-year-old son, Mark.

The slightly startled-looking face of Mrs. Swann popped up from the stairwell that led from the main hall down to the kitchen.

"Why hello, Miss Greene. I didn't expect you home at this hour! Gave me a little turn, you did."

The kindly, worn face of the housekeeper lit up with a smile once the intruder had been properly identified. Mrs. Swann ran both Jade's home and home life with capable efficiency, and Jade had said on numerous occasions that her frantic life-style was only bearable because of the ministrations of Mrs. Swann.

"There's been no word from my niece, Shelley, has there, Mrs. Swann?" Jade asked anxiously.

"Not one phone call since you called me, ma'am. I just came back from Gristede's though. Had to run out for a few things and I thought I'd do it while Mark was still in school. You know how he hates to have to go shopping when we could be playing in the park down by the river."

Jade sighed and picked up the mail from the polished top of the small Louis XIV table that stood in the front hall.

"Well, I'll check from upstairs with my office and my service and see if they've heard anything."

Mrs. Swann's gray-haired head disappeared as

suddenly as it had appeared, and the efficient lady returned to her work downstairs.

Jade plodded wearily up the graceful, winding stairs, her footsteps muffled by the thick, garnet carpeting that covered them. All the former lift she had felt from her gym workout disappeared in the face of the worry that again enshrouded her.

Pushing open the door to her bedroom, she started and almost cried out at the sight of the slim young figure stretched out on her bed. It was Shelley.

"My God, Shelley, how did you . . .?"

The pretty blond teen-ager sat up abruptly and began straightening her clothes, and her features arranged themselves into a petulant expression.

"Now Aunt Jade, don't start yelling at me. That's the last thing I need."

"I damn well *will* yell at you, young lady," began Jade, throwing down her purse and the mail on a chair as she turned to stare at her wayward niece in astonishment and anger.

"First of all, how on earth did you get in here, and second, where the hell have you been? You've had this whole family scared out its wits. Your mother's frantic, your father's going crazy, and you've totally disordered my normally disorderly life!"

Shelley's face fell so pitifully under her aunt's tirade that Jade's heart softened slightly toward the girl.

She dropped down on the bed beside Shelley and put an arm around her shoulder. "What's happened, Shelley? Tell Aunt Jade all about it and let's see if I can help."

Shelley turned large, blue, earnest eyes toward her aunt's concerned face. The faintest shine in them hinted at tears yet to be shed.

"I'm sorry about everything, Aunt Jade. Breaking in and all. But I tried the front door and it was locked and nobody answered, so I went down to the kitchen door and someone must have forgotten to push the latch button because it opened when I tried it. There was nobody home, so I just came up here to lie down and wait until you got home because I'm so tired and all."

Faint blue shadows under the large, sincere eyes indicated an obvious lack of sleep.

Patting her niece's shoulder comfortingly, Jade said "That's really not so important anyway, honey. I just hope you latched it behind you. And I hate to think of the fright you would have given Mrs. Swann if she'd walked in and found you. She was probably out to the store when you came in. But let's talk about all the rest." Jade turned toward the girl and took both of her hands. "Why in the world did you do something like this? You have scared us all out of our wits, you know," she finished reproachfully.

Shelley jumped up and stalked to the window, staring down at the quiet street below.

At last she turned to face her aunt again.

"I just couldn't stand it any longer, that's all," she said in a flat voice.

"Stand *what?*" asked Jade in genuine puzzlement.

"Stand *everything.* Covy High School, Augusta, the *people!* You don't know what it's like up there, Aunt Jade."

Her tone was so woebegone that Jade had to fight back a smile.

"Oh, *don't* I? You forget, I grew up there, too."

"But you left!" insisted Shelley plaintively.

"So did you, obviously," answered Jade, allowing her amusement to show through now, so great was her relief at finding the girl safe and accounted for.

"We're going to have to call your folks, honey. They are going out of their minds with worry over you." Jade made a move toward the pale blue princess phone by the bed.

"Please wait! Not just yet. Please let me talk to you first. Don't make me go back!"

Against her better judgment, Jade paused.

"We can talk a minute, but then we must call. And what do you mean, don't make you go back? What do you propose to do instead?" A faint suspicion was forming in the back of Jade's head as to just what her niece had in mind.

Relieved at her reprieve, Shelley came over and sat on the bed again. Her tone became very serious, very pleading.

"Aunt Jade, couldn't I stay here with you?"

Jade rolled her eyes upward.

"O-o-o-o-oh no you don't! First of all your parents would never permit it; second of all, where would I put you? Third of all, what about school? Shelley, what's gotten into you? This is very unlike you."

Shelley's pleading expression turned sullen again.

"Maybe nobody knows what I'm really like."

Jade sat down in a damask-upholstered slipper chair next to the bed and leaned her head on a hand, studying the girl opposite her.

"Okay, maybe I'll grant you that. But could you please try to explain to me. What's going on up there in Augusta?"

"Nothing, absolutely nothing. That's what's so terrible."

Jade threw up her hands in exasperation.

"Look Shelley, you're a pretty, popular girl. You're a straight *A* student. You're in your last year at Covy High and seniors are always supposed to have a ball. Now maybe just because Augusta doesn't teem with cafe society, or swarm with foreign agents, you're writing it off as a bore. For heaven's sake, life isn't one constant party!" Jade was losing patience with the girl.

"I know that. But try to look at it my way for a minute. I don't know about the pretty part, but sure I'm popular. I've dated ever since my freshman year—and always boys a year or so older. Now I'm a senior. The boys my age seem babyish, and besides, they're all dating freshman girls. All the older boys are away at school. But it's not the boys; it's *everything*. I've been editor of the newspaper; I was on the yearbook staff last year. I've been a class officer. I made the cheering squad. I've been and done *everything* at that school. And grades are a laugh. I can keep right on getting straight A's, even if I stopped going to classes. The courses are a snap for me. The phony rah-rah business of being a senior is crap and you know it. And Mom and Dad are so . . . so . . . provincial."

Jade gave a little snort of amusement at the last comment.

"That's what comes of living in the provinces."

Unintentionally, Jade had given Shelley an opening and she jumped on it.

"That's what I mean. I want to be down here, in Manhattan, where people are doing *interesting* things, where their minds are open to new ideas, fresh discoveries, where life is really happening. I want to visit the U.N.; I want to wander through all the museums; I want to memorize the art galleries. I want to . . . *live!"*

Jade stared at Shelley for long moments. God, she thought, can I ever have been that young, that earnest?

Still, she couldn't help but empathize with some of what the child was saying. Augusta *was* stifling. That's why she herself had moved down to New York after only two years of junior college in Maine. She had often thought as time went on that she had been hasty in what she had done. She should have finished the next two years of school. Yet what did it matter now? Did anyone ever ask Jade Greene, television personality, for her college diploma? In the end, maybe it was all crap.

Jade shook her head guiltily, as if to banish such heretical thoughts. She had to help Shelley figure out what to do next, for her niece had obviously been thinking this over for quite some time, as was evident from the forcefulness of her feelings.

"I'll grant you that a *little* of what you're saying is true. In fact, I've been kind of planning to give you maybe a month's visit here in New York as a graduation present next June. But you've got to graduate! What about school?"

Shelley's face lit up with happiness. She felt her aunt was beginning to consider what she herself had had in mind all along.

"I could go to school here in the city. They have high schools here, don't they?"

Shelley's pathetic eagerness tugged at Jade's heart, but she tried another tack.

"But where could you stay? Wait!" She held up a warning hand. "I don't think I want you to answer that. I can feel the answer coming on," she finished with a grin.

Shelley returned the grin happily.

Her words tumbled out.

"Here, Aunt Jade. I know the sofa in your study converts into a bed. You told me that once you let Mark sleep in there when he was out of school with the chicken pox."

"Boy, you don't miss a trick, do you? I can see that you were taking notes every time I paid a visit home."

Jade's smile disappeared and she became suddenly serious again when she realized how far Shelley had gone in her planning.

"All other considerations aside for the moment,

what about your parents? You know my sister would never for a moment let her darling little girl stay with her degenerate aunt in the big, wicked city. No, Shelley, it won't work. You've simply got to go back. Think of your trip down here in June to keep you going, honey."

With that note of finality in her voice, Jade turned again to the telephone and lifted the receiver.

"I'll just run away again if you make me go back. And next time, I'll go to the East Village like the runaways and disappear, and none of you will ever find me again!"

The little girl sulkiness was back again, and Jade put down the phone with a sigh.

"You're not acting very grown-up about this whole thing. If you're going to pout, we'll never get this thing straightened out."

Shelley came off the bed with a bound and knelt before her aunt on the floor, her hands clasped in supplication on Jade's lap. The tears in her blue eyes were very evident now.

"Please, Aunt Jade! I beg of you. I won't be any trouble at all. I'll take care of Mark for you and I'll take him places and do things with him. I'll clean and I'll scrub. I'll do the laundry and the ironing . . . I'll do anything you like, but please let me stay! It means everything to me!"

Jade felt tears well up in her own eyes. The child was so sincere and her pleading was so touching. The whole thing was pure madness, but being young was so painful at times—most of the time, Jade remembered, looking back on the loneliness of her own adolescence.

"Oh Shelley, baby. Get up off the floor. I don't need a scullery maid, for pity's sake." She pulled the girl up and wrapped her tightly in her arms.

As Shelley's tears flowed unchecked down her

cheeks and wet Jade's own with their saltiness, Jade began to stroke the child's long blond hair.

"This does mean everything to you, doesn't it, darling? Poor baby, I had no idea you were so unhappy up there."

For an answer, Shelley could only gulp and nod.

Pulling back so she could look Shelley directly in the face, Jade made a reluctant decision.

"Okay." There was a long pause. "Okay," she said seriously, "I'll give it a try. I'll call Rose and ask her what she would think of the whole idea . . ."

Shelley's joy was so instantaneous, so overwhelming, that Jade thought the girl would burst.

"Oh, Aunt Jade, oh, Aunt Jade. I never thought you would . . . I mean how can I ever repay you? Oh, Aunt Jade . . ."

Jade held up a warning hand.

"I only said I'd *try*. I'm not guaranteeing a thing. You know your mother, and so do I. We'll have to have something pretty logical in mind for school . . ."

Always one step ahead of most situations, Jade's mind was already racing over the school problem. Obviously Shelley couldn't just be tossed into a public high school in Manhattan. Most of them were pretty bad, and Shelley's naïveté would make her a sitting duck for any kind of influence. A private school would have to be the answer, preferably a private *girl's* school. Preferably a *convent*, thought Jade wryly. And with that, she suddenly knew the solution to the whole problem.

A convent was just what she needed—The Convent of the Sacred Heart up on 91st Street, a very strict, very fancy private girl's school, with a fancy tuition. Jade had already realized that the year's tuition for school would have to be her graduation present to her niece, because Rose and Herb could never afford that sort of thing. But at Sacred Heart the atmosphere would be geared to a good education with a certain amount of insulation from the rude street world of the city. She was sure she must know someone on the Board of Trustees who could help her get Shelley enrolled there. And she resigned herself to giving up a certain amount of privacy for the school year with her niece occupying the sofa in her study.

But looking down again at the shining, glowing face before her, Jade felt like she had just been privileged to give the invaluable gift of happiness to someone. It was a good feeling.

Smiling now, she pulled Shelley to her feet and rose herself.

"Well, I've got some ideas about how we can take care of the school thing. But now, let's face the grueling task of convincing your parents. You go into the study and pick up the extension there. But don't say anything until I tell you to. Let me handle this first . . ."

Shelley skipped off into the other room with so much bounce that she reminded Jade of the adorable little child she used to be when Jade had taken her out for ice cream cones on her yearly family visits to Maine.

As she picked up the phone and began to dial, Jade mused over the lunacy of what she was doing. But she would be making someone happy, and wasn't that what all the money and prestige she had worked so hard for were meant to do?

Her anxious sister picked up the phone in Augusta, Maine, on the first ring.

"It's me, Rose. Jade. Shelley's fine and she's here with me. Now pull up a chair, kiddo, because I've got something I've got to talk to you about and I think you'd better be sitting down . . ."

Chapter 10

Annie threw the last of her makeup and her three bras—strapless, no-bra look, and padded—into her already jumbled model's bag and quickly checked the small dressing room with a glance to see if she had forgotten anything. Her model's bag contained every conceivable item she might need in the course of a day. It was practically a walking dressing room. Finally assuring herself that she had all her belongings, she left.

Making her way through the tangle of cables and discarded props thrown around the floor of the dingy studio, she called a weary "'bye" to the photographer and art director who were huddled in the far corner of the room, poring over a stack of layouts.

Both looked up guiltily and waved, for they had already forgotten about her. The gorgeous, famous black model was to them, after the day's shooting, just another prop.

She pushed open the heavy metal door to the street and went out into the cool, refreshing air of early evening. Though she knew it was filled with smog and pollution, after six hours in a stuffy, dusty studio, it smelled like heaven to her.

The one thing no one ever realized about a model's life, which was pictured as glamorous, exciting, and fun filled, was that models got sore feet. It was an occupational hazard. Annie was sure that this was the reason so many of the girls took enormous shoe sizes. Standing on one's feet for eight hours or so every day was not conducive to Cinderella-size slippers.

Aside from the aches in her feet, Annie became aware of another, more urgent ache—in her belly. She realized that she had eaten nothing since the cup of yogurt she had snatched at a deli after the morning's gym class on her way to her first assignment.

She supposed that she and Ferrago would go out to dinner to the little restaurant they frequented in their Soho neighborhood. Neither ever felt like cooking after a day's work, and Annie was grateful that Ferrago did not force her to go to the health food restaurant where he had lunch by himself every day.

But the pain in her middle persisted.

Hard as she tried, it was impossible for her to ignore the bright yellow sign ahead of her that proclaimed "McDonald's Town House." Ever since McDonald's had opened a string of their restaurants in Manhattan, they had taunted her like personal demons, always beckoning appealingly from unexpected places. For Annie, it would only be heaven if the pearly gates were topped by the twin golden arches.

She strode by resolutely. And then, dragging her feet, she turned slowly back. It was no use. She had no will power. And besides, Ferrago would never know. She didn't believe for a minute all that nonsense about him having spies watching her at all times.

She would just have a small cheeseburger with a

big bag of French fries—and a diet soda, to ease her conscience. She'd still be ready and eager for a medium-size dinner at the restaurant later.

Pushing open the big glass door, she breathed in the familiar aroma of greasy cooking as if it were the perfume of Araby.

There was no one at the counter waiting, so the clerk fetched her food instantly. The restaurant was nearly deserted and Annie looked around quickly, happy she saw no one she knew.

She slipped into a small, plastic booth unit, propped her heavy bag against the leg of the table, and greedily tore into the cheeseburger wrapper on the tray in front of her. With the first bite, her aches, pains, and weariness began to melt away.

The trouble with Ferrago was that he didn't understand her compulsion for junk food. It was a need that went deeper than mere appetite. He might have been raised on the Lower East Side, in a lower class Italian family, but he would never know what it had been like to grow up poor in Harlem.

Annie Clemmon's family had been grindingly poor. Her father had disappeared when she had been too young to even remember him, and she had been third in a family of six children. Her mother, Eulalia Clemmons, had been on and off welfare over the years, but whenever she had been able, she worked as a domestic, cleaning the apartments of the wealthy who lived on the Upper East Side. To this day, whenever Annie was on the Upper East Side for a job and had occasion to grab a crowded Fifth Avenue bus downtown, she was smart enough to stand near some plainly dressed, serious-faced black woman, knowing full well that the seated woman would soon exit in the 50's or 60's to go keep house for the day for some wealthy white family.

So Annie and all her siblings had learned early to fend for themselves. When their mother had to go off to work, she would give them each two quarters— their daily money to "eat off the streets." Most children attending the Robert J. Frost School at 123rd and Madison would split for the street at lunchtime. What the socially conscious nutritionists who planned all those wonderful school lunch programs didn't realize was that the good food they served was often alien and indigestible to the black children who were expected to eat it. Milk made Annie's stomach hurt and canned soup and baloney sandwiches were as foreign to her as the dark side of the moon. In the Clemmons' household, when there was the money to afford it, they dined on scrumptious feasts of boiled greens and side sticking food like ribs and fried chicken.

The most common spots for the children to spend their precious money would be any one of a number of dirty hole-in-the-wall stands that dotted the dilapidated neighborhood and specialized in greasy French fries and gray-looking hamburgers overloaded with bright red ketchup, the lifeblood of the poor man's diet.

The hamburgers were thirty-five cents, and they didn't fill you up much and didn't leave enough left over for anything to drink. But for fifteen cents you could get a large bag of French fries, douse them with ketchup, spend twenty cents for a soda, and still have fifteen cents left to buy yet another belly-filling bag of fries on your way home after school, in case supper was late or, as on some nights, nonexistent.

For all the years she played and survived on the streets of Harlem, the delicious aroma of greasy French fries would make Annie salivate as surely as the bell induced Pavlov's dog. Whenever she felt depressed or lonely, a bag of French fries with ketchup was sure balm for her troubled spirits.

But Ferrago would never understand this. She supposed that maybe his devotion to health food could in some way be traced to his childhood, too. Perhaps it began as an aversion to all those plates of pasta on which he was raised. She knew with a certainty that his almost homicidal aversion to drugs was directly connected to the death of a dearly loved younger brother who had overdosed on heroin. Ferrago was fanatical on the subject and didn't even like it if he caught Annie taking an aspirin for a headache.

Thoughts of Ferrago made Annie gulp the last bite of cheeseburger and scrounge around the salty insides of the French fry bag for one stray bit that might be left.

Gulping the last of her diet soda, she crumpled her napkin and stood up. She neatly emptied her tray into the plastic container provided for refuse, grabbed her bag from beneath the table, and hurried toward the door.

Thus fortified, she contemplated the thought of a pleasant, leisurely supper with Ferrago in much better spirits than when she had entered.

Chapter 11

India was down on her knees beside the tub, just finishing giving the nightly six o'clock bath to her bubbling, bouncing two-and-a-half-year-old son. Toohey loved his bath and he loved his Mr. Bubbles and he loved his Crazy Foam and every one of the thirty-six rubber animals he seemed to feel a bath was incomplete without.

Normally, India's patience would have given out about an hour ago. Five o'clock was dinner time for eight-year-old Heather and Toohey, and they bickered constantly during the meal. This evening, as she had sat with them, India had remonstrated at them only slightly and had sometimes even found herself smiling in amusement at the sheer idiocy of their arguments.

Hiring a sitter and getting out of the house for a couple of hours in the morning to go to her gym class was working wonders for her morale, she realized, not to mention her sanity. She supposed it was simply putting things into perspective for herself. The world did not begin and end with two noisy, quarrelsome, dirt-collecting children. There were real grown-up people out there doing real grown-up

93

things and she had a chance to rub elbows, or rather, stretch muscles, with them twice a week. It made the hours she spent with the children less burdensome, more fun. Aha, she thought, absence does make the heart grow fonder. Only she didn't think that seeing less of one's children was quite what had been intended when that venerable saying had been coined.

Until she had started the class, she mused, she had channeled her frustrations into that time-honored pursuit of bored housewives—being the compleat consumer. There had been endless times when she had tied an unsuspecting Toohey into his stroller and had marched directly to Gimbel's East to spend countless hours browsing and buying, simply out of sheer boredom. She now had an ironing board cover with racing stripes. *Racing stripes,* she reflected wryly, were not essential to the practice of ironing. But Gimbel's East had featured ironing board covers with racing stripes, and so racing stripes it had been. When Bloomingdale's had implied that it wasn't Spring until one had a complete set of enameled cookware painted with daisies, the first flowers to bloom in the Spring had appeared on India's four-burner stove.

Asinine, she thought to herself in her newfound wisdom. And here she was now, secretly savoring the fact that she had been the only person in class today to do a perfectly balanced headstand. It was the sort of thing you wanted to shout to the world. Hey, world, guess who can do a terrific headstand? She had fantasies of being somewhere, at a huge public gathering, where—in the age-old manner of calling, "Is there a doctor in the house?"—someone would say, "Listen, is there someone present who can do a perfect headstand?" Modestly, she would step forward and timidly offer to display her prowess for the throng. How they would applaud! She wondered if the *New York Times* would ever run an ad that read, "We have an opening for a middle-aged lady who can stand on her head."

The absurdity of the whole idea tickled her fancy so that she laughed aloud, which prompted the wet, squirming little figure she was attempting to towel dry to inquire crossly, "What's funny? I'm freezin' a death and you're laughin'!"

She hastily apologized and hustled him into his clean Dr. Dentons. He had the shining, squeaky-clean face of a cherub, she noted, even if his tiny brows were furrowed in annoyance. She kissed him on his turned-up nose and suggested that he run off and pick up the toys strewn about his room before Daddy got home.

Stopping in front of the mirror over the long double dresser she and Drew shared, she peered long and hard at her reflection. Her whole appearance seemed altered. Her newly dyed, uniformly brown hair curled softly about her face, her hazel eyes seemed bright and alert, and the small wrinkles seemed more like laugh lines and less like crevices. And this was what Lanny, the gym instructor, saw when he looked at her, not the shriveled-up hag she had felt herself to be a couple of weeks ago.

She turned away guiltily at the thought of Lanny. Come on now, she chided herself. He's a good-looking young man with kindly, sensitive blue eyes, who offered to help you work out so you would catch up with the class. He's also got to be at least fifteen years younger than you are, and his interest is professional, not personal. Still, the image of his broad, handsome face lingered in her mind.

And that is a sign of approaching old age, she

mused wryly. When attractive young men start to appeal to you, you are heading over the hill.

The sound of Drew's key in the lock interrupted her reverie.

It was followed by the rattle and clank of the chain lock catching and a few choice expletives from Drew.

"Sorry, honey," she called out, hurrying to release the safety chain for him.

Closing the door and unlatching the chain, she opened it again to give him access. "I forgot to take it off before I put Toohey in the tub."

Drew smiled down fondly at her as he dropped a kiss on her brow.

"No matter. If it keeps the burglars away, it's worth the inconvenience. How was your day?" he asked dutifully as he shucked off his trench coat and parked his ever-present attaché case in the entrance hall.

As she followed him into their sunken living room and over to the corner bar, her answer was drowned out in the screams and cries advancing from the other room of "Daddy, Daddy, Daddy's home!"

Toohey threw his little pajama-clad body at Drew's knees while Heather, decorous and prim in her eight years, reached up and embraced him around the waist.

Drew smiled and kissed them both, rumpling Toohey's long blond hair affectionately with one hand and giving Heather a pat with the other.

"Hi! How are all the little people tonight?" he asked.

"I got 100 on my spelling test," Heather announced proudly.

"An' I ate sand in the park with Miz Schmidt," chimed in Toohey.

"Mrs. Schmidt? Oh, that's right. You went to gym

96

class today, didn't you?" he said to India as he disentangled himself from his son and stepdaughter and proceeded to mix some martinis.

"Okay, that's enough. Beat it now for awhile so Daddy and I can talk. Playtime comes after your homework is finished, Heather. And Toohey, I want to see every toy in that room in the toy box, and *then* we'll have story time. Come on now." With this, India shooed the children off and accepted the chilled, silvery drink Drew offered her.

They both moved to their usual evening-talk positions—one at either end of the long blue corduroy-covered sofa—and Drew kicked off his tasseled loafers and propped up his feet on the large, round coffee table in front of them.

Taking his first long sip of the drink, he shuddered happily at its impact.

"How was your class today?" he asked conversationally.

India fought back her desire to launch into a lengthy, detailed explanation of all that had happened, highlighting the story, of course, with her magnificent headstand, and instead decided to inquire first about his day.

Drew leaned his head back on the sofa wearily and said with mock solemnity, "A day like any other day, full of the events that shape the lives and minds of millions of unsuspecting consumers."

India laughed and said, "Come on, it couldn't have been all that bad. I'll bet it was another tough one where you spent three hours interviewing beautiful models for commercials, three over a long business lunch, and then went back to the office to take a nap before beginning the arduous trip home to 83rd Street."

"Ha! That's all *you* know," he answered with a

grin. "It was a bloody battle the whole day through with that thickheaded client who's in town, and to tell the truth, I'd really like to relax a little before going through all the gory details for you. Come on, tell me about the latest events at the rich-lady's sweat palace."

India didn't need any more prodding, and she gave him a condensed version of her hour at the gym, complete with all the funny antics of her classmates and ending with her feat of the headstand. Jade was the only person to whom she referred by name, having astonished Drew last week by mentioning that there was a celebrity among her fellow students.

"And she was there again? Wait'll I tell everyone that my wife rubs leotards with the "Morning Hour" hostess!"

"Please," interrupted India with a laugh. "You make it sound like a lesbian experience!"

"Any of them make a pass at you, honey?" he asked with an unconvincing leer.

"Nope, none of them even asked to feel my muscles," she returned facetiously, draining her glass. "But I did have a handsome young gym instructor who spoke—would you believe—Brooklynese, so I understood every work he uttered."

It was Drew's turn to laugh because he remembered her bewilderment during the first class, when Misha had called out instructions with his thick, unintelligible accent.

"And you know something?" she continued. "It was better when I couldn't understand. Some of those exercises are killers!"

Drew took her empty glass and his own over to the bar for refills.

"Why don't you bring those out to the kitchen and

keep me company while I start our dinner?" India suggested, reluctantly abandoning her snug position among the pillows on the couch.

"Fair enough," agreed Drew, following her with drinks in hand.

"Oh, one bit of news did develop today—and I'll bet you won't turn handsprings over it. I've got another trip coming up."

"When?" was India's succinct inquiry. She hated the shooting trips for commercials that Drew had to make periodically for the ad agency that employed him.

"Second week in October," he answered, handing her her drink while he lounged on a nearby kitchen stool.

India took from the refrigerator the fillet of sole she had bought that afternoon and prepared to poach it for sole *bonne femme*, a favorite dish of Drew's. And fish was nice and low in calories for the slim figure she was pursuing.

"Where to now?" she asked with negligible interest. One trip was pretty much like any other to her since all it meant for her was days and days without Drew's company.

"Paris. We're shooting those perfume commercials over there. It was that or fake it in a studio here, and this client is a real stickler for authenticity. Besides, we need the look of all that Left Bank local color, and I think the copywriter has a yen for some time in Paris. He wrote it so specifically that we could hardly shoot it anywhere else."

"It's a tough life you ad people live," noted India dryly, pouring a little white wine in the bottom of the skillet.

Drew came over to her side and put an arm around

99

her waist for a quick hug.

"Ah, honey, you know these stupid trips. They're all work and boring as hell. Nothing of any interest ever happens."

"You never know," said India, carefully placing the fillets in the pan. "This may be the one that's different."

Chapter 12

Ivan Petrovich and Igor Trogorney whirled through the revolving doors and into the ruby-hued gloom of the Russian Tearoom on West 57th Street. It was a favorite lunching spot of theirs whenever the opportunity to lunch together presented itself, which was rare. Usually one of them stayed at the gym while the other ducked out for a quick bite, or they ordered something sent in for both of them.

Today's luncheon was at Igor's request, a fact that made Ivan very edgy. He lived in constant dread that Igor would discover his fiscal irresponsibility. Igor would not tell him the purpose of the lunch, but he had said it was imperative that the two of them get out together and talk. Ivan was very nervous over what the subject might be.

The blond hostess smiled a greeting at them familiarly and led them to their favorite table in the bar, the last one toward the back on the left.

She pulled out the small, pink damask-covered table and allowed Ivan to slip behind it. As Igor seated himself, she handed each of them a large menu displaying colorful Russian scenes and said she'd be back in a moment for their orders. Ivan nervously adjusted his blue paisley ascot and hoped Igor would quickly say what was on his mind.

Igor Trogorney, with his close-cropped, salt-and-pepper hair, his short, sturdy build, and his ruddy complexion was an almost complete physical opposite of the tall, aristocratic-looking Ivan. Igor radiated peasantlike health and good cheer and generally greeted the world with a beaming smile, whereas the dour-appearing Ivan only smiled when a paying customer confronted him.

Today Ivan noted that Igor seemed especially exuberant, which would hardly be the case if he wished to talk about money. Ivan felt slightly reassured.

"Ivan, I want to talk about money," Igor began.

Ivan's reassurance died abruptly.

A waiter chose that moment to appear and ask if they would like cocktails.

Ivan was about to decline, as was his usual luncheon custom, when Igor beamed happily and said, "Come on, Ivan, let's have a wodka! It's a happy occasion!"

Ivan hesitated only a second before replying in the affirmative. He realized that Igor would scarcely be that cheerful if he had any knowledge of the fifty-thousand dollars Ivan had deposited in their corporate account a week earlier, the total contents of the brown-wrapped parcel he had received at F.A.O. Schwartz's. Nor would he be that happy, Ivan rationalized, if he realized that the gym was now in debt to one of the biggest loan sharks on the streets.

No, it had to be something else. And that, in itself, was cause enough for celebration.

As the waiter disappeared, Igor opened his large menu and began to peruse it. Ivan followed suit, deciding to let Igor proceed with the conversation at his own pace, lest he, Ivan, precipitate something he did not care to discuss.

Ivan's eyes immediately paused at the listing of "Beluga Caviar—$42.00 the ounce." What was a vodka without caviar, he thought ruefully. Then, with regret, knowing Igor would frown on such extravagance, he went on to read the rest of the menu, which he knew almost by heart.

As usual, they both settled on the blinchiki with cheese and sour cream, though Ivan's eyes coveted the blinis with red caviar and sour cream. Still, red caviar was so pedestrian that giving it up wasn't all that much of a sacrifice, Ivan decided.

Finally, closing his menu and laying it aside, Ivan found he could contain his impatience no longer.

"Igor, what is it that you want to discuss? What do you mean, let's talk about money? What is that supposed to mean?" His apprehensiveness gave his voice an irritability he took no pains to conceal.

Igor's equanimity was unruffled. "Can't we at least wait for our wodkas to toast a new venture?" he asked affably.

Ivan scowled and fiddled with his silver as he waited impatiently for the waiter to reappear with their drinks.

Igor hummed a few bars of a Russian melody and smiled an abstracted smile as he reached for a fresh white carnation from the tiny vase on the table, broke off the stem at the blossom, and proceeded to tuck it into the buttonhole of his serviceable blue blazer. While Ivan's clothes were all custom-tailored and designer-labeled, the less pretentious Igor wore clothes that his loving wife of thirty-five years purchased for him at less ostentatious stores such as Macy's or Gimbel's.

At last the waiter approached their table with the

vodkas served the way they liked them—neat and chilled to a frostiness in small shot glasses and topped with freshly ground black pepper.

"Na Zdrovyda!" said Igor happily as they each threw back their heads and tossed down the drinks in one gulp.

"Well?" asked Ivan gruffly as the burning yet icy sensation subsided.

"Well," said Igor, leaning forward in his chair and folding his arms on the table, his face flushed with vodka and eagerness, "what would you say if I suggested that from now on there not only be an Ivan & Igor's gymnasium in the heart of Manhattan, but also one on the West Coast, say in the heart of Beverly Hills?"

"I'd say you'd had one too many vodkas," grumbled Ivan, settling back in his chair and wondering what the hell had come over his comrade of so many years.

Igor held up a restraining hand. "Please Ivan, hear me out. It's something I've been thinking about for a long while."

Ivan sighed a Slavic sigh and waited for Igor to go on.

"Natasha and I have been talking for some time now about how, since the children are grown and married, maybe we should think about moving someplace where it's warmer and pleasanter to spend the years ahead of us. Now warmer—that means Florida or California, right?"

Ivan nodded noncommittally.

"But in Florida all the people are old and retired and what do they want a gym instructor for, right?"

Again Ivan nodded.

"But in California there are many young, beautiful bodies who would love a place to go to work out, right?"

"Igor," Ivan interrupted impatiently, "they *have* many places to go and work out—Richard Simmons' place, Jane Fonda's—"

"Ah, but not with our East Coast flair . . . does Kounovski have a West Coast branch, for example?"

"Walter of Alex and Walter went out there years ago," began Ivan.

"A perfect case in point!" said Igor gleefully. "I saw him last time he was in New York and he told me his place out there was flourishing!"

"Romanians are all liars," said Ivan glumly.

"Ivan, he is a Russian and you know it!" insisted Igor loyally.

"I fail to see what you're getting at," Ivan protested, though, of course, he saw very well indeed. And what worried him was where the money would come from to finance this venture, for Igor was entirely in the dark about their financial situation. He had blindly trusted Ivan's handling of their money.

"I think we should open a place out there," explained Igor patiently, "and Natasha and I will move out there and operate it. You will be in charge of the East Coast operation and I, the West. We will make twice as much money, and while Natasha and I enjoy the magnificent climate of California, you will have the glamour and excitement of New York," he finished with a flourish.

"And we will spend twice as much money trying to maintain two establishments and employing two sets of instructors," complained Ivan, although in his own mind he could begin to see the glimmer of an advantage in having Igor safely stashed away on the West Coast. It would give him the time he needed to repay the debt he had just incurred and get things here bailed out so that the books might once again balance. Still, where the capital to do such a thing would come from had him worried.

"And the money? Does money grow on trees like oranges in this magnificent climate of California?" asked Ivan stubbornly, suddenly hoping that Igor could come up with the miracle it would take to accomplish this.

Igor leaned even farther forward across the table and lowered his voice so that he could not be heard beyond their immediate area.

"Ivan, you are my very oldest friend and I value our friendship. Still, we are unalike in many ways. While you have always enjoyed the delights of the material world, Natasha and I have simpler tastes and have always lived frugally so that we could be comfortable but put some money away as well. I have a nest egg of my own . . ."

As Ivan's dour face began to lighten, Igor put up a hand to restrain him.

"Not much, I warn you, because you know that neither of us has ever taken enormous sums out of the business . . ."

Speak for yourself, thought Ivan ruefully.

"But enough—enough so that if you would be willing to go with me to one of the banks here and we put up the East Coast business as collateral, I'm sure we could raise the necessary funds to begin the West Coast operation within a few weeks. Would you do this for an old friend and his wife who would like to go westward to enjoy the sunshine in their declining years?"

Suddenly Ivan realized how really advantagaeous it would be to have Igor on the West Coast. And who knew? If it turned out to be as sound a business proposition as Igor seemed to think, perhaps some of the profit from out there could be used to offset some of the rather large debts he had incurred here. He was sure that if he could spend a few hours alone with the gym's books, he could make them stand up to the scrutiny of the bank officials if they felt the need for an audit.

Ivan turned the matter over in his mind for only seconds before reaching over and patting his partner's hand. He smiled beneficently.

"Igor, for you, my oldest and dearest friend, I would do anything. You know that. If you like, we can see a banker this very afternoon."

Igor's rosy, peasant face became wreathed in smiles. "Ivan, you are a true friend. Your friendship brings tears to my eyes. I thank you and I know Natasha will thank you when I tell her the good news. I will miss you very much of course, but we will be in touch."

Not too close in touch, Ivan hoped.

He became more expansive. "I will miss you too, my comrade. But life must go on. I wish you success in our new venture. I trust you will find the climate of California salubrious to your health. And now, let us drink another toast. This time, to *your* health. Come, let us order another."

A slight gleam crept into Ivan's eyes as he suggested slyly, "And perhaps a little Beluga caviar with this one? It is, after all, a celebration!"

Seventeen stories above the bustle of traffic on Fifth Avenue, in the massive complex that is known as Rockefeller Center, an unprepossessing middle-aged man sat alone at a large mahogany desk in a small, tidy office. The gilt lettering on the opaque glass door to the office read simply: Lotus Industries,

Importing & Exporting. There was very little furniture in the office. A green leather chair stood opposite the desk, a bulky, old-fashioned black vault stood in one corner, and on the coat rack by the door hung a charcoal gray chesterfield coat and a pearl gray fedora.

The people who occupied the other offices on the floor rarely saw anyone come or go there. The middle-aged man visited the office only intermittently himself. Today he was frowning over a large black ledger that was spread open on the desk in front of him.

With one carefully manicured forefinger, he followed a column down the pale green lines on the page, pausing only when he reached the bottom.

His frown deepened. His finger retraced its path. He did not like what he saw there.

This Ivan Petrovich did not seem to take his commitments seriously. He had been late twice, and the last time the payment was short.

The people the man represented were very serious.

Some steps would have to be taken to convince Petrovich how serious they were.

He reached for the phone.

Chapter 13

It had been no easy matter convincing Jade's sister Rose that her daughter Shelley would be safe living in the "wicked city" with her aunt. It was only the mention of sending Shelley to the Convent of the Sacred Heart that had, oddly enough, done the trick.

Rose's first reaction to this suggestion was, "What would a nice Jewish girl be doing in a convent?"

Jade carefully explained that though the school was run by the Sisters and attended by Catholics, there were non-Catholics who went there and survived—even managing to graduate without conversion to the Catholic faith.

Rose was dubious.

In desperation and exasperation, Jade had finally snapped that if the place had been good enough for Caroline Kennedy, it really ought to be good enough for Shelley Shattuck.

Rose, small town snob that she was, went to the bait like a famished fish.

"*The* Caroline Kennedy?" Jade's sarcasm had been totally lost on her single-minded sister.

"I don't know *what* her mother's thinking of, letting her run loose all over Europe the way she does," Rose mused, suddenly lost in a mother's empathy with Jackie O. The appeal of having her daughter attend the same school the famous former First Lady's had attended was a powerful inducement.

Jade sighed. So like Rose to do the right thing for the wrong reason, she thought to herself. No matter. It was time to move in for the kill while Rose was still lost in visions of being a sister under the skin to the world's foremost celebrity.

"So you think it's possible that you and Herb can entrust Shelley to me for the school year?" she asked.

Jade consciously fought to keep the abrasive tone out of her voice and accomplish her mission. This was no time to replay sibling rivalries, she knew, but a time to consider what was best for Shelley and by this time, Jade was fully convinced that staying with her in Manhattan could truly be beneficial to the child. In fact, she was beginning to look forward to playing wetnurse and chaperone to her favorite niece.

It was just as well that she did not possess the gift of prophecy or her outlook might have been considerably less sanguine.

"Well, I'd have to talk it over with Herb, of course . . ."

Jade smiled into the phone, knowing she'd won.

The last thing that Rose had talked over with Herb had been whether or not he had wanted stuffed derma served at their wedding reception twenty years ago. That had been Herb's biggest and final decision in their entire marital relationship.

"Look Rose, while you and Herb are discussing all this, is it possible that you could pack up a trunk of Shelley's clothes and send it on? The poor kid has little more than the things on her back. I'm going to take her out shopping this afternoon for some stuff to tide her over, but I'm sure she'd like her own clothes as soon as possible. We'll be in touch and I'll let you know how we're doing as soon as we get her settled in. Don't worry and give my best to Herb."

With this, Jade rang off, leaving a slightly bewildered sister on one end and a wildly happy niece on the other.

Jade and Shelley had a perfectly marvelous afternoon combing the tiny, fashionable designer boutiques of Manhattan for suitable teenage attire. Shelley was particularly enchanted with the stores that endlessly blared loud rock music designed to lull the youthful shoppers into hypnotic complicity.

They picked up many more outfits than Jade had planned to buy, chiefly because Jade felt that everything that Shelley tried on looked fabulous on her. Besides, the young girl's enthusiasm and uninhibited gratitude were a powerful intoxicant, and Jade decided to relax and enjoy playing Lady Bountiful.

Everywhere they went, salespeople recognized Jade instantly and fawned over them, making the afternoon pass in a joyous haze for Shelley.

They topped off their shopping expedition with an early supper at the Ginger Man. Then Jade hauled a wearly, deliriously happy niece home to be tucked into her convertible sofa, after which the suddenly exhausted aunt crawled into her own bed to nurse a brandy and soda and ponder the craziness of the day.

The very next morning, as soon as the show went off the air, Jade began her quest for a loose string to tug to get her niece into school at this late date on the academic calendar. After a little digging in her files, she found that one of the members of the Board of Sacred Heart was the wife of a congressman with whom Jade had done a favorable interview only six months before. It took merely a quick phone call to arrange an interview for 9:30 the following morning with Sister Cabot, the mother superior.

Shelley was visibly nervous as the taxi deposited them at the huge, imposing carriage entrance of the magnificent town house at the corner of 91st and Madison.

The school had purchased the building in 1934 from the estate of international financier Otto Kahn. In the twenties, when the mansion had first been designed on a grand scale, Kahn had answered his contractor's questions about budget with "I don't give a damn what it costs," and the truth of his words was evident in the lavishness of the structure. Behind its grand exterior—built in the manner of the Italian Renaissance palaces—were sixty-six rooms, each more magnificent than the last.

Shelley's eyes widened considerably as Jade led her through the carriage drive and opened one of the tall, heavy doors of the entrance.

Upon entering, they found themselves in an enormous, marbled reception hall; a refectory table with a children's craft exhibit on it ran the length of the hall, and at a small desk off to one side sat a young woman of indeterminate age working over a ledger.

"Are you sure this is a school?" Shelley whispered nervously to Jade.

In spite of herself, Jade found she was whispering back.

"A school *and* a convent, so mind your manners, kiddo!"

Shelley's eyes wandered to the left, where there was a large, gilt-framed oil portrait of a sad-eyed woman in a nun's habit. It was lit from an overhead light and there was a low kneeling bench in front of it.

The wall directly in front of her was lined with tall, arched, Gothic windows that faced out onto some sort of greenery-filled courtyard.

The quiet splendor of the place quite overwhelmed the young girl and she stood rooted to the spot while Jade strolled, with more casualness than she felt, over to the corner desk.

The young woman working there looked up and smiled as Jade made her inquiries.

Yes, she would notify Sister Cabot that they had arrived and would they mind waiting just a few moments.

If she recognized Jade at all, it failed to show on her serene countenance.

Jade walked over to where Shelley still stood staring, and, taking her arm, she led her to a small, elaborately carved bench in the corner.

In a matter of seconds, another pleasant-faced young woman appeared from nowhere and led them down a long hall.

Shelley fell behind just a trifle and tugged at Jade's sleeve.

"If this is a convent, then where are all the nuns?" she inquired curiously.

"I'm not so sure that both of the ladies we've just encountered aren't nuns. Remember, this is 1985, and most nuns have—you should pardon the pun—kicked their habits!" Jade whispered back.

Shelley giggled nervously and resumed her inspection of the place as she followed her aunt and their guide.

It was as Jade had guessed. Sister Cabot greeted them warmly, wearing a neatly tailored blouse and simple A-line skirt. There were no coifs or wimples anywhere Shelley looked. She felt a vague sense of disappointment. It was not the way she had envisioned a convent.

Sister Cabot chatted briefly with Jade and Shelley, then offered to escort them on a short tour of the school.

If the pleasant nuns they encountered on their tour looked all too ordinary for Shelley's romantic imagination, the physical plant itself was splendid, beyond her wildest dreams.

Sister Cabot explained that the school was actually made up of two separate mansions that were now joined.

The main one, the Otto Kahn house, had been built as a private home and designed for lavish entertaining. But by the early 1930's, the Kahns' enthusiasm for that type of life had waned and they began to look for a buyer. At that time, the Academy had been located in three buildings on Madison Avenue and 54th Street and had been there since 1881. They had outgrown the space, however, and the religious school began hoping to purchase the spacious house built by Otto Kahn on 91st Street. In fact, for some time, their prayers had included what they called their "O.K. intention." After two years of negotiations, the deal was completed a few weeks after the death of Otto Kahn and the house became a Sacred Heart property.

Sister Cabot took them up to the roof to admire the magnificent view across Central Park of the reservoir and the grand old apartment buildings lining Central Park South. There was playground equipment up there for the younger children, an art studio

114

and private apartments that Sister Cabot explained were used by the nuns.

Shelley and Jade followed her dutifully as they examined the breathtaking original ballroom and a beautiful small chapel where religious services were held.

Shelley was so enraptured by her surroundings that she had quite forgotten her shyness and asked Sister Cabot if the chapel was part of the original house.

Sister Cabot smiled gently.

"I'm afraid not, my child. The Kahns weren't Catholic, you know. As I understand it, this was originally a dining room."

Shelley blushed furiously at her ridiculous gaffe, but Jade covered it quite smoothly with a gracious comment about how fitting it seemed to be celebrating communion in a place that had once been used for dining.

Shelley fell into an embarrassed silence and wondered if she would ever acquire her aunt's *savoir faire.* Her silence lasted only until they reached the library, however.

The library was everything a romantic young girl had ever dreamed that a wealthy man's place of study and seclusion would be. There were rows and rows of books set into richly paneled walls, long tapestry drapes at the tall windows, and, at one end, a small balcony ran the length of the room.

Shelley gasped in admiration.

"It's gorgeous! Do the girls actually get to use it?"

"Of course," answered Sister Cabot with a smile.

"Everything here is used by the sisters and the students. Would you like to see the secret stairway?" she asked with a twinkle in her eye.

Shelley nodded.

To one side of the library was a tiny carved door

that opened onto a small, narrow staircase.

"Go up," urged Sister Cabot, enjoying the girl's delight. "You won't get lost."

Shelley proceeded up cautiously feeling her way along in the dimness. To her surprise, at one turn she encountered a small window. Peering through it, she found that it looked out into the library. What a delicious way to spy! she thought excitedly and giggled in spite of herself.

Reaching the top of the tiny stairs, she found that a passage led out onto the balcony she had admired, and she was suddenly looking down at her aunt and the mother superior in the library below.

Both women turned their faces up to her, enjoying her wonderment at a way of life few people ever knew in these times.

"I feel as though I should make a speech," announced Shelley, basking in the beauty of it all.

"I suggest you try to find your way down again without breaking your neck and we let Sister Cabot get on with her business of the day," said Jade good-naturedly.

Shelley reluctantly withdrew from her lofty position and Jade turned to the nun beside her.

"As you can see, my niece is obviously enchanted with her surroundings. Do all your girls enjoy the place this much, or do they become blasé about it, seeing it every day and studying here?" she asked curiously.

"Oh, I think they stay in tune with it. I'm afraid the big shock for them is when they leave here to attend other schools and find the outside world a pretty ungracious place. We hear a lot about that when they come back to visit us," she finished warmly.

They passed many closed doors, behind which classes were in session and, at Sister Cabot's suggestion, took a quick look at the adjoining house, the

Burden mansion, purchased in 1940.

There the lower school classes were held. The Burden ballroom was even more spectacular than that of the Kahn building, being lined with smoked mirrors and crowned with several magnificent gilt-and-crystal chandeliers.

Sister Cabot explained that it was generally used as a lunch room now, but for special occasions the large folding doors at one end were pushed back and the whole of it was employed.

Peeking behind the folded doors, they saw another room of equal size, where hordes of little girls in gray flannel jumpers were lined up beside a concert grand piano, lifting high, pure voices in chorus practice.

Descending into the marbled main hall of the Burden house, from a curving marble staircase with a velvet-covered balustrade, Sister Cabot and Jade chatted easily about the curriculum; the sister assuring Jade that Shelley should have no trouble fitting in.

Shelley lagged behind them, lost again in dreams. She envisioned the home as it had originally been, with the chandeliers twinkling, musicians playing, and herself in a velvet gown, descending this staircase to confront a throng of upturned admiring male faces.

It was all she could do not to stretch out an imaginary white-gloved hand to graciously accept assistance as she stepped from the bottom stair.

Jade thanked Sister Cabot and bid her good-bye, nudging Shelley as she did so.

Shelley recovered herself just in time to remember her manners and extend her hand to the mother superior.

"Thank you," she gushed. "It's a truly beautiful school and I'm so excited about going here that I really am almost speechless."

Both the older women joined in laughter at the girl's unaffected candor.

Before Shelley knew it, they had exited through the large front doors, and, with a jolt, she found herself out in the real world again.

"Aunt Jade, I just adore it!" she exclaimed. "I can't tell you how much I adore it! I never dreamed there were places like this around!"

Shelley couldn't stop babbling about it.

A quick look at her watch had shown Jade that though it was only 10:25, she had missed her usual class at Ivan & Igor's.

She made a quick decision to catch the next class, hauling Shelley along with her. She always felt so refreshed after a workout at the gym that she hated to skip a day, even if she had to sneak into a later class. Oily Ivan always made room for her.

When informed of their destination, Shelley snapped out of her trance and was immediately fascinated. Every facet of her aunt's life intrigued her.

"Is it a touch-your-toes kind of workout or what?" she inquired.

"We swing from the rings with the greatest of ease, or try to. Aerobics, too. All kinds of stuff, honey. You'll see. It'll be fun. By the way, I think we breezed through that interview with no problems at all. I'll probably get a call at the office about it later today," said Jade, hailing a passing taxi.

Shelley said little, but she missed nothing from the moment the elevator deposited them at the penthouse gym studio.

Jade tossed a new copy of *Seventeen* magazine at the girl and suggested that she make herself at home on the rust-colored sofa while she, Jade, slipped into her leotards.

Shelley took the magazine and sat down, but the copy lay unopened on her lap as she eagerly surveyed her surroundings. The huge curtains that usually covered the floor-to-ceiling glass window-walls of the large gym were open, and she could watch the class now in progress there.

There were four women in the class, three in black leotards and the fourth in bright red. The woman in red was a slim blonde with a turned-up nose. One of the women in black had a medium build, short brown hair, and looked slightly older than the rest. The second black-clad figure had long, flowing black hair tied back from her face, and a slightly rounded figure. But it was the fourth woman who fascinated Shelley. She was black, tall, and pencil-slim, and she moved with extraordinary grace and fluidity.

Shelley thought her quite the most exotic creature she had ever seen. She looked like a princess from an ancient civilization.

As soon as Aunt Jade returned from changing, Shelley began to bombard her with questions.

Jade laughed. "Hang on a second and I will identify all of them for you. That's my regular class. Oh, Darlene," she called over to the pretty reception-ist at the desk who was absorbed in this month's issue of *Vogue*, "this is my niece, Shelley Shattuck."

Darlene looked up, flashed a practiced capped-tooth smile, and returned to her reading matter.

"Now," explained Jade, "the woman in red is Cricket. She's a travel writer—in the country one day and gone the next. Hey, there's a fourth. I wonder who's taking my place?"

Jade walked over to the silver samovar and drew a cup of coffee, craning her neck to see better as she did so.

"Oh, I know her. That's Sidonia Silverstein. Haven't seen her around for awhile. I've interviewed her husband, Mark, for the show. He's an author."

Curiosity satisfied, Jade settled down next to Shelley on the sofa, drew her legs up under her, and sipped her coffee before continuing.

"The other woman in black, with the short brown hair, is India. She's relatively new here. Don't know much about her, but she seems pleasant enough. And the tall, raving beauty is Anastacia."

"She's unreal," breathed Shelley in admiration.

"Oh, she's real enough," laughed Jade. "She keeps the place jumping. But her figure *is* gorgeous, isn't it? She's a professional model, of course. You've probably seen her face a million times in the magazines and on TV. She's one of the hottest models around right now."

Shelley followed Anastacia's every movement with her eyes. She had incredible grace.

"Hey," said Jade, struck by a sudden thought, "I've got an extra leotard in there. Why don't you suit up and work out too? Hey, Darlene," she called out, "got room for another one in the eleven o'clock class?"

Darlene obediently closed her magazine and opened the large leather appointment book.

Her eyes scanned the page.

"Sure, there's only you and Chantal. In fact, you saved Chantal from a fate worse than death. If you hadn't shown up, Lanny would have worked her out alone, and you know how she huffs and puffs. Want me to add your niece?"

"Sure. And put it on my bill please."

Jade dragged a semi-reluctant Shelley back to a dressing room and helped her change.

"Aunt Jade, what if I make an absolute fool of myself?" asked Shelley as she nervously folded her clothes.

"You won't be the first person to do so at this place. You laugh, that's all. It'll be fun!" Jade assured her.

Just then, the ten o'clock class broke and Cricket and India waved a greeting to Jade as they headed for the showers.

Sidonia Silverstein was breathing heavily as she passed them, but she managed a tentative smile at Jade. Sidonia went through life being positive that no one remembered who she was.

Jade made her day by greeting her by name.

Anastacia was still in the gym doing an extra stretch on the trapeze, when Shelley and Jade entered.

Jade introduced Shelley to Lanny and then to Annie.

"Annie, you have a new fan here. This is my niece from Augusta, Maine. Shelley's going to be staying with me this year and going to school here."

Annie flashed Shelley a friendly smile from the trapeze, then dropped down to the gym mat in a heap.

Picking herself up, she reached back to loosen her long black hair and shake it free.

"Cool. Nice to meet you. Don't tell me this aunt of yours is going to make you work out in the torture chamber here?"

Shelley smiled at Annie's description of the gym.

"I—I thought I might try it. I'm not good like you all are."

"No sweat. Easy as falling off a log, once you get the hang of it. Stay loose, honey. See you Thursday, Jade."

With a wave and a skip, Annie disappeared.

Shelley stared after her with open-mouthed admiration.

Jade smiled at the girl's awe. She could see that Shelley had a new heroine. Well, thank God she hadn't asked Annie for her autograph!

*　　*　　*

Annie changed quickly and was searching in her bag for a dime to call the agency and check her bookings, when the pain hit her.

It was like a giant stab in the abdomen, and she doubled over instinctively and held her stomach until the worst of it had passed.

She swore silently. That was the second time today! She had felt the first spasm in the taxi on her way to class this morning.

Annie decided to slip into the ladies' room and check to see if she was getting her period. It was highly unlikely because she'd just finished her last one two weeks before.

A look at the crotch of her cashmere slacks puzzled her. She was staining, but it wasn't like a period; it was a dark brown color.

Annie suspected that it probably had something to do with that damned IUD she'd had inserted a while ago. She had chosen an intrauterine device instead of the pill or that bothersome diaphragm she had been using, but the pain during its insertion had been excruciating. And now she had these awful cramps when she least expected them.

She poked a tentative finger inside herself and probed for the tiny, reassuring knot that told her the device was still in place.

Yep, the little devil was still there, thank goodness. She and Ferrago had made long and satisfying love the night before, and without the IUD, the results could have been disastrous.

She made a mental note to call her gynecologist about it if the pains persisted.

Then she thought no more about it.

Chapter 14

Cricket was happy. She had that delightful, butterflies-in-the-stomach feeling she always had at the beginning of a trip.

Two-and-a-half weeks back in the city had been good for catching up, but now she was ready to relax in the tropical sun, or come close to relaxing as she was able.

Partly because she needed the money and partly to assuage her guilt feelings at covering the Caribbean so soon again, she had contacted one of the bridal magazines and arranged to do a Jamaican honeymoon piece while she was down there, as well as the *Festival* piece.

This would entail checking out more than just the usual spots she always covered for *Festival*, but Cricket loved strenuous sight-seeing and was already making a mental list of places to include on this jaunt that might appeal to honeymooners.

The three-and-a-half hour trip flew by and soon her plane was touching down at the Montego Bay airport.

Seen from the air, with its shiny crescent of sandy beach and glittering group of luxury hotels and seaside homes, Montego Bay looked like a picture postcard. But once down, the postcard image dissolved into more realistic scenes of a bustling island port city—noisy, colorful, shabby, but vibrant.

The Spanish called it *Manteca Bahia,* a name derived from hog lard, because in Spanish days the chief industry had been rendering the fat of wild hogs caught in the hills. Old English maps called it Lard Bay. And up close, Cricket mused, the unglamorous appellation of Lard Bay seemed apt.

Cricket hurried through customs, disdaining the offer of a free rum punch from one of the smiling natives, anxious now that she had finally arrived to check into her hotel and unpack. Then, she thought, a cool swim might be in order, before the sun became too high in the tropic skies.

Another smiling native procured a dusty limousine for her, bundled her luggage in beside her, and she was off.

Tryall Golf & Beach Club, where she had made her reservations, was only a half hour from Montego Bay along the coast, but it was located on 2,800 acres of mountain and seaside plantation and offered respite from the bustle of Montego Bay. The Great House, pool, and grounds were a seventeenth Century plantation-owner's dream with twenty-first Century comfort and luxury. It was a beautiful combination, no matter how one looked at it.

Cricket had been a guest there several times before and the courteous desk clerk remembered her instantly and warmly greeted her by name.

Once in her room, she opened her suitcase and fumbled through it for a bikini. Clothes flew in all directions. There would be time enough to straighten things out and hang them up later, she decided. Cricket believed in living for the moment, and right now a dip in the enormous pool that overlooked the Caribbean was the only thing on her mind.

Once poolside, she broke the water cleanly as she entered with a graceful dive. Surfacing in seconds, she began to go the length with long, smooth strokes. The pool area was deserted except for a lone man sitting at the "Wet Seat Bar." The bar was the pride of the resort. It was housed in a huge, circular, thatched-roof enclosure, half of which hung over into the pool area. Along the side of the bar facing into the pool were small, round bar stools, partially submerged in the water. To reach a bar stool, one had to swim to it, hence the name Wet Seat Bar.

The man sitting there alone appeared to be in his late thirties and had touches of gray at the temples. He was tall, lean, and looking decidedly irritated.

Cricket deduced the latter from the fact that he kept looking at his watch impatiently and then scowling into his drink as he sipped it.

He glanced over in her direction and his irritation appeared to increase.

Playfully, Cricket changed direction and headed toward the bar. Her curiosity was piqued. How could anyone sit around a place as beautiful as this and be in a foul mood?

As she pulled herself out of the shimmering water and sat on the stool next to him, he growled, "About time you got here!"

Obviously he thought she was someone else.

Cricket was so tickled by the situation that she decided to play along.

She instantly assumed a contrite expression.

"Sorry."

"Jesus. You're all alike, damn it! Just let me finish

this drink and we'll take off. They're going to lose the proper light if we don't hurry."

Cricket fought back a smile as she tried to think what to do or say next. The joke was too delicious to give up so easily.

Meekly she apologized again, then ventured timidly, "Uh, who are all alike?"

He slurped up the last of his tall drink and signed the check on the bar.

"You damn models. You think the whole world waits for you. We shot the brunette yesterday and *she* managed to get to the location on time."

"Sounds like you plan to shoot me for tardiness."

The man had turned to slip into the pool, but her last remark halted him.

"You *are* the blonde for the Fresh Hair commercial, aren't you?" he asked, a note of uncertainty creeping into his voice as he studied her face a little more closely.

Cricket's laughter bubbled over.

"No, but don't let that stop you from giving me hell. You do it so well!"

His handsome face flushed and he hung there awkwardly, half in and half out of the water.

"Oh, for God's sake, I'm sorry. I thought you were someone else."

"Obviously."

Cricket giggled again, enjoying his discomfort.

The man pulled himself back up on the bar stool and smiled in embarrassment.

"I really must apologize. I am so used to the New York hustle and bustle that I can't stand it when a cast and crew get down here and act like they're on some damned holiday. That was really stupid of me. Let me introduce myself and buy you a drink to make up for dumping on you like that."

"Aren't you afraid you'll lose your light?" she teased, imitating his tone. All the while, she was studying his rugged features intently. He really was quite good-looking, she realized, and very attractive in his contrition.

A dark-skinned bartender appeared from nowhere and the man ordered two tall rum punches. Then he turned to smile engagingly at Cricket.

"I'm Andrew Travick. I'm an ad agency producer and I'm down here to shoot some shampoo commercials. The damn blonde was due in this morning and didn't show, so I sent the crew on ahead to set up at the location and I'm cooling my behind here waiting for the dumb broad. Lord, I can't tell you how sorry I am that I jumped on you like that!"

"No problem. But now that you describe her as a dumb broad, I think I'm annoyed that I was mistaken for her. Now if you'd told me that she was breathtakingly beautiful and *that's* why you made the mistake . . ."

Andrew returned her smile and the bartender set their drinks in front of them.

Cricket took a long sip of hers.

"Hasn't anyone ever mistaken you for a model before?"

"Many things, but never a model."

"You here on vacation?"

"Work, as a matter of fact."

"May I ask what work that might be?"

"International spying, drug smuggling, that sort of thing."

Cricket kept her eyes demurely downward at her drink so he couldn't see the laughter in them.

"No kidding. Must be fascinating work."

"Has its ins and outs. Sometimes you have to do time . . ."

Andrew looked at her sharply.

Cricket couldn't suppress her smile, much as she struggled.

"You know, I get the strange impression that you're putting me on."

"Touché," she answered. "But don't you think you really deserve it after lighting into me like that?"

Andrew looked shamefaced.

"Fair enough. Friends now?"

"Friends."

Cricket played with the straw of her drink for a long moment before looking up into his eyes and giving him her most dazzling smile. She was finding him quite attractive. She had noticed the golden band on the third finger of his left hand but had chosen to ignore it, as she always did with casual flirtations.

What was an island stay without a little *soupçon* of romance?

"As a matter of fact, I'm a writer."

"Books, magazines, what?"

"A little of everything. Mostly travel, though."

"You're very attractive . . . for a writer, I mean."

"You're pretty attractive yourself . . . for a producer, of course!"

They both laughed easily, but his quick, surreptitious glance at his watch was not lost on Cricket. She had the feeling that the interlude was about to end and that her newfound friend was thinking about his schedule again. She really didn't want to lose him so quickly.

Then she had a sudden inspiration. "You know, you could do me a big favor."

She had his full attention again—for the moment, at least.

He raised his eyebrows by way of reply and she

paused a moment, then deliberately phrased her invitation in the most provocative manner she could invent.

"How would you like to honeymoon with me tonight?"

Andrew's expression looked slightly startled and he stammered in bewilderment for a few seconds before Cricket interrupted him in her most innocent voice.

"Oh, no, nothing like *that*, not what you're thinking. It's just that I'm down here, among other reasons, to do a piece for a bridal magazine, and that means I have to cover a lot of restaurants and bars and things."

She managed a delightfully helpless look. "And it's rather embarrassing to have to go to them all alone."

She was lying in her teeth, of course. There hadn't been a bar or restaurant in her career which Cricket hadn't been perfectly capable of walking into alone and asking for and getting the best seat in the house. But she was also the master of the helpless look when the occasion demanded it. Vestiges of her Southern girlhood stood her in good stead.

Andrew was torn. He never did the nightclub scene when he was on location. He needed his sleep. And he was a married man—a happily married man. Yet, for some reason, he knew he wanted to see her again.

He settled for a token protest.

"I'm not sure I'd be very good company after a full day of shooting. And I have to be up early tomorrow to get this thing wrapped up . . ."

Cricket smelled victory. She moved in rapidly.

"Oh, we wouldn't be out too late. And it would be *such* a help to me. I'm sure you'd be super company. Why don't you meet me in the bar after you're done for the day? Say, about seven o'clock? My expense account from the magazine will pick up the tab for everything. We'll do the whole scene. It'll be *such* fun. And you *would* be saving my life!"

She turned quickly on her bar stool and prepared to dive back into the pool before he could protest further.

"Wait a minute! What's your name?" he called as her slim figure disappeared into the aquamarine water.

He wasn't sure she had heard him.

In seconds, her blond head reappeared and she flashed him a bewitching grin.

"Cricket Wells. And I'll see you at seven o'clock."

With a wave and a splash she dove again, frisking off like a playful mermaid.

What have I gotten myself into this time? wondered Andrew with a shake of his head.

What, indeed?

Chapter 15

He spotted her the second he walked into the lounge. Any man would have had to have been blind not to. The day in the sun had touched her already-tanned skin with a dazzling glow, her blond curls looked as though they were lit by a key light, and her clingy emerald green and pale blue print dress caressed her figure from top to bottom.

She was sitting at a tiny table in the corner and the several male occupants of the bar were making a concerted effort to appraise her without being obvious about it.

In the half-light, her teeth flashed whitely against the contrast of her bronzed skin as she saw him and threw him a smile and a friendly wave.

He quickly made his way over to her table, wondering for the hundredth time why he was doing this, why he felt guilty about it, and why he'd been thinking about it all day long in a corner of his mind.

Cricket immediately banished all his doubts with her obvious delight at his arrival.

"Hi. I was afraid you'd back out and leave me all by my lonesome!"

He slipped into the chair beside hers.

"Couldn't do it. Being rude to you once a day is about my limit. That model finally showed up and then the shooting ran late."

He ordered a frozen daiquiri to match hers and lit her cigarette for her.

"All right, bride, what's on the agenda for tonight?"

"God, you sound like we've been married for twenty years instead of being on our honeymoon," Cricket proclaimed with a giggle.

Andrew usually hated it when women giggled, but Cricket's laughter was like everything else about her—light, bright, and shimmering.

After joining in her laughter, Andrew succumbed to one last pang of conscience. He sobered and said, as casually as he could, "I *am* married, you know."

Cricket matched his mood with mock solemnity. "It's better that way. When you're honeymooning, that is."

Quickly pulling out a local guidebook before the conversation could bog down, she eagerly began describing the restaurant she had picked out for dinner. Then she went on to the various bars they should check out after dinner.

Andrew gave himself up to the pleasures of the evening.

They dined at an elegant restaurant on a terrace overlooking the Caribbean. Tiny candles on each table were the only illumination, and Cricket's eyes looked twice as sparkling as they reflected the twin, twinkling flames.

The food was bountiful, delicious, and most of it completely unidentifiable to Andrew.

"Like it?" Cricket asked as the waiter placed yet another steaming dish of seafood in front of them.

Andrew dabbed at his chin with an enormous

damask napkin. "Fantastic, but I have to confess that half the time I can't tell what I'm eating."

Cricket's laughter rippled again. "Most of the time, it's probably better that way. But for your information, that last was smoked dolphin with lemon sauce. Wasn't it delicious?"

Andrew groaned. "I ate dolphin! My kids will kill me!"

The native orchestra began a dance tune with a sensuous tropical beat.

"Would you care to dance?" Andrew asked politely.

"You sound like a prim little boy at dancing school. I'll bet you went to dancing school, didn't you?"

Andrew smiled. "Yes, as a matter of fact, Miss Know-it-all, I did go to dancing school."

Cricket warmed to her topic. "I'll bet you went to dancing school and prep school and a proper Eastern college."

"You read palms, too?" he asked with a raised eyebrow.

Cricket adored his eyebrows. "Tell me where you went to school. And where you grew up. And what you were like when you were a little boy."

No man could have resisted her flattering interest. How many years, Andrew wondered, had it been since an attractive woman had turned her full attention to him and wanted to know what he—Andrew Travick—was *really* like? Models didn't count. In his field, the woods were literally filled with them, eager, anxious nymphets who, once they learned he was an agency producer, were transparent in their feigned attention to him. They were all frantic to get a job, any job, to get ahead, be successful. They were usually perfectly willing to jump into bed with any man who came along who could further their interest. Nubile narcissists with empty heads, their sole concerns were their faces, their bodies, their careers. Andrew had long ago become immune to their plastic charms, their instant availability.

But Cricket was different. She was obviously successful in her field, feminine as a flower, and childlike and charming in her enthusiasm.

Andrew found himself telling her the story of his life over the thick, rich coffee they enjoyed after dinner.

"And after Choate, there was Princeton, where—would you believe—I majored in Political Science? How did a nice young Princeton boy with such a degree become an ad agency producer, you might ask."

"I was just going to."

Andrew started to speak, then broke off in embarrassment. "Hell, I must be boring you to tears with all this. Just tell me to shut up, will you?"

Cricket protested sincerely. "No. I really want to know. What *did* happen? What did you really want to do with your degree?"

Andrew shrugged. "I guess I had some wild idea of going into the diplomatic corps . . ."

"Aha! I knew it! Deep down inside you too have the wanderlust!"

Andrew grinned.

"Yes, blithe spirit, there *is* a gypsy in my soul. But tell me about the gypsy in yours. How did you ever get started in the travel-writing business?"

Cricket recounted the story of her early years in Paisleyville, and what it was like to grow up as a girl in a Southern society.

"I couldn't hack it. And besides, I wanted so

desperately to be free . . ."

"Free from what?"

"Ah, there's the rub. I'm not quite sure. I'm not quite sure even now. All I know is that I can only stay so long in one place and then I simply have to go, move, be someplace else with other people."

"Isn't there any one special person, or isn't that any of my business?" Andrew asked gently.

"There was, once. There was a boy back home in Paisleyville. But he wanted the one thing I couldn't give up."

"And that was . . .?"

"My independence. My me-ness." Cricket shook her head as though to change the scene as well as the mood.

"So there you have it, the story of my life. Cricket Wells. Girl Vagabond. Which reminds me. We've got to move on. Miles to go before we sleep and all that."

Andrew signaled the waiter and Cricket swiftly and unobstrusively signed the check and rose to go.

The evening, after that, blended into a colorful, shifting montage of island night life.

They danced native dances in dark bars, they drank outrageous concoctions of rum and other unidentified ingredients which Cricket insisted they wouldn't have enough of until they got sick. They laughed at pointless, silly jokes and Andrew decided he hadn't had so much fun since adolescence.

Throughout the whole evening, both felt a dreamlike unreality, as though there would be no morning after, no time or space to follow. Just now. And here, wherever "here" happened to be.

And then suddenly, as they closed the last bar, they both realized that it was almost over.

As Andrew pulled the car into the parking space at Tryall, he turned off the ignition reluctantly.

Cricket sat for a moment, staring pensively at the huge picture-book moon that hung suspended over the Caribbean waters. Impulsively she turned to Andrew. "One last fling for our mythical honeymooners?"

Andrew found himself eager to hear anything she had in mind that could postpone the end of the evening.

"A walk along the beach in the moonlight. What a perfect way to end a perfect night!"

"You're on," Andrew said with a laugh. "Last one to the beach is a rotten egg!"

They ran and laughed and slipped and skittered as they hit the silky sand in a dead heat.

"You can't do this with shoes on," Cricket announced and promptly slipped out of her silver sandals.

Andrew sat down on a small stone fence bordering the sand and followed suit.

Dangling their shoes from one hand, they strolled the long, smooth beach, which seemed pale and magical in the moonlight.

"I see the moon, the moon sees me. The moon sees someone that I long to see . . ." began Cricket in a light, high voice.

Andrew joined in.

"God bless the light that shines on me, and shines on the one I love." They finished together, slightly off-key, and laughed in chorus at their giddiness.

"I haven't heard that song in . . . well, at least a million years," said Andrew.

Ever daring, Cricket began to venture further out along the water's edge, playing tag with the incoming waves. She tucked up the hem of her dress under the legs of her bikini underpants, which gave her gown a fetching, native-sarong look.

Andrew smiled at her playfulness and enjoyed the sight of her unself-conscious beauty in the moonlight.

Suddenly he saw a larger wave heading toward her and reached out quickly for her hand to help her maintain her balance.

It seemed the most natural thing in the world to continue to hold it as they strolled on.

They talked of their favorite poets, surprised each other by both naming *Faust* as their favorite opera, and discovered that they shared a mutual hatred of artificial flowers and anything made with anchovies.

They talked of places she's been, favorite cities and favorite hotels, and places they'd both like to visit.

"You must travel a lot as an agency producer."

"Not as much as you might think. For financial reasons, we're shooting more and more stuff in studios in New York. This fall I'll be doing more traveling than I sometimes do in a year. I'm flying to Paris the first week in November to meet with a perfume client and map out a new product introduction. Otherwise, we agency folks are sticking closer and closer to home."

"Quelle domage!"

A companionable silence followed, then Cricket broke it at last.

"You're a nice guy, Andy Travick."

"And you're not so bad yourself, Cricket Wells. For a writer."

They giggled. It seemed amazing to Andrew that after only one short evening, they already shared private jokes. It had been that kind of evening.

In fact, Andrew reflected, she probably knew more about him after one evening than most people would ever find out—except for India, of course.

He pushed India from his mind as quickly as she

137

had entered it. India had no place in this evening. She didn't belong here. It had been an innocent evening and would remain so. He would do nothing to hurt India.

But this evening was out of time and space, a short holiday into unreality, a brief luxury he would permit himself to indulge in. He knew he would never see Cricket Wells again. He couldn't.

"I hate to be the one to say it, but those are the first rosy fingers of dawn creeping up over the horizon."

Andrew blinked in disbelief.

Where had the evening flown?

They crept stealthily through the silent halls of the Great House and stopped at the door to Cricket's room.

"I'd ask you in," whispered Cricket, "but I know you're not that kind of boy."

"You betcha. Straight arrow all the way, that's me. Did I tell you that I was an Eagle Scout?" Andrew whispered back.

Cricket giggled.

"That may be the *only* thing in the world that we missed talking about!" he concluded.

She suddenly sobered and said sincerely, "Thank you for a lovely evening, Andy. You're a very nice, square person. And I like you very much."

Unconsciously, she leaned closer to him.

"I feel like a teenager again and I wish I'd known you then. In fact, I wish I could wrap you in tissue paper and ribbons and tuck you away among my souvenirs."

Impulsively, she reached up, put her arms around his neck, and planted a gentle kiss on his lips.

Somewhere inside of Andrew, the ghost of a yearning twisted in his middle, and, in spite of himself, he wrapped his arms tightly around her waist and returned her kiss.

The tender kiss grew passionate and Andrew felt heat flood his groin and his organ stiffen in response.

Cricket pressed closer and wished she never had to let him go.

It was Andrew who at last reluctantly pulled away.

They stared at each other for a moment, both dazed by the rush of their emotions.

Then, without another word, Cricket turned and put her key in her lock and Andrew spun away and strode with determined steps down the long hallway to his room.

The agency crew wrapped up the shoot the next day and by afternoon they were ready to leave. During every moment Andrew spent in the vicinity of Tryall, he was in an agony of mixed emotions, hoping against hope to catch sight of Cricket again before he left, frightened because he wanted to so much.

By the time he had settled his bill, he still had not had even a fleeting glimpse of her.

It was just as well, he told himself.

He really didn't trust himself ever to see Cricket Wells again.

Chapter 16

A cool autumn breeze blew through the vast expanse of the Soho loft that Annie and Ferrago shared.

It was a welcome relief after an unseasonably hot October day and a long, fevered session of love-making. Annie had come in ready to drop from a day that had started with her regular workout at Ivan & Igor's and had ended with standing for five hours at a commercial shooting at which everything had gone wrong.

Ferrago had sensed her weariness the moment she walked through the door. Then he had solicitously cooked a steak for them and tossed a huge salad so that she wouldn't have to change and go out for dinner.

Afterward, while Ferrago cleared things away, she had fallen back on the king-size bed they shared and dropped off into a gentle sleep.

She awoke to feel his hands softly caressing her flesh under the long, peach silk caftan she had slipped on earlier. As always, the weariness fell from her and she responded eagerly to his touch.

Even in the midst of her passion, she drew a

comfort and security from their lovemaking that never ceased to surprise her. She was wise enough in cocktail party psychology to wonder sometimes if he represented a father-figure to her. She had never known her father and often speculated about him, always with feelings of guilt, however, for she sensed that he, like her mother, might not approve of the interracial liaison she had made.

Two years ago her mother, Eulalia Clemmons, had married Ed Simmons, a hardworking black man who drove a taxi sometimes as much as fifteen hours a day to provide for his wife and the children still at home. They had a neat, clean apartment in Harlem now, and her mother could enjoy the luxury of staying at home and looking after the house and children instead of cleaning for wealthy whites, as she had done for years.

Annie visited them on the second Sunday of every month and took presents for them all. They loved seeing her and hearing stories of her glamorous life. They were very proud of her success.

But the part of her life that she kept a deep, dark secret from them was her relationship with Ferrago. She had told them that she shared an apartment with another black woman and kept up the pretense all these years.

Her mother was a traditional Southern black who had mellowed somewhat in later years in her feelings toward whites, but she still had a deep-seated distrust of them, and was not entirely comfortable with the fact that Annie's working life threw her into constant contact with them.

Her stepfather had been a Black Muslim some years back, when that movement had been rampant in Harlem, and now he nursed a hatred that bordered on the pathological.

Annie was always very careful to display copies of black magazines in which she appeared, playing down the extensive layouts in the white fashion magazines. Her stepfather always beamed when he saw her on television in any one of the numerous "black" commercials she had made for the large companies who now routinely shot slice-of-life spots both in black and white versions.

But she knew that they would have been shocked and appalled if they had had any idea that she was living with a "honky"—the term her stepfather continually used when referring to whites.

It seemed odd to her that in today's climate, the white world she lived in casually accepted intimate relationships between the races while her family in Harlem scorned and denigrated them. How had things come full circle in so short a time? she often wondered.

Most of the time, her separate identities did not bother her. But the second Sunday in each month, after a day of visiting at home, she always found herself moody, depressed, and laden with a guilt that took several days to shake.

She would finlly exorcise it by going on a shopping spree and purchasing all the presents she would go home bearing on the second Sunday of the following month.

Ferrago noticed the heaviness of her depression after these visits, but wisely he never probed into it and accepted the fact that Annie's family was a thing apart—her own thing, to be kept in a private part of her life.

The mood from last Sunday's visit had persisted even through today, but tonight she had given fully of herself in their lovemaking, and as he had plunged deep inside her again and again, she had risen to his thrusts eagerly.

"Oh God, baby! I love you," she had panted.

"Annie. Annie. So sweet. I love the way your body holds me. I want to drown in you."

They had gone on and on until both had spent themselves.

Now, as she lay with her head against his chest and felt the gentle breeze waft over her naked body, she knew the tiredness of the day had drained from her and evaporated in the explosions of her orgasms. Feeling the almost imperceptible change in Ferrago's breathing, she knew he had drifted into a deep sleep.

She lay quietly for a long time, drawing strength from the security of his arms and comfort from the intensity of their sex. For however long they lasted, she knew they would continue to be good together.

At last, succumbing to an uncontrollable urge to urinate, she slipped silently out of the bed and crept to the bathroom.

She decided not to flush after relieving herself, lest the noise awaken Ferrago. Because her cramps seemed to have cleared up recently, she slipped in a probing finger to check for the reassuring little knot of her IUD.

She poked around, at first tentatively, then frantically.

The knot was gone. And she had no idea how long it had been missing.

Chapter 17

Jade headed for her office on Friday as soon as the show went off the air. She had a pile of correspondence to catch up with before she left for the afternoon's interview.

She raised her eyes in slight surprise when she noticed that Linda, her secretary, was not at her desk.

That wasn't like Linda. She knew Jade usually wanted to plow through the day's business as soon as the show wrapped. From the half-empty coffee cup and the spread-out papers, she knew Linda was in today.

But where? she wondered.

Entering her own office, she found her mail neatly stacked and sorted as usual. She decided to glance through it and wait.

Faithful Linda was bound to return momentarily, Jade rationalized.

It was a good fifteen minutes before the young, blond-haired woman stuck her head in the door.

Jade looked up quickly. Something in Linda's face told her something was up.

"Got a minute?" the secretary asked.

"I was about to ask you the same thing. Come

on in."

The young woman came in, glanced briefly over her shoulder, and after a moment's hesitation, closed the door behind her.

She sat down on the edge of the chair facing Jade's desk.

"What's up?"

"Well, I'm glad you're sitting down because this is a big one."

Jade leaned forward. "Okay, you've got my total attention. Now what's going on?"

Linda took a deep breath.

"Well, for openers, Victor McNally is leaving."

Jade let out a long whistle.

"Our illustrious head of programming? That *is* news. Where's the memo on it?"

"No memo—yet." She stopped Jade before she could protest. "Ladies' room. That's where I've been."

Jade didn't know whether to laugh or be exasperated.

"You heard it from his secretary, right?"

"Wrong. Heard it from Johnson's secretary who always has coffee with McNally's secretary. She read the notice on McNally's secretary's desk. Upside down," she added with obvious admiration in her voice.

"This network had a secretarial system that could put the CIA to shame. So when's the memo coming out?"

"At the speed McNally's secretary types? About next month, I'd say!"

"Seriously, Linda."

"It'll be in our IN box in the morning."

Jade sat back and considered this latest development. It was hard to predict how this would affect

146

her, or the plan she had in mind.

"Lord, I don't know why I even bother to read my memos and call reports. I always hear what's coming next from you."

"You jest, but the ladies' room is the real information center around here. Know why Hansen's secretary goes to the john so much?"

"Kidney problems?"

"No. Hansen caught on to the jungle drum system as soon as he got here. Every time he saw Mr. McNally's secretary go to the ladies' room, he'd go out to Sue Ellen's desk and suggest that she touch up her makeup. Sue Ellen got the message—fast!"

Jade looked with mild amusement at the serious, scrubbed face of her secretary, so earnest and forthright.

"I've been thinking, Linda. It wouldn't hurt if you powdered your nose a little more often."

Linda was indignant.

"Listen, Jade, I'm the only secretary here with a period that lasts for thirty days. And I change my tampon every hour. You sometimes hear more from inside the stalls," she explained.

Jade laughed, then swiveled around in her chair and finally got up and strode to the window.

Her thoughts were a million miles away as she looked down and stared unseeingly at the first ice skaters of the season lazily circling the Rockefeller Center rink.

Linda's voice broke into her reverie. "Aren't you even interested in knowing who his replacement will be?"

Jade turned with a start. "You mean you know that *too?*"

Linda answered a trifle defensively. "Well, I know the candidate list . . ."

Jade dropped down in her desk chair again and leaned her chin on a cupped hand.

"Okay. Shoot. Who's my new boss going to be?"

"Well," began Linda, warming to her topic, "there's Hansen, who's really panting for the job."

"Obviously, if he'd stoop to bathroom intrigue."

"Then there's Gottchalk, down on twenty. But he's a weak contender . . ."

"What do you guys do, handicap them?"

"Then there's a guy on the West Coast whom everyone is convinced is a shoe-in . . ."

"Named?"

"Parkinson, that's it. But he's got a funny first name."

Jade's mouth tightened. "Griggs," she said in a flat voice.

"Yeah, that's it, Griggs. Griggs Parkinson. You know him?"

Jade's emerald eyes turned to green ice and her expression darkened. "Yes. I know him."

Linda stared in surprise at her employer. She had never heard Jade sound quite so forbidding.

"Old friend?"

"Old enemy."

Bitter memories of cruel words she would never stop hearing flickered through her mind as the silence between them lengthened.

Finally Linda spoke timidly. "Bad news, I guess?"

"*Very* bad."

"Well, I guess I'd better be—"

Jade came back to the present and felt contrite for the girl's stricken look.

"Hey, it's not your fault. We don't kill the bearer of bad tidings anymore," she remarked, striving for a light note. Get your book and let me get rid of some dictation I've been meaning to catch up on."

Linda rose obediently and started toward the door to fetch her pad.

"Hey, you forgot to tell me one thing," called Jade.

Linda paused expectantly.

"If McNally's secretary's typing speed is so bloody slow, how come she's been the program director's secretary for the five years he's been here?"

Linda looked astonished at the naïveté of the question.

"Didn't you know? She sleeps with him."

Jade watched the retreating woman's back and wondered who the innocents were around here—the youthful secretaries or the battle-scarred news reporters?

Chapter 18

India thought she detected something different about Drew's attitude after his return from the shooting trip in Jamaica, but she was reluctant to question him about it. It eventually occurred to her that the change might not be in him, but in her.

She knew she was letting her twice-a-week sessions at Ivan & Igor's assume an importance all out of proportion to the rest of her life. She lied to herself and said it was because this was her only contact with adults in the outside world. Yet in those unguarded moments as she lay in bed at night waiting for sleep to come, she thought about Lanny and *knew* why Tuesdays and Thursdays were important to her.

The incident that had occurred last Tuesday, for instance, had been trivial enough, and yet she had since relived it a hundred times in her reveries during the day and at night.

She had arrived at the building that Ivan & Igor's occupied about five minutes before the hour, later than usual, but Mrs. Schmidt had been delayed in her arrival to take care of Toohey.

She had popped into the empty elevator, pushed the penthouse button, and tapped her foot impatiently as she waited for the automatic mechanism to close the door.

Just as the door was about to close, Lanny rushed in, obviously also behind schedule.

Seeing that India was the other occupant of the car, he flashed her a boyish smile in greeting.

As the car began its rapid ascent, India mentally searched for something clever to say.

Suddenly the elevator car jerked to a halt just as sharply as it had started. It jerked again, then dropped about a foot with stomach-lurching abruptness and stopped dead.

Lanny looked surprised, then irritated, as he punched the alarm button.

India felt her legs go weak. She reached out for the railing around the wall to support herself.

Lanny turned and, seeing the expression on her face, inquired quickly, "Are you all right?"

India attempted a smile. "I guess so. I thought for a minute I was going to faint."

Rapidly taking control of the situation, he suggested that she sit down on the floor of the elevator and lean back against the wall while they waited for help to come.

He dropped down easily beside her.

"These damn things do it all the time, you know. Are you frightened?"

India swallowed loudly and found her voice. "I guess so. I was hit by a wave of panic there that was *unreal.*"

"Some people react like that to being trapped in an elevator, but I think it's just a stupid nuisance. They'll probably spend half an hour looking for the Super before they get us out of here."

As he saw the fright creep into her expression again, he hastened to reassure her.

"Hey, wait, don't go off again. I'm kidding, honest. They'll probably have us out of here in no time. Let's talk about something else, to take your mind off the situation."

India stared into his large, friendly, blue eyes and read the concern in them. She suddenly began to feel better. Managing a small laugh, she said, "Okay. As my little son would say, 'Let's talk—*you* start.'"

"Want me to tell you my life story? Now that'll put you to sleep."

He smiled easily as he leaned back, legs apart, knees bent, and hands clasped casually between them.

India responded like an eager child.

"I'd love to hear your life story. Make things up if it's not sufficiently diverting," she added.

Lanny laughed. "You're funny. You sound like you've heard it already. Hey, speaking of life stories, I don't mean to be nosy, but where in the world did you ever get a name like India? Were you born there?"

"No, nothing so romantic. My mother read a book—one that was written way before your time—called *Gone With the Wind.*"

Lanny pulled a mock frown.

"Come on, I'm not *that* young. I saw the movie."

"Rerun, of course?" she asked with a twinkle.

"Rerun," he admitted.

"Well, anyway, my mother loved this book so much that it was either India or Scarlett."

They both laughed.

"Beats the hell out of Scarlett," he conceded. "Besides, somehow it . . . suits you," he added shyly.

India found herself blushing. She didn't know if it was the way he said it or the way he looked at her, but she had an intuitive flash that he felt attracted to her, too. It was heady knowledge.

She began to relax and chatter easily. She found out that he'd grown up in Brooklyn, gone to high school there, became interested in gymnastics and had hoped to train for the Olympics. Feeling he was now too old to be a serious competitor, he looked forward to someday opening a gym of his own.

"I think that would be wonderful. You're so good with people—even the *klutzes*," she said with a grin.

He grinned back. "It's the klutzes that you *have* to be good with. They could hurt themselves."

India even felt at ease enough about their predicament to discuss the old question of whether or not, if an elevator dropped, one would be better off jumping up and down rapidly on the theory that there was a fifty-fifty chance one could be up in the air when the car hit bottom.

Lanny furled his shaggy brows.

"Somehow it just doesn't sound like a workable plan."

At just this moment, the car began to inch upward ever so slowly and they both scrambled to their feet.

India looked at her watch. They had been trapped there thirty-five minutes and it had seemed to her more like five.

She felt a pang of regret at the rescue.

"Looks like we're being saved," Lanny offered. There was no enthusiasm in his voice.

They both stared upward at the flashing lights that indicated the floors they were passing. Though they were moving slowly, the floors went by much too fast for India.

Suddenly they felt awkward in their aloneness together.

Lanny put a tentative hand on her arm.

She turned expectantly and looked up into his eyes.

"This sounds silly but . . . it's been fun. Let's have coffee together sometime, huh?"

He looked as though he half expected her to reject his offer.

India beamed. "I'd love to. It *was* fun—once I got over my panic. Thanks for being so . . . understanding."

He brushed aside her thanks with embarrassment.

"Forget it. Hey, what do you bet Ivan chews me out for being late?"

They exchanged guilty grins as they realized that they both disliked Ivan.

As the elevator doors slid open smoothly at the penthouse floor, the first person they saw was an irate Ivan standing in the middle of the reception area.

At the sound of the elevator, he spun around and glared at Lanny. "And where the hell have *you* been all morning?" he demanded.

Chapter 19

Thursday's ten o'clock exercise class found all four of the regulars there, for a change.

Because Sacred Heart had a teacher's meeting holiday, Jade had even permitted Shelley to come to class.

The second Shelley spotted Anastacia, she asked Jade if it would be all right if she went in and changed with Annie. Jade waved her on and told her to make it quick, then slipped into a dressing room already occupied by an unusually exuberant Cricket.

"Where have you just gotten back from now?" asked Jade, removing the beige camel-hair sweater she had worn over an ivory satin blouse for the morning's show.

"The Islands, and I'm in *love!*" announced Cricket as she wriggled into her red leotard.

"That explains your obnoxious good cheer," retorted Jade, dropping the matching beige skirt to the floor and stepping out of it.

Cricket turned and closely scanned her reflection in the brightly lit makeup mirror on the wall.

"Doesn't it show on my face? Don't I look radiant?" she teased.

"You look tan enough to make me green with envy. Do you plan to go around looking healthy this whole coming winter? I *could* learn to hate you."

Cricket flopped down onto one of the green-velvet-covered benches that lined either side of the dressing room and lit a cigarette.

"Well, that all depends. I'm contemplating a trip to Paris, but for reasons other than a good tan."

"The plot thickens."

"You betcha."

India slipped into the dressing room to change and, seeing both Jade and Cricket already there, paused as though to go find another room.

"Come on in, there's always room for one more," sang out Cricket.

Giving them a smile of greeting, India dropped her purse and gym bag and began to disrobe.

"Aren't you even going to ask me about him?" prodded Cricket to Jade, exhaling a large cloud of smoke.

Jade was almost into her leotard by now.

"Why? I'm sure you're going to tell me anyway."

"His name is Andy and he's the guy I've been looking for all my life."

"And finding every two minutes, if memory serves me well," retorted Jade with a grin, giving a final pat to her mane of copper hair.

"There's one tiny problem."

"There's *always* one tiny problem. Don't tell me. Let me guess. He has only six months to live, right?"

"Wrooooong! He's married."

Jade made a face.

"Good luck!"

India studiously tried to avoid looking as if she were listening, which was ridiculous because she obviously couldn't help but listen in such close quarters. Besides, she rationalized, Cricket seemed to have no compunctions about broadcasting her affairs to the whole world.

India sighed in spite of herself. Cricket lived such a carefree life, she mused. Even when she fell in love with a married man, she could dismiss such a horrendous complication as a "tiny problem."

India's fingers shook slightly as she unbuttoned the front of her blouse and thought about the fact that in five minutes she'd be face to face with Lanny again.

Her problem as she had begun to think of it, was far from tiny. An adult married woman was infatuated with a gym instructor perhaps half her age. She wondered how Cricket would like *them* apples.

Cricket chattered on, oblivious to anything but herself. "I don't think she understands him though . . ."

Jade held her side in mock agony. "Please! Spare me the clichés!"

Cricket snubbed out her cigarette. "Hey! I've got a terrific idea. You free for lunch? You can give me advice to the lovelorn from an *older* woman!"

Jade bopped her over the head with her flowered gym bag for the gratuitous insult.

"As a matter of fact, I just got canceled out for lunch. I'll do it if we can talk about some of *my* problems for at least two minutes."

The two women left, chatting as they went.

"*You* got problems?"

"Oh boy! Have *I* got problems!" Jade's voice floated back into the dressing room as they made their way into the gym.

India hung up her clothes neatly and tried to control the inner trembling she felt. She had made

159

up her mind that if Lanny asked her for coffee, she would accept. There was absolutely nothing wrong with having coffee with a friend, she told herself. Nothing at all.

Cricket was strolling along 61st Street heading for the restaurant when she spotted Jade getting out of a taxi in front of the green canopy of Mme. Romaine deLyon's just ahead. The restaurant was a favorite of both women and specialized in every kind of omelette imaginable.

Cricket quickened her step and Jade paused to wait for her as she saw her coming down the street.

As Cricket drew close, the women each raised their large, dark sunglasses to the tops of their heads and let them rest there, in the familiar mutual salute of Manhattan women.

"Hi," said Jade. "I was afraid you'd beat me. I got tied up back at the studio."

"I stopped over at my office after class and grabbed my mail. Let's hope we're early enough to get a table."

The tiny restaurant accepted no reservations and handled its clientele on a first-come basis. The flowered tablecloths gave it a tearoom atmosphere, and an outsider would hardly suspect how many wealthy and renown people lined up there to enjoy the delights of Mme. Romaine's famous omelettes, which were cooked, one by one, in her small kitchen and were well worth waiting for.

After they had been seated and each had ordered a glass of white wine, Cricket quickly chose an "artichoke, ham, and cheese omelette" and Jade settled on "mushroom, asparagus, and cheese" for hers.

Cricket pushed the menus aside and lit a cigarette. "Now what's this about your having problems? I thought your life was glamorous, dazzling, and problem-free."

"Aside from the 'glamorous,' you could be describing my laundry," commented Jade dryly. "I thought we were here to discuss *your* love life."

"Oh, we'll get to that, I assure you. But it's been ages since we've had lunch together, so we've got oodles of catching up to do. Are you still seeing that handsome senator from California? What's-his-name?"

"Kendall Court. And that's part of my problem."

"Shoot. I love to enjoy someone else's agony."

Jade fiddled with the stem of her wine glass for a few seconds before answering. Unlike Cricket, she had trouble opening up and discussing her personal life. But she knew she'd feel better after talking it over with someone, and the strange, half-close, half-distant friendship she had with Cricket—whom she rarely saw outside of exercise class—was the perfect relationship in which to hash it over and talk it out.

She took a deep breath and began.

"Well, as you may or may not know, the good senator is coming up for reelection next fall."

"And he wants your vote!"

"Shut up and listen, clown. And he's thinking about his image."

"Meaning, he shouldn't be seen all over New York every time he's in town, with a no-good TV personality-type lady!"

Jade smiled. "You're hopeless. No. Believe it or not, the damned opposition, for want of anything better to go after, is starting to circulate ugly rumors about the forty-three-year-old senator who's never been married—that maybe he might be a . . .

161

closet queen."

Cricket hooted so loudly that the people at the next table gave her indignant looks.

"You must be kidding! He's about as queer as Casanova! I'd sleep with that gorgeous man in a second!"

Jade gave her another "you're hopeless" look and remarked, "I thought you were in love."

"I mean, of course, if I weren't in love," shot back Cricket, trying to look demure and failing completely.

"That's what I adore about you. You're such a lech. If you weren't a woman, you'd be a dirty old man."

"Okay, so I'm a dirty old woman. But that's *so* ridiculous. What's the real problem?"

"Okay, so after three years of a perfectly lovely relationship, Kendall is starting to make 'let's get married' noises."

"Marry him," was Cricket's succinct advice.

"You're a fine one to talk. Why don't you get married, if you think it's such a red-hot thing?"

"I told you, he's married."

"Details. Anyway, seriously, you know I was married. And it didn't work out."

"If at first you don't succeed, try, try . . ."

"Go to hell. You're not being any help at all. No, I am honestly not sure that I ever want to get married again. It just doesn't seem to mix well with my job and my life. Besides, can you see me having a long-distance marriage, with him in California and me in New York? It's too absurd."

"Your feet are going to get awfully cold at night when you're old and gray."

"Electric blankets have a way of giving without expecting you to sacrifice your life in return."

"So you don't want to get married and he does. Do you love him?"

Again Jade fiddled with her wine and finally took a sip.

"Yes. I guess I do. And that's the hell of it. I suppose as a way of forcing me to come to a decision, the last time I saw him we had a blow-up, and he gave me an ultimatum."

"Shit or get off the pot."

"You have such an elegant way of putting things, but yes, that's about what he said."

Cricket sighed. "You *do* have problems. Now, about *my* love life . . ."

Jade held up a hand. "Wait! That's only the beginning."

"Jesus, I'm going to have to have another glass of wine if your life gets any worse."

Jade signaled the busy waitress for two more.

"It gets worse. Now we get to Shelley . . ."

"Speaking of Shelley, where is our new Miss Teenage America? I thought she had the day off."

"She does and Anastacia invited her to go along on her bookings for the rest of the day. I hadn't the heart to say no, Shelley was so excited."

"So, what's the problem there? Being mother to a teenager making you feel old?"

"It's not making me *feel* old; it's actually aging me. She's a sweet kid, but so naïve and"—Jade shrugged—"I just never know what she'll get into next."

"Like?"

"Like I come home the other night and she's on my private phone."

"Big romance?"

"Big obscene phone call."

"Happens all the time."

"But she's talking to him at great length!"

163

"As long as she doesn't make a date with him!"

"No, listen to this. This guy has called before and she's talked to him and he told her that if she could get him to climax—over the phone, mind you—then he'd stop calling."

"Better over the phone than in person."

"Be serious, Cricket. She is sitting there talking sweetly to this pervert about his 'problem,' and when I finally get her off the phone and yell at her, she says she feels *sorry* for him and she's trying to help him. She calls it *therapy* and accuses me of being unfeeling!"

"Jade, you are making this up!"

Jade crossed her heart. "I swear, it's true! Could I make up anything so ridiculous?"

"Good Lord, you're right. She *is* naïve. I didn't know they made 'em like that anymore."

"They do in Augusta, Maine."

"Maybe you should ship her home before she gets in real trouble."

"I thought about it, believe me, but I can't bear to do it. She'd be heartbroken, and besides, my sister Rose would say, 'I told you so.'"

"Well, what about that convent you've got her in? Doesn't she have hip friends from there to run around with, girls who'll protect her and give her the scoop?"

"Oh, she's met some girls from there. But she's much more fascinated with someone glamorous like Anastacia."

"Annie seems like a good kid."

"I guess so. But she obviously travels with a fast crowd, older than Shelley is. What have I gotten myself into this time?"

Jade leaned her head on her hand.

164

"Beats me. *Now* is it my turn?" asked Cricket flippantly.

"Almost," said Jade. "Then there's my job . . ."

"Good grief, there's more?"

"The network is bringing in a new head of programming, a guy from the West Coast named Griggs Parkinson, and this guy is the bastard of the whole damn world!"

"You know him personally, or is this just hearsay?"

"Years ago, when I first started at the network, he was a junior executive."

"And?"

"And we had one run-in so ugly, I honestly don't care to talk about it."

"Oh, come on. Tell."

"No, really. It's something I've spent a lot of time trying to forget."

"So give him a wide berth."

"I'd like to, but I've got a little plan of my own I've been trying to lay pipe for, and this royally screws it up."

"Tell Momma about your little plan."

Jade hesitated only a fraction of a second. She knew she could trust Cricket.

"Well, the anchorman on the six o'clock news is planning to retire, and I've been trying to get my ducks in a row to angle for his spot."

"Wow! First woman anchorperson on a major nighttime news program. You do think big!"

"Yeah, but I haven't an icicle's chance in hell with Parkinson in the driver's seat just as the spot comes up."

Both women sat silently for a moment.

Jade honestly felt better after spilling it all out to

someone, so she attempted to shake off her depression and to look cheerful and interested in Cricket's problems.

"But, as they say, enough of me. Tell me about your problems."

"Me?" asked Cricket. "Damn, lady, compared to you, I've got no problems at all. Here come our omelettes. Let's talk about something cheery like death and taxes!"

Chapter 20

Annie had had to wait two weeks before she could get an appointment with her gynecologist. The waiting was pure hell, because she lived in the shadow of the fear of pregnancy.

She did not confide in Ferrago about what had happened, though she wasn't sure why. It wasn't out of a feeling of not wanting to worry him; it was more that if she *were* pregnant, she wanted it to be her problem alone. Perhaps she was afraid to hear what he might say if she were. She had no idea whether or not he would suggest they get married. She was sure of the intensity of his feelings for her, but not of their duration. They had never made any long-term commitments to each other.

On the other hand, even if he wanted to marry her, she knew she could never have the baby. How could she ever take a little half-black, half-white baby home to her family in Harlem? It would mean a complete break with her family once and for all. And they were her roots, her stability, the place where she always felt whole again.

For that matter, how could she even take Ferrago up there and say "This is the man I am going to marry?"

She lived in a nightmare of uncertainty for two weeks, ate little, slept less, and was little more than desultory in her lovemaking with Ferrago. Only Jade's niece, Shelley, provided some diversion.

On Columbus Day Annie took Shelley to her bookings with her after the gym class, and Shelley had so much fun doing it that, on impulse, Annie suggested the next week Shelley cut classes for one day. Annie would book out for the day and they would have lunch and sightsee all over Manhattan. Annie knew that Jade would be furious if she ever found out. For that matter, so would Ferrago.

But this only added delicious spice to the day's outing. Annie felt young and silly with Shelley, which was odd, considering the differences in their backgrounds and upbringing. Perhaps it was Shelley's freshness and naïveté that seemed to offer shelter to Annie and allowed her to enjoy a childishness that she had never had the luxury to enjoy when she was growing up. Sometimes Annie felt that she had had to grow up much too fast, and she wished she were young and carefree, like Shelley, without problems hanging over her head.

The day had been delightful. They had promised each other to do it again someday and both had sworn never to tell.

Annie had not worried about being pregnant all day; that is, until she walked back into the loft that night and lied about the hard day's shooting she had endured. Then the gloom settled over her once again.

Now she was on the gynecologist's table and his gentle fingers were probing her insides.

"Yes, your body definitely seems to have rejected it," Dr. Gallagher was saying. "But you haven't any idea when this happened?"

Annie shook her head no and watched his face with wide eyes, trying to read his expression.

His countenance told her nothing.

At last she summoned enough courage to ask.

"Do . . . do you think I'm pregnant?"

"I think it's really too early to tell yet for sure, but you don't appear to be. Why don't you get your clothes on and come into my office for a little talk."

Annie obeyed and dressed quickly with nervous fingers. Soon she was sitting beside his huge mahogany desk, where her file folder lay open in front of him.

"Annie, some people's bodies reject the IUD and we don't know why. But yours seems to be one of those. Now we must look for an alternate form of contraception. You *do* want to continue to use some form of contraception, don't you?"

Annie nodded.

"Well, since we've ruled out the IUD and you told me when I fitted you with that that you didn't want to use a diaphragm, I think the only alternative is the pill."

Annie's eyes widened in alarm.

"Now, wait a minute. I don't know what you've heard about the pill, but the pill is perfectly safe for a young woman your age and you can go on using it for years with a large degree of safety."

"I just don't like taking drugs," said Annie stubbornly.

Sudden visions of what Ferrago would say if she were pill-popping every day entered her mind.

Dr. Gallagher spoke more sharply.

"You don't want to be pregnant, do you?"

Annie's defenses began to crumble. She never again wanted to go through the fear and torment she had been feeling for the past two weeks. She knew she couldn't face an abortion. She'd rather try to convince Ferrago of the innocence of the birth control pill than *that*.

Dr. Gallagher spoke more gently.

"Annie, I don't mean to be harsh with you, but I must tell you that I am getting very tired of young women who take a casual attitude about what form of contraception they use and then come running back to me in a few months for an abortion. I am not against legalized abortion, but I am against people who use abortions as a form of birth control. Abortion is a last measure when birth control, conscientiously practiced, has failed. Too many people are becoming too careless about it now that abortion is legal."

Annie agreed and decided that she had to give the pill a try.

"Now, I'll write you a refillable prescription for a month's supply, but I want you to check back with me in six weeks and tell me if you've been feeling any side effects."

"You're sure I'm not pregnant?"

Dr. Gallagher smiled. "I can't promise anything. But there are none of the physical signs present and I'm sure if you wait a week, you'll get your period. Try not to worry. That can delay it, you know. And start taking these pills right after you have it. Regularly, you hear?" he finished with a smile and a wag of his finger.

Annie promised she would and left his office with a much lighter heart than when she had entered.

She had the prescription filled at the drugstore right next to his office and then headed for the nearest Baskin-Robbins for a triple-scoop chocolate cone to celebrate her narrow escape.

Chapter 21

The last week in October was unseasonably cold in New York. November appeared to be crowding into the calendar before its time and the nip in the air seemed to pump new excitement into the tempo of life in Manhattan.

Lanny asked India to have coffee with him after Thursday's class, explaining that he had some free time since the eleven o'clock class had been canceled.

She had rehearsed her acceptance so often that it actually came out sounding casual, even to her own ears.

They went to the coffee shop on the main floor of the building that housed the gym, and lingered over their coffee so long that the noontime regulars arrived on the scene and gave them dirty looks for tying up a booth at rush hour.

At last, with obvious reluctance, Lanny reached for their check. India reached at the same time and their hands brushed, then held. They stared into each other's eyes unblinkingly as they sat, their hands clasped across the table.

"I wish we could have dinner together sometime," Lanny said at last.

"I do too," said India, so softly that he had to lean forward to catch her words.

She stood up abruptly and made her way to the front of the restaurant, leaving Lanny to fumble in his pocket for change for the waitress.

Cricket had made up her mind. She canceled her five days at Costa Brava for the first week in November and arranged to do a special piece on the Louvre Museum in Paris for *Festival*. She wasn't sure, once she got there, how or where she would find Andy. But somehow she would. Her luck always held. It wouldn't desert her now.

He had made no attempt to contact her since the Jamaica trip. This surprised her. She had been positive that he would.

But since he hadn't, it was time to arrange an "accidental" meeting. Cricket had great faith in planned coincidence.

Ferrago had taken the news of Annie's birth control pills far better than she had expected. He had merely shrugged and said something about it probably being the safest thing. Annie had at first been gratified that he hadn't made a bigger fuss, then felt slightly disappointed to realize that her health was not truly his first concern. His sexual pleasure seemed to take precedence.

Still, it was wonderful to be able to enjoy sex without having to worry about an unwanted pregnancy.

The only cloud on Annie's horizon was that the pill had seemed to upset her metabolism, and she was alarmed to notice that her weight had started to creep

172

up. She would virtuously fast for a day or two, and it would drop back down again. But her frequent forays into McDonald's and Burger King finally began to take their toll and, for the first time in her life, Annie found herself a combat soldier in the battle of the bulge.

Jade arrived in her office one Friday morning in late October after the show had gone off the air and found a huge florist's vase containing four dozen long-stemmed American Beauty roses. Their fragrance assaulted her nostrils even as she crossed the threshold.

Jade wondered if they could possibly be a conciliatory gesture from Kendall Court and her heart pounded a little faster as she hurried over to her desk.

She searched through the greenery for a clue to the identity of the sender.

At last she found a tiny white card hidden deep among the ferns.

It read: "Don't you want to welcome me to the East Coast? How about dinner some night?"

A chill ran up her spine as she recognized the sender.

The signature was simple: Griggs.

Chapter 22

Ivan was in his office early on Monday. With little more than a grunt, he accepted the cup of hot coffee that Darlene placed before him.

After she had left, he closed the door to his office and returned to his desk to slip rapidly through the stack of mail before him. It included only bills, checks, and a few announcements, as far as he could determine.

He leaned back in his heavily padded leather chair and heaved a sigh of relief.

Thank God. No word from them, he told himself with relief.

Ivan was genuinely frightened. The letter he had received the week before had shaken him. It had clearly spelled out what might happen to him if he did not bring his account up-to-date with his "friends" at Lotus Importing.

Before that, there had been a phone call, but it had been made in such a friendly, innocuous manner that Ivan had felt it had only been a polite reminder. He realized now that he had been wrong.

Going once more through the stack of mail before him, he saw a letter he had missed. But the familiar handwriting and the California postmark reassured him that it was only news from Igor on the West Coast.

Perhaps Igor had good news, he thought. Perhaps there was even a check in the envelope.

Ivan tore it open with eager hands, but no stray piece of paper fluttered to the desk. It contained only a single sheet covered with Igor's spidery scrawl.

"Greetings, my good friend," it began. "I hope the world goes well with you. Life out here is beautiful and Natasha and the children are all well and enjoying themselves."

Yes, yes, thought Ivan impatiently. Get on with it.

His eyes rushed ahead, stopping over the words "Business is showing no profit as yet, but we have high hopes for the first of the year."

The first of the year might be too late.

"I wish you well and, if I do not hear from you before then, I hope your holidays will be happy ones."

Drivel. Ivan tossed the letter into the tooled leather wastebasket by his desk.

He leaned his graying head onto his carefully manicured hands.

Where had he gone wrong and how had he gotten in so deep?

Long ago he should have stopped the back-gammon games that he played weekly with his wealthy friends, but he kept hoping that he could recoup some of his losses that way. Instead, he had gotten in deeper.

No longer could he permit himself to grasp at that straw as a way out. He needed to put his hands on some more money fast or at least show his "business associates" that there were good, solid prospects for more money coming in.

He had already gone back to them once for more money to take care of the vigorish. By this time,

Lotus Importing had become a half-owner of the East Coast operation of Ivan & Igor's, a carefully kept secret from both Igor and the women who patronized the gym. At the end of each month, Ivan was expected to bring a payoff of half the profits to a mutually agreed upon location in the city.

Last month, Ivan simply had not shown up at the appointed time, and at the end of last week, he had received the letter.

Ivan got up and went over to the complex stereo machine and put in a tape, hoping music would relax him and help him think. Then he returned to his chair and slumped down in it.

Pachebel's *Kanon* flooded the air as his weary brain raced like a squirrel in a cage. Over and over again he reviewed all the possible solutions to his problem.

He could not turn to any of his friends for a loan. He was already in debt to most of them with his gambling. He couldn't imagine trying to sell his co-op apartment. To begin with, the market wasn't great right now, and besides, where would he live?

He glanced at the twinkling star sapphire, set in heavy gold, that graced his pinkie finger, and he thought briefly of trying to pawn some jewelry. There was the solid gold lighter that the wealthy duchess had given him some twenty years ago, in return for "favors received."

He sighed at the memory and wondered if he could find anyone who would pay for the use of his body today? It was an aging machine, kept in good repair, but aging, nevertheless. It was good for little more than instructing vain women in the myriad ways of preserving their own bodies.

Idly he opened the first envelope in the stack in front of him. It contained a check from Jade Greene for her own and her niece's exercise classes for the previous month.

How simple life was for a famous television personality! He had read only last week of an enormous contract renegotiation for one of them and a salary that went well up into the six figures.

He tapped a toe unconsciously to the exquisite, intricate music that he used to love to play as he worked out on the parallel bars, many years ago.

Somewhere in the depths of his crafty mind, a light began to flash. There was no way he could increase his list of gym patrons enough to take care of his extensive debts, but there was a simple, modern method of reaching many more women—the miracle of television!

What if he, Ivan Petrovich—still not too bad looking with clever makeup and proper lighting— could manage to convince the officials at a network to let him to a daily exercise show—an elegant exercise show, done to the strains of chamber music? If he could get a contract—even for only thirteen weeks to begin—not only could he get some money, but he could also prove that there would be more money coming in. And if all went well, it would be *big* money!

His febrile brain raced.

Jade Greene was the contact he needed. The way to his salvation lay right here in his own gymnasium. She was very important at the network. She could put him in touch with the proper people, say the right things about him, and he would do the rest. All he needed was to do a little planning and figure out how to approach Jade with his idea.

He would present his plan to her, outline the kind of show he had in mind, and simply turn on his irresistible charm. He had great faith in his personal charm.

At last, things were looking up.

Chapter 23

On Tuesday morning, Ivan was in the gym bright and early. He could scarcely wait for the members of the ten o'clock exercise class to begin arriving. He was bursting with plans for his own TV show and wanted to feel Jade out about it as soon as possible. His first step would be to ask her to have coffee with him after class, to make sure they had complete privacy for this important discussion.

The first person to get off the elevator was not Jade as he had hoped, but a rather dispirited Anastacia. She gave Darlene and Ivan a halfhearted hello and went to change into her leotard. Her usual bounce and vivacity was obviously lacking this morning.

Ivan glanced again at the class listings for the morning to be sure that Jade planned to appear. He saw only one cancellation and that was for that Cricket girl. Probably traveling again, thought Ivan.

After only a few moments, Anastacia reappeared, suited up for class, and went up the stairs to the floor above, where the scale was kept. She came down again in seconds, looking, if possible, more despondent than before.

Anastacia sat down, picked up a current magazine,

and pretended to flip through it, but it was easy to see she had no real interest in it.

At last, she stood up and walked over to Ivan. "Ivan, may I speak to you a moment, please?" she asked somewhat timidly.

Ivan fought down his impatience and tried to slip his practiced smile into place.

"Yes, my dear? What is it?" He did not want to be tied up with the black model when Jade made her appearance.

"I'd rather talk to you privately, if you don't mind," she said, indicating his office with a slight nod of her head.

And I'd rather not talk to you at all, he thought irritably.

But Ivan could not afford to be rude to anyone in his present financial situation. And so he turned reluctantly and ushered her into his private office.

Slipping into his chair and into his polished professional manner, he attempted to look interested. "Now, lovely Anastacia, what is troubling you today?"

"Ivan, I have a problem . . ."

"Please let me know if I can be of help."

Ivan was used to the women of his gym coming to him with all sorts of problems. He had helped them solve everything from where to find the best hairdresser or the best doctor for tennis-elbow, to where to find a good abortionist—before such things had become legal. Of course, in the case of the professional people to whom he referred his patrons, he always received a healthy kickback. This fact remained unknown to the gym clients, naturally. But Ivan felt that his referrals were certainly worth money to the people involved, and he had no qualms about accepting suitable remuneration for his recommendations.

As he looked more carefully at Annie, he wondered what her problem might be. Much too young to need a plastic surgeon; unmarried, so she could hardly need a good divorce lawyer.

Annie sat and squirmed so long without speaking that Ivan could scarcely contain his impatience. Jade might be coming in, even now, he silently speculated.

"Well, I guess you know that I model . . ."

"Yes, yes," said Ivan a trace too quickly. "I have seen your pictures *everywhere*. Beautiful, beautiful."

"Yeah, well, I'm kind of having a weight problem, which of course is *death* in my business, and—"

"Please do go on. You know you can tell me anything, my dear."

"Well, I was wondering, it kind of seems to settle around my middle and . . ."

Annie was struggling, more out of guilt than anything else, knowing full well that the problem around her middle was attributable to too many hamburgers and French fries and ice cream cones eaten on the run between assignments. These had never affected her weight before, but since the pill, they were beginning to take their relentless toll and she found herself powerless to resist them.

If anything, her will power was growing worse and worse in that direction. She knew Ferrago would have no sympathy for her, because he would insist she was poisoning her system with that food. Then he'd either lecture her endlessly on her eating habits or force her to cut out the birth control pills, a possibility that she couldn't bear to face.

It was only this desperation that made her turn to Ivan, a man who generally intimidated her with his overpowering manner. But she did accept his expertise on the human body, if only because she had heard him expound on it so often.

"And I was wondering if there were any special exercises you could give me, to do during classes and maybe at home to help me . . . uh, well . . . keep my waist trim, you know?"

Ivan stared hard at her, wondering if she were putting him on.

"You aren't pregnant, are you?" he asked sharply.

Annie squirmed and blushed rosily under her normally coffee-beige skin. She hadn't expected Ivan to get so personal. She briefly considered telling him about the birth control pills, but decided against it.

"No."

Ivan was thoughtful for a moment. Then a sudden inspiration came to him, one that would bring in a few dollars on the side.

"Ah, yes. Well, I understand your problem— completely. It could be just a bodily imbalance. Do you take vitamins?"

Annie thought with distaste of the rows of natural vitamins that Ferrago kept at home.

"No."

"Hmmm, considering your profession, when you are on the go so much, with so little time for regular meals, it could be a matter of some therapeutic shots to help you," he went on smoothly. "They would also curb any appetite spurts you might have," he added, noting a slight reaction on her part when he mentioned regular meals. For all he knew, she gorged herself on junk food.

"Shots?" Annie looked dubious.

"For your health, my dear, strictly for your health. Vitamins and tonic and such. Now, I have the name of a wonderful doctor over on Park Avenue right here somewhere," he assured her, fumbling through his address book though he knew exactly where the number was. And well he should, for he had sent enough patients over to the doctor—those who decided they had weight problems or energy problems or whatever. And the good doctor was very expensive and very prompt in sending Ivan a generous finder's fee.

"Ah, yes. Here it is. Dr. Adrien Davis."

He quickly scribbled the name and number on a piece of paper and handed it across the desk to Annie.

"Call him as soon as you can and get over to see him. Many of our gym clients here go to him and are very well pleased. His shots will make you feel alive, vigorous, and on top of the world. Your weight problems will vanish like ice in the summer sun."

Ivan beamed his most fatuous smile at her and stood up by way of dismissal.

Annie took her cue and rose also.

"Thank you, Ivan. You've been very helpful. I never thought of it as a bodily . . . what was it you called it?"

"A bodily imbalance. It happens to many people, my dear. I am so pleased to have been of help to you. Let me know how you feel."

Ivan all but shoved her out of his office door in his haste to be rid of her. He followed closely behind her, closing the door as he went.

He glanced quickly through the plate-glass wall into the gymnasium, only to be greeted by the sight of Jade, already in her leotard, warming up with Lanny for the class.

Damn! he swore silently. The black bitch screwed up my timing and I missed her!

He quickly decided he would lie in wait for her after the class. Ivan was determined to begin laying the groundwork with her for his very own television show. He couldn't afford to waste any time.

It was a dispirited class that day, though none of the women seemed to notice the moods of the others, so wrapped up was each in her own problems.

Annie was nervous and missed her timing in her handstand three times. She was torn with indecision. Ivan's suggestion had opened up a whole new avenue of action to her. Yet she was nervous at the thought of seeing a strange doctor without telling Ferrago. He might raise absolute hell about it if he found out. And to tell him would necessitate her telling him about her problem, which brought her right back to where she began. Her dilemma raced around her mind like a worried puppy.

India had been the first one into the gym that day, having entered while Annie was talking to Ivan, and in the few minutes she and Lanny had been alone, he had asked her almost shyly if she'd like to have a bite to eat with him tonight. She hadn't expected the invitation quite so soon, though they'd met for coffee twice now. She thought quickly. Drew was going to be late tonight. She could ask Mrs. Schmidt to come back and stay with the kids. She could tell Drew that she went to a movie for the evening. She actually *could* have dinner with him. And so she had blurted out yes, and then Jade had come walking in, and now she was wondering how and where she could meet him and how and when he could tell her where. The thought of the evening had her in such a state of confusion and guilt that she almost fell off the trapeze and would have except for a firm, restraining hand from Lanny that lifted her gently back in place.

She shot him a smile of gratitude and practically melted at the one he returned to her.

184

Jade, on the other hand, went through her paces with a vengeance, almost overshooting the lower uneven bar as she swung around the upper one. She was thinking about what had happened after her show earlier . . .

The first thing she saw on her desk was a message that made her blood boil. It read: "Mr. Parkinson called. Said he would pick you up for dinner tonight at seven o'clock. Dress."

She crumpled the message with one swift gesture and bellowed for Linda to come into her office.

"Did you take this damn message? What the hell does he mean? And who the hell does he think he is telling me to *dress*? That lousy bastard can go screw himself for all I care!"

Linda stood in the doorway, looking bewildered at Jade's outburst. She had never seen her so furious.

When Jade finally paused for breath, Linda apologized profusely.

"Golly, I'm sorry Jade. I thought *you* had made the date. He called himself. It wasn't even his secretary. And he sounded so pleasant and self-assured that I just assumed . . ." The young woman's voice trailed off helplessly.

"Never assume anything," said Jade bitterly, sitting down now that the first blast of her fury had spent itself.

Linda looked for a way to rectify her error.

"Gee, do you want me to call him and tell him that you're busy? It does seem kind of nervy just to call like that . . ."

Jade was sitting silently, still fuming inwardly but wondering what the hell Griggs had up his sleeve now. Did he possibly think that she'd fall all over herself at the opportunity to go out with him? What was going on in his malevolent mind? She knew that

Griggs Parkinson never did anything without a reason, and generally a sinister reason, at that.

The memo she had received had said that Griggs would assume his duties on Monday—yesterday—but he hadn't even called his first staff meeting yet. Was there some reason he wanted to talk to her alone before that event took place? Further, would it be to her advantage to talk to him alone first? She still had not entirely given up her plan to try for the spot on the evening news, though the possibility certainly seemed a great deal more remote now with Griggs at the top.

Jade's curiosity began to battle with her instinctive loathing of the man. She had dismissed the sending of the roses as bitter sarcasm on his part. But now there was this.

Curiosity won out. She could play as cagey a game as he could. Let him take her out to dinner. She would be polite, remote, and listen. She would read what he had in mind before deciding how to proceed with her own plans.

She shook her head wearily at her expectant secretary.

"No. Forget about it. I'll go out to dinner with the son of a bitch. I'll just drink something milky first to coat my stomach so I don't throw up at the sight of him."

Linda tactfully withdrew . . .

A chance remark of Lanny's brought Jade out of her reverie and also served to convince Annie to see Ivan's doctor. Catching the black model as she spun off the bars, he casually remarked, "Good grief, Annie, you're getting heavy," meaning it more in jest than in earnest.

It was the push Annie needed. She decided she

would call Dr. Davis right after class—and then stop for a milkshake, to make herself feel better.

India needn't have worried about where to meet Lanny. Under the cover of handing her a towel after class, he whispered to her, "Is six-thirty at The French Shack okay?" and she merely gave him an affirmative nod and a happy smile as she went off to dress. She briefly reflected that thirty-nine was a late stage in life to begin practicing such duplicity.

For Jade, the vigorous exercise had been a catharsis. Now she dressed quickly and stormed out of the gym, more determined than ever to figure out what Griggs Parkinson's game was and beat him at it. So wrapped up was she in her own plots that she virtually ignored Ivan's frantic signals to her from the telephone where he was tied up with a call. Instead she stomped into the elevator and pushed the button for the main floor with a vengeance she would have liked to have directed at Parkinson's pretty nose.

The elevator doors closed just as Ivan managed to disengage himself and hang up the phone.

He swore softly under his breath.

Chapter 24

Jade was short-tempered with everyone when she returned home from the office that afternoon. She sat and had a martini at the kitchen table while Shelley and Mark had their dinner at six o'clock, prepared by the ubiquitous Mrs. Swann.

She snapped at eight-year-old Mark for having his elbows on the table, sharply corrected Shelley for interrupting when she tried to speak, and crossly remarked to Mrs. Swann that the food bills were running awfully high.

Abruptly she stood up and apologized to everyone. "I'm sorry. I'm really being beastly tonight and I don't mean to be. I've got a business dinner date that I'm not looking forward to and I've got to go dress for it. See you all later. Mark, homework before TV. Shelley, that goes for you, too."

With that, she moved to drop a kiss on the top of Mark's head and one on Shelley's cheek as she passed her chair.

Mrs. Swann nodded to her but wisely said nothing. She knew Miss Greene too well to be offended by a mood. She could also tell immediately when something was troubling her usually pleasant employer.

And tonight, Miss Greene was obviously troubled.

Jade climbed the several flights of stairs to her bedroom and took out a long, saffron-colored chiffon gown by Halston.

Dress indeed!

Tonight, she would dress to *kill*.

Carrying her martini with her, she wandered into the large adjoining bathroom and began running a steaming hot tub of bubbles. She hoped that a long bath would take the kinks out of her body and her mind.

After placing her martini on a tiny, white, marble-topped table next to the oversized tub, she shed her clothes rapidly. As she stepped into the fragrant froth of bubbles and settled back, she felt herself relax. She closed her eyes and gave herself up to the pleasant sensation.

Griggs Parkinson, she mused silently. How strange life is.

There had been a time, long ago, when that name would have aroused happy feelings, not the festering hatred she felt for him now.

How young she had been, and naïve—fresh out of Augusta and a sheltered childhood.

Her father had owned a string of movie houses all through New England, and she had spent much of her youth in darkened movie theaters, watching the flickering images on the screen. Knowing she had no talent for singing or dancing, she had dreamed of being an actress, but her strong, handsome features had not been the sort that Hollywood cherished in those days.

So, after a brief fling at junior college, she had decided on a career in journalism and had headed for the big city of New York to fulfill those dreams.

She had begun with a small job on a New York

newspaper as Jade Greenberg, which was her real name. Then she had gotten a spot as a combination secretary-researcher with the network.

Earnest, dedicated, and hardworking, she had soon become known around the network as an ambitious young woman with her eye on the future.

It was there that she had met Griggs Parkinson.

Griggs had been a junior executive then. Her equal in ambition, he was far ahead of her in polish and sophistication, with a keen sense of self-promotion. He was the network's brightest "bright young man."

She remembered the first time she had seen him around the office and had been impressed with his dark good looks, his classic features, his dazzling smile. Just your average, Greek-god-like gentile prince, she had thought wryly. He was quite obviously prep school, Ivy League, and all the right clubs.

She actually had been shocked the first time he had asked her out. She had envisioned him dating pretty post-debs and sitting around glamorous places like The Stork Club sipping champagne.

Instead, they had gone to a quiet little restaurant in the Village and had talked for hours about journalism, television, and the kind of programming that would be watched in the future.

His manner had been light and easy and his smile engaging.

He had been the first man in the whole city who seemed to take a real interest in her and gradually Jade's shell of self-protection had softened a bit. She began to look forward to their chatty little dinners together and exchanging bits of news about the network. She had even opened up enough to confide in him all her secret ambitions about one day being an on-camera reporter. She began to have daydreams about what a striking couple they might make someday—he a network executive, and she a noted television journalist.

Jade felt, for the first time in her life, that she was in love—really in love. She could scarcely believe that a man as polished and perfect, as warm and as tender as Griggs could return her feelings, but she decided that it was all part of the wonder of love.

She started to shape all her hopes and dreams around a future with Griggs.

Her rosy bubble had burst in a startling manner one day when she stopped in the coffee shop on the main floor of their building. Dog-tired from running all over the city that morning on a story and bedraggled from having been caught in a sudden cloudburst, she had slipped into a high-backed booth toward the rear of the restaurant, hoping she wouldn't see anyone she knew.

With a hot cup of coffee in front of her, she had taken her notebook out of her large purse and was going over the notes she had made in the course of her research.

All at once, she heard a familiar voice from the booth directly behind her.

It belonged to Griggs and she instinctively cringed lower in the booth, hoping he wouldn't notice her in her disheveled state, drenched from the rain, her makeup smeared.

She listened to the other voice and realized that it belonged to Griggs's boss, Frank Ellsworth. It was obvious they had just dropped in for a late morning coffee break.

Deciding she would wait until they left, she turned back to her notes and thought no more about it until, with a shock of recognition, she heard her own name mentioned and realized that they were talking about *her*.

Frank was saying, "Hear that you're dating that kid from research, Jade Something-or-other. You serious about her?"

The faint incredulity in his tone irritated her and she found herself listening involuntarily, waiting for Griggs's reply.

"Jade Greenberg. Yeah, well, I've taken her to dinner a few times."

"And?"

"And nothing." Griggs's tone was one of dismissal. He sounded as though he wished Frank would drop the subject.

"Well, what gives? She's hardly in your league."

Griggs's laugh, which she had always found so engaging, grated on her in its artificiality.

After a pause, he said, "Listen, what can I tell you? She's a pushy little Jewish broad with inflated ambitions, who's obviously willing to sleep her way up the corporate ladder. I just don't want to be the one who missed getting a piece of her ass on the first rung."

Jade felt faint. She could hardly believe her ears. Their mingled laughter at his last remark echoed like thunder in her head, where the blood rushed and pounded in her temples.

Her face burned and she wanted to run from the restaurant and home to her tiny apartment. She sat in frozen horror at what she'd overheard, and it was only by dint of sheer will power that she managed to stay glued to the booth until the interminable time when they finished their coffee and left.

She had never felt so hurt or humiliated and didn't know how she could have been so taken in. Griggs had kissed her good night and there had been times when they'd sat and kissed on her couch in the apartment, but that had been all. It must *not* have been all that he'd had in mind for the future.

She was torn with pain, and yet there was a strange relief that she'd found out what he was like before she had let herself go any farther with him. She had already become too involved—too involved and open and honest, and this was what she had received in return for her love and caring. Her gentile prince had turned into a toad.

Jade never answered any of his calls after that and went out of her way to avoid seeing him at the network. She passed Frank Ellsworth many times in the hallways and her face always burned with shame and she averted her head whenever she saw him.

Griggs had stopped calling her after a while. His career had advanced with the meteoric ascent that had been expected, and he'd been transferred to the West Coast several years later.

Jade's career too had lurched forward, sparked by a lucky accident.

Her boss had broken his leg while out on assignment, and Jade had had to rush to the location and do the news story. They had put her on camera and she did so well that the network began to let her cover feature stories.

She had shortened her name to Jade Greene, and her strong, handsome features began to become familiar to viewers of MBB. She worked hard and never missed an opportunity.

The "pushy little Jewish broad" made her way slowly up the ladder, but she played the game by her own rules.

She never slept with a man to further her career in business. And she never opened up herself or her soul to anyone again the way she had to Griggs Parkinson.

Eventually she met Ross Fleming, the producer for daytime soaps at MBB. There quickly followed a sedate and unimpassioned courtship. They married without the flames of passion and divorced without the fires of recrimination, simply agreeing that two careers were too demanding in one family.

Mark, her son, saw his father on weekends, and, though Ross was with another network now, Jade and he occasionally met for lunch to discuss Mark's well-being and his future.

Jade knew that her pushiness was now politely referred to as "aggressiveness" and that her knowledge and hard work had earned her the respect of those she worked with.

But she had never forgotten or forgiven Griggs Parkinson.

A sudden sense of how late it was growing made Jade finally throw off her reverie and leave the sanctuary of the hot tub.

She expertly applied her makeup, slipped into her dress, and brushed her copper hair until it shone with flicks of fire. She was just applying perfume to the crevice between her breasts when she heard the downstairs bell ring.

Grabbing a matching saffron-colored evening coat from her closet and a tiny gold evening purse from her dresser, she took one last, reassuring look at herself in the mirror and hurried out of her room and down the stairs.

She slowed her step as she turned the curve of the staircase and saw him waiting for her below in the foyer.

He turned and looked up at her approach.

Griggs appeared urbane and dapper in his impeccably tailored black dinner jacket and Jade saw that time had only served to enhance his dark good looks.

The touch of gray at his temples and the streak of the same color in the lock of hair that fell engagingly across his forehead seemed so perfect that they might have been done by an expert hair colorist. And knowing Griggs, thought Jade, they just might have been.

She had heard news of him over the years and of his expert business maneuverings and none of it had been very complimentary. He was sharklike in his dealings and always accomplished what he set out to do, without adding the unwieldy burden of friendships along the way. He had married an heiress somewhere along the line, she remembered reading, and had shed her a few years later—probably walking off with a good deal of her fortune Jade speculated.

He smiled when he saw her, and his smile was as charming as ever.

"Jade."

His resonant voice made a greeting of the single word.

Jade attempted to make her smile as gracious as possible and wondered at the churning of emotions in her chest that he still had the power to summon.

"How kind of you to invite me to dinner. And how presumptuous of you to assume that I would accept."

Jade tried to make her smile a little brighter to take some of the sting out of her words and cautioned herself against letting bitterness get in the way of finding out his plan.

But Griggs only chuckled as he helped her on with her coat. "My, you haven't changed a bit in years," he remarked. "Still able to strike with a rapier tongue."

His black stretch limo was waiting for them at the curb. The chauffeur standing beside it leapt to attention at the sight of them and expertly handed Jade into the car. Griggs exchanged a few whispered words with him and then they were off, threading their way into the tangle of midtown Manhattan traffic.

"I had originally thought of taking you to Twenty-One, but then I realized that with your . . . ah, notoriety . . . and my new job, we'd be all over the columns tomorrow and probably wouldn't have a moment's privacy to talk there, anyway."

Translated, that means you're not sure you want to be seen in public with me, thought Jade ironically.

"So we're going to a little Italian place uptown that I discovered. The food's quite passable and it's quiet and dark."

The little Italian place turned out to be *Paroli Romanissimo* in the east eighties, a tiny, tastefully appointed restaurant with fantastic food and prices to match.

Griggs scorned one of the three tables elevated on a platform along the right wall of the restaurant, favoring instead a small loveseat and table at the far end. The lighting was dim, the ambiance, elegant. Jade adored the place on sight, even though she had been prepared to scoff at anything Griggs might like.

Griggs was able to scan the large menu before Jade had a chance to peruse it. When she reached for it, he placed a restraining hand over hers.

"Please, let me order for us. I know the chef and the food here. And I think I remember your tastes well enough to choose something you'll like," he added reassuringly.

Jade cringed. It was the first reference he had made to their former relationship, and it suggested an intimacy that made her uncomfortable.

Outwardly, she merely shrugged and said, "As you wish."

After a moment's consideration, he instructed the

waiter that he would begin with *calamaretti*, tiny baby squid delicately deep-fried, and Miss Greene would have the clams *oreganata*. Then he requested veal *piccata* for two, an order of noodles *Alfredo* to be split between them, and two tossed green salads, all accompanied by a well-chilled bottle of *Verdicchio*.

He waited until the waiter had fetched them each an icy martini before he turned to Jade and spoke again.

"It's been a long time."

Dear lord, if his material doesn't pick up, I'm going to die of boredom, thought Jade, and then decided she simply must stifle her cynicism.

"I suppose I should say congratulations on your new job."

"Let's even drink to it."

They each took a long sip.

"And *I* should congratulate you on how famous you've become. Even out in the primitive wilds of the West Coast, you're a household word."

Jade wondered if he were hinting at her often-voiced disdain for the California life-style. She decided to play a waiting game, preferring to let him lead the conversation where he would.

He turned serious and examined her face for long minutes.

"What ever happened to us, Jade?"

Another winner cliché, she mused silently, deciding he had been working on soap operas for too long. Countering with a cliché of her own seemed safest.

"Was there ever any 'us'?" she returned, trying to sound as sincere as he.

He wrinkled his handsome brow.

"We never made it in bed, did we?"

There was honest perplexity in his question, and Jade could restrain herself no longer.

"Thanks a lot for the compliment of not remembering." Her bitterness was evident, even to Griggs.

He had the grace to look abashed.

"That wasn't too tactful of me, was it? But there have been a lot of years between, you must admit."

Suddenly changing his tack, he commented casually, "I've run into your friend Kendall Court quite often out on the Coast."

The shift in subject and the mention of Ken's name threw Jade entirely. She forgot her pose of disinterested observer momentarily.

"Now, what's *that* supposed to mean?" she snapped.

Griggs allowed himself an amused smile. "It's gratifying to know that I can still get a rise out of you and that you are not altogether the cool, composed lady you are trying to play with me tonight."

Jade turned sullen. "I'm not trying to 'play' anything with you. I am merely trying to enjoy a pleasant evening with an old"—she paused and selected her next word carefully—"friend."

"Well, in answer to your question, it's not supposed to mean anything. It was merely a statement. Of course, I do happen to know that you have been seeing him quite regularly, and I also happen to know that, as of now, you two have both decided to call the whole thing off."

"My, my, how fast news travels."

Griggs gave her a long look again.

"So perhaps, now that you're at loose ends, we might see each other now and again."

Jade almost gasped aloud at his nerve. Local boy returns to the scene of his beginnings as a conquering hero and decides that "pushy Jewish broad" is not quite so objectionable now that she has sufficient fame and status to make her acceptable.

Jade could hold her tongue no longer.

"You would lower yourself to be seen in public with a 'pushy Jewish broad'?"

Griggs looked puzzled.

It amazed Jade that words that had stung her so badly and had stayed in her mind for so many years had been totally forgotten by him.

"I'm not sure what that's supposed to mean. But then I've never understood what happened to us either. So I'm willing to forget what you said, if you are."

It was probably as close as the bastard could come to an apology, thought Jade. Then she realized again that she would have to get her emotions under control if she were going to accomplish anything.

She attempted to change the subject and asked him if he had any special plans in mind for reshaping the network.

He warmed immediately to the topic and launched into a lengthy description of his goals and his methods of realizing them.

Jade found she was listening with interest, in spite of herself. It was the closest they would come to their old relationship, which had been built on this safer theme of business.

"I happen to think that one of their biggest problems is their daytime scheduling. Those game shows are a lot of garbage."

Jade agreed heartily. "But are you suggesting we fight soaps with soaps, so to speak?"

"No. I think women today are looking for something more challenging. Look at the ratings of some of the daytime specials for women that they've done. The networks are coming too dangerously close to underestimating today's woman's intelligence and interests."

"What do you suggest—public interest shows to while away the day?"

"No. But I think the market's ripe for a lot more shows centered around today's woman, her problems, and methods for self-improvement and self-enrichment. Look at Donahue's ratings."

It was an interesting thought, particularly coming from a man who almost perfectly fit Jade's definition of a male chauvinist.

She looked thoughtful.

"I'd really like your ideas on the subject, Jade."

It was the closest to humble she's ever heard him sound.

"I'd have to give it some thought."

"I realize that. But you should understand some of the problems."

The excellent dinner had been eaten while they talked, almost without Jade noticing it.

"That, in fact, is probably going to be the theme of my first network meeting on Wednesday. But I wanted to give you some lead time to work on the problem."

Jade could hardly believe her ears. If she hadn't known the son of a bitch so well, she might have fallen completely for his sincerity.

But Griggs was never as simple as he seemed on the surface, and she reminded herself to keep her guard up. Fool me once, shame on you. Fool me twice, shame on me, she recited silently.

His next line convinced her that she'd been right to be suspicious.

"Say, my brand-new co-op is only a block or so from here. How about coming up to see it and have a nightcap?" His voice was all innocence.

Jade smiled sweetly, once again in control of the situation.

Her voice dripped sweetness as she answered, "You're a *darling* to suggest it, but, Griggs, no one should know better than you, as the new head of MBB, how early a hard-working girl reporter like me has to get up in the morning."

Griggs reached for the check. "I'll drop you at your place."

The first round was hers, and he was smart enough to acknowledge defeat gracefully.

Chapter 25

Only a few blocks away, India was letting herself into her apartment. She paid Mrs. Schmidt, checked on the children, and wandered into the living room to sit and stare at the walls.

Drew wasn't home yet. She was just as glad. It would have been painful to face him now, the taste of the evening still in her mouth, an evening warm and delicate with promise.

The French Shack was a small, noisy, unpretentious restaurant, with prices low enough to fit a gym instructor's budget. Yet the whole evening had been heady as they had again played the tantalizing game of things unsaid.

On impulse, India went over to the stereo and put on some Tchaikovsky, whom she considered everyone's first favorite composer.

As the familiar notes of the First Piano Concerto echoed through the living room, she tiptoed out to the kitchen and poured herself a glass of Beaujolais and then returned to savor it, in melancholy solitude.

The music, or perhaps the mood, brought tears to her eyes. Tchaikovsky wrote music for unrequited love. His themes were haunted with loneliness and made one's insides ache.

What were her insides aching for, she wondered, feeling a pang of guilt at the answer.

She was aching for Lanny, not Drew, her faithful, patient, wonderful husband. How had it ever come to this? She was, she repeated to herself, a happily married woman at last.

Heather had a wonderful stepfather, Toohey was a delightful child—why was she cataloging her children first?—she had a good, settled life and a marvelous husband. So why, why, why was she involved in this?

Some deeper, wiser part of herself answered.

Thirty-nine was a painful age. She was facing a long future, a future in which she would be forever India Travick, mother and wife. And yet still she hoped for the Cracker Jack prize in the bottom of the package.

Was Lanny the prize she had been looking for?

The music hurt, it was so beautiful.

She lit a cigarette and admired the long, lazy curls of smoke that drifted from it.

Could she face the fact that she would never be any more attractive, never be any younger, possibly never be any thinner than she was right now? Could she face all that and still resist the impulse to rush into Lanny's strong young arms?

He was so handsome and so without guile in his now open admiration for her. She knew that if she gave him any more encouragement, they would sleep together.

It wasn't that he pushed the subject at all. It was simply that she would have had to have been blind not to read the message in his large, candid, blue eyes. He wanted her. And the knowledge that he did made her ache with longing for him. India had always found it hard, when someone loved her, not to love back.

Perhaps that was why she had married for the first time. And now she wanted desperately to love Lanny, to be with him, to know how it felt to have him hold her and love her.

Even as she thought it, she knew it was a cheap gamble. Why couldn't she weigh it rationally, against what she had now?

Because loving was never a rational bargain, she told herself. She knew in her heart that she loved Drew, but she knew just as well that she was *in* love with Lanny.

Still, there was more to lose than to gain, more to risk than to realize, and she had finally, at long last, acknowledged that it was a game with no winners and had accepted the fact that it was too dangerous for her to ever meet Lanny again, when she heard the sound of Drew's key in the lock.

The music ended and the stereo switched off just as the beam of light from the hallway sliced through the foyer and Drew's familiar face appeared around the door.

"You still up?"

She crushed out her cigarette and gave him a weary smile.

"Just waiting for you, love. That's all."

Chapter 26

Annie fidgeted nervously as she waited. She had picked up and put down three magazines in the ten minutes she had been sitting in Dr. Davis's waiting room. She sneaked glances at the people around her, trying to stare without appearing to do so.

They were an oddly assorted group—several obviously wealthy young women in *couturier* clothes, a dignified young Madison Avenue type, a long-haired man in jeans and a sequined T-shirt who looked strangely familiar, and a European-looking gentleman with high, polished black shoes and a nubby silk suit. Nobody seemed poor, or old, or, for that matter, sick.

The sequined-shirted fellow was staring back at her with a blank, glazed look. Everyone else was making a great show of not noticing anyone else. One by one, each would be called, in turn, by the receptionist, disappear into the office, and never reappear again. There must be a back exit somewhere, Annie surmised. Either that or he was killing them off and piling them up in the back of his office, she thought grimly.

At last the receptionist beckoned to her. Annie

noticed that none of them had been called by name. She had gone over and given her name quietly to the woman when she had first arrived. The woman had merely placed a tick mark on the list in front of her and nodded to indicate that she was to take a seat. Perhaps the woman was mute, Annie thought, or perhaps Annie's imagination was working overtime.

Annie tentatively twisted the knob on the office door and entered.

The door opened into a large office lined with books. There were several other doors leading from it. Only a small medical table in the corner to the rear of the large desk gave a clue to the occupant's profession.

Dr. Davis himself sat behind the desk, poring over some papers in front of him. He was a gray-haired man with a balding spot atop his head, and he wore gold-rimmed spectacles and a slightly grimy-looking white lab coat.

As Annie closed the door behind her, he looked up and gave an automatic smile of greeting. "Hello, hello. Come in please. Sit over here." He indicated a leather-covered chair beside his desk.

Annie sat down somewhat timidly. She was always in awe of doctors and an unfamiliar physician increased her timidity.

After several more minutes of paper shuffling, Dr. Davis put aside whatever he was perusing and reached into the right-hand desk drawer for a white card. Fixing her with a kindly stare through his gold-rimmed glasses, he began.

"Name?"

Anastacia . . ." She paused. "Uh, Anastacia Clemmons." One couldn't go to the doctor with only one name.

He then asked her address, phone number, height,

and weight.

"Age?"

"Twenty."

"And who recommended you?"

"Ivan. Ivan Petrovich of Ivan & Igor's."

"Ah, yes," commented Dr. Davis and duly noted this on her card.

Finally, he put the card in the corner of the huge, leather-bound blotter holder that covered his desk and rose from his chair.

Excusing himself for a moment, he disappeared through a small door at the side of the office, only to reappear seconds later with several tiny vials in his hand. He busily began to mix these together at the little medical table that Annie had noticed earlier.

At last, looking satisfied with his concoction, he proceeded to fill a syringe with the mixture and attach a needle to it.

Turning expectantly, he seemed surprised that Annie did not have the sleeve of her sweater pushed up in readiness.

"Well?" he asked.

Annie felt confused. She hesitated to question a medical authority, but she did know that doctors usually examined one and asked lots of questions about whether or not one had had the measles or mumps during childhood.

Her dark eyes grew large at the sight of the needle. "Aren't you going to examine me or anything? I mean, don't you want to know what's bothering me?" She sounded genuinely puzzled.

Dr. Davis allowed himself a small smile of understanding as he realized how naïve she was.

He adopted a fatherly attitude.

"Now, now. What's bothering you is not as important as what's going to make you feel better.

It's the cure we're after here, not the disease."

His voice was so comforting and paternal that it did not occur to Annie in her fright to sort out the non sequiturs in his statement.

Obediently she began to roll up one sleeve, never taking her eyes off the dangerous-looking needle.

Dr. Davis wiped her arm with a piece of cotton, all the while continuing in a chatty monotone designed to soothe her fears.

"Now, this will sting a little at first and you may feel a few strange sensations . . ."

He plunged the gleaming needle into her slim arm. Annie winced at the pain but was unable to pull away because he held her arm firmly with his other hand. She watched in horrified fascination as the liquid in the syringe disappeared slowly, slowly, into her arm.

". . . a little light-headedness perhaps, but that will quickly pass and be replaced by a glorious feeling of euphoria . . ."

His voice droned on but Annie ceased to make sense of it because it was as though an opaque cloud had dropped over her eyes. She shook her head once to try to clear it but stopped because the motion caused her to be hit with a wave of dizziness.

She became dimly aware that the doctor had withdrawn the needle. She heard his voice coming to her as though from a great distance.

"Are you all right Anastacia? That didn't hurt now, did it?"

He seemed to be placing her jacket over her arm and shoving her purse under her other arm as he steered her toward a large door on the other side of the room.

Opening this, he gently pushed her through it, saying something about "three times a week at first and then twice will be sufficient. Call my office for your next appointment . . ."

The next thing she realized, Annie found she was standing on the sidewalk of the cross street off Park Avenue. Idiotically, as she stood there dazed, waiting for her head to clear, she realized that she had been right. There *was* another exit from his office and that's why she had never seen anyone come out of there. The whole thing seemed strange, so strange.

And then, slowly, her mind began to clear. She became aware of the sounds and sights around her in a most vivid way, a way she had never experienced before. The sunlight was blindingly beautiful and the traffic noises blared and glared like the brass in a jazz band. She blinked a few times and found herself smiling. She experienced a surge of energy and joy that made her feel as though she could conquer the world.

Confidently, she turned her feet toward Park Avenue to find a taxi. Her step was bouncy and vigorous as she leaped off the curb, unconscious of the fact that the light was against her. Horns shrieked and brakes squealed as traffic ground to a halt to avoid hitting the slim, swinging figure.

None of this fazed Annie. Her mind was shouting, I feel *terrific!*

Annie had no way of knowing that she had just had her first shot of speed. And she *loved* it.

Chapter 27

Ivan was furious at himself for his botched attempts to corner Jade Greene.

Still, he had to admit that selling her on the idea of his own exercise show might take quite a bit more persuading than a simple chat before or after class. Even in his ivory tower of egocentricity, he knew that she led a complicated, fast-paced life and her initial response to his suggestion might be merely to say that she'd think about it and then forget the whole matter.

He really needed a staging of some magnitude to impress upon her the grandioseness of his scheme, an opportunity to dazzle her with his competence as both an instructor *and* an athletic performer.

Slowly a plan took shape in his mind. Perhaps he could stage an exhibition, but he knew that an exhibition needed a setting. A party might do, but a party needed an excuse. Then he thought of the coming holidays.

Mundane, he concluded.

Then suddenly, in a blaze of inspiration, he had it. It would not merely be a Christmas party. It would be a *Russian* Christmas party—a party to celebrate the glory and tradition of his cultural heritage.

Like all great ideas, in retrospect it seemed perfectly simple. In the Russian Orthodox community, Christmas traditions were always celebrated according to the Julian calendar. The Russian Christmas was always observed thirteen days after the Christian holiday, thus enabling Ivan to throw a sumptuous gala sometime in January. He calculated that that would be long enough after the usual morass of holiday parties to stand out. It would also give him enough time to carefully map out his scheme of presentation.

Somehow he would have to stall his creditors until then. Perhaps he could hint at the prospect of his own TV series.

He would need at least two months to arrange for all the props, the traditional food, the musicians, the flowers, and the decorations. And most of all, he would need time to perfect some scripts for his exercise show, one of which he could present almost in its entirety as his own gymnastic exhibition. But spotlighting only *his* ability might not be enough to draw Jade and perhaps a network biggie, as well as enough of his other glamorous exercise students to provide a glittering background assemblage. She must see how he was adored—no, worshiped!

But again, how simple! he thought. What would appeal to his self-centered clientele more than participating in their *own* ego-stroking demonstration!

Most of his students were easily proficient enough to perform, and none of them, he'd venture, had ever had an opportunity to show off for their lovers and friends.

Ivan's mind was racing along at top speed now. He would give a magnificent party to celebrate an exotic, ethnic ritual, highlight it with exhibitions of athletic proficiency given by his star pupils, and cap it with a stupendous performance of gymnastic expertise by none other than himself, the prince of the ivory leather gym mats and the free-swinging chrome trapeze.

The plan was elegant in its simplicity. Surely it would be obvious to everyone attending that he would be fantastic as the star of a new syndicated exercise show.

Ivan's mind began to course ahead feverishly with the preparations, and sometimes he was almost overcome with wonder at his own brilliance. So wrapped up was he with his fabulous scheme that he was able to put behind him the nagging worries about the seriousness of the "hints" his creditors were now dropping.

An exercise show of his own would make him a media celebrity and allow him to be less involved with the gym and more involved with show business. He was tiring of the gym and its petty problems and was becoming almost paranoic with worry over his financial problems, for the people with whom he did financial business seemed to have an uncanny knowledge of the day-to-day business of his exercise salon.

In an off moment, he had even wondered if anyone on his payroll might be in league with his underworld connections. It was a thought so ridiculous that he tried to put it out of his mind. And he almost succeeded.

Chapter 28

Cricket was at first surprised, then alternately irritated and puzzled when she didn't hear from Andy after her return from Jamaica. Could his memory of the time they had spent together fade as easily as her tan had? Hadn't any of it meant anything to him? She couldn't believe that he hadn't been as intoxicated as she had over that fleeting but painfully poignant kiss at her door. She had found herself thinking of little else in her spare moments of daydreaming.

She also felt surprise at her own feelings. Was this the footloose, love-'em-and-leave-'em world traveler she had always pictured herself to be? What was there about Andy that she couldn't get him out of her mind?

At rational moments, she would ask herself if it was because he was a married man. But she dismissed this thought because in her continent-crossing life she had known many married men, and most of them were less appealing than the single ones because of their dedication to the mundane. The sameness of their come-ons had always wearied her.

No, it was not a case of forbidden pleasure that had her in this state of intoxication. Rather, there was a sincerity about Andy, a willingness to share and a childlike delight in discovery that she had never sensed in any man before.

She cursed herself when she couldn't fall asleep at night and saw only Andy's face in the darkness of her room. She railed at herself when she jumped whenever the phone rang. Even the office phone set her teeth on edge. She went through one weekend of pure anger at him for not having the same feelings she did.

And so she proceeded to her plan of an accidental meeting, with which she had merely flirted before. She was determined to do what she had to do to see him again.

She remembered that he had said he would have a meeting in Paris the first week in November. She knew Paris like the back of her hand. She had told him in passing of her favorite hotel, L'Abbaye, on the Left Bank in the St. Germain des Pres area. He had asked her to spell it, because he had said he was tired of staying at the large, American-type luxury hotels, and she had assured him that L'Abbaye was nothing like that.

Cricket now placed two calls. The first was to her editor informing him that she was penciling in a short European jaunt the beginning of next month. Then she dialed thirty-three, the international code for France, followed by a phone number from her address book.

After a few minutes of static and ringing, a polite voice answered. *"Allo. L'hotel del L'Abbaye. A votre service."*

A small, pleased smile played around the corners of her mouth before she spoke. Sometimes, she reflected, one was forced to give fate a nudge.

Chapter 29

India felt herself flush with guilt when Andrew casually mentioned his trip to Paris the following week. She knew immediately that such guilt stemmed from the fact that instead of the sinking feeling that usually hit her when an impending separation was at hand, she was feeling her breath and heartbeat quicken with anticipation.

She fought to keep her voice as casual as his. "How long will you be gone?"

He looked up from his newspaper with a faintly annoyed expression.

"About a week. Earth to India. Don't you remember when I told you a couple of months ago that I had to be in Paris the first week in November for those perfume meetings?"

Now the guilt was at her own forgetfulness.

She answered truthfully, "I guess I do. It's just that time has gone by so quickly lately that I didn't realize next week was November already." *That* part was certainly true enough, she mused before continuing. "Okay, let's try it again," she said, this time making her tone light. "What day do you have to leave?"

Andrew rewarded her with a smile.

"You know me. A transatlantic flight wipes me out for awhile. So, much as I hate to be away, I thought I'd fly over on Saturday night and then have Sunday to recuperate. My first meeting's on Monday."

"Passport in order?" she inquired perfunctorily.

Drew's passport was *always* in order. *Drew* was always in order.

Stop it, she chided herself. You're mocking the very things you've always admired about Drew. What's the matter with you lately?

Unfortunately, she knew the answer to that one.

Andrew misinterpreted her sigh. He stood up abruptly, letting the newspaper fall to the carpet, and came over to sit by her side on the sofa. Putting one arm around her, he said sympathetically, "Don't be blue. It won't be long. I'll try to wrap things up as fast as I can and make it back before the following weekend."

He leaned over and nuzzled her cheek in consolation.

India had never felt like such a rat in her life. Try as she would, she couldn't banish Lanny's face from her thoughts. Lord, had she sunk this low? she wondered. Her husband was making loving gestures toward her and she couldn't think of anything but another man!

"Unless you'd like to fly over and meet me for the following weekend? Want an illicit weekend in Paris with your husband, baby?" he teased softly.

India shook her head, as much to try to shake her thoughts of Lanny as to signify no. "Don't be ridiculous, Drew. What would I do with the children, check them into a locker at the airport?"

The thought of the children helped anchor India

in reality.

"What about your magic Mrs. Schmidt, the one who comes in on gym days?" prodded Andrew, only half-kiddingly.

"Oh, I don't think she'd consider staying for a weekend," answered India doubtfully, suddenly envisioning the excitement of a few days in Paris. Then cold reality returned abruptly, and she continued, "Besides, we really don't have the kind of money to go jetting off to Europe for the weekend. Company expense, yes. Our pocketbook, no way."

Andrew shrugged amiably.

"You're right, as always. And *I'm* the romantic. Don't worry, I'll take you there someday."

"Someday when I'm old and gray," retorted India, her normal domesticity returning.

Yet that night, when Andrew reached over for her in the darkness, she found herself stiffening involuntarily. And she hated herself for it.

The Hotel de L'Abbaye, located on the tiny rue Cassette, just off la rue de Rennes, was once a seventeenth century abbey and later a school. It had been lovingly restored to a small, lovely inn that stood behind heavy, dark-green, fifteen-foot street doors. Once through these formidable doors, one entered a large stone-paved courtyard adorned with huge pots of greenery and, in the summer, bright splashes of flowers. The formal entryway had marble floors, tasteful eighteenth century antiques, and looked into a combination living room and lobby that was filled with low sofas surrounding a marble fireplace. Fresh flowers bloomed from vases artfully placed throughout the whole of the downstairs.

Cricket stopped at the small front desk to the left of

the entryway when she arrived Monday morning from Charles de Gaulle Airport.

The desk clerk was bent over the register. Though he looked up with a question in his eyes, it was only a moment before recognition dawned.

"Ah, Mademoiselle Wells! *Bonjour, bonjour! Votre chambre est pret.* It is the one you requested," he added in English, in the low tone of a conspirator.

Cricket signed the register, noting the names listed, favored the clerk with a smile and *"Merci,"* then turned to follow the porter who had worked there forever. He wore, as always, a dyed-looking brown wig and a uniform of the same color. His demeanor never varied; he was solemn, serious. He stood aside to let Cricket enter the tiny elevator that would whisk them up to her floor.

Just as they were proceeding down the dim hallway in the direction of her room, Cricket's ear caught the sound of a door opening ahead of them.

Cricket fought hard to keep from laughing when she saw the look on Andrew's face as he emerged from his hotel room.

"Bonjour," she said gaily. *"Comment ça va?"*

The porter was struggling with the key to her door, which was exactly opposite the door of Andrew's hotel room. Both doors were in a tiny hallway with yet a third door that could close them off from the main hall so that they could be used as a suite.

"Quelle surprise," she said casually while Andrew struggled for composure. His first look had been one of utter shock, but it had been quickly replaced by confusion, dawning comprehension, and, at long last, what Cricket hoped was a subtle smile of pleasure.

The brown-clad porter finally succeeded in opening the door to her room, then walked in to deposit her sole piece of luggage, a tapestry suitcase.

Pausing only long enough for Andrew to mumble a greeting, Cricket swept into the room after the porter, tossing over her shoulder, "Are you free for dinner tonight, by any chance?"

At Andrew's mute nod of assent, she said, "Seven o'clock. In the bar in the lobby for aperitifs. See you." Waving airily, she closed the door and left him standing dumbstruck in the dim hallway.

While the porter shuffled around opening blinds and turning on lights in the bathroom, making time for her to locate some coins, she smiled smugly to herself.

"First round goes to the lady with the well-worn passport," she thought.

After tipping the porter and letting him out—Andrew had vanished, to her relief—she quickly unpacked her few things and planned her day. First she would have a bite to eat and then, just what any reasonable woman would do on her first day in Paris—go shopping.

Cricket had carefully planned some meetings for Tuesday and Wednesday with the Louvre people. Her convenient excuse for the trip had been that she had been asked to review the upcoming Renoir show that would begin in Paris, then tour the USA for a year, but she'd left today free for her personal business. And the climax of her day of personal business, according to her meticulously worked out schedule, would consist of dinner with Andy tonight in some romantic bistro. Well, she mused maybe *dinner* wouldn't be quite its climax!

She took a taxi to the Right Bank and shopped at her favorite haunts on la rue de Foubourg Saint-Honore before enjoying a light lunch in the rear of Fauchon's on la place de la Madeleine. Then she took a taxi back to her hotel to bathe and rest for her evening.

After an afternoon nap in the center of the huge, cloud-soft queen-size bed in her room, she felt fully refreshed from her flight and decided a long, bubbly bath would bring her back to her energy peak. She knew she would need all her energy tonight.

It was while she was luxuriating in a fragrant hot bath in the oversized tub in her marble bathroom that she heard the door across the tiny hall open and close.

She glanced at her watch, which she had placed on the small table at the side of the tub. Six o'clock already. Andrew's meetings had been long. Well, she thought, there was still time enough for him to wash up and change. She had no intention of being the first one in the bar.

At five minutes to seven, she again heard his room door open and close. She was just drying herself with the enormous bath sheet L'Abbaye always thoughtfully provided.

She smiled a happy smile. Tonight was going to be interesting. *How* interesting would remain to be seen.

Unhurriedly she sprayed herself from head to toe with the new perfume she had purchased that afternoon. Then she threw on a lacy bra and filmy bikini panties and slithered into a golden-russet silk sheath she had picked up that day at her favorite boutique. It set off her blond hair and put amber glints in her dark brown eyes. She wished her Jamaican tan hadn't gone so sallow. She was unaware that the excitement she felt gave a special glow to her skin that was far more becoming than mere suntan. Bone pantyhose and beige kid pumps completed her ensemble. Her only jewelry was a pair of gold hoop earrings. She filled her tiny silk purse with her makeup and, after one quick check in the mirror, she prepared to rekindle her acquaintance with Andrew Travick.

Down in the intimate bar set off to one side in the palm-filled lobby, Andrew fidgeted. It had taken him a morning of inattention at his meetings to cope with the unsettling reality of Cricket being here in Paris and right here in this very hotel, at that. He had struggled with feelings of guilt, excitement, and eager anticipation. He had barely been able to concentrate, so anxious was he for seven o'clock to arrive. But the questions he had stored up all day for her vanished as he caught sight of her entering the lobby.

She looked breathtakingly lovely and exceedingly chic. She stood out enough to turn heads, even in this sophisticated city of chic women. Several men paused in their conversations as she passed.

Andrew rose as she approached him and extended his hand awkwardly. She took it and leaned over to kiss him lightly on the cheek before settling in beside him on the brocaded settee.

As if on command, the porter, now dressed for his role as bartender, appeared to take their orders.

Cricket favored him with a small smile and said, *"Une Lillet blonde, s'il vous plait."*

Turning to Andy, she raised her eyebrows for his order.

Andrew fumbled and mumbled something that sounded like "the same" and then corrected himself. "No, wait. I guess I'd like a martini. A vodka martini, I guess."

The waiter stood rooted to the spot. He found English difficult enough to decipher, without

225

having to contend with mumbling as well.

In a clear, pleasant voice, Cricket repeated Andrew's order, adding, "S'il vous plait." The waiter bowed and vanished.

Andrew looked at her with respect and commented, "Your French is fluent."

Cricket smiled and said she found it handy.

"Lord, I haven't cracked a French book since Choate," laughed Andrew, adding, "At the places I've stayed, I don't need French."

"That's why I want you to see my Paris," said Cricket lightly. "It's quite different, you know."

The waiter returned with their drinks and placed them on the small table in front of them.

After his departure, Andrew and Cricket lifted their glasses and formally clicked them together before drinking. Their eyes held for a long moment, yet neither said anything.

Cricket was the first to look away. She sipped her Lillet and looked around her. The silence was suddenly awkward.

"Well," began Andrew and then he stopped.

"Well," mimicked Cricket and then she smiled.

"What you're doing at L'Abbaye is probably as good a place to start as any," said Andrew.

"What *you* are doing at L'Abbaye should be the question. Remember, it's *my* favorite hotel," she retorted.

"Yeah, I remember. You told me about it—the last time we met, as I remember. I'm here for perfume meetings, if you recall."

Cricket's bland expression looked devoid of guile.

"That had totally slipped my mind. I'm here to do a piece on the Renoir show," she said chattily. "When did you get in?"

"I flew in Sunday morning. Slept and messed

226

around most of the day, trying to shake my jet lag."

"I got here this morning—as you know," she added with a grin.

"Quelle coincidence!" marveled Andrew with a smile.

"See. You're catching on," said Cricket approvingly. "We'll have you chattering in French like a . . ."

"Tourist!" Andrew shot back, laughing.

Cricket's laughter matched his own and their merriment seemed to dissolve any strangeness between them.

"A nice coincidence, if you want my opinion," mused Cricket after another sip of her aperitif. "Now,"—she turned to look directly into his eyes— "are you ready to put yourself into my hands for dinner at a small bistro, some strolling, some music, and some general atmosphere absorbing?"

Andrew's eyes crinkled at the corners as he smiled.

It was a nice smile, Cricket decided.

"The last time I did that, as I recall, we had a wonderful evening. So I'm all yours. Wherever you lead, I shall follow."

Cricket's eyes sparkled in anticipation as she remarked, "I think we're going to have a wonderful evening . . . again."

After a delicious dinner at an intimate bistro on la rue Saint Benoit, where Cricket was greeted as an old friend, they turned toward the Seine to stroll along the quai.

The moon cast a path of silver on the surface of the dark water. Across from the quai loomed the Louvre and in the center of the river floated the ancient Ile de la Cite. Except for a slight chill in the air, the setting could not have been more perfect, thought Cricket.

Andrew seemed totally absorbed in the sights and

sounds around him. The casual way he took her hand as they strolled seemed almost an afterthought.

"A *centime* for your thoughts," said Cricket.

"It's so beautiful, I haven't words. I have never seen Paris like this. It's always been, you know, business dinners, tourist spots . . ." He shrugged in the darkness. *"You* know."

"And after dinner," Cricket teased, "did you go to the Lido or the Moulin Rouge?"

"The Moulin Rouge," answered Andrew automatically, then realized that she was teasing him.

Cricket laughed at his embarrassment.

"Don't be ashamed. All tourists go there, at least once."

"Only once, if they're smart," muttered Andrew.

"At the prices they charge, only the tourists can afford to go there," offered Cricket.

Andrew lapsed into silence.

"Well, let me show you some tourist spots on the Left Bank, if you're game," she challenged.

Andrew's assent was less than enthusiastic.

"No, don't be put off by the tourists. Some of the places are fun. Have you ever been to a *cave?*" she asked, giving it the French pronunciation.

Soon they were making their way through a church close on la rue St. Julien le Pauvre to a tiny entrance marked "Caveau des Oubliettes." Cricket explained that this cave used to be a fourteenth century prison and that the word *oubliette* meant a dungeon with a trap door at the top as its only opening. Victims were pushed through it into the Seine to drown.

"Sounds really weird. What do they put in your drinks?" whispered Andrew as he ducked his head to follow her through the low opening into the cabaret.

Inside, it was dark and smoky, with groups of

people crowded around miniscule tables in a stone, vaultlike room with a low ceiling. Singers strolled about in period costumes singing *chansons* of old, and encouraging the crowd to join in.

Jammed together at a table, they ordered wine and Cricket whispered under the noise that the only thing to do was to relax and sing along.

The hours flew by in a blend of laughter and music, and Andrew was surprised to see how late it was when they had at last paid the check and left.

Once outside, they both gratefully filled their lungs with the cold night air.

"The French smoke like chimneys," commented Cricket.

"Oh, was it smoky in there? I hadn't noticed," said Andrew, coughing.

Turning back toward the Abbey, they strolled hand in hand past crowds of people still milling, though it was well into the early hours.

"Don't they ever go to bed?"

Cricket considered this. "Well, they *must*, sometime, if their romantic reputation is deserved."

"Am I to gather that you don't know if it's deserved or not?"

Cricket grinned in the darkness. "Who, me? I'm just a pure little Southern belle from the U.S. of A."

"You sure get around, for a little girl from the U.S.A."

Her "hmmmmm" was noncommittal.

"But wherever I go, Paris is my absolute favorite city."

"Really?"

"Really. I like other cities. I like Rome. I like Venice. I like London. But I *love* Paris. It's only possible to *love* one."

Her words seemed to hang in the air as Andrew's

thoughts turned, for the first time that night, to his wife. He should feel wretched about being with Cricket, about enjoying himself with another woman, but he couldn't seem to. Tonight seemed unreal, dreamlike and unrelated to real life.

He wished it could go on. And he knew it couldn't.

They had to ring the bell outside the tall, green street doors to gain entry. The everpresent porter opened the door a crack and, seeing who they were, admitted them.

They took the elevator and walked down the hall, neither saying a word. Andrew opened the outer door to their rooms. At their facing doors, Andrew turned and looked into Cricket's eyes. He couldn't read their expression.

Still neither spoke.

Finally Andrew put his hand under her chin and lifted her face to his.

"Thank you for a lovely evening. I like your Paris, my little Cricket."

He kissed her gently on the lips and turned quickly to go into his room.

Cricket opened her door, crossed her threshold, then leaned against her door, lost in thought.

At last, she peeled off her clothes, slipped into a diaphanous sea-foam green nightgown she had bought that day, and turned off the lights.

After brushing her teeth, she went again to the door of her room and twisted the knob as quietly as she could. Softly opening it, she found herself face to face with Andrew.

He was in his pajamas and he was reaching to lock the outer door that turned their two rooms into a suite. After slipping the bolt, he took her by the hand and silently led her into his room.

The lights were off there also, but the same full

moon that had traced a path on the Seine softly illuminated the room with a magical glow.

They stood close together but not touching, staring deeply into each other's eyes.

The moonlight laced Cricket's blond curls with silver and her skin shone luminously, as though lit from within. Drew thought he had never seen such loveliness.

Cricket seized the moment and moved into his arms before reason or reflection could stay the outcome she desired.

From somewhere deep inside of Drew came an anguished groan as he gathered her warm, fragrant body tightly to him. Her bare skin felt as delicate as the down of a peach, and the scent of apricots seemed to cling to every soft curve of her. He wanted to drown himself in her sweetness.

Drew knew then that there was no turning back from the inevitable ending to this glorious night, when both Paris and Cricket had enveloped him in their spells.

Cricket's lips sought his and captured them eagerly. They were her willing prisoner.

Surrendering at last to the passion dammed up inside him, he slipped her nightgown from her shoulders and carried her to the bed. They fell together across it, locked in the urgency of their desire.

Their lovemaking was frenzied and fierce, climaxing rapidly and then building to yet another crescendo. It was as if, freed at last from constraints, their hunger for each other knew no boundaries, and they gloried in it, swept along by its power and fury.

At long last, spent and exhausted, they fell asleep in each other's arms.

Sometime in the middle of the night, Cricket

stirred and Drew awakened at her gentle touch. They made love once again, but this time without the desperation of their earlier coupling. Because the thirst of their passion had finally been slaked, they could now slowly savor the wine of their pleasure.

When at last they drifted off in the small hours, Cricket sighed in Drew's ear and whispered, "Wait until you hear the birds in the morning. They sing in French."

Chapter 30

After Andrew had kissed both children and given India a final hug before his departure, India had walked him to the apartment door and put on the chain.

She wouldn't be going out anywhere, even on a Saturday night. It made her smile to remember how important a Saturday night date had been to her once.

And then she sighed with the memory. So much was past.

Stop it, she chided herself.

Restlessly she went to the bar in the living room and poured herself a hefty scotch and soda.

Then, realizing how late it was—almost seven o'clock—she went to the kitchen to make something for the children to eat for dinner. She didn't feel any hunger for food.

Looking across the courtyard to the window that faced her apartment, she noted the woman who lived there was in her own tiny kitchen. Probably doing the same thing, India thought, looking for something to feed her family.

But what could feed *her* appetites?

She felt restless, itchy, as if she'd like to jump out of her skin.

She took a deep swig of her drink and looked in the freezer for help.

Later, after she had tucked both children into bed, she paced the apartment from one end to the other.

She was feeling the effects of the scotch and no food, yet still she didn't feel hungry.

You might as well do it, she told herself. You know you're going to.

She went to the phone and dialed Mrs. Schmidt's number.

"Mrs. Schmidt? This is India Travick. Do you suppose you could sit for me Tuesday night, as well as in the morning? Yes. I have a dinner engagement.

India didn't know how she got through the days until Tuesday. Sunday was cold and sunny, and she took the kids to Central Park and they played and ran until they were exhausted. She watched *60 Minutes* Sunday night and could not have said what she'd seen, once it ended. Monday she got Heather off to school and took Toohey in his stroller up and down Madison Avenue, looking in boutiques at expensive clothes she didn't need.

By the time Tuesday arrived, she felt as though she were marching toward an unavoidable appointment. She had a moment of panic as she considered that Lanny could be busy that night. Well, she'd know soon enough, she told herself. If he were, she'd catch an early movie by herself.

Jade and Annie were already in the dressing room when she slipped in to change. Annie seemed unusually revved up and Jade seemed distracted and unusually quiet.

234

India's heart was pounding, even before the warm-up exercises.

Lanny was in the gym waiting for the class to begin.

The moment he saw India, his face lit up.

"Hi, India. Jade. Annie. Everybody ready for some heavy-duty stretching today?"

India felt light-headed with happiness. She didn't even worry about how she would find a way to talk to him after class. Everything would work out beautifully. She was certain of it.

"Okay, let's go. One and two and . . ."

India made sure she was the last one to get her stretch at the trapeze. It seemed to her that Lanny held her body arched in midair a bit longer than he had held the others.

As she let go of the trapeze and hit the mat, she coiled into a perfect forward rotation and came out of it with a little leap to her feet, her arms thrown up in perfect finishing form.

"Wow. You're looking good today, India," commented Lanny.

Her eyes sparkled at his compliment. She smiled at him and said in a low voice, "Feelin' good too. Are you free for dinner tonight, Lanny?"

A brief flash of surprise appeared in his eyes, but he quickly returned her smile and said, "Sure. What time and where?"

India had only rehearsed this part a thousand times.

"Do you like Japanese food?"

He nodded.

"Nippon House? Six-thirty? In the bar?"

His nod was almost imperceptible, but it made her heart sing. She grabbed her purse and towel and headed for the showers before he could see her idiotic

235

grin of delight.

She all but flew home, paid and thanked Mrs. Schmidt, and said she'd see her at six o'clock.

When she checked her weight on the scale that afternoon before she showered, she was pleased to see that her weight had dropped by twelve pounds in the last month.

She felt as excited and attractive as a teenager.

Getting out of the taxi at Nippon House, India realized why tonight felt so different. *She* had instigated it. *She* had planned it in detail. She couldn't write any of it off to impulse or chance. It had been as carefully calculated as a mathematical equation, and there would be no turning back.

She didn't want to turn back. She wanted to be young and desirable and carefree for one whole, wonderful evening. And for once, she didn't want to be anybody but herself or any place but here tonight having dinner with an attractive man.

Lanny rose from the straw mat in the bar the minute she came through the door.

She approached him and felt suddenly shy.

Fortunately the bar was dim enough so that he couldn't see the flush that rose to her cheeks.

"Hi," he said happily. "I don't know why I'm lucky enough to get to see you tonight, but I'm glad you're here."

He took her hand and helped her settle herself beside him. They ordered drinks and grinned foolishly at each other. When the drinks arrived, they clicked glasses and their eyes met.

"To us," said India simply.

After he drank and put down his glass, Lanny looked at her seriously and said, "I guess we'd better talk. Is something wrong, India?"

She knew immediately what he meant. He meant, has something happened to your marriage? Are you hurting, in trouble? Has a turning point in your life occurred?

She looked down at her hands, which were twisting the drink stirrer slowly, over and over.

She had trouble putting into words what she wanted to say.

"No," she said slowly. "Not really. Nothing important."

He waited patiently for her to go on.

"I could lie, but I guess I'm too honest to be a good liar, so I'll just blurt out the unflattering truth." She took a deep breath. "My husband's away for the week."

She looked into his eyes, seeking censure or disapproval. She found none—just those beautiful, soulful eyes looking intently back into hers.

"And?" he prodded when she did not go on.

"And," she said, staring down at her nervous hands again, "I wanted to see you." She quickly looked back into his eyes when he said nothing. "Aren't you going to say anything? Don't you think it's awful of me, a married woman, to wait until my husband's out of town and then make a date and run out for dinner with a single man? Don't you think—"

He put one strong, square hand over her two fluttering ones to stop their endless twisting, then interrupted her.

"Nothing you do could ever be 'awful', India. Stop flogging yourself. There's nothing wrong with the way you're feeling."

Her hands relaxed under his warm touch and she let them go limp in his gentle grip.

"Thank you," she said, feeling a sudden dewiness

237

rise to her eyes.

He looked into them, long and lovingly.

"I feel the same way. I'm sure you know that. I'm a big boy. I know the rules. I know the limits to the game. But that doesn't change the way I feel about you. It's not something I can help—or that you can either, I don't think. It just happened. It doesn't have to hurt anyone. Can't we just enjoy the time we have together without recriminations?"

A slow, tender smile came to his lips as he continued. "I *like* being with you. And I'm glad you're here—for whatever reason. Now, tell me what you were like when you were a little girl, so I'll know what turned you into the woman you are." His smile widened to a grin as he felt the tension go out of her.

India laughed a thoroughly relieved laugh. "What a dumb thing to want to know about. I was a dopey little girl, totally nonathletic, as I'm sure you can tell from our gym workouts. I grew up in the Midwest where the people are friendly and the land is flat . . ."

Their conversation flowed easily and without a pause. It was unlike the other time when they'd had dinner together and had stayed with comparatively impersonal and safe subjects, like movies and books and daily happenings.

India felt as if she were unfolding layers of herself and feelings she had kept stored away, and Lanny responded in kind with bits of himself. He was funny and kind and totally undemanding.

They had two more drinks before they realized simultaneously that they were starved. It was the first genuine hunger that India had felt since Drew had left on Saturday night.

A lovely young Oriental woman in a kimono led

them over the tiny bridge to the dining room, where they deposited their shoes in a rack and proceeded, in stocking feet, to a small, secluded table in an alcove.

With athletic grace, Lanny dropped easily into a cross-legged position at one side of the low table.

India eased herself down to the floor with what she hoped was a modicum of grace.

"Saki?" asked Lanny, though India was sure he already knew the answer.

"Why not?" she giggled, feeling slightly giddy. "Might as well be completely soused as halfway there."

He had such beautiful eyes, she thought. And such a beautiful face, all sloping planes and chiseled angles. His softly waving brown hair looked slightly in need of a trim. That and his white turtle-necked shirt under a tweedy sport coat gave him the look of a medieval knight—a knight with a full, sensuous mouth that seemed as if it would be gentle with its kisses.

India had long ago discarded caution and she luxuriated in the uninhibited freedom she felt.

They giggled their way through the tableside preparation of *sukiyaki* and their awkward attempts to get it to their mouths with chopsticks.

The warm saki, sipped from fragile little cups, caressed her insides. And Lanny's beautiful eyes caressed her face all through the meal.

When at last neither could eat another bite, they decided to ask for fortune cookies. It was the only possible dessert, since consuming them was not required.

"I thought fortune cookies were Chinese," said India.

"Maybe the Japanese have microchip fortune cookies."

"Is that like chocolate chip fortune cookies?" asked India and then giggled at her own inane joke.

Their waitress put a little plate of cookies on the table between them.

"You first," urged India.

Lanny reached into the pile and withdrew one.

Cracking it open, he read, "When fortune smiles, the wise man smiles back."

His handsome face melted into a smile.

"Well, I've been smiling all night, so I'm right on the money. Now you," he said.

India took one and broke it open. "A matter of the heart brings spring into winter." A serious expression flickered on her face only momentarily before she asked, "Do you think the baker in the kitchen has been spying on us? These seem awfully appropriate to happen by chance!"

Lanny grinned. "I'm all for chance. It's been doing fine for me so far. In fact, I only wish I'd been clever enough to have thought to make up some fortunes of my own and slip them to the chef to serve to us."

"Oh ho," said India teasingly, "just what would you have slipped into a cookie, if you'd have your way?" she asked.

Lanny's features became serious.

"Oh, maybe the address of my apartment, for instance, and a message that you are urgently needed there."

Their eyes held for long moments as the import of his words sank in.

"Is that what you really want?" asked India at last.

"Isn't it what *you* want?"

India flushed in answer to his query.

Lanny signaled for the check and paid it quickly.

Then they rose stiffly and went to retrieve their shoes.

As they left the restaurant, a tiny warning flickered in India's brain. Suppose there had been someone she knew in the restaurant, some friend or business acquaintance of hers or Andrew's.

Well, just suppose, she thought defiantly. Let someone see her. She had a right to go out. She had a right to have dinner with a friend. She was not supposed to be a cloistered nun just because her husband was out of town. On the other hand, she realized, if other people had noticed the way she and Lanny had been looking at each other over dinner, they would not have mistaken the couple for platonic friends.

The cool, crisp, night air was refreshing. She turned to look questioningly at Lanny, realizing she had no idea where he lived.

"Want to walk?" he offered. "It's only a few blocks up from here on Lexington."

Nodding her ascent, they turned eastward. She reached over and took his arm. He squeezed it close to him, though whether in affection or reassurance, she could not be sure.

They walked up five blocks on Lexington. Neither spoke.

At last, Lanny paused. "We're here."

India looked up and saw that they were in front of a hardware store. Beside the entrance was another door, which led to a small entryway.

Lanny opened the outside door for her to enter first, then fumbled in his pocket for his inner-door key.

India surveyed the short row of mailboxes in the wall. She saw the plain white card with the carefully lettered words "Lanny Collins" in black ink. The impersonal card suddenly made everything real. She had never before known anything of his world

241

outside the gym.

"It's a few flights up. I hope you're up to the climb," he commented, looking down into her eyes in the gloom of the small entryway.

India's eyes never wavered. "I, sir, go to a gym twice a week and am in tip-top physical form. Lead on!" she commanded.

The hallway up was also dim, but from what India could see, it looked reasonably clean and well kept.

By the third flight, she was puffing slightly and her legs had started to ache.

Lanny looked back and reassured her. "Just one more flight. You okay?"

India nodded, not wanting to waste precious breath by speaking.

At the next landing, Lanny stopped at the first door in the hallway and inserted his key. "Let me get some lights on so you don't trip."

India was not sure what to expect. In all her fantasies, she had never included any thoughts of where Lanny lived.

When the lights flared and she stepped inside, she paused and surveyed her surroundings like an animal sniffing a strange territory.

She was standing in a large, well-appointed living room. Everything around her bespoke care and good taste, though none of the furnishings were lavish.

There was a deep, brightly striped sofa to one side in front of a stripped-to-the brick wall. Next to it was a small, open-hearth stove. Two canvas sling chairs had been placed around a low table holding candles, and several large, brightly colored pillows were strewn on the floor.

There was a profusion of green plants—hanging ones in rope hangers, as well as standing ones—that made a small glade in one corner of the room. The blond wood floor was covered with several rough-woven throw rugs in colors that picked up the stripes of the sofa. On one wall hung a beautiful wooden stringed instrument with a bowed back and ivory inlays on the front.

Lanny was taking India's coat and hanging it up as her eyes made their inspection. She fastened her gaze on the instrument.

"That's lovely, the, the . . . thing on the wall," she said. "What is it?"

Lanny followed her glance. "Oh, that. It's a Persian lute. It was an extravagance, but it was so beautiful that I had to have it."

"Do you play it?" she heard herself asking, as much to fill the silence as anything.

Lanny laughed carelessly.

"I pick at it. But no, I am not going to serenade you. That would be cruel and unusual punishment. And that's *not* why I asked you here," he tossed over his shoulder as he knelt to put a match to the firewood already laid in the stove.

As the fire leapt to life, Lanny turned and lit the candles on the coffee table.

Still India stood rooted to the spot where she had paused, just inside the door.

The obvious question was poised on her lips, but she couldn't bring herself to ask it.

Lanny moved unhurriedly around the room, adjusting a light, flicking on the stereo, pushing some magazines aside. Then, his domestic shuffling accomplished, he turned and looked at India.

"You might as well say it. I can read minds. Or yours, at least. 'Just why *did* you ask me here?' Right?"

India fought back a smile. He *could* read her mind.

He crossed to where she was standing and took her

by the hand. Leading her over to the couch, he sank down and indicated that she should join him.

"All of a sudden, you look like you're sorry you came. Don't be. Nothing will happen that you don't want to happen. And as to why I asked you here, I'll tell you why, even if it sounds silly. I wanted to see you here, to see you surrounded by my things; to see you in the place where I spend so much time. I think about you a lot, India, and I wanted to be able to picture you here when I thought about you from now on. I wanted to be able to look around and remember how you looked here." He paused and looked at her seriously. Then his mobile mouth broke into a slow, gentle smile. "Now, that's pretty silly, isn't it?"

It didn't seem silly to India at all. And the words "nothing will happen that you don't want to happen" echoed in her head. What she *wanted* to happen was exactly what she was afraid of.

Suddenly remembering his obligations as a host, Lanny jumped up. "How about some wine? Would you like that?"

"Very much," managed India, still unsettled by her conflicting feelings.

Lanny brought a bottle of red wine from the kitchen and two crystal balloon glasses.

After he poured the wine and handed a glass to her, his expression grew serious again.

"India, please relax. Take off your shoes; let down your guard. I swear I won't bite you," he teased.

India returned his smile. "I know it sounds corny, but I haven't been in a single man's apartment for a very long time."

She did slip off her shoes, then curled her feet up under her. She ventured a sip of the wine. It was very good.

She found herself gradually unbending, and the

earlier, pleasantly relaxed mood of the evening returned. "You said you thought about me a lot. I didn't know that."

"Well," said Lanny, studying the tips of his loafers, "I guess you know now." Then he looked up at her and flashed that delightful grin that showed his deep dimples and turned India's insides to pudding. "Don't you think about me?" he probed good-naturedly.

She flushed. "You know I do."

"So admit it."

"I admit it. Guilty."

"But you're *not* guilty. I wish you wouldn't think of it that way. I think there's something inside each of us that responds very naturally to the other. And I don't think we should feel guilty about it."

"What did you think of me the first time you saw me?" queried India, her curiosity overcoming her better judgment. After all, she might not like what she heard.

Lanny leaned back and clasped his hands behind his head. "Well, I thought, Here's a very attractive, intelligent woman, who's rather shy, has pretty hazel eyes, and I would like to know her better. You looked, well, intimidated, I guess would be the best word."

India laughed delightedly.

"I think intimidated sums it up very well. I had never been to a place like Ivan & Igor's before in my life. I had never seen such svelte, sophisticated women, and they were doing such athletic things with so much skill that I was overwhelmed. I felt like a new kid on the first day in a new school—all overweight and awkward."

You weren't overweight," protested Lanny kindly. "But you have lost some pounds, haven't you?" he added.

"Looking at myself in all those mirrors twice a week was a very sobering experience," said India lightly. "I kind of lost my appetite."

They each sipped their wine reflectively.

Finally India said, "Do you do this often? No, I mean, I don't mean it *that* way. I mean have you ever seen any of the other women from the gym outside the class? Or isn't that any of my business?"

Lanny frowned slightly. "Of course it's your business if you want to know. And no, of course not. Those women are like creatures from another planet. They're lacquered and tended and self-absorbed, like a bunch of rich Barbie dolls. I have no interest in any of them."

"Annie's nice and so are Cricket and Jade." India found herself suddenly defending her classmates.

"Sure they're nice. Annie's a lot of laughs, but she's tense and troubled somehow underneath all that bravado. Cricket's funny, but she's moving on a fast track and I guess I don't feel there's a lot of depth there. Jade Greene is one tough lady who knows what she wants and is out to get it."

"And me?" whispered India.

Lanny turned to look her full in the eyes.

"You're *you*, and you're special. You're a real person. And I guess I've fallen in love with you," answered Lanny softly. Then he reached over and took her wine glass from her hands and placed it on the coffee table.

They moved simultaneously toward each other as Lanny folded her into his arms. She returned his embrace and felt tears well in her eyes. His lips searched for her mouth and he kissed her long and deeply.

They both drew nourishment from the kiss. It was as if they could not get enough of each other.

246

When their lips finally parted, Lanny whispered into her ear, "I've wanted to do that for so long, so very long. That day in the elevator, I wanted to take you in my arms and tell you not to worry, that everything would be all right. I knew you were terrified, but you tried so hard to be brave."

India smiled at him through misted eyes.

She pulled back and looked at him. "I was. I really was. And it seems so silly now. I just felt claustrophobic all of a sudden. I was so glad you were there."

"So was I."

As he drew her close again and began to caress her, she grew brave enough to ask the question that had been nagging at the back of her mind.

"Lanny, how do you feel about the fact that . . . that I'm older than you are?"

"Are you?" he murmured in her ear.

She pulled away just slightly to look at him.

"You know I am."

"So?" he asked unconcernedly, reaching to bring her close again.

"How . . . how old do you think I am?"

"Twelve?" he asked in a voice muffled by her neck.

India giggled in spite of herself.

"Be serious."

"I am."

"How old?" she persisted.

"I'll give you a fast thirty-two or thirty-three," he said finally, since she wouldn't be put off.

"I'm thirty-nine."

"Horrors. Over the hill. The end of the line." And he began nuzzling her again.

"How old are you?" she asked plaintively.

He finally realized that she would not be happy until this was discussed.

"Truth?"

"Truth!"

"Twenty-four. But I'm getting older every minute."

India looked thoughtful.

"That's fifteen years difference."

"I had no idea that you were a math whiz," he teased.

"But doesn't that bother you?"

"No. If it bothers you, why don't you just adopt me? I could use a good home."

Now India looked pensive. "It really doesn't matter to you."

"No, and it shouldn't matter to you either."

He took her in his arms again and kissed her, tenderly this time. *"That's* what should matter to you," he whispered afterward.

"It does, darling. It really does."

"So?"

India sighed. "So, would you think I was forward if I asked to see the rest of the apartment?"

"I thought you'd never ask," he said, scooping her up in his muscular arms and heading toward the bedroom.

His bedroom was sparsely furnished, but it was clustered with plants. His bed was simply a double mattress and box spring on the floor, which he had covered with an Indian throw.

He knelt before carefully placing her down upon it, like a fragile piece of china. India stared at him hesitantly before asking, "Could you turn down the lights, please?"

Lanny obliged, leaving only one small light burning on the Oriental chest against the wall, though he chided, "Didn't it ever occur to you that I want to be able to see your body? It's such a lovely body, India."

What could have been an awkward moment flowed easily as Lanny shucked off his sport coat, peeled his turtleneck over his head, then knelt on the mattress beside her to gently unbutton the beige satin blouse she was wearing.

India could not take her eyes off his broad, smooth chest. She had looked at the way he was built in the gym, but the short-sleeved white shirt he always wore concealed the beauty of his softly sculptured muscles. She ran her fingers over his chest unconsciously.

All the while, he was crooning softly, "My beautiful, beautiful India, so lovely and curved like a piece of sculpture."

Before she was even aware of it, he had unwrapped her gently, like a precious gift, and his long, hard body was pressed comfortingly against hers.

What surprised her later, when she thought about it, was how tender and gentle his lovemaking had been. In expecting the raw, untamed passion of a young man at his sexual peak, she had seriously misjudged him. Every step of their coupling had been loving and giving. He had seemed far more concerned about her responses and satisfaction than about his own. No one had loved her that considerately and caringly in her life. Yet that, if anything, seemed only to intensify and inflame her desire.

For each, the whole of the act seemed infused with the joy of pleasuring the other.

In the drowsy afterglow of their loving, they both drifted off into a gentle slumber, from which India awoke first, casting a guilty glance at her wristwatch.

Moving cautiously so as not to awaken Lanny, she slipped off the low bed, gathered her strewn clothes, and crept toward a door that she assumed was the bathroom.

Once the door was safely closed, she flipped on the

overhead light.

She stared at herself in the mirror over the sink as she was flooded with the merciless glare of the ceiling light.

Instead of looking old and haggard, she saw herself pink and glowing, with a radiance she wouldn't have believed possible.

Her brown hair was tousled and her makeup rather blurred, but she saw with surprise that she looked more like a love-fulfilled movie heroine than the middle-aged housewife she knew herself to be.

She quickly washed her face and dressed, knowing she had to hurry if Mrs. Schmidt were not to begin worrying over what had happened to her.

As she left the bathroom, she was surprised to find Lanny up, dressed, and pulling the bedclothes together. At the sound of the door, he looked around anxiously.

"Hey, you weren't planning to sneak off and leave me, were you?"

As India struggled with a reply, he crossed swiftly to her side and kissed her on the cheek.

"Because I'm not letting you go home alone at this hour of the night."

India protested that it was only a quarter to twelve, but Lanny was firm.

"You're not running around the streets of Manhattan alone at this hour."

"Just let me run a comb through my hair and splash some water on my face, then I'll get us a taxi."

When she started to protest, he interrupted her.

"I'll only drop you at your door—I'm not about to compromise you in front of your neighbors—but I will not let you go alone, and that's it!"

True to his word, he let her out at the canopy of her apartment building, even before the doorman could reach the taxi door, and whispered, "Call you tomorrow."

As she rang for the elevator, India wondered if she really needed it or if she couldn't just float up the eight stories to her apartment.

The next day, after getting Heather off to school, she mooned around the apartment waiting for the phone to ring.

Stop it, she told herself. He may not call at all.

But when a bell rang, it was not the phone but the apartment house intercom.

The doorman announced that a messenger was on his way up.

India stood at the half-open door of her apartment, twitching with curiosity. When the elevator door opened and a florist's delivery boy approached her with a long, white florist's box, she broke into a smile. She had a feeling she knew whom they might be from.

Overtipping the delivery boy, she closed the door, dropped the box on the hall table, and tore at the package like a child at Christmas. Inside were eleven long-stemmed yellow roses.

The card said simply, "I'll give you the twelfth when I see you. I love you. L."

Oh lord, she told herself, I shouldn't be so happy. I know it.

But she was.

Chapter 31

Not too many blocks away, Annie was standing in a brightly lit photographer's studio, waiting to do yet another take on a shoot that had started at seven o'clock to film a fashion collection.

She wore a long, sinuous, white jersey gown that hugged every curve of her long, sinuous body. Rock music was blaring, as it always was at a shoot, and Annie's body worked endlessly and repetitiously in time to the music.

She felt good, she felt gorgeous, and she felt thin. She also felt a little nervy, maybe, a little more trembly than might be desired, since she was having trouble holding absolutely still for any pose that demanded a long exposure, but all in all, she felt fine, really fine.

It was as though there were a rhythm inside her body that kept her moving without her volition. In fact, the makeup girl had gotten annoyed when she had tried to do her last touch-up.

"Annie, for Heaven's sake, stand still for one minute, will you?" she had snapped.

Annie had merely flashed her brightest smile and had slipped away from under her puff, saying, "I'm cool, honey. Just cool, Don't need that stuff."

The makeup girl had stalked away mumbling.

Maybe she was feeling *too* good. It was as though she were on a constant high. Yet she never ran out of energy and she ate like a horse when she felt like it, without gaining a pound. Of course, her hunger seemed more infrequent now, too.

All at once, she remembered that it was Wednesday. She'd have to stop at the doctor's office after she left here. She was getting a shot on Mondays, Wednesdays, and Fridays now.

When she had first started with Dr. Davis she had been so afraid that Ferrago would get wind of what she was doing. But now, except for making sure he never discovered the needle marks from the shots, she barely worried about it.

She didn't sleep as well as she used to, for she was experiencing periods of wakefulness every night, but other than that the shots were worth the trouble. Even with the pill, she had no weight gain. And she could even indulge in an occasional junk food binge.

In a business where every ounce one put on was like a five-pound gain to a normal person, these shots were definitely worth both the time and the money they cost.

"Hey, Annie! Get your fanny over here. We're ready to go!"

Annie bopped her way across the floor, snapping her fingers in a rhythm all her own.

Ivan got a very disturbing phone call that afternoon. He told the voice at the other end that he was going to need more time. He explained that the networks wanted him for a regular exercise series and that he'd be able to make a payment in mid-January.

The voice at the other end did not sound very convinced. Ivan decided he'd have to start working on setting up the idea with that Greene woman after her class tomorrow. He'd have to get a commitment from her about bringing the right people to the Russian Christmas party. The stakes were getting too high to waste anymore time.

Ivan felt a bead of perspiration form on his upper lip, even though his office was cool.

Ivan hated to sweat.

India had just put Toohey down for his nap that afternoon when Lanny called.

Hearing the sound of his voice when she picked up the phone made her go weak inside.

"Lanny! The roses are gorgeous! Thank you so much!"

"I miss you," he said by way of reply. "Is there any way I can see you today or tonight or whenever?"

India sighed. "I miss you, too, but I can't see how I could do it. I couldn't possibly get Mrs. Schmidt again tonight."

"Could I possibly come there later? Maybe after the kids are in bed?" The hopeful note in his voice was heartbreaking.

India shook her head at the phone. "I can't imagine how. They're both in bed and asleep by eight-thirty, but I just think it would look so odd to the doorman if I suddenly started receiving a strange gentleman caller late at night when my husband is so obviously out of town."

"That's the disadvantage of being wealthy and living in a fancy apartment building," he retorted, attempting a light tone but unable to conceal the disappointment in his voice. There was a long silence, then Lanny added, "By the way, do you know when he's coming back yet?"

He didn't have to tell her who "he" was.

"No. It could be late tomorrow or even Friday. I just don't know," said India regretfully. Her earlier jubilance at hearing his voice was dissolving into gloom.

Sensing her mood, Lanny said, "Look, don't worry. We'll work things out. I just wanted to tell you how much I miss you. Let me handle things.

India puzzled over his change of attitude but at last said good-bye and hung up.

Later that afternoon the phone rang and it was Drew calling from Paris. He explained that his meetings were going longer than expected and he couldn't possibly be back until Saturday.

After he rang off, India decided she'd take her chances. She called Mrs. Schmidt and asked her to sit again for her Friday night. Let her think what she would. Every moment was growing too precious to waste.

She took a long shower after she put the children to bed. Then she curled up in a flannel nightgown and robe and tried to read a book.

At five minutes after ten, the apartment intercom buzzed. The doorman announced that her pizza had arrived.

Mystified but curious, India told him to send it up. When she opened the door, she almost laughed out loud.

There was Lanny in sneakers, blue jeans, and a black jacket, with a black cap pulled low over his eyes and a huge pizza box balanced on one hand.

"You order da pizza, lady?" he asked in a horridly exaggerated Italian accent.

She grabbed him by the arm and pulled him into

256

the apartment, smothering her laughter at his outfit and whispering, "You idiot! Get in here before the neighbors hear you!"

He placed the pizza on the hall table and took his other hand from behind his back. In it was the twelfth yellow rose.

Then he took her in his arms and kissed her. "I couldn't get through the night without seeing you. Besides, your rose might have wilted. I hope you're hungry for pizza."

"I'm hungry for you," was all India could say, still shaken as she was from the unexpectedness of his appearance.

She led him into the living room, put the pizza on the coffee table in front of the couch and the rose in a bud vase, then went to get them two beers from the refrigerator.

Suddenly the thought of pizza was irresistible. She realized that she hadn't eaten any dinner.

They sat on the floor beside the coffee table and eagerly devoured the pizza, washing it down with long gulps of cold beer.

"This is hell on my diet, you realize," said India between bites.

Lanny looked at her with loving eyes.

"You don't need to diet. I love you just the way you are," he sang.

"Flatterer," she said, sinking back on the floor, thoroughly stuffed. "I must say, you certainly find novel ways to work your way into my life."

Lanny took the remaining piece of pizza.

"Well, I'm a master of disguise. What can I tell you? Say, the doorman won't think it's odd that I don't come back down right away, will he? I mean, they won't start searching the hallways for a mad-pizza-deliverer-turned-rapist or anything, will they?"

"I seriously doubt it. Max is much more careful about screening who comes *into* the building than who goes out. I think I could stroll out naked and he'd be sitting there dozing."

"Aha, but *I* wouldn't be. Want to try sneaking by me naked?" Lanny attempted a leer and failed.

"No, dopey. The kids are asleep in the next room."

"Will we wake them?" he asked with sudden concern.

"Nope. Once they're asleep, you could drive a tractor through and they wouldn't turn a hair." She was pleased by his concern. "Oh, by the way, I have good news and bad news."

"Shoot me the bad and get it over with," said Lanny carelessly.

"Drew called."

Lanny's face darkened. "You were serious. You meant really bad news."

"Well, sort of. He's not coming back until Saturday afternoon."

"But that's *good* news."

India's eyes began to twinkle mischievously.

"If you think that's good news, wait 'til you hear the rest."

"So?" Lanny wolfed down the last of the crust and closed the pizza box.

"So, how would you like company for dinner Friday night? I wantonly called Mrs. Schmidt and signed her up for then. I decided I don't give a damn what she thinks."

For an answer, Lanny leaned down and kissed her. Then he sat back briefly to look into her eyes before kissing her again.

"That's *wonderful* news. Where would you like to go?" he asked softly.

"Anywhere. I just want to be with you," she

258

answered simply.

"I know. Want to come to my place and I'll cook us dinner?" His face lit up at the idea.

"Can you cook?"

"Can I cook?"

"I'm asking the questions," she retorted playfully.

Lanny warmed to his subject. He jabbed a finger at her. "You show up on my doorstep at six-thirty Friday night and you will enjoy the most delicious dinner of your life!"

India laughed with delight. "I keep discovering wonderful new sides to your personality."

"And I keep being amazed at how wonderful you really are."

He leaned over and kissed her again. It was as though he couldn't get enough of her.

"Have I told you how cute you look in your little flannel nightie and robe and scrubbed face? All you need are fuzzy slippers to look like a teenager."

"I happen to *have* fuzzy slippers," she said with mock indignation.

He groaned. "I should have known."

Lanny sipped the last of his beer.

"Another?"

"No, I shouldn't stay too long. I've gotta work tomorrow and you've gotta work out."

"My God, I almost forgot! Tomorrow's gym class."

"Ah, how quickly they forget," he said, rolling his eyes.

"Will you be able to act normally with me tomorrow?" she teased.

"Try me," was his smug reply.

India sighed.

"Well, *I* may find it difficult not to grab you and kiss you."

"Use a little will power. You'll make the other ladies jealous."

"*I'll* be jealous if you lay a hand on any of them too personally."

"Never do. Haven't you noticed? It's all part of my craft. I am the charming, impersonal young gym instructor."

"Well, I'll keep my cool by remembering that I'm having dinner with you the next evening."

"What about tomorrow night?"

"Honestly, Lanny, I don't think I can get Mrs. Schmidt again. It would look too strange. Even the kids would notice and maybe say something in front of—"

"Who said anything about going out?" he interrupted.

"Oh, lord, you're not going to try the pizza gag again, are you?"

"What's a matter? Missy no like Chinese food?"

Lanny crinkled up his eyes in a futile attempt to look Oriental.

India howled with laughter. "You're impossible!"

"Wait'll you see me in a kimono!"

They kissed a long while at the door and Lanny left at last, reluctantly.

India checked on the children, then climbed into bed for a long, dream-filled sleep.

Chapter 32

India carefully timed her arrival at Ivan & Igor's the next day so that she wouldn't be so early as to be conspicuous, nor so late that she'd be rushed while changing into her leotard. She wanted to look good.

Darlene looked up and gave her the usual bored greeting.

"Morning, India."

India grabbed her gym bag from the hook and found an empty changing room. She could hear Annie and Jade chatting in the next room. There was another voice, too, a young voice that India couldn't place. Nor did she much care. She had seen no sign of Lanny when she had come in. She applied more lipstick and fussed nervously with her hair.

As she walked out to have a cigarette in the waiting room, she saw Misha, one of the other instructors, coming down the spiral staircase.

Darlene looked up from her coffee.

"Hi, Mish. How goes it?"

Misha answered something undecipherable in his heavy accent.

Darlene's thickly mascaraed eyes glanced up at the clock. It read nine fifty-eight.

"Hey, look at the time. No Lanny. You may have to take his ten o'clock."

Misha grunted in acknowledgment.

India's heart sank. What could have happened to him. Had he been mugged on his way home? Had he been hit by a car on his way to work? Her imagination raced.

Just at that moment, the elevator doors opened and Lanny stepped out, looking flushed and rushed and full of good cheer. He was heartbreakingly handsome thought India.

"Morning, Darlene, Mish. Hi, India! What's happening?"

He strolled to the reception desk and looked down over Darlene's shoulder at the appointment book, scrupulously avoiding meeting India's eyes.

"What's happening is that you're late," said Darlene sourly. "Ivan would kill you if he found out. You know you're supposed to be here quarter to, latest." She scolded.

"Couldn't help it, hon. Hot date last night," he said flippantly, tossing an outrageous wink at India.

She blushed wildly, in spite of herself.

I'll get you for that later, she thought.

Lanny turned back to the book and ran his finger down the page carelessly, unperturbed by India's bright color.

"So who's here? India, Annie, Jade. No Cricket?"

"She's booked out for the week—out of the country," commented Darlene languidly. "Jade brought her niece Shelley though. That okay?"

"She can pay, she can play," tossed Lanny over his shoulder, heading into the gym.

Almost as an afterthought, he called back, "Coming, India?"

India snuffed out her cigarette and rushed to join him.

When she entered the gym room, he had already peeled off his jacket and was vigorously jumping up and down with casual grace.

How could he be so calm, wondered India.

When she joined him on the mat and began to jump, he wordlessly mouthed I love you, which caused India to flush all over again. Today was going to be difficult, to say the least, she thought.

Never missing a beat, he bellowed out, "Jade and Annie! Get out here! Time's awasting."

India concentrated on jumping with all her might.

Jade and Annie scurried in, followed by Jade's pretty teenage niece, Shelley, who was poured into a neon orange leotard and looked as perky as a puppy.

Her blatant youthfulness struck India like a body blow. Now *there* was someone who was closer to the right age for Lanny, she thought miserably. Stop it, she remonstrated herself. He chose *you*.

The women formed a ragged line beside India and joined in her exertions.

"So where's Cricket?" queried Annie as she jumped.

"Out of the country," answered Jade, matching her rhythm.

"She's out of it completely, most of the time," cracked Lanny.

Shelley grinned broadly, obviously enjoying the camaraderie.

Lanny, noticing her smile, asked pleasantly, "Why aren't you in school today, juvenile delinquent? Playing hooky?"

India was shocked by the stab of jealousy she felt at his solicitude for the girl.

Pull yourself together, she cautioned. She was also getting breathless from the jumping.

"Holiday . . . teacher's meeting," gasped Shelley, trying not to lose the beat. She was not yet as skilled as the other women at working out and talking at the same time.

"Lanny," pleaded India in what suddenly sounded like a whine to her ears, "haven't we done this long enough?"

Lanny smiled at her. She forgave him all.

"You're right. Eeenough!"

The women halted abruptly.

"Now that we've got the old blood flowing, let's limber up. Cross over and touch toes. One and two and . . ."

India threw herself into the exercises with a vengeance and tried not to think. Thinking today, she decided, was dangerous.

Annie's lithe form flowed flawlessly through the warm-ups. Seeming never to tire, she switched gears effortlessly and fluidly.

When it came to the individual floor work, Lanny said casually, "Come on, India. Start us off."

Suddenly self-conscious, India walked to the end of the mats and waited nervously for his commands.

"Two forward rotations, legs apart, two backward and land on your feet, please."

Easy for you to say, she thought dryly.

She managed the two forward ones gracefully and paused only a fraction of a second before rolling into her backward rotations. But when she hit the last one and attempted to rise in one smooth movement, she staggered and Lanny was at her side in an instant, his gentle hands grasping her body and lifting her effortlessly to her feet. Those gentle hands felt like branding irons to India, so conscious was she of his touch.

"Thanks," she said, flustered.

"You're doing fine," was his only answer, then he turned his attention to the next person.

The next person was Jade. Her movements were precise and crisp, as always. When she ended her routine, she stopped, then sagged and groaned.

"God, I ache!"

Lanny walked up behind her and began kneading her shoulder muscles.

"You're tense as a board, that's why. Loosen up," he admonished cheerfully.

India felt her stomach churn again. She was being foolish. Lanny always did that to the women—helpfully, casually, impersonally. It was just that today she was so painfully conscious of whom he touched and *how*.

Shelley was next and she was engagingly awkward.

Lanny had to guide her body and help her through every inch of her routine. He was kindly, patient, and encouraging to the girl. And India wanted to kill him with her bare hands.

At last it was over and India thought it was the longest class she had ever been through.

Lanny gave her an extra long stretch on the trapeze and India felt him give her a reassuring squeeze as he reluctantly let her body swing loose. He mouthed "later" to her as she left the gym.

The other women were calling such farewells as, "Thanks Lanny. Have a good one," as they gathered their things and trooped back into the showers and dressing rooms.

Ivan, looking what was for him relatively pleasant, was waiting as they filed by.

"Jade, my dear, may I have a word with you after you're dressed?" he requested in his most unctuous manner.

"Sure thing, Ivan," answered Jade, looking at Annie and shrugging as Ivan moved away to talk to Darlene.

"What was *that* about?" India heard Annie ask Jade from the next dressing room.

"Beats me. And I was going to ask if you wanted to stop for coffee."

India heard Shelley squeal with delight. "Oh, *could* we?"

"Sure," answered Jade expansively, "You two go on downstairs and I'll join you after I find out what 'the Terrible' wants."

Annie acquiesced and then hollered over the partition.

"What about you, India? Got time for coffee?"

India was momentarily stunned.

The women had never asked her to join them before. But, why not? she told herself.

"Sure thing," she sang out. "I'll be right there."

Ivan ushered Jade into his private office with great ceremony and offered her a chair.

He did everything but bow and scrape, she thought wryly. Come to think of it, he had bowed slightly.

"What can I do for you, Ivan?" began Jade flippantly, wanting to get this conversation over with and knowing how Ivan loved to discourse and sermonize. "Did my secretary forget to mail last month's check?"

Ivan's craggy visage took on a pained expression.

"Please, please, Jade. Do you think I would be so crass as to hector you about your bill?"

"In a word, yes. So what's up?"

Ivan bent forward at his desk, leaned on his elbows, and made a little tent with his fingers.

"I wanted to talk to you about an, ah, an idea I have had."

Jade's expression showed polite curiosity.

"A little business proposition, you might call it."

All Jade's antennae snapped into position. She couldn't conceive of a business in which she'd like to get involved with Ivan.

"Exercise is nowadays big business, yes? Miss Fonda, that funny little Simmons fellow, all those books and videos—"

"No one should know that better than you," interjected Jade with a bite that was lost on Ivan.

"Ah, yes. Now, you are involved with the media; you are powerful at your network—"

"Ivan, I am as powerful, as you put it, as this morning's ratings—no more, no less. Get to the point."

"Ah, yes. Well, I have a little idea for a television show, a fantastic television show, a television show with the potential for attracting a fabulous, upscale audience, a—"

"An exercise show, you mean," said Jade flatly.

Ivan's pained expression returned.

"Please! Not a mere exercise show—an exercise show starring me, Ivan Petrovich. I would not only demonstrate the exercises, but I would perform athletic demonstrations that would inspire women to greater heights of gymnastic ability. I would coax and cajole them to care for their bodies like fine machines. I would show them how a well-tended body can remain in fine physical condition later on in years . . ."

Jade noted that Ivan was practically flexing his biceps as he spoke.

"Ah, Jack La Lanne, eat your heart out," muttered Jade with amusement.

Ivan halted and stared hard at her.

"Pardon?"

"Just a little joke, Ivan. Go ahead. What do you want me to do with your 'little idea'?" she asked, more out of curiosity than compliance.

"Have you ever seen me perform, Jade?" asked Ivan almost condescendingly.

"No, I'm afraid I've been spared that pleasure."

Her irony was wasted on Ivan.

"Ah, well, perhaps next week I shall show your class *my* workout. Anyway, I want to throw a little party to, ah, enhance my idea. I thought perhaps a Russian Christmas party. I would like some of our best pupils to perform—you among them of course. And I will perform. I would like not only that you attend, but that perhaps you would bring this new important man at your network. I have read about his big job in the newspapers. Mister . . . what is his name . . . Griggs Parkinson, I believe? I would like your cooperation in convincing him that this is a feasible idea. After all, is not *your* superb body a credit to my ideas of conditioning and working out? You've been coming here for years. And who knows, perhaps you might want to do a little feature on one of our classes for a segment on your show . . ."

Jade had been letting him run on and spin out his fantasies of fame and fortune, but the last bit caught her attention. It might be an interesting feature, showing how the elegant women of Manhattan keep their figures trim and healthy. She was certainly always on the lookout for new pieces.

Right now, she was chomping at the bit with her co-host status on *The Morning Hour*. She really wanted to make the move to the evening anchor spot, but now that everyone had gotten wind of its availability, the competition was building up. She needed all the extra showcasing she could get to stand out from the pack. Unfortunately, no matter how good her work was, the ultimate go-ahead for filling the post would probably have to come from Griggs. She'd had dinner with him on two different occasions now and had walked the fine line of trying to keep the evenings strictly business while being as pleasant to him as she could.

Griggs, for his part, had gone out of his way to be charming, and when Griggs turned on his charisma, he was difficult to resist.

Jade spent her time with him rigorously resisting being taken in by his charm. She had no intention of becoming romantically involved with him again, not even for the sake of business—most especially not for the sake of business. She'd never used her body to get a break yet, and she wasn't about to start now.

However, she reflected now, maybe Ivan's idea about a chic exercise show *did* have some potential. Maybe it could fit into Griggs's daytime programming package. He still hadn't solved the daytime ratings race yet. Maybe, just maybe, there might be something in it for her.

Ivan was still droning on about the glories of his physical theories and Jade decided it was time to get out of there.

"Ivan," she broke in, "I promise that I will give some thought to your project. Our network has literally hundreds of ideas in treatment right now, but let's see what we can do with this one."

"And you promise that you'll come to the party?"

"Yes," said Jade.

"And bring your Mr. Parkinson?" finished Ivan.

"I shall bring him if I have to sling him over my shoulder and carry him," answered Jade with a smile, anxious to get going.

"Ah, Jade, you are a lovely person—"

Jade cut him short by abruptly excusing herself.

She threw on her clothes and dashed down to the coffee shop to join the group.

"So what did Ivan the Terrible want?" asked Annied without prelude as Jade slid into the booth next to her.

Both India and Shelley were already sipping their coffee. Annie was toying with a diet soda.

"Would you believe his own TV show?" retorted Jade before giving the waitress her order. "Coffee, black, please."

The three women burst into laughter.

"You're joking, aren't you?" asked India as the laughter subsided.

"I am dead serious and so was he," Jade assured them.

"That old fart has more nerve than King Kong," commented Annie.

Shelley looked from one to the other of them while they spoke, as though she were an observer at a tennis match.

"Well, what the hell. It might not be the worst idea in the world. And lord knows, you see enough bad ideas on television. There must be room for one more," said Jade. "Oh, yes, and he's going to give a Russian Christmas party, to which we are all invited in order to watch him perform," she added.

More laughter.

"When is Russian Christmas?" asked Shelley.

"I think, in the Orthodox Russian Church, it's sometime after ours," explained India, searching her memory.

"Can I go?" Shelley eagerly asked.

"Yes, you can go," answered Jade indulgently.

Shelley still wore her wonder of the city's ways in her eyes.

Annie looked across at Shelley. "Hey, has this old auntie of yours taken you to any swingin' parties?" she asked the younger girl.

Shelley thought for a minute. "Let's see . . . we

went to a publisher's cocktail party for Norman Mailer . . ."

Annie hooted. "Be still, my heart. Such excitement! A publishing party. What laughing, what dancing—" Annie stopped immediately when she saw how Shelley's face fell at her sarcasm.

"No, don't look so sad, honey. I just meant there are more exciting parties to go to than literary teas." She cast an accusing look at Jade. "That the best you can do for this kid?"

Jade shrugged. "What can I tell you? Getting up at 3:00 AM to do a TV show every morning isn't so conducive to having an active social life, you know."

India was fascinated, in spite of herself. She too had thought that all Jade did was go to glamorous parties. It never occurred to her that Jade's hours were rigorous and demanding.

Annie bent toward Shelley. "Listen, Ferrago and I are going to a party at a loft down in Soho next Saturday night. Some artist he knows, plus lots of the rag trade folks . . ."

At Shelley's puzzled look, Annie explained. "Rag trade means the fashion crowd, the clothes peddlers. Anyway, how would you like to go with us? If Ferrago says okay, of course."

Shelley looked expectantly at her aunt.

Jade looked doubtful. "I don't know about that, Annie," she said thoughtfully. "That's kind of a fast track for Emmy Lou, fresh off the farm here. Drinking and drugs and God knows what else—"

"*Please*, Aunt Jade."

"Oh, come on, Jade. You know how fanatic Ferrago is about drugs. He's real straight-arrow. And what the hell, the kid's old enough to have a glass of wine, isn't she?"

"The kid had better stick to coke, if she knows what's good for her. And you know what kind of coke

271

I'm talking about, Annie!'' finished Jade quickly, anticipating a smart rejoinder.

Shelley's face brightened as she sensed her aunt weakening.

"Give me your phone number, honey, and I'll call you tomorrow night," promised Annie.

Turning to India, Jade said conversationally, "What are you up to this weekend? Any fabulous parties on your agenda?"

India flushed at Jade's personal interest in *her*, a noncelebrity if ever there was one.

"Nothing too exciting, I guess. My husband's getting back from Paris on Saturday, so I imagine he'll be tired."

"Paris is cool. What's your husband do, India?" asked Annie.

"Advertising. He's a producer." After a moment, she added shyly, "I used to be in fashion. I was a sportswear buyer."

"Hey, I'll bet that was fun. Buyin' the stuff has got to be more fun than standing around in those threads," said Annie.

"Oh, come on," protested India, "I think you have the most glamorous job going."

"Well, the hours are better than Jade's, I'll admit. Gettin' up at three o'clock in the morning! Woo!"

Annie sipped her drink reflectively, then suddenly commented, "Now Cricket has the really fabulous job. How would you like to fly all over the world and get paid to write about it?"

Jade shrugged. "She has her problems, too."

"Like what?" probed Annie.

"Like she's mixed up with a married man. And I think this time she wishes he'd leave his wife for her."

"Fat chance," commented Annie. "Besides, what's so great about marriage? You tried it and didn't like it, right Jade?"

272

Jade gave Annie a warning look, then flicked her eyes over toward India.

"For some people it works out, Annie. For some, it doesn't," said Jade philosophically.

"Well, I'll take a red-blooded lover over a husband any old day!"

"Why not have both?" India blurted out before she knew it, and she couldn't believe she had said it. She smiled broadly to show she was kidding and was relieved when the rest of them laughed.

"Now that's the spirit!" said Jade. Then, noticing the time, she added, "Come on Shell, we've got to run. See you all Tuesday!"

The women gathered their things and spilled out into the street to go their separate ways.

India caught a bus up Madison Avenue and wondered anxiously if she really would see Lanny that night.

The Chinese food she hadn't ordered was announced by the doorman and arrived promptly at nine-thirty that night.

This time Lanny wore a battered trench coat and dark glasses, and carried two large brown paper bags, one in each arm.

India laughed in delight when she opened the door and saw him. "Hey, you promised a kimono! I don't settle for a London Fog and shades, you know!"

She took the bags from him, accepted a kiss on the cheek, and went into the kitchen to get some plates.

Lanny shed his coat and followed her.

Pulling her away from her food unpacking, he took her in his arms and kissed her.

"Did you miss me?" he whispered.

"You know I did. It was a very long day."

Then she found herself telling him all about coffee

with the ladies and Ivan's idea for a TV show.

When Lanny heard that, he looked thoughtful.

"Boy, he sure does have some weird ideas. But you know, I get the feeling he's in some kind of financial trouble."

"Why do you say that?"

She handed him the plates to take into the living room.

"I don't know, really. It's just bits and pieces of things I overhear. But he's into all kinds of funny things."

Ivan's problems were soon forgotten over an enormous feast of lemon chicken and moo shu pork, barbecued ribs and egg rolls.

"No fortune cookies?" asked India as they wiped their sticky hands on bunches of paper napkins.

"You're my fortune, Cookie," said Lanny, leaning over and giving her a duck-sauce-flavored kiss.

Together they cleaned up the mess they had created and chatted about everything and anything—anything and everything, that is, except India's husband's return.

When India at last kissed him good night, he held her close for a moment longer and said, "You're sure I'll see you tomorrow night?"

"Wouldn't miss it," she whispered.

Then he was gone.

Annie was frightened.

It was during a five-minute break in the fashion shooting that they were doing. They were shooting on the Brooklyn Bridge and her hand shook so, she could scarcely hold the Styrofoam cup of coffee steady enough to drink it.

It was chilly this Friday in early November, but not cold enough to account for her violent tremors. She

274

was praying that no one else would notice it.

She put the cup down on the equipment case next to her and pulled the brilliant pink marabou coat she wore more tightly around her.

Get hold of yourself, she lectured silently. This is just nerves—nerves and lack of sleep.

The sleeplessness was getting worse, too. She could barely sleep an hour through in the night. And her appetite was almost nil. Her sleek figure was getting a bit too angular, even for the gaunt, half-starved fashion ideal of photography.

She knew deep down inside that all this had something to do with the vitamin shots she was getting, but she didn't want to admit it, even to herself.

She tried again to bring the coffee cup to her lips and almost spilled some it its steaming contents on the expensive, midnight blue sequined ballgown she was wearing.

The stylist was at her elbow in seconds.

"Jesus, Annie! Watch what you're doing! That dress is so pricey, we practically had to have a Brink's guard here."

The woman was mopping up the liquid that was dripping from the cup and down Annie's hand and arm. She stopped abruptly. "What's the matter with you? You're trembling like a leaf. You sick?"

Annie nodded no, put the cup down again, and moved back to take up her position in front of the camera.

She was frightened enough to decide that she was going to skip her appointment today at Dr. Davis's. This was just too scary.

And the worst part was that she couldn't talk to Ferrago about it. She had always talked to Ferrago about everything. He was her lover, her brother, her father, and her confessor. But this was one confession she knew she had to keep to herself.

She took a deep breath, lifted her chin, and threw back her head in that haughty, arrogant way that she knew the photographers loved.

She'd lick this thing. And the first step was no more shots.

India fairly flew up the steep steps to Lanny's apartment that night. It had been so long since they had been together, all by themselves, without her children sleeping in the next room.

Lanny was waiting at the open door of his apartment wearing a dish towel tied around his slim waist that looked like a ludicrous decoration over his blue jeans.

She was in his arms in an instant and he kissed her as though he would never stop.

When at last they both paused for breath, India became aware of the delicious aroma of beef Stroganoff permeating the apartment.

"Mmmmm, something smells good!"

Lanny smiled. "Yeah, and it's you. Come into the bedroom with me. The food will keep."

Lanny brought a bottle of wine into the bedroom and they drank and talked and made love over and over again. It was after ten before they even thought about food again.

After a marvelous late supper of Stroganoff, salad, hot crusty bread, and cheese, India helped him do the dishes and tidy his minuscule kitchen.

"I really should be going," she began reluctantly. Both had scrupulously avoided discussing when they would be able to do this again.

"Yeah, I know. Just let me grab a jacket and we'll get a cab."

In the taxi, Lanny held her hand tightly but

said nothing.

India turned to look at him in the flickering light from the traffic and street lamps.

"Lanny, don't worry."

Lanny tried for a silly smile and a "What, me worry?" expression.

"I mean it. It'll all work out. I'll work something out. I promise," she said solemnly.

"So, I guess it's 'See you in class'?" he asked as lightly as he could manage.

"Don't be silly. I'll call you sometime either Sunday or Monday. Will you be home?"

"Certainly. All alone, by the telephone, as the old song goes."

India stared hard into his magnificent eyes and tried to memorize them. "Just remember, I love you."

"Me too you," he answered in a hoarse whisper and leaned over to kiss her softly.

They were at her building already.

She scrambled out of the taxi without looking back.

Drew got back from the airport late Saturday afternoon.

When India heard his key in the door, she froze. Then, in the midst of yells and hugs from the children and a squeeze and a kiss for her, India found herself behaving perfectly naturally.

Drew had brought Toohey a stuffed clown and Heather a silver charm of the Eiffel Tower, and for India there was a lovely Hermes scarf.

He said the trip had been tiring and India said she thought he looked a little more drained than usual.

"You, on the other hand," he said, "are blooming! What have you been doing all week? Is it your hair or what?"

Heather looked up from admiring her present and said, "Mommy's been going out!"

In that instant, India could have strangled her own daughter. Instead, she found herself saying smoothly, "Well, it was going to be a surprise, but I've enrolled in a French course."

"What brings this on? I go to Paris and *you* take French?" His expression was amusedly quizzical.

"I confess that it was your trip that made me think of it. But I've been doing so much for my body, with dieting and the gym and all, that I decided I should get my mind working. I enrolled at the New School evenings and took a couple of catch-up lessons last week."

India could not believe how easily the lies rolled from her own tongue. She made a mental note to pick up a French textbook.

"Next week I'll be in a regular Wednesday night session. That okay with you?" she added casually, almost as an afterthought.

"Sure, I guess so. I'll be happy to baby-sit. It just surprises me, that's all."

Andrew headed for the bedroom to unpack, and India gratefully escaped to the kitchen to begin doing something about dinner. The ease with which she dissembled was almost frightening, she thought as she prepared the meal.

Andrew turned in early because, as he explained, it was midnight by his internal clock and he couldn't keep his eyes open.

India tucked in the children and waited until the clock said ten before she dialed Lanny's number. When his lovingly familiar voice said hello, she felt weak inside.

"How would you like to have a steady date every Wednesday night?" she asked in a quiet voice.

Chapter 33

Tuesday morning at eight o'clock Ivan was the first person to arrive at the gym. Checking Darlene's appointment book, he realized that the ten o'clock was the first class of the day. Today he would impress that Greene woman.

Changing into the standard instructor's costume of a white polo shirt with the tiny crossed gold dumbbells emblem, skin-tight moss green trousers, and olive kidskin gymnastic slippers, Ivan let himself into the larger of the workout studios and went through a brisk floor routine to warm up.

He then carefully adjusted the parallel bars to the height he needed and proceeded to swing through an intricate series of maneuvers.

His sixty-eight-year-old body moved with feline grace. The suppleness and fluidity he displayed would have done credit to a gymnast one-third his age. His timing was flawless and his moves so languidly effortless that they belied the long years of practice such a performance demanded.

Ivan was at his most comfortable on the bars or the rings. There he felt released from the constraints of gravity. When he was working at full capacity, the momentum he built up took him from position to position as naturally as water flowed. There was a mindless satisfaction in the clockwork rhythm of his routine, to which he gave himself up with gratitude this morning.

When Darlene stepped off the elevator at nine o'clock, she was momentarily startled to see Ivan through the glass walls separating the waiting area from the gym. He was poised for a flying dismount; a maneuver he then executed with military perfection, landing lightly on his feet, arms thrown high in a triumphant pose.

Darlene paused for only a moment, then crossed mechanically to her desk to begin her daily tasks.

She made a single, brief phone call.

Ivan checked the adjustment of the parallel bars one more time. Satisfied, he came into the outer room and greeted Darlene cordially.

"Ah, good morning, Darlene! It is a beautiful day, no? Coffee, please, in my office, as soon as it is ready, yes?"

Darlene merely nodded in acknowledgment and went to start the coffee.

Ivan disappeared into his inner sanctum.

It was a good forty-five minutes later when Misha and Lanny arrived, followed shortly thereafter by Cricket, Annie, and Jade. India did not get there until five minutes to the hour. Her bus had crawled down Fifth Avenue in traffic.

The women were chattering while changing, as usual, when they heard Ivan's voice boom out over the tops of the dressing rooms. "Ladies, please hurry. I have something special in store for you this morning!"

Cricket rolled her eyes as she scrambled into her fire-engine red leotard. "What do you suppose he has in mind now? Some backbreaking new warm-up?"

Jade was already clad in her black outfit and was patting a tendril of her copper hair back under the white sweatband she wore around her head. "No," she replied, "unless I'm mistaken, I think we're about to witness the birth of a TV star!"

Cricket was mystified, having been away when Ivan had first confided his brilliant plan to Jade, but she followed Jade into the gym to see what was up.

Annie and India were already inside with Lanny.

They all lounged in casual poses while Ivan stood planted, feet apart, in front of the parallel bars, in a rigid stance of expectation.

"Good morning, ladies," sang out Ivan in his most dulcet tone.

Jade and Cricket moved over to join the rest of their group.

"Now, please sit and make yourselves comfortable," he invited. "I am about to give you a little exhibition of the kind of gymnastics to which you may all aspire."

Cricket smothered a giggle, but all four women and Lanny dropped down to the mat, crossing their legs Indian fashion and waiting curiously.

"Now, I have in mind to give a party sometime soon, at which we will all perform for our friends and relatives . . ."

At this Cricket guffawed aloud, but a stern look from Ivan hushed her. "A little party to celebrate an ancient tradition, that of Russian Christmas. This demonstration may also prove to be a prototype for"—here Ivan paused dramatically and looked from face to face in the group—"my new television show." He ended with a flourish.

A moment of silence greeted this proclamation. No one was quite sure what the proper response was supposed to be.

"Entitled *Callus* perhaps?" quipped Cricket.

The group tittered, but Ivan, not understanding her pun, plowed on. "I think the American public would like to see how you, the wealthy, well-known women of Manhattan, keep your fabulous figures so trim, so healthy. I think they would like to see the possibilities that this kind of physical conditioning opens up to them."

"Sure," whispered Jade. "Every woman in the Midwest wants to know how to swing from her chandelier."

"Shhhhh!" snapped Ivan, conscious now that the ladies were not taking him as seriously as he wished. Very well, he would *show* them, he resolved silently.

Irritation visible in every muscle, he turned sharply away from the group and, with one graceful leap, mounted the uneven bars.

He did a few preliminary swings around, up, and over, then prepared to step easily into one of his flashiest moves—a one-handed stand on the uppermost parallel bar.

The women's full attention was directed toward him now. In spite of his pomposity, Ivan was a commanding figure on the bars.

He effortlessly upended himself on one hand and seemed to hang suspended for an instant. In the next second, the bar gave a tremor, quivered, and crashed to the floor. Ivan's slim body came smashing down into a heap on top of it.

Someone screamed.

Everyone seemed frozen in place by the horror of what had just taken place in front of them.

Lanny was the first to his feet, moving swiftly over to where Ivan's lifeless form lay.

Lanny felt delicately on Ivan's neck for a pulse.

The older man's eyes were closed and his athletic figure lay crumpled at awkward angles.

The women came alive and rushed over to the inert body.

"Is he all right?"

"What happened?"

"Is he hurt?"

They babbled in panic.

Lanny took charge. "He's unconscious, but I get a pulse. India, have Darlene get an ambulance. Jade, get a blanket from his office. Don't touch him. I don't know if anything's broken."

India rushed out to Darlene's desk, where the lacquered receptionist sat staring in round-eyed horror at what had just happened beyond the glass wall.

When she didn't respond to India's pleadings, India grabbed a phone and dialed 911, the emergency number, herself.

"Please get an ambulance as fast as possible to Ivan & Igor's gym. Someone's been hurt!"

She gave the address in a clear voice and slammed the phone down.

Turning, she almost collided with Jade, who was running into the gym with several white, fluffy blankets.

Lanny covered Ivan carefully, saying that there was always a chance of shock.

India saw with alarm that a tiny trickle of scarlet blood had begun to dribble out of the corner of Ivan's mouth.

"Listen, there's nothing any of you can do here. Why don't you get dressed and go about your business. I'll be here with him. I can give you all a call later to let you know about his condition, once the medics get here," Lanny said at last.

The women started to protest, but Jade overrode them.

"He's right. We really can't do anything else."

"The ambulance should be here in seconds," said India with more confidence than she felt.

The women turned reluctantly to go gather their clothes in the dressing rooms.

Before they had even completed changing, they heard the rush of feet that signified the arrival of the ambulance. The last sight they had of Ivan came as he was being borne out on a stretcher, covered by a long, white sheet up to his ashen countenance. In the swift glimpse they had of him, he suddenly looked every year of his age and more.

Lanny telephoned India later that afternoon from Lenox Hill Hospital.

"Hi. I'm at the hospital. He's going to be all right, I think. They thought at first that his back could be broken, but now they think it might be only a bad sprain."

"Did you talk to him? Is he all right?"

"We said a few words, but then they put him out with a shot. It's pretty painful, I guess."

India breathed a sigh of relief. "That was scary to see. What happened anyway? Was the equipment defective or something?"

Lanny hesitated. "No. That's what's so weird. I thought to check the bars, right away, to see if they'd broken and we'd have an insurance claim against the manufacturer. So while I was waiting for the medics, I looked it over."

"And?"

"And nothing. Nothing was broken. The only way that could have happened was if the lever that locks the bar in place had been loosened. I could kick myself for not checking it before he began."

India remembered vaguely that Lanny always went from one side of the parallels to the other, checking the adjustment before any of the class ever performed on the bars.

"But that's not expected of you when it's not your class working out. I thought a gymnast was always expected to check out his own stuff."

"He is. And I couldn't believe that a gymnast as experienced as Ivan hadn't done that. So I mentioned it to him when he came to and I was with him in his room."

"What did he say?"

"Well, I couldn't be sure he even understood me. He was pretty foggy. I just said something like, 'You should have checked to be sure the bar was tightened.' And he mumbled something and then closed his eyes. I didn't want to repeat it because I didn't want to sound like I was accusing him of carelessness—not when he's there on the bed, maybe crippled for life."

"He won't be, will he?"

"No. The doctors said that as far as they could tell, he'll be in a brace for awhile and then he'll slowly regain his former mobility. They also said that it's a darn good thing he's in such fantastic physical shape, or he might have killed himself. He's just lucky his neck wasn't broken."

India shivered at the thought.

"I don't think I'm going to be so red-hot anxious to get back up on the bars again."

"Don't be silly. First of all, I *always* check those things and make sure they're extra tight. Second of all, I always spot for each of you very carefully."

"Ivan would have been highly insulted if I had moved over to spot for him," finished Lanny with a little chuckle. "He's such a hard head."

"Lucky for him his head *is* so hard or he could have cracked his skull," commented India.

"Yeah. Well, I'm going to hang around here for a while and then get back to the gym. Misha, Alex, and I will have to take all our own classes today, plus work in Ivan's private lessons as well. Gonna be a *long* day."

"Will I see you tomorrow night?" asked India anxiously.

"Wild horses *or* broken Russians couldn't keep me from that appointment!" Lanny assured her. "Seven o'clock okay? I know I'll have to take one of Ivan's six o'clock classes."

"Sure."

"And listen. Tomorrow night I'll give you a key. That way, if I'm ever late, you can let yourself in."

They said good-bye and Lanny made several more calls, to Jade, to Annie's service, and to Cricket's office to leave word that Ivan the Terrible was alive, albeit not terribly well.

Chapter 34

It was the next day before Ivan regained anything resembling full consciousness. Even then, he grew cold all over when he considered his little "accident" of the day before.

He had tightened those bars himself, thoroughly—twice. The first time had been when he had begun in the morning, and the second, when he had finished his routine about nine o'clock.

Someone had loosened them after that—on purpose. Someone had cold-bloodedly plotted his "accident."

He was certain he knew the people behind the whole thing. But there had been no strangers in the gym that morning.

Someone on his own payroll, or one of his clients, had adjusted those bars after he had secured them. He went over the people who were in the office at the time.

Darlene had been there—too stupid—and Lanny—too honest. He was a good boy. He had come to the hospital with him, he had been told, and waited around to see if he was all right. There was Misha, a recent immigrant who barely understood

English—English, no, but maybe treachery, yes.

Then there were the ladies of the ten o'clock class. But surely none of them would tamper with his equipment. His head hurt with the possibilities that were swirling around in it.

Only one thing was certain. The people to whom he owed money were not fooling around anymore. They were serious—deadly serious.

He had to take some kind of action.

First he would move his Russian Christmas party up by several weeks. To hell with the actual date. He would give it shortly after Thanksgiving. There was no time to lose. Secondly, he would put into action his other plan—the one he hadn't really wanted to use. He did not want to stoop to the kind of dishonesty that was practiced by the people from whom he borrowed money.

But if he did not learn to "stoop" fast, he might never walk again, the sharp pain in his back reminded him.

When the nurse came in to give him his painkiller, he asked her to pass him the phone first and permit him to call someone privately. Then she could shoot him into oblivion once again.

Ivan found that it was hideously painful even to move his fingers feebly to dial the number.

A man's voice answered after two rings. Ivan slowly and weakly told him what was needed. The man promised to see that it was done in the next twenty-four hours. Then Ivan dropped the phone back into its cradle and pushed the button to summon the nurse.

Sometimes one had no choice in these matters.

Jade was working at her desk. This morning's program had gone well, she knew. She now had about two hours to get something on paper in terms of daytime scheduling proposals before her business lunch with Griggs Parkinson.

She was mulling over whether or not this was the time to mention Ivan's exercise show. After his awful accident yesterday, she had no idea how soon he'd be back in commission. Yet if she didn't mention it now, when? And with all this daytime programming junk, how and when was she going to make her pitch for her own move to anchorwoman on the evening news? It had to be done with the skill of a brain surgeon—or a cat burglar, she thought wryly.

Just then the intercom buzzed at her elbow. It was Linda, her secretary.

"Call for you on line four. It's Sister Catherine from Sacred Heart."

"Thanks, Linda. I'll take it."

Jade stabbed at the button on her console with a long, brightly polished nail.

"Good morning, Sister Catherine. What can I do for you?" asked Jade cheerily, fighting a sinking feeling in her stomach as she wondered what Shelley had done now.

"Good morning, Miss Greene. I wanted to have a few words with you about how Shelley has been doing."

Her worst fears confirmed, Jade jumped into the conversation.

"Certainly, Sister. Would you like me to come by so that we can talk?"

Sister's chuckle was reassuring.

"Oh, it's not as serious as that. Yet," she added.

"Well, then, perhaps you can tell me over the phone. What seems to be her problem?"

Sister hesitated, searching for the right words. "Well, it's more a problem of, let's say attitude."

"She hasn't been disrespectful, has she?" asked

Jade quickly, a note of concern creeping into her voice.

"Oh, no, no. Nothing like that," Sister said hastily. "It's more a question of, shall we say, lack of concentration on her school work. She's daydreamy, which is certainly not all that uncommon in a girl her age. But her homework is often undone, and her daily work reflects this. She doesn't seem to be putting in study time at home, and I wondered if perhaps the city experience is consuming too much of her outside time."

Sister let the possibility hang as Jade rapidly considered what to say next. She really had just been assuming that Shelley was studying every night and doing her homework.

Jade always seemed to have a book to read after dinner for the next day's show, or newspaper reading to catch up on, or something that demanded her attention once she'd finished eating with her son and niece.

She had just naturally assumed that Shelley disappeared into the study to do her homework. She knew the girl didn't go out on school nights. That rule had been established early on. Whatever was the child doing with her time? Jade knew whose job it would be to find out.

She sighed. She'd have to have a talk with Shelley tonight and she told the sister that she would certainly see to it and to please not hesitate to call her again.

After hanging up the phone, she turned wearily back to her desk. No one had ever told her how onerous it would be to look after a teenager. Was Mark going to be so time-consuming when he hit that magical age of thirteen—too old for a governess and too young to be responsible? Jade thought guiltily that she had been so wrapped up in her own network maneuvering that she hadn't taken the proper time with Shelley.

This also made her give thought to the upcoming Thanksgiving holiday. She had planned to send Rose and Herb tickets to fly down to spend the weekend in New York. Upon further reflection, she decided perhaps the best way to handle it would be to fly herself, Mark, and Shelley up to Augusta, to spend the weekend up there. It was hardly a scintillating prospect, but maybe it would do Shelley good to see the old hometown she had left, in all its dreary monotones, and to let her realize that her stay in Manhattan was dependent on how well she did in school. That had been the original agreement, and it might be time for a little environmental reminder, thought Jade.

Yes, she decided, that was the best idea—that and a little talk with Shelley tonight. Now, if she could only solve her business problems as cannily.

Cricket was surprised that it was Wednesday night and Andy still hadn't called her. Their week in Paris had been nothing short of divine.

Her booking of the room next to his had been inspired, because after that first night, the rooms had been used as a suite. She and Andy had gone their separate ways to business meetings in the daytime and then had returned to meet at the end of the day in the suite for cocktails and lovemaking.

She had taken him to all her favorite haunts and he had been enchanted by her Paris—and by her, from the way he had behaved.

They had laughed and drunk wine and danced every night until the small hours. And Andy had never once guessed that it had been anything but a wonderful coincidence that she had been in Paris when he was.

Men were so touchingly naïve, she thought. Even in high school, they had always assumed that *they* asked the girls out, when almost any girl could have told them otherwise. The procedure varied only slightly. A girl would take an interest in a boy, make excuses to bump into him in the halls or after school, and, simultaneously, send out not-always-subtle messages by way of her girlfriends or boy chums to get the word to the fellow in question that she would certainly be interested in dating him. After a few weeks of this concentrated effort, the boy in question would call the girl—the knowledge that his invitation would be accepted would give the necessary courage—and ask her out. Naturally, the boy would always assume that the developing relationship had been all *his* idea. And it was ever thus, thought Cricket cynically.

As usual, she was not averse to giving fate a hand. She reached for the Manhattan phone directory and looked through it for Andrew's address.

Yes, there it was. There was only one Travick in the Manhattan directory. Running her finger across the column, she saw his address was on East 75th Street. "My God, only a few blocks from my own apartment!" she exclaimed aloud.

She'd give him a few more days and then she'd have to make sure that she ran into him on the street. She didn't want the memory of those Paris nights to begin to fade.

He was one of the sweetest, most attractive men she'd met in ages, and she couldn't get him out of her mind.

Why were all the best men married?

Annie was having problems focusing. She

couldn't seem to keep her mind on anything, and physically she felt terrible. She was weak and shaky all the time, and in a cold sweat most of the time.

Tonight was a perfect example. She and Ferrago were supposed to be having a cozy dinner at his favorite health food restaurant and she was having trouble following what he was saying. Ferrago didn't seem to be noticing, because he was completely wrapped up in the plan he was outlining to her.

"The way I see it is, you've reached the top of your profession right now. Young to do so, I'll admit, but we both know a fashion model's life is a brief one anyway. There's always a newer, younger face coming along. So where do you go from here?" he asked her theoretically.

Annie was busy pushing her vegetable lasagna around on her plate. She knew she needed food for strength, but even though she'd stopped taking the shots from Dr. Davis, her appetite had not returned.

Fortunately, Ferrago did not expect an answer. He went enthusiastically ahead.

"Oh, you could try doing rock videos or something, but I've got even bigger ideas. I see you as being the first truly successful model making the transition from the still photographer's lens to the big screen. What do you think of that?" He paused dramatically to get Annie's reaction.

Her reaction was a gut one—fear. "Me? Ferrago, what are you thinking of? I look good up there because I know how to stand, and turn, and move, and use my face and give photographers what they want. But I don't know anything about actin'!" she protested.

"The big screen would just make me look like a big fool. Look at what's happened to the other models who've tried it. You know the ones I mean. The critics chew them up and spit them out for breakfast." Annie put her fork down on her plate with shaking fingers. "I just *couldn't*," she stated flatly.

"Nonsense," said Ferrago. "You can do anything. You're the right person, at the right time, in the right place. And the right race!" he finished with a smile.

"Now, to begin with, I've got connections to get you a screen test, sometime within the next few weeks. And"—he put a hand up to silence her forthcoming protests—"I've got you signed up for acting lessons, starting Friday. You'll work with the best coach in town. Annie, you've got to trust me, trust my instincts. I know what I'm doing. Haven't I always done right by you?" he asked protectively, reaching across the table to hold her hand. "Trust me, honey."

Late that night, two men carrying enormous cases let themselves into Ivan & Igor's darkened penthouse gymnasium. Swiftly and silently they went about their work.

A huge machine was installed in Ivan's private office. To it, myriad of wires were connected and concealed throughout the gym.

In each of the dainty, prettily decorated dressing rooms, a tiny microphone was secreted. Two even tinier microphones were installed in each of the three workout rooms. One was even installed under the masseuse's table.

Several hours later, satisfied that their work was completed and expertly done, they let themselves out with a key and disappeared into the thronging, faceless crowd that milled, even at this time of night, along 54th Street.

Chapter 35

Thursday's ten o'clock class was very subdued. Lanny and India had discussed Ivan's accident in detail the night before over dinner, and the other women didn't seem to care to remember it today, much less make comment. Annie, however, found herself sneaking a look over to where Ivan had fallen, half expecting to see blood stains.

Lanny tried valiantly to get some spirit into the class, but they all seemed listless and dragging. Cricket was inwardly occupied, wondering how long she should wait before calling Andrew, Annie could think of nothing but her forthcoming acting lesson, and Jade was mulling over the unsatisfactory talk she had had with Shelley the night before.

It seemed that Shelley was just having trouble buckling down. She would watch TV too long and too late at night, and though she seemed restless and eager to finish school, she refused to attempt the work necessary to accomplish this. Jade decided that bringing her to the gym more often would at least work off some of her physical energy, which seemed at present to have no outlet.

And her lunch yesterday with Griggs had been a

horror. While she tried to discuss network business, she had felt his hand under the table on her knee. It had taken all her restraint not to slug him in the jaw, right there in the Four Seasons. She wondered how long she could continue walking this thin line.

When Lanny tried to get them to work out on the parallel bars, they declined, to a woman. He assured them that they were perfectly safe and even did a few exercises on them himself, but still he could get no volunteers. Tuesday's scene in the gym was still too vividly imprinted in the minds of all of them.

Finally, he settled for some work on the trapeze. But as they left, he called after them, "Okay for today, but I warn you, next Tuesday, you're all going back up there again!"

They called back their good-byes and various thank-yous, but it was a dispirited group that changed back quietly into street clothes without the usual accompaniment of idle chatter.

And somewhere in the depths of a sinister machine, in a hidden corner in Ivan's office, a large spool of tape ran around and around and around.

By Friday, Cricket decided the hell with it, picked up her office phone, and called Andy at the ad agency where he worked.

"Morning," she began breezily. "This is your big chance to buy a starving writer a decent lunch."

Andrew hated the way his heartbeat sped up when he heard the sound of Cricket's unmistakable voice. "Hey, nice to hear from you," he said with a casualness he did not feel. "Gee, I'd love to, but I've got a big business lunch today. The work really piled up while I was away last week."

"Cancel it," was Cricket's comeback. "Why don't

we meet at twelve-thirty at Twenty-One?" she continued. "I'll make the reservations in my name."

While Andrew struggled with his conscience and tried to come up with a plausible reason for whatever decision he made, Cricket moved smoothly ahead.

"See you there," she said brightly and rang off before he could utter another word.

Andrew looked helplessly at the dead phone in his hand, hating himself for his weakness.

Annie had butterflies the size of American eagles in her stomach as she approached the address that Ferrago had scribbled on a piece of paper for her. Her appointment with the acting coach was at twelve sharp. She switched her heavy model's bag to the other hand and looked nervously at her watch. It said eleven forty-five.

Something across the street caught her eye. It was the beloved golden arches.

Suddenly, with a hunger more psychic than physical, Annie darted out into the street and dodged her way through traffic. She knew that something would have to steady this horrible shaking inside her. Something would have to strengthen her to get her through this ordeal.

The something turned out to be a Big Mac, a large order of fries, and a large chocolate milkshake.

Food didn't even taste good to her anymore, but the hunger she was feeling was far deeper than that of the body.

She finished it down to the last greasy sliver of a fry, then grabbed her things and rushed across the street.

It was high noon, exactly.

Chapter 36

That weekend India and Andrew seemed to have an invisible wall between them. They did the usual things: an outing to the Museum of Natural History with the children on Saturday and a leisurely reading of the *New York Times* on Sunday morning, but communication seemed to stay at a minimum.

Sunday afternoon Andrew asked her what she wanted to do for the Thanksgiving holiday.

"Gee, I hadn't really thought about it," India remarked, looking up from the crossword puzzle.

"Maybe we should drive up to some quaint inn in Connecticut and have dinner out. Might save you the trouble of cooking a big Thanksgiving feast just for the four of us."

"That's not a bad idea," India agreed. "You'd better come up with a place soon though, so we can make reservations. Most places in the country get booked up very fast."

"I'll ask around the office and see what's good up there," offered Andrew before they fell silent once more.

*   *   *

Jade tried to devote her weekend to entertaining Mark and Shelley. She took them skating at the Rockefeller Center skating rink and, afterward, to the Palm Court of the Plaza Hotel for hot chocolate.

It was as they were sipping their hot chocolate that Jade divulged her plan for Thanksgiving. "How would you both like to fly up to Augusta with me for Thanksgiving?" began Jade brightly.

"Oh boy!" said eight-year-old Mark, all but jumping up and down. The idea of flying in an airplane had him thrilled.

"Oh lord," groaned Shelley, putting down her cup of chocolate so sharply that some of it sloshed into her saucer. Her face assumed a pained expression.

Jade turned toward her pretty niece. "Hey, is that any way to greet the idea of spending the holiday with your folks?" she chided.

"I'm sorry, Aunt Jade. I didn't mean it that way. Of course I'll be glad to see Mom and Dad, but it's the idea of going back to Augusta that sounds so boring."

Shelley's face took on such a plaintive expression that Jade had to stifle a laugh. Then she steeled herself for what she knew she had to say next.

"Look honey, Augusta may be boring, but you may be spending your last semester back there if you don't get on the stick at Sacred Heart. You remember our bargain. You promised to make good grades at school. Now your midterms were all C's and B's. Those are not great grades for someone who was an A student back at Covy High. You have finals coming up just before the Christmas holidays, and if I don't see some A's out of that, I am packing you up at the end of January and shipping you north again. I don't want to sound like the world's meanest person, but for someone as smart as you are, there's no excuse for not getting top grades."

Shelley looked properly chagrined.

"Aunt Jade, I swear I'll pull *A*'s for the semester. I will study every night from now 'til finals. I will not disappoint you. But please, please, please don't make me go back to Augusta for the last of my senior year. I would die—just absolutely *die*."

"Okay, okay. No cheap theatrics, please. But remember it's up to you. I know you can do it if you put your mind to it. Now, in the meantime, I'm going to get flight reservations for Thanksgiving, and I want you to look properly homesick when you see your folks again," Jade ended with a smile.

Shelley rolled her eyes heavenward. "Talk about theatrics; that'll take *some* acting!"

"Drink your cocoa, you impertinent whipper-snapper," commanded Jade good-naturedly.

There was really so much of herself in her niece that Jade found the girl irresistible.

Cricket's luncheon with Andrew had ended where she had wanted it to end—back in bed in her apartment. They'd made a date for lunch the following week before they said good-bye.

Over the weekend, her folks had called from Virginia and asked if she were coming home for Thanksgiving. On impulse, Cricket had replied that she was planning on it. She had suddenly decided that four days out of the city and out of Andrew's life might be the best thing in the world.

She booked herself out of New York on the Wednesday night before the holiday and got a late flight back from Virginia on Sunday night.

She'd drop that little number on Andrew during their lunch next week, she thought to herself, adding, damn it, fella, I've *got* to get you to miss me!

Although Ivan was out of the hospital by the end of the weekend, he was firmly encased in a back brace from his neck almost to his hip and his movement was very limited.

Monday he limped into the gym with the aid of a cane. After greeting Darlene, he closeted himself in his office for the whole day, listening to endless hours of chatter on tape—fast forward, stop, play.

"I'm seriously considering a face-lift. Honest."

"At thirty-two? You're insane!"

Fast forward, stop, play.

"And then *he* said, 'Why don't you enter a monastery, if you feel that way about it?' And *I* said, 'A monastery? You mean a convent!' And *he* said, 'No, I *meant* a monastery.'"

Sounds of loud laughter.

Fast forward, stop, play.

At last Ivan punched the "off" switch in disgust. He had been listening to drivel—hours and hours of drivel. Didn't anything ever happen to any of those women that meant anything?

Ivan stared morosely at the enormous stack of unopened mail on his desk, most of it probably bills. There would be some checks also, but not enough—never enough.

He heaved a deep, heavy, Russian sigh. It was time to begin planning his gymnastic exhibition. He fingered his leather-tooled desk calendar. Two weeks—that was the longest he could wait. He would set a date two weeks from now and order the food and the music and get the ladies working on a program. The idea of a chic exercise show was a good idea—a salable idea—and he knew it.

He would sell the show and get the package worked up, even if he was in a back brace. He could get Lanny to do some on-camera work for awhile if necessary. All he needed was a firm commitment, a signed contract, *and* a fat check for his part. He would begin making the arrangements tomorrow.

As he hobbled out of his office, he carefully locked the door behind him.

Annie and Ferrago planned an enormous dinner for the Thanksgiving holiday, inviting all the people they knew in the city whom they considered strays—people who weren't going home to families for the holidays or who had no families with whom to celebrate. New York was full of such lonely people every holiday and on no day was the loneliness more poignant than on Thanksgiving, the traditional time for families to gather.

They planned to serve nothing but untraditional food. Ferrago had arranged for the delivery of an immense order of Peking duck from his favorite Chinese restaurant and several friends were bringing various ethnic dishes of their own heritages, all of which would result in a groaning board of exotic delicacies from every corner of the globe.

Annie would have preferred a Big Mac, but knew there was no hope for it. She went dutifully to her acting lessons but felt wooden as a stick, and she was positive that she would be laughed off the screen when Ferrago set up her test. In an attempt to calm herself, she would stop regularly, either before or after her lesson, at the McDonald's across the street from her studio. Her nerves remained as frazzled as ever, but the greasy food comforted her soul.

Early on Thanksgiving morning, Annie surreptitiously placed a call to her family in Harlem to wish them a happy holiday and explain that an important business dinner would keep her from joining the family for their turkey feast. She felt guilty doing this, but she had no desire to spend the holiday without Ferrago and knew that her mother would never welcome him into their home.

Their guests had been told to drop up to their loft any time after noon, so Annie slipped into something festive and glamorous. She chose a floor-length velvet caftan in a glowing mustard gold that swished around her and made her coffee-colored skin and long black hair look even more exotic. Large, slender gold hoops in each ear were her only adornment.

Their enormous loft was divided at one end with partitions that reached almost to the ceiling. That section held their bedroom, bath, and kitchen.

The rest had been left more or less open, with a pillar here, a pillar there, and lots of low furniture and treelike plants strewn throughout. The floor-to-ceiling windows flooded the immense open area with light, and whenever he chose, Ferrago could set up any kind of shooting space he needed. He often photographed at home and the loft was frequently covered with large rolls of seamless paper.

Today Annie had bought armloads of flowers and had arranged them in unexpected places. It had taken dozens upon dozens to fill the spaces. From the ceiling in one corner hung a large basket full of colorful birds of paradise. They looked as beautiful and exotic as Annie herself.

Along one wall, Ferrago had set up rows of saw horses with planks stretched across them to form a buffet table that stretched almost twenty feet. Over this, he had thrown some long bolts of shimmering gold cloth, and Annie had arranged big bowls of autumn leaves at infrequent intervals. The table also held stacks of heavy white plates and an odd assortment of table utensils, which had been collected from every shooting on which Ferrago had ever worked. Mismatched glassware that included everything from Waterford crystal to jelly glasses completed the service. Before the afternoon was over, every available inch of space would be crowded with platters and casseroles, breads, and desserts, wines and cheeses of every conceivable kind.

The first guests began pouring in at about twelve-thirty P.M. It was an eclectic gathering. There were many faces from the fashion world—models with whom Annie worked, editors, and other photographers; there came also a large group of local Soho artists, a smattering of musicians and writers, Ferrago's lawyer and his two small children, two set designers, and a bag lady. Everyone was made welcome and all mingled freely. Good humor was the order of the day.

Unfortunately for Annie, one of the first people she bumped into was a commercial producer with whom she had often worked.

"Hey, Anastacia, you look absolutely smashing! Ferrago tells me we may lose you soon to Hollywood. That the straight story?"

Annie blushed deeply beneath her mocha-colored skin. "Rumor, honey, rumor. They'll take one look at me and put me right back in the funny papers, where I belong."

Ferrago had come up behind Annie during this exchange and had slipped a protective arm around her waist.

He leaned over to whisper through her cloud of black, cascading hair. "Do not, repeat, not put yourself down, baby. You are going to be *great.* Get

305

used to it."

Annie smiled sweetly and slipped away to greet another group, though, as always, she got knots in her stomach when Ferrago started talking like that. She loved him, she couldn't live without him, but she couldn't see how she could ever live up to his expectations.

She paused briefly at the buffet table to pour herself some wine and nibble a piece of banana bread.

A stunning-looking woman who appeared to be about seven feet tall entered the room on the arms of two shorter, nondescript men. The woman was deeply tanned, with long, streaked blond hair, and these features were enhanced by a flowing white jersey dress. Twined in her hair were huge brown feathers that wafted behind her when she walked.

"Hi, Carmela," Annie greeted her with a light kiss on her cheek. The two had often worked shootings together. Their unusual looks made a striking combination.

"*What* are those in your hair?" asked Annie.

"Turkey feathers, my dear. What else would you wear for a Thanksgiving repast? I *am* part American Indian, you know."

"Which part?" someone inquired good-naturedly.

The talk ranged from theater to politics to recipes, and had Annie not felt so nervous about her upcoming film test, she would have thoroughly enjoyed herself. She was usually comfortable in such a mixed Manhattan bag of artists and up-and-coming movers and shakers. There were even a politician or two present, and a neighborhood priest.

By late afternoon the din was deafening. The crowd had swelled to fill the loft and people seemed to be having a good time. In one group, someone had brought out a flute and was playing, accompanied by someone else on a balalaika. Rock music blared from Ferrago's elaborate stereo at another end of the room.

Ferrago mingled and bantered, Annie noted. He was well liked and respected in this crowd. And Annie watched Sadie the Bag Lady as she sipped wine from a Waterford crystal goblet while deeply engaged in conversation with a young sculptor.

Sadie was a familiar figure in their neighborhood. She carried two shopping bags and wore her entire wardrobe on her back in all seasons. She and Annie often chatted when they passed on the street and Annie had included her so that she wouldn't end up having to take her holiday meal at the Salvation Army. Sadie knew many of the people there and was enjoying herself immensely.

Only one unpleasant episode took place to mar the conviviality of the day.

At one point, Ferrago looked over to where Carmela was enscounced in a pile of cushions on the floor, the center of an animated group. Carmela was carefully rolling a one-hundred-dollar bill into a tight tube.

The muscle in Ferrago's jaw tightened as it always did when his anger began to build. Pushing through the crowd, he stood towering over her, looking down at the little heap of white powder on the coffee table in front of Carmela.

"What the hell is that and what the hell do you think you're doing?" he demanded in such a loud voice that the conversation in that immediate area died abruptly.

Carmela looked up and gave him her most angelic smile. "Why, it's nose powder, honey, and I'm preparing to powder my nose."

Ferrago swung and somebody near him grabbed his arm so that he missed Carmela, but his gesture

307

scattered the expensive powder all over the table.

Ferrago uttered a string of profanities at the top of his lungs, ending with a shouted invitation to Carmela to "get her ass out of here."

Drawing herself up from the floor to her full seven-foot height, Carmela strode off across the room with feathers streaming out behind, flung her red fur poncho over her shoulders, and, trailed by her two nameless companions, slammed out the door.

She reappeared seconds later to dash to the buffet table, snatch up her loaf of homemade challah bread from the spread, tuck it under one arm indignantly, and slam out the door once more.

This last action brought embarrassed titters from the people closest to the altercation and soon the din of conversation rose again and the incident was forgotten.

It was forgotten by everyone, that is, except Ferrago, who made his way over to where Annie was standing. She had witnessed the scene in its entirety but had been powerless to move to intervene.

"Does she do that while she's on jobs with you?" he snarled in a low, angry voice.

Annie lowered her eyes. "Sometimes," she said softly.

Ferrago put his hand under her chin and jerked her face up so that he could look directly into her eyes.

"Then I don't want you taking any more jobs with her, understand? I don't want you around scum like that! I mean it, Annie."

His tone was so ferocious that all Annie could do was nod. Everyone knew how Ferrago felt about drugs.

Late afternoon passed into early evening, the buffet table became a shambles of half-eaten platters of food and half-empty bottles, and no one showed any signs of departing.

Annie gathered a few dirty plates that were close by and wended her way through the crowd to the kitchen. Might as well start stacking a few things now as later, she thought.

The sight that greeted her there made her smile broadly. There at the kitchen sink was Sadie the Bag Lady, sleeves rolled up and arms deep into a sink full of suds, sporting one of Annie's aprons, which read, "Who invited all these tacky people?"

She was smiling her big, toothless smile at Ferrago's lawyer, Arnie, who was also in shirt sleeves and busily drying dishes as fast as Sadie could wash them. They were deep in animated conversation and did not even notice Annie's arrival at first.

Annie put down the dishes she was carrying and crossed over to kiss first Sadie and then Arnie on the cheek.

"Bless you both. Aren't you two the domestic scene, though?"

Arnie returned her smile. "She's trying to convince me that I should get out of law, and I'm trying to convince her that she should get off the street."

Annie laughed.

"I'm staying out of this one. May the best person win. Sadie, you *must* take some of this food with you when you go. We'll be eating leftover stuffed grape leaves and sushi for weeks," Annie sang out over her shoulder as she exited.

"I don't eat *bait!*" called Sadie after her with a cackle.

Finally, at about midnight, the crowd began to thin. First people began to leave in a trickle, and soon it became a flood. Everyone left thanking Ferrago and Annie, insisting it was the best Thanksgiving ever.

309

Annie realized they had been partying for twelve straight hours and she was suddenly conscious of her aching feet. But still, she reflected, the room was a shambles.

Reading her thoughts, Ferrago took her gently by one hand and led her toward the bedroom.

"Relax, sugar. It'll all be here when we get up in the morning. You look beat, so let's hit the feathers."

Annie did not need much convincing. She dropped her velvet caftan to the floor as she stood by the bed and stretched languidly.

Ferrago, already stripped and under the covers, lay watching her appreciatively.

A small furrow crept into his brow as he surveyed her.

"Annie?"

She looked at him expectantly.

"You puttin' on some weight?"

Annie wished she had undressed in the dark.

"Maybe a pound or two. Why? And I ate like a horse today. It's Thanksgiving, Ferrago," she ended plaintively.

Ferrago bounded out of bed.

"Yeah. It's Thanksgiving, but that looks like more than a pound or so to me. And you *know* why. By next week I'm going to have you in a screen test, and every pound will look like a ton."

He practically dragged her into their bathroom, switched on the light, and pushed her at the doctor's scale that stood in one corner.

"On!" he commanded.

Annie meekly stepped on the scale and wished the ground would swallow her up.

Ferrago fiddled with the weights until he struck a balance.

"Ye Gods, Annie! You're up *seven* pounds! What

are you doing to yourself?"

Seeing her forlorn expression, his voice softened.

"I'm sorry, darling. And look, I'll grant you that you probably ingested about two pounds of food today alone. But the other stuff has *got* to go. I mean it. I want you to look great for your test. I want you to be a big success."

He took her naked body into his arms and patted her back as though she were a baby.

"Come on, it's late. Let's get some sleep and we can worry about it tomorrow," he said consolingly.

Much later, as Annie heard the comforting sound of Ferrago's light snoring, she resolved to go back to Dr. Davis on Monday. She couldn't let Ferrago down now—not after he'd gone to so much trouble for her career.

Chapter 37

India, Andrew, Heather, and Toohey had spent a pleasant day at the Silvermine Tavern in Connecticut eating an enormous Thanksgiving turkey dinner. India and Andrew didn't talk to each other too much, but the children's chatter more than filled the air with happy conversation. Both children fell asleep in the car on the drive back to the city and India noted that Andrew seemed completely wrapped in his own thoughts.

By Sunday, Toohey was running a slight fever, so India put him to bed with some aspirin and Andrew took Heather to the zoo in Central Park. When Toohey fell asleep for a brief nap, India headed straight for the phone.

She hated herself, but she dialed Lanny's number. She so much wanted to hear his voice.

He answered on the first ring.

"Happy Thanksgiving," said India softly.

"And the same to you." She could hear the smile in his voice and was pleased that he was glad to hear from her.

"How was your Turkey Day?" she asked.

"Pleasant. Went out to Brooklyn with the family.

My sister and her husband and kids were there and we all ate too much. The usual. And yours?"

"More or less the same. We drove up to an inn in Connecticut and had a big feast with all the trimmings."

As they chatted aimlessly for awhile, India mentioned Toohey's illness and her hope that it was only a twenty-four-hour bug. Lanny told her how much he missed her and that he couldn't wait for Tuesday. India said she felt the same way and she hung up reluctantly, only because she thought she heard Toohey stirring.

Cricket got back to her apartment late Sunday night. The traffic had crawled home from the airport. She wondered if Andy had missed her. She had missed him.

She checked her answering machine for messages. A few that related to business were waiting, but nothing of any importance.

While in Paisleyville, she had seen all her old friends who were home for the holidays and had spent lots of time visiting relatives, but she had returned to Manhattan as always with the grateful feeling of being truly home.

Ironically, she was going to have to look at her trip schedule once again and figure out where she should be going for the next few months. She wondered if Andy had any trips scheduled.

Might be worth quizzing him about, she mused silently.

Annie had gotten in touch with her service over the weekend and had booked out for eleven o'clock on

Monday, at which time she found herself sitting in the drab little waiting room of Dr. Davis's office.

When she was ushered in to see the doctor, he didn't look the least bit surprised to see her again. She explained her weight gain problem but also stressed that she did not want to go on the shots again. Secretly, she was afraid that Ferrago might see the puncture marks on her arm.

Dr. Davis only nodded understandingly and said he could give her some pills that could effectively handle her problem.

Annie then hesitatingly confided to him that the shots, while controlling her appetite, had made her very jumpy.

Again, the kindly doctor nodded and said he could also give her some other pills, which she could use when she needed to relax.

It all sounded perfect to Annie. She took the pills gratefully and paid him in cash. As soon as she was out of his office and onto the street once more, she popped one of the first set of pills into her mouth and swallowed it without water. Then she headed for her noon appointment with her drama coach.

By the time she reached his studio, she felt her old bounce returning. One of the effects of the shots, which she had forgotten about in her physical misery, was the wonderful feeling of self-confidence they had given her. She needed that now more than ever.

Maybe she *could* do it—pull off an acting gig. Maybe she *could* make Ferrago proud of her. She felt now as if she could lick the whole world.

That night, after having virtuously consumed only a plain yogurt and an apple as her day's total ration, she and Ferrago joyously made love. But even the release of her multiple orgasms didn't seem to relax her. As soon as she heard the deep, even breathing that signaled that Ferrago had dropped off to sleep, she crept into the bathroom with her handbag.

There she fished into her tampon case, where she had decided to stash her two sets of pills, and withdrew a small orange capsule. She took one, washed it down with a swallow of water, and tiptoed back to bed.

Moments later, she was deep in a dreamless sleep.

Tuesday morning, as soon as she came down to her office from the set, Jade received a call from her niece, Shelley.

Shelley reminded Jade that she had no school that day—it was another holy day—and asked if she could go to Ivan & Igor's with her aunt.

Jade said she thought it would be a splendid idea and told Shelley to take a cab and meet her there. She wanted Shelley to get more exercise.

As soon as Andrew and Heather left the apartment Tuesday morning, India made a rushed, hushed call to Lanny to try to catch him before he left for the gym. She explained that Toohey's fever had been very high yesterday and she'd called the doctor, who had told her to keep him in bed for today, even though it was lower now. Toohey had become cranky and wanted his mommy with him, so she'd canceled Mrs. Schmidt for the morning and wouldn't be able to make it to the gym class.

Lanny sounded disappointed but said not to worry. If Toohey was feeling better tomorrow, India could do a makeup at his Wednesday ten o'clock class.

India was sorry not to be able to see Lanny, but she also felt sorry for runny-nosed little Toohey. She said she was sure he'd be better so she could make Wednesday's class.

Then she called Ivan & Igor's, spoke to Darlene, and rescheduled her appointment for Wednesday at ten o'clock.

At nine-forty-five on Tuesday, when Cricket arrived for class, there was not another soul to be seen. Even Darlene was away from her desk.

Wondering if she'd be the only one in class, Cricket stopped at Darlene's big appointment book, which lay open on her desk, to see who else was scheduled. Running her finger down the column to ten o'clock on Tuesday, Cricket saw her own name, Cricket Wells, followed by Jade Greene, followed by Anastacia, followed by another name with a heavy line through it. Cricket peered closely and could just make out the name under the black line.

India Travick.

Cricket looked again and blinked.

A wave of shock crashed over her.

Now suddenly, it was unmistakable. *Travick.* She could see it clearly.

Just then Darlene rounded the corner and headed back to her desk.

Looking faintly annoyed, she said coolly, "May I help you, Cricket?"

Cricket gave a guilty start and felt herself flush. "No, no, not really, I was just looking to see if I was the only one here today . . ."

"Jade's already changing, India's cancelled, Annie's still due, and Jade's niece is coming today. That answer your question?" asked Darlene.

The faint touch of snottiness in the receptionist's voice was lost on Cricket, so shaken was she by what she had just seen in the book.

Slightly dazed, she grabbed her gym bag and headed for the changing room. "Jade?" she called out tentatively, needing desperately to confide in someone.

"In here," sang out Jade from the far room.

Cricket opened the door, closed it behind her, and sank down on the little velvet-covered bench.

Jade turned around to greet her friend and the smile froze on her face as she saw Cricket's stricken expression.

"Hey, what's up? You seen the proverbial ghost or something?" Her concern was evident in her voice. She paused in her undressing, sat down on the bench next to Cricket, and took her hand.

Cricket didn't answer for a moment.

"Hey, it's me, Jade. What's up?"

Slowly Cricket turned to face Jade. "Did you know India's last name?" she asked faintly.

Jade looked puzzled. "No. Why? Does it matter? What's this—twenty questions?" She tried to laugh a little to lighten the other woman's mood.

"It's Travick," whispered Cricket in a hoarse voice.

"Travick?" Clearly the name didn't mean a thing to Jade. "So?"

"So that's my guy's last name. Travick. Andy Travick. The man I met in Jamaica. The one I followed to Paris. The man I'm in *love* with, Jade, is *Andy Travick*." Cricket paused to let the import of her words sink in.

318

Jade's forehead wrinkled.

"But, but couldn't there be *two* Travicks? I mean now that I think of it, I don't think Andy is India's husband's name. I think she called him Doug or something. Drew! That was it—Drew!"

Cricket shook her head despairingly.

"No. There's only one Travick in Manhattan. I looked him up in the phone book. Andrew Travick. One East 75th Street. Oh God, Jade!"

"Andrew," said Jade slowly. "Yes, she did call him Drew. And you called him Andy. I get a funny feeling you're right. Oh dear! Andy and Drew are one and the same."

"And the same is India's husband," finished Cricket. "God, I feel like such a rat! I'm having an affair with India's husband!" she said in a low, clear voice.

"But she doesn't suspect, does she?" asked Jade anxiously.

"Not that I know of. But Jesus, I didn't know I knew his wife. It's"—Cricket shuddered—"it's weird, that's all."

"Well," said Jade thoughtfully, "now that you do know, the question is, what are you going to do about it?"

Again, Cricket shook her head. She got up and slowly began to undress. "I don't know. I just don't know. I'm already in over my head. I really don't know."

"Best thing to do is put it out of your mind right now. She's going to dash in here any minute and you're going to have trouble looking normal."

Suddenly Cricket came back to reality. "No, she's not. That's good, at least. That's how I found out. I was looking in the appointment book. She cancelled out for today."

"Thank God for small favors," breathed Jade. "At least that postpones one part of it. Look, hop into your leotard and let's get moving. We can talk about this later and figure something out."

Jade leaned over and gave Cricket a reassuring hug. "Maybe you should change gym classes or something," added Jade, searching for a solution.

"Maybe I should change *gyms*," offered Cricket morosely, reaching for her red leotard.

Meanwhile, Annie and Shelley had shared the same elevator coming up and had headed for a dressing room together.

Shelley was extremely happy to have run into Annie again and Annie was looking cheerier and feeling more chipper than she had in ages.

"So how was your Turkey Day?" Annie asked Shelley brightly as she closed the dressing room door.

"Okay," said Shelley.

"Only okay? Mine was terrific. You should have been there. What'd you do for the holiday?" chattered Annie as she started to strip.

Shelley recounted the whole, deadly trip to Augusta and ended with her Aunt Jade's threats of returning her there if her school work didn't perk up.

"What's the problem, honey? That old school can't be so tough. Just pull yourself together and you'll ace it," said Annie encouragingly.

"Well," began Shelley tentatively, and she lowered her voice slightly so that it wouldn't carry to the other dressing rooms, "it's a little more complicated than that."

Annie gave her a quick look, wondering what the naïve girl had gotten herself involved in this time.

"You see, I've been skipping classes sometimes,

and I'm really far behind now. I've been so afraid that Sister would tell Aunt Jade about it, but I don't think she's found out."

"Okay, so now it comes out. Dare I ask where you've been going when you've been skipping?" Annie was trying her best to play the big sister. She really liked Shelley and wanted to help her with her problems.

Shelley's face became animated with happiness.

"Everywhere, just everywhere! It's so wonderful; I've seen so much!"

This Annie couldn't figure out. "So where's 'everywhere'?" she asked in puzzlement.

"I mean just every place in this city. One day I went to the Frick Museum, I've spent *hours* in the Metropolitan, I've been to the Guggenheim . . ."

Annie had to chuckle in spite of herself. "This is wild! You been cutting classes to go overdose on New York culture? That may not be all bad."

Shelley had the good grace to hang her head.

"Well," she admitted slowly, "it hasn't *all* been culture. I spent a lot of one day in Bloomingdale's, and lots of times I've hit Times Square movies, then one day I took the subway out to try to find Coney Island . . ." Her voice trailed off.

Annie tried very hard to sound stern.

"So it hasn't exactly been an art expedition. It seems it's more like you're trying to swallow the whole Big Apple in one gulp."

Shelley nodded affirmatively and looked miserable.

"How'd you get away with not being missed at school?" Annie was curious, in spite of herself.

"Sometimes I forged Aunt Jade's signature; other times the biggest cuts were study hall, where they didn't notice I was gone. But I missed time when I should have been getting research and reading done. Worst of all, the work has just piled up like crazy. I mean I've got whole novels to read and finals are coming up next week, and if I stayed up day and night from now 'til then I probably wouldn't be able to catch up.''

Tears welled up in Shelley's eyes, then slowly spilled over and wandered forlornly down her cheeks.

Annie reached for a tissue from the dressing room shelf and tossed it at her.

"Come on, come on. All is not lost yet. You still got a week, right?''

Shelley gulped and nodded as she mopped at her face.

Annie had an idea, but she knew it wasn't a great one.

"Listen, if you buckled down now and really tried, do you think you'd have a shot at it?''

"If I literally worked almost all night, every night until exam time, maybe I could get some *B*'s . . . but I'm tired and I'm discouraged and I'm ashamed. . . .''

"Okay, so stop being all those things." Annie started digging in her bag for her tampon case.

"I got something here to help. I got these pills for my dieting, but man, they really jazz you up. If I didn't take another pill at night to relax me, I'd never get any sleep. I will give you enough to get you through the next couple of weeks. They'll also give you some self-confidence that you can do it. But you gotta swear—and I mean *swear*—you will never let your auntie find out. She would kill me if she knew. For that matter, Ferrago would kill me if he knew *I* was taking this stuff. But you take one of these every morning, and you go to those classes, and you come home and hit those books—take another if you need it to stay awake—and you will be able to do super-human things!"

Comprehension was slowly dawning on Shelley's face, and it was quickly replaced with a smile of gratitude as she stretched out eager hands to catch the pills Annie was pouring out.

"I shouldn't do this, but you got yourself in a mess and I think you can get out of it—with a little help from your friends, as they say. These make you feel real good, like I said—like you can do *anything*. And I think maybe you need a little confidence right now," said Annie compassionately.

Shelley looked up nervously.

"What's in them, anyway? Are they okay to take?"

"Honey, I got them from a doctor that Ivan sent me to! 'Course they're okay. It's not junk I picked up on the street. I wouldn't do that. Trust me. But you gotta do your part. You gotta study, okay?"

Shelley assured Annie that she would. She quickly wrapped the pills in a Kleenex and put them in her purse. Her whole mood lightened. She rapidly tugged on her leotard.

Annie smiled at the girl's happiness. It was nice to be able to help turn someone's world around.

"Annie," yelled Lanny from the gym, "you coming or not?"

"Shelley!" joined in Jade. "Get a move on!"

The two women exchanged a conspiratorial smile and dashed out to join the others.

Ivan was in the gym with Lanny and the others. He was stiff and uncomfortable in his back brace, but he knew he had to get things organized for the party.

"Good morning, ladies. Lanny and I have been discussing what we will do for an exhibition at the party and we have come up with certain ideas."

His stern glance suddenly took note of Shelley.

"You are . . . ?" he scowled toward the younger woman.

"My niece, Shelley," filled in Jade. "She comes with me sometimes, Ivan."

Shelley flashed her aunt a grateful look. She was not used to Ivan and his brusque ways.

Ivan's scowl was immediately replaced by an oily smile.

"Welcome," he said in his most unctuous tone, knowing that any relative of Jade's would have to be welcome as the flowers of spring.

"Yes, now. . . ." He returned to the subject at hand. "Jade, you might want to do a little routine on the rings. I believe you are very proficient there, am I right?"

Jade managed not to laugh and instead commented lightly, "Well, I don't fall off on my ass, if that's what you mean, Ivan."

Lanny nodded agreement. "Yeah, Jade's very good there. She can do her whole routine while the rings are in motion. You *are* good there, Jade," he said.

"So, yes," mumbled Ivan, making notes on a small pad he held in one hand.

Annie, standing to one side, had been jumping up and down in place to get her blood pumping. She was impatient to get on with the morning's exercises.

Ivan turned his attention to her. "You, Anastacia, could do very well with a floor routine, is that not so?"

Annie grinned. "Sure, what the hell. I've never fallen off the floor yet, Ivan," said Annie flippantly.

Ivan frowned at her frivolity and turned instead to Lanny to confirm Annie's abilities. "Forward and backward walk-overs, that sort of thing?"

Lanny nodded a confirmation.

"Does she do any aerials?" asked the older man.

"She hasn't yet, but I'm not so sure I couldn't get her into a few by the party," answered Lanny affably.

Annie shrugged and made a face. She knew that aerials were stunts in which nothing touched the floor, as in a no-hands walk-over or a back flip without any part of the body hitting the mat.

"Why do I think I'm about to fall off the floor?" she asked of no one in particular.

Ivan ignored her.

"Why don't you rig up the safety belt today and see if she could manage a few?"

Lanny promised he'd give it a try.

Next Ivan turned to Cricket, who was curiously quiet today.

"Now, what do you think you would like to do, Cricket?"

A flash of her old humor returned momentarily.

"Get out of town!"

Ivan was annoyed that these women refused to take anything seriously. They were such flibbertigibbets, and he had so much riding on this. They could be his most convincing selling point for doing his own show. If these idle, flighty women could be shown exhibiting the kind of physical fitness he had taught them, he could dazzle the TV people. If only they would be serious! he raged inwardly.

"Why don't you let me see you work out on the parallel bars?" suggested Ivan.

Cricket protested instantly.

"Ivan, for Heaven's sake! I'm not even warmed up yet!"

Lanny rushed into the breach.

"She could probably do quite well on those, Ivan. But she's right. She's not warmed up. Let me work with her. She can do something—if she's going to be here for the party."

Lanny shot Cricket a questioning look. He knew her trips were frequent and sometimes unannounced.

"Oh, I'll be here, as far as I know," said Cricket wearily. Then she felt another stab of anxiety. That damn party! Would India and Andy be there? She dismissed the worry instantly. India had not been coming to Ivan & Igor's that long. She wasn't that proficient. She wouldn't be performing and probably wouldn't even bother with the whole thing.

"Count me in, I guess."

That settled, Ivan turned toward Shelley.

Jade quickly intervened. "Shelley is a newcomer, Ivan. I'll bring her along, but don't expect her to do any tricks."

Shelley breathed a sigh of relief as Ivan nodded in agreement.

"Certainly Jade; whatever you say. But"—and here he put on his most charming smile and looked over at Shelley—"she is so very sweet and attractive. Surely you would have no objection to her taking part in a group demonstration of our warmup work, would you?"

Jade shot Shelley a questioning look.

Shelley smiled to show her willingness.

"Okay," said Jade. "A little class demonstration should be all right."

Ivan then turned to Lanny and ran through a short list of other women from other classes who he thought might be suitable to participate and asked Lanny to contact them during the next few days.

"If any of them are not coming in for classes, try to reach them by phone. We must have this locked up by midweek, so everyone will have time to practice and feel sure of herself."

Lanny promised he would, and Ivan hobbled out

of the gym and disappeared into his private office, much to everyone's relief.

Cricket had been afraid he would stand around and observe the class and that always made all the women nervous. He was such a taskmaster.

"So how does it feel to be Ivan's replacement in the 'reeelly big shew'?" Annie asked Cricket facetiously.

Cricket looked distracted. "Oh, on the bars, you mean. Yeah, sure. Terrific."

Annie was surprised. Cricket wasn't her usual effervescent self today. Wonder what's eating her? thought Annie.

But such thoughts were quickly forgotten as Lanny began a really strenuous warmup to make up for the time lost consulting with Ivan.

"Okay, let's hit it! One and two and . . ."

All four leotard-clad figures began jumping in place with a vengeance.

Chapter 38

India could scarcely wait for Wednesday morning. Toohey's temperature was normal and he was even looking forward to seeing Mrs. Schmidt as a welcome diversion. Making sure he knew he was to stay in bed and after loading him down with crayons and paper and toy soldiers and picture books, India gave him a hasty kiss and took off.

She got to Ivan & Igor's at ten minutes to the hour and was greeted by Darlene as mechanically as usual.

Even as she was changing, she heard Lanny's wonderful voice.

"Hi, Darlene. We got many for the ten o'clock?"

India marveled at how casual he managed to sound.

She heard Darlene's nasal reply. "India just came in, Brooke cancelled, and Liza hasn't shown up yet."

"Okay." Raising his voice so that he knew he could be heard, he shouted out, "Come on, India. Get a move on and let's get going!"

"Coming," she yelled back.

She was breathing rapidly, from the excitement of seeing him again and also because she was slightly nervous at being with a strange class. She still didn't feel that sure of herself in the gym routines yet, though she knew that Lanny would keep her from looking foolish.

She loved the way his face lit up at the sight of her. And her smile was every bit as bright, she knew.

"Hi," they said simultaneously.

Lanny laughed and said they ought to get started because the missing Liza was notorious for being late.

India felt slightly foolish at being the only one in the gym with Lanny, but as he began jumping in place opposite her, she did the same.

Since she was the only person he had to drill and she mirrored him perfectly when he switched from one exercise to the next, he didn't even bother to count aloud. They moved together, opposite each other, in perfect rhythm and total silence for many minutes.

Noticing that India was tiring, Lanny called out, "Enough," and they both stopped for a moment.

"Looks like you're going to have a private lesson," he observed, glancing at the clock on the wall.

It showed ten past the hour.

"It's funny, but it's much more tiring working out by yourself," said India.

"That's why private lessons usually run only thirty-five to forty-five minutes."

Looking around him to check the sight lines from the waiting room through the glass walls of the gym, Lanny said quietly, "And if we move over here a bit to work, no one will be able to see what we're doing."

Laughing in spite of herself, India said, "What'd you have in mind?"

"Nothing that I'd dare try here," he retorted, "but somehow you always inspire a need for privacy in me."

India quickly moved toward the corner of the room where he was standing and faced him.

They began an easy stretching routine and started to talk.

"Did you miss me?" asked Lanny mischievously.

"God, you know I did! It's been a whole week since I've seen you. Our dinner last Wednesday night seems like a million years ago. Of course I missed you."

"Sometimes I wish there were two of you," said Lanny pensively.

"One for you and one for my family?"

"You got it."

"You'd get tired of me," India teased.

"Try me," was the prompt reply.

"I guess neither of us expected it to turn out this way," said India between deep bends.

Lanny looked at her with such love in his eyes that she almost melted.

"No," he said softly. "And if it weren't for seeing you every Wednesday night, I don't think I could stand it. I love you, you know."

"I know. I feel the same way."

"Do you think it would ever be possible for us to spend a whole night together?" he asked wistfully.

"Don't know." India was brief because she was running out of breath.

"Stop for a minute, darling. You need to take a rest."

India obliged willingly.

As Lanny moved over to her side, she automatically drew away.

"Don't," she said in a whisper.

Lanny grinned. "Okay, have it your way. I just want to see how you'll do going over in a back bend all by yourself."

India blushed and laughed. "Oops. Sorry. I forget we're in a class. Okay, come on. Put your arms around me. You know I can't do it alone."

Lanny responded swiftly.

"I never need a second invitation to put my arms around you."

For a moment, he was all instructor again. "Okay, slowly now. Bend with your legs first, sight over behind you at the floor, ease down just a bit . . . and now drop," he commanded.

India let herself drop and was pleasantly surprised at the ease with which she caught herself on the palms of her hands.

"You're getting better," said Lanny approvingly. "I really wasn't touching you at all. I just had my hands lightly under you, ready to catch, in case."

From her arched position, India beamed at his approval.

"Now what, chief?"

"Now move your hands back, inch them along, and try to get them closer toward your feet so you get a higher arch."

India started to laugh.

"I lose my sense of direction in this silly position," she spluttered.

Suddenly her beautiful arch collapsed and she fell to the floor laughing.

"Boffo finish, but not exactly Olympic material," said Lanny, reaching down a hand to help her up.

When he pulled her to her feet, their faces came so close that he reached the extra inch and kissed her lightly.

"Lanny!"

"Sorry about that. I couldn't help myself."

"You're not sorry at all, and you know it."

"And you are right!" he said. "Okay. Two

rotations forward, legs together, and land on your feet."

India groaned before responding.

"That's hard and you know it."

"That's hard and you can do it." He mimicked her tone of voice.

India even surprised herself when she smoothly executed two forward rotations, legs straight as an arrow, and landed on her feet.

"You are getting better and you don't even realize it!" said Lanny. "When am I ever going to teach you to appreciate how really wonderful you are?"

India shrugged modestly.

"Bars?" asked Lanny next.

"Sure, but you've got to help me there, you know.

The parallel bars were in full view of the waiting room, so India and Lanny were carefully business-like as she went through her routine.

"Even that's getting better, and those are tough moves," commented Lanny when she had finished.

After a quick workout on the rings, Lanny told her to hang loosely from them, and he walked her out into a long stretch for her back.

Reluctantly, he let go of her at last and whispered "See you tonight" in her ear.

She nodded.

"Seven?"

"Six-thirty. I'm dumping Ivan's six o'clock class on Alexander. I can't wait until seven to see you."

India smiled and then called out loudly, for Darlene's benefit, "Good class. Thanks, Lanny."

"The pleasure was all mine," he said softly after her departing figure.

The night was cold and India couldn't find a taxi

so she decided to walk the eight or so blocks to Lanny's apartment. Later, she decided that that had been her first mistake.

As she walked briskly along the darkened neighborhood streets, she was aware of footsteps behind her. She paid no attention at first, but then she began to notice that the sound of them seemed to slow when she slowed and quicken when she quickened.

She tried to sneak an unobtrusive glance over her shoulder, but she could not catch sight of whoever it was. Then she tried the ploy of crossing the street. To her alarm, she heard the person behind her cross also.

She began to feel her first prickles of panic. She hurried her pace and tried to stay well out onto the sidewalk.

It was only a few more blocks now.

When she was within a block of Lanny's, she could control her panic no more and she broke into a run. She heard the footsteps behind her begin to pick up.

She slammed into the entry door of Lanny's apartment, with the key already clutched in her numbed fingers.

She fumbled with the lock for only a moment before the key slid smoothly in and turned. She slammed the door shut behind her and raced up the first flight of stairs, not even pausing to look back.

When she heard no sound of anyone trying to force the door downstairs, she slowed her speed a bit but still kept going breathlessly.

As she turned up the last flight of stairs to Lanny's apartment, she heard his door open.

To her immense relief, he was standing there waiting for her.

One look at her face however, and he was all concern.

"India, what's the matter? What happened?" He

grabbed her in his arms before she could even answer him. "You're shaking like a leaf!"

Without meaning to, she burst into tears.

He led her inside and over to the couch.

"Come on, what's the matter, darling? You're all right now. There, there," he said, folding her in his arms again.

Through her muffled sobs, she told him what had happened.

"Let me get you a good, stiff drink," he offered and went into the kitchen to mix her a scotch and soda.

"There now, drink this. You'll feel better.

India obediently drank her drink.

Lanny meanwhile fumed at her. "Look, I hate to lecture you in the state you're in, but you should never, repeat, never wander around the streets of Manhattan alone after dark. Understand?"

She nodded like a repentant child.

"I was so anxious to get to you and there wasn't a cab in sight," she offered by way of explanation.

"Honestly, India. I can understand that, but I never want you to put yourself in jeopardy like that again, understand?"

Snuffling, again she nodded.

Lanny went into his bedroom, grabbed a comforter off his bed, and brought it back to tuck around her. As he leaned over her, he kissed her cheek tenderly and said, "You mean too much to me to ever have anything happen to you."

She returned his kiss gratefully. Then he moved from her and lit the fire that was already set in the small, open-hearth stove.

"That should get you warmed up soon. You still look frozen."

Then he brought his tiny Panasonic TV set over, put it on the coffee table in front of her, and switched on the evening news.

"That should keep you entertained while I get the spaghetti and meatballs going. Now, stay put, drink your drink, and warm up. Dinner'll be ready in a jiffy. We have to feed you to keep your strength up," he finished with a smile.

India smiled back and snuggled down under his comforter happily.

It was so nice to be looked after and fussed over. It seemed like such a long time since anyone had taken care of her, instead of the other way around.

Lanny insisted on serving supper to her on the coffee table and otherwise coddling and babying her. "Come on," she protested. "I'm not an invalid!"

"You need someone to look after you, India. And I'm applying for the job."

"Sorry it has to be only part-time," she whispered in his ear as she leaned over to kiss him.

"Me too," said Lanny. His regret was obvious in his voice.

Later he took her into the bedroom and made love to her tenderly and sweetly. She found it very hard to get dressed and leave the warmth of his bed that night.

Thursday morning at nine-forty-five Jade sailed into Ivan & Igor's like a battleship under full steam. She didn't even bother to return Darlene's happily chirped, "Good morning, Jade."

She tore her gym bag off its hook, slammed into a dressing room, and dropped her purse with a thud on one of the upholstered benches. Her expression looked like a thundercloud about to turn into a storm.

Several moments later, Cricket popped in, looking

336

all around her cautiously. "She's not here?" she asked in a low voice before dropping her things to change.

"Who?" snapped Jade, then, seeing Cricket and realizing what the other woman was talking about, she changed her tone. "You mean India. No, I haven't seen her."

"Hey, what's up with you? You look like you'd like to slug someone," remarked Cricket, relaxing visibly once she realized they were alone.

"I would and his name is Parkinson!" snarled Jade.

"Ah, yes, the illustrious head of your network, as I recall. What's he done now? Aced you out of that spot you wanted?"

"No, not yet. But I suppose it's only a matter of time. And I suppose I'd better get used to the idea."

"So, what's he done?" asked Cricket curiously. She pulled her leotard from her gym bag and began to squirm into it.

Jade was already changed, so she sat down and began to puff angrily on a cigarette.

"This morning he drops into my office all sweetness and light, to discuss, I thought, the daytime programming. I brought up the evening slot that was opening up and told him how much I'd like a crack at it. And without so much as batting an eyelash, he smoothly says he's interested in buying some property in Connecticut for a weekend house now that he's settled here on the East Coast and how would I like to go up to the country for the weekend with him, to act as an adviser, as he so quaintly put it."

"And?" urged Cricket.

"And I said most politely that the place I had for weekends was in South Hampton and that my

337

knowledge of Connecticut real estate would therefore not be all that helpful, figuring he'd take the hint."

"So?"

"So he steamrolled right over that remark and said he'd heard that there were some pretty old inns up there and that it might be nice and cozy to relax in front of a roaring fire and drink mulled wine in the northwestern corner of Connecticut!"

Cricket gave a final tug to her leotard and reached down to pull on leg warmers. "And you said . . ."

"I wanted to say 'screw you,' but it was all too clear that that's exactly what he had in mind!"

Cricket chuckled.

"Don't laugh. As far as I can see, I made my pitch and he made a counter proposal and I don't care for his terms. And furthermore, I'm damned angry about it!"

Cricket flopped down beside Jade on the bench.

"Look, maybe he's really crazy about you and he just wants to be all alone with you for a romantic weekend."

"Yeah, and maybe Adolf Hitler was really a great humanitarian, but I wouldn't want to put any money on it," snapped Jade sarcastically.

"Oh, ho! Do I catch a shade of religious prejudice in your meaning?" asked Cricket, arching one daintily penciled eyebrow.

"That's putting it mildly. That bastard is the biggest anti-Semite since Hitler. I know from past experience," she added icily. "Furthermore, I resent mixing business with pleasure or having that monster try to put the make on me with a professional promise dangling. Griggs Parkinson is an ass and a phony and I have no intention of sleeping with him for either business or—heaven for bid—pleasure."

"Don't knock it 'til—"

"Oh, shut up, Cricket! I really hate the bastard and I resent being put in this position."

"So what do you do now?"

"I pray he gets hit by a truck. Oh, yes, and what's even worse is, after this stupid conversation, I have to smile nicely and ask him to Ivan's damn Show and Tell in two weeks."

"My, my, we are a bit upset today—"

At this point their conversation was interrupted by Lanny calling out loudly, "Front and center, everybody. It's showtime!"

"Damn!" said Jade as she ground out her cigarette.

"Come on, you can work out your aggressions on the flying trapeze," said Cricket gaily.

Her gaiety vanished however when she entered the gym and the first person she saw was India, who was jumping up and down in place.

Cricket tried unobtrusively to move as far away from the woman as she could. Even the sight of India's happy face irritated her today. She had been mulling over what she had discovered on Tuesday and even had briefly considered telling Andy that she was in a gym class with his wife, but she had quickly dismissed that thought as pure folly. She certainly did not want to risk scaring him off with fear of a possible slip or, worse yet, the thought that she might precipitate a confrontation.

No, it was just as well that Andrew Travick had no knowledge of how closely his twin lives were to crashing into each other.

Lanny was waiting expectantly for them to line up when Annie bounced into the room.

"You can start now. Miss Olympic Gold is here!" she called out.

"Let's get going, ladies," said Lanny. "Jump in

place and then let's start stretching it out. Ready? One and two and . . ."

The four women in front of him began jumping in time to his count and his eyes flicked over them impersonally as they warmed up.

Annie seemed her bright and lively old self again; for a few weeks there Lanny had noticed that she really had been dragging. Jade looked like she was mad as hell about something and was determined not to take it any more. Cricket looked, well, somehow uneasy. She kept losing the count and when Lanny would call it to her attention, she would swear under her breath and change her pace jerkily. That wasn't like the easygoing Cricket that Lanny was used to.

And India, well, India was her usual wonderful, beautiful self. Lanny had to make a conscious effort not to let his love show in his eyes when he looked at her. He couldn't help wondering what kind of a jackass she was married to that didn't appreciate what a special human being she was. She was so real in this world of aritifcial women, so warm and human in a coterie of cool and calculating females who had success programmed into every fiber of their beings.

"Okay. Enough. Let's try some individual floor work. India, would you like to lead off?" he asked as dispassionately as he could.

India moved over to stand next to him on the mat and waited expectantly for his instructions.

Chapter 39

After class, Lanny asked Annie if she could stay awhile and work on some aerials. As long as her mood was so buoyant, he decided, he might as well take advantage of it. She agreed readily and waved a good-bye to her departing classmates.

India ducked into a dressing room by herself while Cricket headed into the same one she and Jade had shared earlier.

"So do you have time for some coffee or are you headed out for an appointment?" asked Cricket as they dressed.

"Let's stop for some. I don't really have time, but if I go back to the office now and run into that bastard, I just may slug him."

"Nice talk. I thought a good workout would get rid of all your aggressions."

"It'll take more than that to get rid of how I feel about his latest ploy," Jade said bitterly as she threw on her clothes.

Soon they were sitting in a booth in the coffee shop downstairs, and Cricket decided that her best bet would be to talk about less inflammatory subjects.

"So how's your little boy, what's his name, Mark?"

"Precocious, of course," answered Jade with amusement. "Shelley asked him the other day what he'd like to be when he grew up, and do you know what he said?"

Cricket arched an eyebrow in question.

"He said he wanted to be a corporate raider!"

"And he's what—eight years old? That's precocious, I'd say."

"I think he secretly watches the *MacNeil-Lehrer Report* instead of *Mr. Rogers*," declared Jade.

"Speaking of Shelley, how's she doing?"

Jade's face lit up. "Shelley finally seems to have gotten her act together. She's really buckled down and is working hard at her schoolwork. I hear her in there studying until all hours of the morning. I knew she could do it if she'd just try to apply herself. I guess my threat about the return-trip ticket to Augusta really shook her up."

"Sometimes it takes a little gentle persuasion," observed Cricket.

Jade lapsed into silence and Cricket searched for another topic. "By the way, did you see Ivan when you came in this morning/"

"I went tearing in there in such a rage that I wouldn't have noticed King Kong in pajamas!"

"Well, he was hobbling around in his back brace and he went to great pains to explain to me that he can only stand up or lie down."

"And you said?"

"I merely commented that he'd be great at a cocktail party or an orgy but that I wouldn't invite him to any sit-down dinners for awhile."

"I'd say, 'You didn't,' but knowing you, you *did*!"

Cricket chuckled. "I did."

Jade sipped her coffee and stared off into the distance.

"Well, we might as well talk about it. What are you going to do now that Mr. Not-so-wonderful made his pass and you turned him down?" Cricket asked.

Jade sighed.

"Do what we women always do. Go back to the office and work twice as hard as every man in sight to get that nighttime spot."

"It was ever thus," commented Cricket wryly. "I must say that that's one of the things I like about the travel writing biz. I think you find less sexism there than in most professions."

"Just tell me one thing," burst out Jade abruptly. "Why is it that when a woman actively pursues something, they say she's pushy, whereas when a man does it, they call him aggressive?"

And before she knew it, Jade was pouring out the whole ugly story of what had happened with Griggs years before, including the fact that she had fallen half in love with him and had overheard his odious comments about her.

"No wonder he's so high on your shit list. He is *not* a nice man."

"That's putting it mildly."

"Well, speaking of nice men, do you ever hear from your senator, Kendall Court?"

"No, and I don't really expect to. His career plans call for a wife right now, and I can't do that number."

"But why? You were in love with him, weren't you? Was your first marriage that bad that you won't try it again?"

Jade turned pensive. "I was and am still in love with him, I guess. And no, it's not that the first time turned me off that much. It just has to do with what we were talking about before—role-playing. He needs a wife-type, and I don't think I can fill that role with a job like mine."

"Come on, there are lots of two-career marriages nowadays."

"I don't mean to sound elitist, but not with the kind of job I have. I mean, I sometimes get a call to do a remote from halfway around the world with only an hour's notice. I have Mrs. Swann, my housekeeper, to fill in with Mark, but where do I get a fill-in wife? Not to mention the fact that we live on different coasts. No, I've thought about it and thought about it and there's no way that I can see that it would work."

Cricket said nothing and Jade continued.

"Listen, if you're so all-fired sold on marriage, why don't *you* try it?"

"I have one small problem. He's already married, remember?"

"India's husband, you mean?"

"One and the same, as they say."

"You're really that sure that you're in love with him?"

"Oh, Jade, he's special. Andy is really one of the most wonderful men I've ever met. You'd love him!"

"No thanks," said Jade dryly. "I think he has quite enough women loving him now!"

They sat in silence for a few moments, then Jade spoke.

"You know what they say about women who fall in love with married men? It's a kind of safety net. He's already married, so there's no danger of your getting permanently involved."

"Don't tell me about not wanting to be involved, especially around the holiday time. You know how you can tell which woman is having an affair with a married man?"

Jade nodded negatively.

"She's the one with lots of presents around the tree

and nary a date in sight!"

"That could be one of the most persuasive arguments I've ever heard for marriage. At least you always have a date for New Year's Eve! Lord, remember how important that used to be—way back in the dark ages?"

"Tell me about it! I used to start worrying about it sometime right after Labor Day!" Cricket agreed with a laugh.

"Speaking of dates, I can't imagine that your friend Andy is very available on nights and weekends. When do you see each other?"

"We have lunch about once a week—lunch that usually ends up back at my apartment, I might add. And I think he really feels very guilty about it. I told you, he's honestly such a sweet guy."

"They say the nice ones are always married."

"Yeah, and they say nice guys don't win ball games either, so maybe you can triumph over your buddy, Griggs What's-his-name."

"Honey, he's been accused of many things, but never of being a nice guy!"

Cricket reached for the check. "This one's on me. You've got enough trouble back there at the network ranch without being accused of padding the expense account!"

The two women parted with an affectionate hug outside on the street.

"See you next week," said Jade.

"Don't let the bastards get you down!" called Cricket in reply.

Ivan was feeling very good about the party. The food was ordered, the waiters hired, the decorations planned, and the exhibitions rehearsed. Though he was in constant pain from his back injury and he was careful to avoid dark streets at night, he felt that he had obtained a temporary reprieve at least. Nothing untoward had happened since his accident, and he thought that perhaps his debtors felt he had been sufficiently punished for the moment.

Besides, his other "little plan" had begun to bear fruit. It was not something he ever wanted to have to use, but he thought of it as an "insurance policy." If all went well and the network people were as intrigued with his television show idea as he thought they would be, he would never have to use it.

In the meantime, Ivan decided he could use all the insurance he could get.

Annie's screen test was scheduled for early that morning and she was in good spirits. Her weight was down, she felt good, and Ferrago kept telling her how wonderful she would be.

"You'll knock 'em dead, kid! You really will! They will fall out of their trees when they see you up there on that screen. You never looked better, and remember, that camera *loves* your face! You're going to be a smash!"

The funny thing was, for the first time in her life, Annie believed him.

She dressed very carefully, choosing a soft knitted cashmere sheath in a brilliant electric cherry color, a shade so vibrant that it almost seemed to throb with light. It showed off her mocha skin and long, shining black hair to their best advantage. Her large dark eyes seemed to sparkle and snap. She *looked* like a star, she realized.

Tucking her well-thumbed copy of the script they had given her in her model's bag, she went out to the living room area of the loft, where Ferrago was waiting for her.

"So, what do you think?" she asked, twirling around for his inspection and approval.

Ferrago took in every detail of her appearance carefully.

When at last he spoke, he spoke slowly.

"I think we'd better start making plans to move west, that's what I think!"

She ran into his arms and hugged him. Then they skipped down the stairs and out into the street to find a cab that would take them uptown.

India was in a terrible quandary as to what to do about Ivan's stupid Russian Christmas party. Ivan had requested most sincerely that India take part in the exercise warmup demonstration, along with Shelley and several other attractive women. She felt flattered because she knew it meant that Ivan thought she looked good enough to show off, and, of course, Lanny had told her how carefully Ivan had picked and chosen. Yet her better judgment told her she should stay far, far away from the whole thing. Why in the world should she want to expose her husband and lover to each other?

The matter had been complicated by the fact that Ivan had sent out pretentious engraved invitations, and hers had arrived on a Saturday when Drew had been home and had opened the mail.

She had come back from running an errand that day and had found the children chattering about how Mommy was going to be in a show at her gym.

She had seen the opened invitation on the hall table and had tried to treat it nonchalantly.

To her horror, Drew had seemed to think the

whole thing was marvelous.

"This sounds like fun. Will you be one of the 'student exhibitions' it mentions?" he had asked.

India had stammered a little and had told him that she'd been asked to be part of it but had thought that Drew would think it a bore.

"Not at all. I'd love to see this fancy gym of yours. Hey, you've been going there long enough now. I'd love to see what goes on."

India had cringed inwardly at his choice of words and had tried another tack.

"It'll probably be awful. I understand from Jade that Ivan is using the whole thing as an excuse to snag the attention of some network people with an eye to getting his own television show."

It had been the worst possible thing she could have said. Drew's attention had been instantly hooked.

"You're kidding? That means your buddy Jade Greene will be there? I'd love to get a look at her in person!"

"Oh, for God's sake, Drew, grow up! Aren't you a little old to be a celebrity hound?" she had snapped and had been instantly sorry.

Drew's face had fallen at the sharpness of her remark. He had looked so hurt that she had found herself trying to make it up to him.

"I didn't mean to sound so waspish. I guess I'm just self-conscious about my gym work. Sure we can go if you'd like to," she had told him in a much softer tone.

Drew had brightened.

"Great. I'm really looking forward to it. Get Mrs. Schmidt lined up for that night. We'll make an evening of it. It says, 'dress optional.' Shall I drag out the old dinner jacket so we can impress your elegant classmates?"

India had felt wretched at his boyish enthusiasm.

She had also felt like a rat. She knew she would have to warn Lanny. She was sure he could handle it—probably better than she could. Sometimes he seemed a lot more mature than she was.

Damn, she cursed inwardly. It was going to be a weird party.

It took all of Jade's composure to enable her to stroll casually into Griggs's office at the beginning of the next week and toss Ivan's invitation onto the desk.

A promise was a promise and she'd promised Ivan that she'd deliver Parkinson. Besides, she rationalized, the exercise show was still not a bad idea and the more good ideas for which she could take credit, the harder it would be for Griggs to elbow her out when the time came for him to make a decision.

Griggs looked up and gave her his most practiced, charming smile.

"Oh, hi there Jade. What have we here?" he asked, picking up the creamy, engraved invitation.

Jade made a tremendous effort to match his pleasantness. It wasn't easy.

"Just an invitation to a thing that's happening at the gym I go to—Ivan & Igor's place. I'm sure you've heard about it. Lots of females working out to keep their bodies in shape. Ivan is giving a party and a gym exhibition, and I'd like you to take a look. I think it has possibilities as a daytime feature."

Griggs's smile widened and he raised his well-groomed eyebrows.

"Am I to have the pleasure of escorting you to this *soiree?*"

He's all but licking his chops, she thought sourly. Don't get your hopes up, you lech!

"I thought if you wouldn't mind, it might be fun,"

she said with excessive casualness.

"The pleasure is mine, my dear. Shall we have dinner first?"

"Sorry, can't possibly do that. I'm going to be part of this three-ring circus at one point, and I don't do tricks on the rings on a full stomach."

Griggs looked even more intrigued.

"Well, well. I get to see the famous Jade Greene perform! This should be quite an evening."

The understatement of the year, thought Jade.

Cricket found herself looking forward to Ivan's dumb party with a kind of fatal fascination. She wasn't sure whether or not India was going to be there, because she didn't care to get cozy enough with the woman to ask her, things being the way they were.

But, what the hell? she thought. Why should it matter? It would most likely shake the daylights out of Andy, but maybe that would be for the best, too.

Their weekly lunches were a regular thing now, but their relationship seemed to have reached a sticking point. When she had Andy in bed, she knew he was helpless to resist her, but once they were out of bed, she could feel him try to remove himself emotionally. It was as though he couldn't bear to face how truly involved with her he was. As long as his denial mechanisms were in place, he could keep her compartmentalized. She didn't want to be compartmentalized. She wanted to *star* in his life.

The more determined he became to keep her at arm's length, the more determined she became to break down his defenses. Perhaps seeing the two women in his life side by side would be the best thing that could happen.

Cricket was confident she could outshine *any* competition when she put her mind to it. And she had already determined that she was going to look absolutely ravishing that evening.

Her biggest advantage was that, of the three people involved, she was the only one who knew that the confrontation would occur. Her biggest problem that night would be acting perfectly cool and composed.

She felt certain she could carry it off—and come away the winner, the way she always had.

Ferrago told Annie that the reaction to her screen test was very positive. The people who had seen it on the East Coast were ecstatic. They were waiting now for the West Coast Reaction.

"I really think you've got it made, kid. I think this is just the beginning of a great new career for you!"

Annie was sky-high with excitement. She was happy that things were looking so good and happy because she hadn't let Ferrago down.

Their bubbly enthusiasm made them feel as if they could conquer the world.

When she mentioned the party at Ivan & Igor's, Ferrago said expansively that he'd hire a limo for the evening so a future star could go in style, as he put it. He also told her that she'd better find out from Ivan where Igor's place in L.A. was, because she'd be doing her sit-ups out there before she knew it.

Annie knew that her aerials were going to be a breeze, because she felt like she was walking on air.

She was also going to cut out all the pills once they were settled out there. There wasn't a pill in the world that could compare with the heady intoxication of success.

Chapter 40

On the Saturday night of the party, it would have been difficult to recognize Ivan & Igor's as a gymnasium. Ivan had outdone himself. Beginning with the scarlet carpeting he had rented to have installed in the downstairs foyer and the colorfully costumed Cossack he had hired to run the elevator for the evening, Ivan had transformed the whole of the place into a gaily decorated twinkling, greenery-bedecked fantasy of a Russian Christmas.

Normal lighting had been replaced with tiny, glittering bulbs that sparkled from the depths of the boughs that graced the ceiling and walls of the waiting room. Darlene's large desk had been covered with an enormous, colorful paisley shawl and served as a spacious bar, presided over by a tall, Russian-looking bartender wearing a high fur hat.

The main gymnasium had been turned into a ballroom. In one corner a small group of costumed musicians tuned their instruments and, against the wall, a long buffet table was set with a multitude of silver chafing dishes and staffed by a group of elaborately dressed Russian waiters—Ivan had hired all his help from off-duty personnel at The Russian

Tea Room. There were no traces of the normal gym equipment. Innumerable candelabra had been set around the room to give off a romantic glow and the ceiling had been lowered by means of billowing draperies in brilliant jewellike colors. There was even incense burning in small containers secreted around the room, enveloping everything in an exotic scent.

Presiding over the whole of this Slavic fantasy was Ivan himself, looking debonair and distinguished in his elegantly cut velvet dinner jacket. In order to be properly dressed for this festive occasion, he had forced himself into a smaller, cagelike back brace, which was so constraining that he could hardly breathe. It was completely concealed, however, by his ivory satin evening shirt, brocade cummerbund, and damask vest. It had taken him ages to manage to dress himself, but the result was more than worth the effort. Except for a certain stiffness in his bearing, no one would realize he was so corseted. It irked him beyond belief that the brace prevented him from making his usual slight bow from the waist, but he compensated for this with a gracious nod of the head as he greeted his guests.

Among the first wave of people to arrive was Cricket, looking completely dazzling in a long white gown covered from décolletage to hem with crystal-beaded fringe that danced and glittered with every movement of her slim figure. Her blond curls sparkled, rainbow crystals showered in tiny water-falls from her earlobes, and her dark brown eyes danced with anticipation.

"Ah, my dear Cricket," gushed Ivan. "You look positively ravishing tonight!" He pressed her hand to his lips.

"Perhaps I'll get ravished then," she shot back at

him as she tossed her white-fox evening coat to an attendant.

She was swirled into the group that surged toward the bar, leaving Ivan to greet the next arrivals.

Griggs Parkinson had been less than pleased when he had called for Jade and had discovered that Jade's niece, Shelley, was accompanying them to the party, but he had put a good face on it and had said something about "the unexpected pleasure of escorting two lovely ladies for the evening."

They did look lovely. Jade's more mature attractiveness was in no way diminished by Shelley's youthful freshness. Shelley was delighted with the way she looked in her first black dress, a simple, short, velvet frock, lavishly trimmed at the collar and cuffs with creamy, knotted, Irish lace. The dress showed off perfectly her blond prettiness and Jade had helped her do up her hair in a wispy knot, with tendrils of curls framing her face.

Jade's was a sophisticated look. She wore an emerald satin gown with a strapless bodice and a gracefully wrapped skirt that just touched the floor. Her copper hair glistened in a sleak, upswept coiffure, and her sparkling green cat's eyes were matched perfectly by the diamond and emerald ear clips she wore. She looked radiant and, more importantly, she looked successful—something that was vital in her business.

She made the proper introductions between Ivan and Griggs when they arrived, and Ivan's obsequiousness was almost painful to watch. He told Griggs that he was deeply honored that so important a personage would grace his little "family get-together," and he expressed his most sincere wishes that Griggs would find it an "interesting evening."

Griggs accepted Ivan's fawning with an amused diffidence.

Shelley squealed with happiness when she spotted Anastacia and Ferrago through the crowd, and Jade told her to go over and join them if she wished and that they would catch up with her later.

It would have been hard to miss Anastacia in any crowd. She stood out like a glittering beacon, even in a roomful of New York's glitterati.

Annie wore an orange-to-citron-shaded ombre chiffon gown that made her tall, lithe figure look as though it were being licked with tongues of flame. Her glistening long black hair fanned out from her face like a gigantic lion's mane and she carried herself with a style and assurance visible to everyone in the room. She was laughing and chatting with a group, her arm linked possessively through Ferrago's. Ferrago was content to play the passive escort and he beamed with an almost paternal pride as Annie recounted the excitement of her screen test.

Shelley pushed through the crowd and Annie greeted her enthusiastically, exclaiming over how pretty she looked tonight.

"Isn't this exciting? I see so many famous people here. I had no idea they all came to Ivan & Igor's," whispered Shelley in an aside to Annie.

"That's because you only see your Aunt Jade's class. Ivan hustles them through here all day and lots of them take private lessons in the rooms upstairs, so you never see them. They want the world to think they were born with perfect bodies," whispered Annie in return.

"Did you see all that food? I don't even know what half of it is."

"It's all Ivan's Russian specialties, and don't go

stuffing yourself, because we have to put on our little show yet, remember?''

Shelley giggled. "Good grief, I almost forgot. What time do we do that?''

"Ivan will slip us a high sign when we're supposed to disappear and change. I'm sure he wants to wait until some of this booze puts the crowd in a receptive frame of mind. I wish he'd hurry it up, though. I'm dying for some champagne, but if I drink any now, I'll fall flat on my fanny in my floor routine.''

India and Drew had just walked in and were still out in the reception area, chatting with Ivan. India couldn't help glancing around nervously as the two men talked. She didn't see Lanny anywhere in the crush, and she half-dreaded, half-wished to get their meeting over with.

India had chosen a simple chocolate-colored panne velvet theater suit to wear tonight. She wore pearls at her ears and throat and looked a great deal more calm and composed than she felt. No one observing the attractive and stylish young matron with her arm linked casually through her husband's would have guessed at her inner turmoil.

Suddenly, in the midst of the conversation, she felt Drew's whole body stiffen and she searched wildly around with her eyes, guiltily thinking he had seen Lanny and had guessed her secret.

To her relief, the only familiar face she saw was Cricket's as her classmate waved and made her way toward them through the crowd.

Andrew stood rooted to the spot as Cricket approached them, wondering what in the world Cricket was doing here and thinking frantically how he could explain his acquaintance with her to India.

To his utter astonishment, when she reached them, it was to India she spoke, not to him.

357

"Hi, India! What do you think of this madhouse?" asked Cricket with a grin, flicking her eyes only momentarily over Drew's face with no sign of recognition.

He was flooded with relief so great that he was dumbstruck.

"It's good fun, isn't it? Oh, Cricket, this is my husband, Andrew. Drew, this is one of my classmates, Cricket Wells."

Cricket looked up innocently into Andrew's eyes and said demurely, "How nice to meet you." She had been about to add wickedly, "You wife's told me so much about you," but one look at his stricken countenance had made her spare him the agony.

Drew mumbled something unintelligible.

Had India been less wrapped up in her own private agitation, she might have noticed his discomfort, but so preoccupied was she that it all went right by her.

Cricket made idle chatter for a few more moments before moving away to another group, much to Andrew's relief.

At last India caught sight of Lanny's handsome face through the throng. Swallowing bravely, she gave Drew's arm a little tug and said, "Come on. there's someone you ought to meet. It's my gym instructor."

Lanny noticed instantly that they were headed his way. He had been watching India from afar from the moment she'd stepped off the elevator. But he had felt it would be more tactful to let her approach him, rather than the other way around.

He stood prepared to face the coming ordeal and reminded himself to try not to dislike her husband.

India handled the introductions more smoothly than she had thought possible, and Lanny was formally polite to Andrew. He couldn't bring himself to meet India's eyes, however. India felt an overwhelming surge of love as she watched his beautiful face and saw how hard he was trying to remain dispassionate. She felt she could see into his mind and read the pain that was registering there.

It was with much gratitude that she heard him say it was time for the women to go change into leotards because Ivan was about to usher the guests into an upstairs gym where the exhibition would take place.

He stiffly said good-bye to Drew and wove his way through the crowd to round up the other gymnasts.

"Seems pleasant enough," said Drew, though India couldn't remember having asked his opinion. "You never mentioned how good-looking he was."

She rushed off to change, mulling over whether or not Andrew had meant anything by his comment.

The dressing rooms seemed crowded, even though there was a total of only sixteen women taking part in the exhibition. The bulk of their formal gowns occupied much of what was usually free space. Cricket and Jade were squeezed into a corner of their usual room.

Jade asked Cricket *sotto voce* how it was going.

Cricket whispered back that the person in question seemed a trifle uncomfortable, but that she herself was handling it rather well.

Jade smiled at Cricket's utter confidence in her ability to handle anything.

Meanwhile, Ivan was most politely hurrying people up the spiral stairway to the largest of the upstairs gyms.

"We will adjourn for a few moments to the upper

level, so that you might see what my pupils have accomplished." He smiled as he indicated the way the crowd should proceed.

Inwardly, he was wincing with pain from that infernal back brace. He had laced it too tightly in his vanity and now he was suffering the consequences. There was nothing he could do at the moment, but as soon as the show was over and he had properly settled people back in the main room, he vowed he would absent himself long enough to adjust it.

The upstairs room maintained the look of an elegant gymnasium, though Ivan had arranged to have all the equipment at one end and several spotlights rigged to focus on that area. In that corner stood Lanny and Misha, looking faintly uncomfortable in their standard white shirts and green gym pants amidst the formality of the guests' attire.

Ivan strode to that end of the room and clapped his hands for attention. Then he made a short, flowery speech about the loveliness of his ladies and the beauties of a well-maintained body. He stole a quick glance at his watch, knowing that the taped music he had programmed to accompany the demonstration would begin promptly at eight-thirty. It was eight-twenty-nine.

He indicated the end of his talk with a jerky nod of his head and basked as the expected applause came from the assemblage.

At exactly eight-thirty, the first notes of a Bach fugue flowed from the various concealed speakers in the gym, and Cricket, waiting with the others just outside the room, whispered one word to Jade. "Pretentious."

Jade nodded agreement as the women moved into place inside, where Lanny would lead them efficiently through the paces of a carefully choreographed warmup.

The whole exhibition flowed smoothly. The women felt self-confident and were all secretly pleased to have been given the opportunity to show off their hitherto unviewed acrobatic skills.

Cricket had worn a white leotard for her turn on the bars and as she whipped through her solo routine, spotted by both Lanny and Misha, she felt like she was in the main ring at the circus.

Jade worked in tandem with another woman on a second set of rings, and their precision drew a round of applause when they dropped to the mat and did quick somersaults to their feet simultaneously for a finale.

Annie was a flash of vitality in her floor routine and India found herself wishing that she had been coming to the gym long enough to have qualified for a solo turn.

Shelley was just excited to be there.

Then it was over. Ivan wisely had paced it swiftly and had kept it short enough to that people were left wishing for more. The enthusiastic applause that greeted the close signaled that it had been a success.

The women all reentered the room on the run, took swift bows, and disappeared to the changing rooms.

Ivan had nervously kept his eye on Griggs Parkinson's reaction to the show, and what he had noted had been encouraging. Though Griggs had seemed at first only politely attentive, as the show had progressed, his expression had become interested and calculating. Ivan planned to corner him later for a private chat.

First he had to shepherd this group safely down the stairs, get the party moving again, and then seek some sanctuary to remove and relace the back brace, which was killing him.

Back in the changing rooms, the women were chattering and laughing, flushed with success and exertion. Ivan had thoughtfully provided magnums of champagne, chilling in silver buckets, in each dressing room. The sound of popping corks mingled with their squeals of delight.

India didn't bother with a glass of champagne but quickly changed into her velvet suit. The only thing on her mind was getting back downstairs to Drew's side and preventing any further contact between him and Lanny. Her best bet was to keep a safe distance between them. She didn't trust either of them not to in some way betray their feelings.

Still in their gym clothes, Cricket and Jade poured tall flutes of the bubbly and toasted each other. Noting that some of the others were grabbing glasses and taking them downstairs so that they could mingle with the guests, Cricket suggested they do the same. "Come on," she said to Jade. "You look smashing in your leotard! Let's go down and accept some accolades on our sterling performances."

Shelley was with Anastacia, who was thirsty and pooped from her routine, so they sat and drank for awhile, until the others had left.

Shelley kept telling Annie how magnificent she had looked out in the spotlight.

"Yeah, well, maybe when I get to Hollywood, they'll find out I'm so good that I don't even need a double for the action scenes! You know what I feel like doing? I feel like *dancing!* Let's go downstairs and get Ivan to put on some *good* music and show this crowd how to boogie, okay?"

Shelley thought that anything Annie did was fine with her, so she trailed behind her, down to the floor below.

The din from the group in the main gym hit a

loud pitch as people mingled with those who had performed and congratulated them on their proficiency. People who might have been reluctant to approach Jade in her role as TV celebrity had no such inhibitions about seeking her out now and telling her how marvelous she had been on the rings. Others who had been part of the show enjoyed standing around in their leotards, basking in the admiration of the others and enjoying their newly gained star status.

Ivan looked about with satisfaction as he observed the elegant and animated crowd. The musicians were taking a break, the waiters were serving champagne and food, and all was going exactly according to plan. Now was his time to sneak off and fix his brace. Then he would make his move on Parkinson.

He let himself into his private office and pulled the door shut. Just beyond it was his personal bathroom, where no one but himself ever ventured. He disappeared in there, bolted the door behind him, and began the arduous and difficult task of stripping off his evening finery and getting down to his iron corset.

Timing, he told himself, was everything.

Back in the gym, Annie was intent on tracking Ivan down.

"Where the hell did the Terrible disappear to?" she fretted to Shelley. "He's got to have some music we could dance up a storm to. I don't believe even Ivan collects only chamber music."

"Gee, I wish I'd known. I've got some great new tapes back at the house," offered Shelley.

Annie grabbed two more glasses of champagne from a passing waiter's tray.

"Here, drink up, honey. Ivan bought the good stuff for tonight."

The two young women sipped and searched the room with their eyes. Ivan was nowhere to be seen.

"I wish I knew where he kept his magic machine. He's *got* to have some other tapes there."

Shelley flashed a giddy smile.

"I know where *that* is. I've watched him in his office while I sit in the waiting room!"

Annie giggled. "Now why didn't *I* think of that? You game? Let's go do some programming of our own."

Annie and Shelley fought their way through the crowded room, giggling conspiratorial giggles.

They were delighted to find his office door unlatched and, fortified with Dutch courage from the champagne, Shelley led Annie over to where the machine was concealed. She threw open the cabinet and said, *"Voilà!"*

Annie's eyes lit up. Sure enough, there was the stereo equipment, with a stack of boxes containing tape reels right next to it.

"Hey, that's more like it!" she cried, starting to finger her way through the tapes.

"Damn, the trouble with these is that most of them are unmarked. I suppose Ivan knows what's on each and every one, but it beats me what they are. Wait, this one says Bach fugues. Here's a Mozart. Damn, it's all highbrow crap!"

"I found something," said Shelley, poking in another cabinet. "Says 'The Latest Material.'"

"Do you suppose that's Ivan's quaint way of referring to the newest music, or is that the name of a rock group?" asked Annie.

"Heck, let's try it. There's nothing else here."

Annie reached in for the box, opened it, and pulled

out a tape reel.

"Lord, he's got enough leader on here," she muttered. Her long, slim fingers slipped the tape in, replacing the reel of exhibition music. She fiddled with it until she had it threaded. Then she hit the "play" switch.

"I hope this plays in the main gym as well as in the upstairs room. Come on, let's go back outside and see. If there's no sound, I'll hop back and push all the buttons until we get some action!"

The women let themselves out of the office, leaving the outer door slightly ajar, just as they had found it. They darted through the crush, back into the gym.

Nothing could be heard above the babble of conversation and laughter.

Annie and Shelley stood next to a speaker and exchanged disappointed looks. But just as Shelley was about to return to Ivan's office, a familiar voice boomed over the speaker.

The din in the room began to die down as the unexpected blast of sound flooded every corner.

"Don't you think that's dangerous?" a concerned female voice asked on the speaker system.

"My husband said it's not as though he's *stealing* the money; he's only borrowing it."

There was a loud gasp from the far side of the room. Little ripples of whispers ran through the crowd, then stopped as another voice came on.

"Lord, I feel like such a rat! I'm having an affair with *India's* husband!"

Andrew Travick felt as though someone had kicked him in the stomach.

India's expression froze as she recognized Cricket's voice.

Someone in the gym said, "Ye gods, Ivan's been

bugging the *dressing rooms!*"

Another voice yelled, "Somebody turn that damn thing off!"

Lanny's face was impassive, but he moved to block the door of the gym. What he had just heard could have an enormous impact on his and India's life, and no one was turning it off while *he* stood guard.

Cricket's expression never changed. So Ivan had been playing games with all of them, she thought angrily.

Annie got a sinking feeling in her middle, but she stood rooted to the spot, frozen in fright.

"You see, I've been skipping classes sometimes, and I'm really far behind now . . ." said a young voice.

With the next words, Annie's worst fears were realized.

"I got something here to help. I got these pills for my dieting, but man, they really jazz me up. If I didn't take another pill at night to relax me, I'd never get any sleep. But you gotta swear you will never let your auntie find out . . . she would kill me if she knew. . . . Ferrago would kill me if *he* knew."

The tremulous voice of the young girl asked, "What's in them anyway?"

Again, there was a buzz of conversation in the room. The whole thing had turned into a nightmare game of Twenty Questions, with everyone trying to identify the anonymous voices.

Unfortunately, the speakers knew and recognized their own voices all too well.

The next voice was instantly identifiable to a major portion of the national population.

". . . I resent mixing business with pleasure or having that monster try to put the make on me with a professional promise dangling. Griggs Parkinson is an ass and a phony and I have no intention of sleeping with him for either business or—heaven forbid—pleasure . . ."

This last was greeted with smatterings of laughter throughout the room. The indignation and vehemence in the voice elicited chuckles from many.

But one person in the room was not laughing. Griggs Parkinson stood his ground, but his face had gone dark with anger.

The tape ran through another splice and India heard her own voice say, "I guess neither of us ever expected it to turn out this way."

Lanny's voice answered, "No, and if it weren't for seeing you every Wednesday night, I don't think I could stand it. I love you, you know."

Lanny's immediate concern was for India, and he sought to catch a glimpse of her face through the crowd.

The women in the gym had recognized Lanny's voice at once, but now there was loud conjecture concerning the identity of the female to whom he spoke.

Ivan chose this moment to rejoin the party. There was something in the tenor of the babble of the crowd that made his skin prickle. Something had gone awry.

He had been right—timing *was* everything.

He barely got out the words, "What's going on here?" before Ferrago smashed him to the floor with his fist.

The spell of the tapes was broken and the voices over the speaker ran on unnoticed as pandemonium broke out.

Ferrago was shouting, Lanny was trying to grab him to keep him from hitting Ivan again, and people were getting shoved around as the crowd surged and voices rose loudly in contention.

Andrew turned to India and said with infinite weariness in his voice, "I think we'd better get out of here."

Griggs Parkinson elbowed his way toward the door, glowering. Jade watched him go and then looked around for Shelley. She saw her with her arms around Annie, who was sobbing loudly. Misha and Lanny had released Ferrago, who now headed toward Annie with an ugly expression on his face. Jade decided she ought to get Shelley out of this before it got worse.

Cricket had seen Andrew and India enter the elevator. She wished with all her might she could be a fly on the wall, in their apartment tonight. Actually, the bit of tape she'd heard that had knocked the socks off her had been the part about India and Lanny. Lord, it's always the quiet ones you have to wonder about, she mused silently.

Shrugging, she headed for the dressing room to get out of her leotard. She was pleased to see that the champagne bottle in there was still half full. She poured herself another glass and began changing back into her fringed gown, oblivious to the mounting roar of angry voices from the other room.

Chapter 41

Ferrago had all but thrown the money at the limo driver as they pulled up in front of their downtown loft. He had not spoken a word to Annie since they had gotten into the car. Annie had retreated to a corner of the seat and had sobbed softly all the way home.

He stormed ahead of her up the stairs and into the apartment. Switching on all the lights, he proceeded into the bedroom and began pulling down pieces of her Louis Vuitton luggage.

Annie stood in the doorway of the bedroom, watching him meekly. Finally she managed to ask, through her tears, what he was doing.

He turned on her, eyes blazing. "What am I doing? What the hell have *you* been doing? Drugs, that's what! You've been popping pills behind my back all this time! Diet pills, ha! Speed—that's what you've been taking! Pills to relax you, huh? It's probably Valium! You think you can quit any time you want, but you're *wrong*, you idiot! You're hooked! After all I've told you! After all I've explained about what dope can do! Do you think I'm going to take a junkie out to Hollywood? Think again. I'm sick to my stomach to look at you! I went through it once. I saw my brother go down the tubes. I'm not gonna do it again. I'm not gonna waste my time with a loser. I'm not gonna stand by and watch drugs destroy you. Why the hell don't you go back to Harlem, with the other junkies where you belong?'' he screamed at her.

Then he began to cry in loud, racking sobs that made him sound like an animal in pain.

Annie stood, stock-still, his cruel words flicking against her like whips from a lash. Tears poured down her cheeks.

At last she moved slowly across the room. She walked around the pile of expensive luggage and dug in the back of the closet until she found a battered, old, vinyl suitcase. She then turned to her dresser and took out some lingerie, two pullovers, and a pair of jeans. She placed these in her valise and snapped it shut.

Then she unzipped her orange chiffon evening dress. It fell around her feet like a heap of dying embers. She pulled on a pair of flannel slacks and a sweater.

Picking up her case, she walked to the door of the room and turned to look one last time at Ferrago. Tears streamed down her cheeks. Ferrago's body was still heaving from emotion, but he refused to look at her.

"Good-bye," she said softly and let herself out the door.

As she went down the long flight of steps, she considered what had happened and what she would do next.

Yes, she'd go back to Harlem. Who was it who said, "Home is where they have to take you in, whether they want to or not?" Momma would take her in.

But she'd come back to this life again. This time

she'd come back on her own terms. She knew she'd been wrong about the pills. She'd get rid of the pills. If they were addictive, as Ferrago had said, she'd go through a program to kick the habit. The pills had to go. But there was more wrong with her life than that. She'd been wrong to look to Ferrago for everything—for direction in her career, for what to wear and where to work, for protection and love in a cold, threatening world. Had she rushed willingly into his arms for love or simply to hide from the hurts that were bound to happen when one struggled for success? She had learned to love Ferrago deeply, but now she had to learn to stand on her own two feet. She didn't want to go to Hollywood. She didn't want a screen career. And it was time to do what *she* wanted. It was time she grew up—past time, she told herself as she hailed a passing cab.

Giving the driver an address in Harlem, she leaned back in the taxi and closed her eyes.

She was suddenly very tired.

After the taxi had deposited Jade and Shelley at Jade's town house, Jade said, "Let's go in and fix ourselves some coffee."

Wordlessly, Shelley followed Jade through the darkened house into the kitchen.

Mrs. Swann had thoughtfully left a light burning there and now Jade filled a kettle and put it on the stove. Then she pulled up a stool to the breakfast bar and indicated that Shelley should do the same.

"I think we'd better talk," began Jade.

Shelley looked at her aunt with large, sad eyes. The bleak, unstinting glare of the kitchen light and the black velvet of her dress combined to make her look pale and tired, like a child whose bedtime is long past.

"I suppose you're going to send me home," she said finally, with a touch of teenage sullenness.

Jade thought for long moments before she answered.

"That would be the easy way, wouldn't it? I could say, 'Shame on you, Shelley. You've been a bad girl, so now you've got to go home.' But I'd like to *talk* about what happened. And *why*. Your cutting the classes isn't even worth discussing. That was irresponsible and you know it. There's no point in belaboring the fact. But taking pills from Annie—pills that even she knew were dangerous—that was just plain *stupid*. . . ."

Shelley had the good grace to hang her head, though she began to mumble, "Everybody does it sometimes . . ."

Jade pounced. "No, that's just not true. Everybody *doesn't* do it. But the point is, what if everybody *did* do it and it was *wrong?* Would the fact that everybody was doing it justify *your* doing it? Growing up is learning to stand up for what you believe in; daring to be right when everyone else is *wrong;* having some principles and being willing to stick up for them."

Shelley's expression had yielded some of its petulance. She blinked and let her aunt's words sink in.

Meekly she ventured, "Like not being willing to sleep with somebody to get what you want?"

Jade nodded and gave a hint of a wry smile.

"Yeah, something like that. That was a great moment of idealism, wasn't it? Did you see Griggs's face when I blasted out that thrilling statement?"

Shelley gave a timid smile at her aunt's willingness to make light of what had happened.

"Is it . . . is it going to cost you the job you

wanted?" she asked.

The whistle on the kettle shrieked, temporarily destroying the intimacy of the moment.

Jade slid off the stool and prepared two cups of instant coffee. She brought the cups back and sat one in front of each of them.

She stirred hers with a spoon, stared down into the dark liquid, and spoke distractedly.

"Yes . . . probably. I don't know. Maybe. Who the hell knows?"

"Well, don't you *care?* Isn't that *awful?* Can't you *do* something? It's not *fair!*" protested the young girl.

Jade's smile was ironic now. "No. You're absolutely right. It's not fair. So what? John Kennedy said that life isn't fair. It's *not* fair. Yes, I do care. And what I'm going to do now is what I have always done—pick myself up, dust myself off, and keep right on working my tail off. There'll be other jobs, other networks. Learning to accept the rotten breaks that come with life is part of growing up too."

Jade put her spoon down and grew very earnest as she continued. "You see, what you've been seeing in Manhattan is the glamorous side of life. You've been seeing successful people enjoying the rewards of their successful lives. And I think it's been giving you a warped view of reality.

"Annie told me a story once, after I had complimented her on how fabulous she had looked in a very beautiful gown on the cover of *Vogue*. Annie just laughed that raucous, uninhibited laugh of hers and said, "Man, you should have seen that dress from behind! It was about four sizes too big for me and they had the whole back of the thing fastened tight with clothespins. I was wearing dirty sneakers and vamping around in that fancy dress all tucked up with plain old wooden clothespins!"

Jade paused.

"Well, you saw the seamy side of our lives tonight. You saw the back all held together with clothespins. It seems Ivan was planning to indulge in some petty blackmail. He was going to try to sell people's seedy secrets for money for who-knows-what reasons. You heard about some people having trashy affairs that they shouldn't have been having, others using money that wasn't theirs, and you saw your broken-down auntie riding off into the sunset like Sancho Panza on the lanky nag of her principles. Some glamorous life, huh kid?"

Jade gave a throaty chuckle and looked over at Shelley to determine if her niece was really understanding how phony all the tinsel was.

Shelley began to laugh too, shyly at first, then with genuine amusement.

"You know, Aunt Jade, you're right. Mr. Parkinson *did* look as though somebody had hit him with a wet fish. What a scuzzball he is!"

"More than you'll ever know, sweetie. More than you'll ever know! I'd say that the story of this little evening will be all over Manhattan tomorrow, even though some of the people who were there will be more than willing to forget about it."

Shelley grew serious again.

"And I understand that I have to go back to Augusta. I really do. I didn't ever actually think it could work out anyway . . ."

"Wait a minute. Just a minute," interrupted Jade wearily. "Who said anything about your going back to Augusta?"

Hope flickered in Shelley's eyes. "But, but . . . ?"

"You think I'm going to admit to my sister Rose that I can't raise one small niece properly for one small year in New York City? I'd never hear the end

374

of it."

"Oh, Aunt Jade!"

Shelley flew off her stool and threw her arms around Jade and started weeping copious tears.

"Hey, come on. It's all right. You're staying. Don't cry." She hugged her niece and patted at her back ineffectually. "And you're going to toe the mark, to," she said gruffly. *"Remember* that!"

Shelley released Jade, gulped back a sob, and nodded vigorously.

"Yes, I will. I really will. And Aunt Jade . . ."

Jade swallowed a lump in her own throat and looked inquiringly at her niece.

"You know something? I really am proud of you. I *really* am."

Jade smiled at the girl through misty eyes.

"And I'm not just saying that 'cause you're letting me stay, either!"

"Come on. It's past everybody's bedtime."

"Just because everybody is doing something . . ." piped Shelley.

"Don't start! Don't you start with me, you pipsqueak!"

Jade put a playful arm around Shelley's shoulder and led her up the stairs.

India and Drew maintained a leaden silence all the way home. India paid Mrs. Schmidt and Drew walked her home.

When he let himself into their apartment, India was sitting on the couch, waiting for him.

"Do you want to talk, India?"

"I guess we'd better."

"Want a drink?"

"Might as well."

Drew mixed them each a scotch and handed India her glass.

"Where do we start?" asked Drew.

India took a long swig of her drink.

"I don't know." She had been in a state of shock ever since she had heard Cricket's voice saying, "I'm having an affair with India's husband." It had continued playing over and over in her head like a scratched record. "I'm having an affair . . ." "I'm having an affair . . ."

She looked up at Drew with tears in her eyes.

"I didn't even know you *knew* Cricket . . ."

"I didn't know *you* knew her," said Andrew and immediately felt foolish at the inanity of their remarks.

"Why, Drew?"

"I might well ask you the same thing," countered Drew with an edge of bitterness in his voice.

"Do you want a divorce?"

"Do *you?*" asked Drew.

India put her drink down and held her head in her hands.

"I don't *know*. I just don't know anything right now."

Drew reached over to put his arms around her, but she pulled away.

"No, please don't. Not now. We've got to talk."

Rebuffed, he said, "Okay. So talk."

"I guess I just wonder why you did it," she said slowly.

In spite of himself, Andrew began to bristle. "Why *I* did it? What about you and that gigolo gym instructor of yours?"

India lashed back. "Don't talk that way! Don't say things like that about Lanny! He's a nice, decent young guy who just got mixed up with—"

Andrew gave her an ugly sneer. "Nice, decent young guys don't get mixed up with other men's wives!"

"You don't understand at all!"

Drew sat quietly, thinking, sipping his drink.

"No, I guess I don't. I've thought and thought about why I did what I did. I can't blame it on anyone but me, but I never *wanted* it to happen. And I never wanted to hurt you. It started out pretty innocently and then, well, then it just sort of took off . . ."

Now it was India's turn at bitterness. "Right under my very nose, I guess."

"No, not really. And if you want all the gory details, I met Cricket on that Jamaica trip, quite by accident. Then she turned up in Paris when I got there, and I was surprised—"

India looked startled. "You mean you schemed to meet her in Paris? And you offered to take *me* along on that trip!" Her eyes widened. "How could you be so cruel?"

"No, I did not scheme to meet her in Paris! I told you, she got there right after I arrived and I was astonished that she was there. She offered to show me around because she's been there so often, and, well, it just got started. I don't know how . . ." Drew sat back in misery.

"Didn't she ever mention that she knew me?"

Drew gave a crooked imitation of a smile. "At the risk of sounding trite, your name never came up."

"*That* was cruel."

Drew was genuinely abject.

"India, I'm sorry. I didn't mean it that way. And I'm sorry if I tried to make a joke. The truth is, I'm just so damned miserable. I thought I was miserable before, because I was sneaking behind your back, and I kept promising myself that I wouldn't do it anymore. But now I find out about you and that guy, and well, it just seems so hopeless. Do we have anything left?" he asked softly. "And more important, I guess, is, do you *want* to have anything left?"

India shook her head. "I don't know. I'm so confused. I can't decide anything tonight. I knew that what I was doing was wrong, but it . . . it just sort of happened, too. It happened at a time when I was feeling old . . . and useless . . . and unattractive, and I suppose it was flattering that a younger, attractive man could be attracted to *me*. My feelings are all mixed up. I never stopped loving you. But I couldn't help loving him, too. I know it doesn't make any sense."

"None of this makes any sense. It's all like an awful, awful dream. I wish to hell I'd wake up," Andrew said miserably.

They sat in silence for a long while.

At last India said, "I'm willing to try to talk about it tomorrow, if you are. I love you too much to just walk away from all we've had."

Andrew turned and searched her face with his eyes.

"Me too. I mean, I'm glad you're willing to talk about it. I feel the same way. I don't know what we can do, but maybe we can find some way out together."

They stood up.

"Do you want me to sleep out here tonight?" Drew offered.

India shook her head.

"No, that's silly. The kids would think it was strange. It's a big bed. Maybe I can get a sitter tomorrow and we can go for a long drive somewhere and just talk and try to figure something out."

Andrew leaned over and gave her a very tentative kiss on the forehead.

"I'm willing to try, India. I'm willing to try *anything*."

Cricket waited all day Sunday for Andrew to call her, but her phone never rang.

What was going on with those two? she wondered. Her curiosity was driving her as crazy as anything else.

Finally, on Monday, she picked up her phone and called Andrew at his office.

"Well," she began brightly, "what's happening?"

There was a long pause and she was afraid he was going to hang up.

"Andrew?"

"I'm here." Another long pause. "Nothing, Cricket. I guess nothing is going on."

"Are you going to leave India?" she asked impatiently, annoyed that she had to pry the words out of him.

"No, I'm not."

"Is she leaving you?"

"I hope not."

"Well, I guess everything is all fine and dandy at home now then," she said sarcastically.

"No," he said tiredly, "things are not."

"So where the hell does all this leave *us?*" she demanded.

"Nowhere, Cricket. Absolutely nowhere. And I guess that's basically where we've been all along. I'm sorry," he added.

But Cricket didn't hear the last. She had already slammed the phone down angrily.

"Damn!" She jumped up and stalked up and down the length of her living room. The spineless bastard! she told herself. Didn't have the guts to leave. Gutless wonders, that's what they all were! She had been right in the first place. Stay loose, stay unattached, and keep moving.

The thought of being on the move was suddenly very appealing. She checked her watch. Her secretary would be in the office by now. She placed a quick call and told her that she was leaving on a trip. She phoned the airline and booked a ticket through to the Yucatán. She'd find a place to stay when she got there.

The clock told her she had two hours to make the plane. She headed for the closet that held her warm-weather clothes. A few days in Mexico were just what she needed.

And when she got back, she'd buy a Jane Fonda record.

The Christmas holidays came and went in a blur for India and Andrew. They went through the familiar rituals mechanically. There were moments of great formality and excessive politeness, because the ground they were treading on was still too fragile to take for granted.

There were inevitable moments of tenderness, such as on Christmas Eve when they put up the tree and hung the children's stockings. They had shared such joy in the past, and it all flooded back in bittersweet memories. There were even feeble attempts at jokes.

And there was one terrible, strained moment when the phone rang. India answered it, and it was Lanny.

She was about to hang up, but then she looked over and saw Andrew watching her.

"Hello, Lanny," she said softly.

She turned and looked Drew full in the eyes as she spoke.

"No. I'm sorry. I'm sorry about everything. I'm all right, but"—she faltered and then her voice grew stronger—"I can't see you anymore. Not ever. Yes, me too. Yes. Good-bye."

She hung up the phone, still looking at Drew.

He crossed over to her side, took her in his arms, and said, "Thank you."

And then, that moment too was past.

New Year's Eve they stayed home, put the children to bed, and watched the crowd in Times Square on television.

At midnight, they kissed each other and wished each other a Happy New Year. Then they went to bed and made love, for the first time in a very long time.

About two weeks later, as they prepared to sit down to a late Saturday breakfast, India handed Drew the front section of the *New York Times* to read and, noting the date, said wryly, "Happy New Year."

Andrew looked up blankly.

"It's the Russian New Year," commented India. "Don't know why *that* stuck in my mind."

As India sat down to her coffee and unfurled the second section of the paper to read, she gave a gasp of horror.

"Oh God, Drew, listen to this!"

She read aloud.

Yesterday morning at eight-forty-five the body of Ivan Petrovich was found in his midtown penthouse gymnasium. His skull had been smashed by heavy barbells and the body had been tied and was found hanging upside down from a pair of gymnastic rings. The woman who found him was one of the gym's regular customers who had come in for an early class. Police are calling it a homicide and an intense investigation is now under way to find the killer or killers . . ."

Here India's voice ran out of steam and she stopped in shock. Her eyes filled up with tears.

"How terrible!" I mean, he wasn't a very nice man or anything, but dear God, who would want to do a hideous thing like that to him?"

Drew looked back at her.

"Honestly India, I know it sounds flip, but I could think of roughly twenty or so people who would have done it gleefully, after that party of his."

India still sat staring, shocked by the brutality of the crime.

Andrew reached over and patted her hand.

"India, pull yourself together. I imagine he was mixed up in all kinds of things with all kinds of people you knew nothing about."

She dabbed at her eyes with her napkin.

"I suppose you're right."

After a while, Drew said, "I guess you'll have to find a new gym to go to."

"As a matter of fact, I may not have time for going to a gym anymore. I was thinking seriously of trying to get a job as a buyer again. I wanted to ask you what you thought of the idea."

She looked to Drew for his approval.

"I think that's a great idea, India. I think you'll be a lot happier. We can get someone to stay with the kids, and Toohey will be going to nursery school before you know it."

"That's sort of what I was thinking, too. Motherhood is a job that eventually self-destructs. And I want to have something of my own to do when the kids are too old to need me."

Andrew sipped the last of his coffee and nodded in agreement. India was so sure of herself, so strong lately. He realized that she wasn't her old self any longer. She had become new—someone new and infinitely more interesting. And Andrew knew that he loved her very much.

Seeing his empty cup, India asked, "Want some more coffee?"

"Sure. Thanks," he answered.

India got up to go to the kitchen to get the coffeepot.

As she grabbed it from the stove, she glanced idly out the window and looked over to see what the woman across the courtyard was doing.

The window was empty.

THE BEST IN REGENCIES FROM ZEBRA

PASSION'S LADY (1545, $2.95)
by Sara Blayne

She was a charming rogue, an impish child—and a maddeningly alluring woman. If the Earl of Shayle knew little else about her, he knew she was going to marry him. As a bride, Marie found a temporary hiding place from her past, but could not escape from the Earl's shrewd questions—or the spark of passion in his eyes.

WAGER ON LOVE (1577, $2.50)
by Prudence Martin

Only a cynical rogue like Nicholas Ruxart would choose a bride on the basis of a careless wager, and then fall in love with her grey-eyed sister Jane. It was easy for Jane to ignore the advances of this cold gambler, but she found denying her tender yearnings for him to be much harder.

RECKLESS HEART (1679, $2.50)
by Lois Arvin Walker

Rebecca had met her match in the notorious Earl of Compton. Not only did he decline the invitation to her soiree, but he found it amusing when her horse landed her in the middle of Compton Creek. If this was another female scheme to lure him into marriage the Earl swore Rebecca would soon learn she had the wrong man, a man with a blackened reputation.

DANCE OF DESIRE (1757, $2.95)
by Sarah Fairchilde

Lord Sherbourne almost ran Virginia down on horseback, then he silenced her indignation with a most ungentlemanly kiss. Seething with outrage, the lovely heiress decided the insufferable lord was in need of a royal setdown. And she knew the way to go about it . . .

Available wherever paperbacks are sold, or order direct from the Publisher. Send cover price plus 50¢ per copy for mailing and handling to Zebra Books, Dept. 1744, 475 Park Avenue South, New York, N.Y. 10016. DO NOT SEND CASH.